A Treacherous Likeness

Lynn Shepherd

corsair

Constable & Robinson Ltd
55–56 Russell Square
London WC1B 4HP
www.constablerobinson.com

First published in the UK by Corsair,
an imprint of Constable & Robinson Ltd., 2013

A copy of the British Library Cataloguing in
Publication data is available from the British Library

ISBN 978-1-78033-168-3 (paperback)
ISBN 978-1-78033-170-6 (ebook)

Typeset by TW Typesetting, Plymouth, Devon

Printed and bound in the UK

1 3 5 7 9 10 8 6 4 2

LYNN SHEPHERD studied English at Oxford before working in the City and then PR. She has been a freelance copywriter for over ten years and has also published an academic work on 'the father of the English novel,' Samuel Richardson. Her first book for Constable & Robinson, *Tom-All-Alone's*, was published last year to critical acclaim.

Praise for *A Treacherous Likeness*

'A persuasive and imaginative tour de force of extrapolative fiction ... The multi-layered plotting is extraordinarily satisfying ... A complete joy.' *The Tablet*

'A dark, new and excitingly authentic version of a literary enigma ... refreshingly readable ... beautifully executed ... intelligent, revealing and exciting in the sheer power of its possibility.' *Lancashire Evening Post*

'Evocatively conjuring early Victorian London ... a compelling story of love, loss, death, and deep duplicity.' *Good Book Guide*

'A compelling and brilliantly evocative piece of writing.' welovethisbook.com

'Her conclusion has haunted me ever since I finished the book.' *Independent on Sunday*

'A lingering literary mystery.' *Herald*

Also by Lynn Shepherd

Murder at Mansfield Park

Tom-All-Alone's

'. . . as the human heart,
Gazing in dreams over the gloomy grave,
Sees its own treacherous likeness there . . .'

Percy Bysshe Shelley, *Alastor*, 1816

Author's note

What follows is a work of fiction, but it is one based on fact.

A Treacherous Likeness reconstructs events in the lives of some of the most celebrated members of the circle of 'Young Romantics' – the poet Percy Bysshe Shelley, his wife Mary, her step-sister Claire Clairmont, and Lord Byron, who was the father of Claire's child.

The Young Romantics have inspired hundreds of books, plays and films over the last two centuries, and there have been many accounts of that famous summer they spent together on Lake Geneva in 1816, when Frankenstein was conceived. But all the same there remain many inexplicable gaps and strange silences, where the biographers can offer us only speculation.

A Treacherous Likeness is an attempt to weave a new story between those gaps, and create a narrative to connect those silences.

In the notes at the end I set out what here is fact, and what is invention, but I've tried throughout to remain faithful to what I've read of the lives and characters of these extraordinary and complex people. The story history tells us is one of death and love, of secrets and betrayal. My own version of that story is darker yet, but I do believe it is one plausible answer to many of the mysteries about the Shelleys that still persist even now, and have never yet been fully explained.

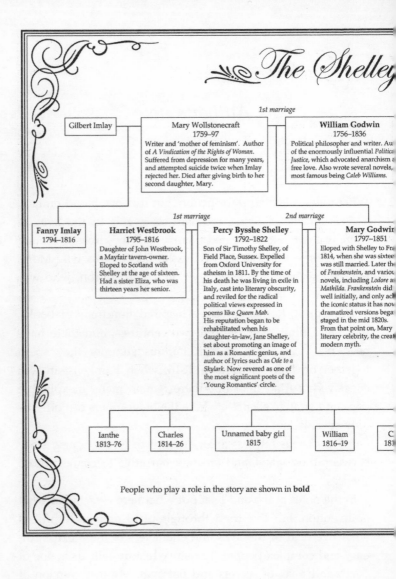

The Shelley

1st marriage

Gilbert Imlay

Mary Wollstonecraft
1759–97

Writer and 'mother of feminism'. Author of *A Vindication of the Rights of Woman*. Suffered from depression for many years, and attempted suicide twice when Imlay rejected her. Died after giving birth to her second daughter, Mary.

William Godwin
1756–1836

Political philosopher and writer. Au of the enormously influential *Politica Justice*, which advocated anarchism a free love. Also wrote several novels, most famous being *Caleb Williams*.

1st marriage   **2nd marriage**

Fanny Imlay
1794–1816

Harriet Westbrook
1795–1816

Daughter of John Westbrook, a Mayfair tavern-owner. Eloped to Scotland with Shelley at the age of sixteen. Had a sister Eliza, who was thirteen years her senior.

Percy Bysshe Shelley
1792–1822

Son of Sir Timothy Shelley, of Field Place, Sussex. Expelled from Oxford University for atheism in 1811. By the time of his death he was living in exile in Italy, cast into literary obscurity, and reviled for the radical political views expressed in poems like *Queen Mab*. His reputation began to be rehabilitated when his daughter-in-law, Jane Shelley, set about promoting an image of him as a Romantic genius, and author of lyrics such as *Ode to a Skylark*. Now revered as one of the most significant poets of the 'Young Romantics' circle.

Mary Godwin
1797–1851

Eloped with Shelley to Fra 1814, when she was sixtee was still married. Later th of *Frankenstein*, and variou novels, including *Lodore* a *Mathilda*. *Frankenstein* did well initially, and only ac the iconic status it has now dramatized versions bega staged in the mid 1820s. From that point on, Mary literary celebrity, the crea modern myth.

Ianthe
1813–76

Charles
1814–26

Unnamed baby girl
1815

William
1816–19

C
181

People who play a role in the story are shown in **bold**

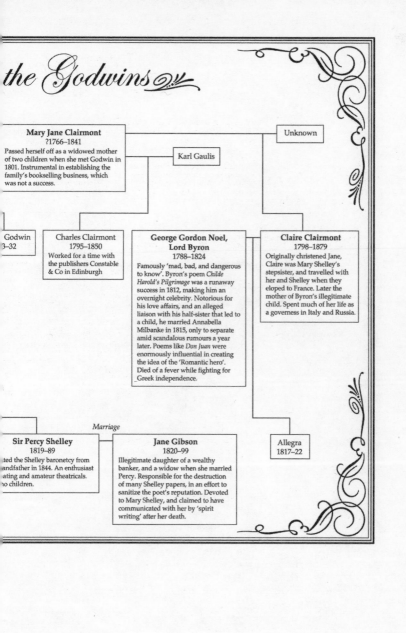

the Godwins

Mary Jane Clairmont
?1766–1841

Passed herself off as a widowed mother of two children when she met Godwin in 1801. Instrumental in establishing the family's bookselling business, which was not a success.

Karl Gaulis

Unknown

Godwin
3–32

Charles Clairmont
1795–1850

Worked for a time with the publishers Constable & Co in Edinburgh

George Gordon Noel, Lord Byron
1788–1824

Famously 'mad, bad, and dangerous to know'. Byron's poem *Childe Harold's Pilgrimage* was a runaway success in 1812, making him an overnight celebrity. Notorious for his love affairs, and an alleged liaison with his half-sister that led to a child, he married Annabella Milbanke in 1815, only to separate amid scandalous rumours a year later. Poems like *Don Juan* were enormously influential in creating the idea of the 'Romantic hero'. Died of a fever while fighting for Greek independence.

Claire Clairmont
1798–1879

Originally christened Jane, Claire was Mary Shelley's stepsister, and travelled with her and Shelley when they eloped to France. Later the mother of Byron's illegitimate child. Spent much of her life as a governess in Italy and Russia.

Marriage

Sir Percy Shelley
1819–89

ted the Shelley baronetcy from andfather in 1844. An enthusiast ating and amateur theatricals. no children.

Jane Gibson
1820–99

Illegitimate daughter of a wealthy banker, and a widow when she married Percy. Responsible for the destruction of many Shelley papers, in an effort to sanitize the poet's reputation. Devoted to Mary Shelley, and claimed to have communicated with her by 'spirit writing' after her death.

Allegra
1817–22

PART ONE

1850

CHAPTER ONE

The West Wind

We began before thick in autumn fog; we open now in the fury of a west and winter wind. Above us high loose clouds drive across a steep grey sky, and beneath our feet the dead leaves are driven before the unseen air like ghosts from an enchanter. Yellow and black and pale and hectic red, they swirl in dry squalls into narrow corners and lift in sudden gusts from the muddy gutters. It's no weather for walking and as yet only the muffin-seller is braving the bluster, bent half double against the freezing wind and struggling to keep both his hat on and his basket covered. No weather for walking, and no weather for idle lingering either, so we will take shelter for a moment in a graceful Georgian doorway and survey this graceful Georgian street. To the south, the level leaden drab of the river; to the north the heave of early-morning traffic on the Strand. But here all is quiet, and the only other passer-by a large black cat making its way purposefully across the cobbles and down the area steps of the house opposite, a rat dangling from its mouth like a rather rakish moustache. Few lights burn yet in the upper storeys, even if the servants in the cellars have been up and busy these two hours and more. Though there is, it appears, one exception. In that same house opposite, there is one uncurtained casement high above the street, and if we move just a little we can see a figure standing at the window.

It is a young man. His face pale, and his eyes deep-set and drawn. Or, at least, that is how it seems from here. Perhaps it is merely the reflection in the bluish glass, or perhaps he has been wakeful all night, and stands there now, prey to the same dark concerns. One thing is certain: we may be interested in him, but Charles Maddox does not even register our presence as he gazes down at the almost empty street, listening to the rattle of the window-panes, which is the only sound to trouble the tall and silent house. He sighs, understanding the exact pitch and weft of that silence, and knowing that it signifies there has been no change. Two floors below, in a larger and more elegant room than his, by a fine marble mantelpiece and a fire kept always carefully tended, his great-uncle lies unmoving in the same cold repose that has afflicted him now for more than three weeks. He breathes still – lives still – but it is a chill and twilight life, from which there may be no returning.

Charles turns back to the room. He has lived here more than a month now, and his attic space is finally taking the look of permanent occupation. Gone are the tea crates that brought his possessions halfway across town and up three flights of stairs, and in their place there's a line of new shelves all along one wall. His books are now arranged in rows, his collection in clusters, the latter accompanied by more or less neatly written labels: *Ethnographical*, *Zoological*, *Historical*, *Mineralogical*. The books, in the main, are scuffed with overuse; the objects, by contrast, have been positioned

4

with care. The coins are laid in chronological order on a piece of new red velvet, and the shells and pieces of coral have been freed at last from the glass jar they've been stored in since Charles was still at school. And if you look a little closer, you'll see that this assortment of apparently unrelated items has not only been placed to best advantage, but as far as possible from the floor, though it's hard to tell whether this is to protect the objects from the cat, or the cat from his own curiosity. Thunder, incidentally, is far too busy at this precise moment, feasting on his prize rat, to be interested in Charles's curios, none of which is remotely palatable (though one or two of the brightly coloured stuffed birds on the top shelf do seem to be a little bald and abraded here and there, which may suggest that Thunder has his owner's dedication to proper scientific methods, and has proved their inedibility with the odd practical experiment of his own).

Charles wanders now to the washstand and stands a moment, looking himself in the eye. The face that stares back at him in the mirror is rumpled from sleep, and the dark bronze curls unruly, but the cuts on his brow have left no scar. Much that he cares. The bowl on the stand is edged with ice, but when he goes to the door he finds no hot water waiting. He's just drawing breath to bellow down at Billy when instead he sees his great-uncle's former henchman making his slow way round the bend in the stairs, the steaming jug clenched in his gnarled hands. There was a time, years since, when there was no man more feared in the shadowier strata of London society than Abel Stornaway, though looking at him now you'd never think it: his legs are bowed, his back bent, and wisps of hair hang limply from his speckled, wrinkled skull. Age has withered him, just as it has the man he served, but Abel has waned only in body, while it is the mind of the master thief-taker that the decades have decayed.

Abel perches the jug on the washstand and eyes Charles as he unwraps the dressing on his right hand. It may be that you have met Charles before, in which case you will know how and why he came by this injury. You will know, too, that patience is hardly the first characteristic that comes to mind in relation to this young man, and will be surprised – perhaps – that he is still wearing the bandage when the hand must, by now, have almost healed. Though as the final strip of cloth falls away you can perhaps see why: with the bandage in place, the damage is masked; without it, there is no evading the fact that one finger is missing. Charles is not usually loath to confront reality, however unpleasant; indeed, his rather bull-headed determination to do just that, and make others do so too, has got him into trouble more than once. But there is clearly something about this particular reality that he cannot bear, or cannot bear quite yet, and it does not escape Abel's beady eye that a clean bandage was ready laid out and is even now being quickly fastened.

'What was it you wanted, Abel?' says Charles, a question that would sound to anyone else like the opening of a conversation but is really, as both men know, a changing of the subject. 'You usually send the boy up with the water, so there must be something.'

'You remember the calling card that was left, Mr Charles? Have you done owt about it?'

Charles shakes his head and goes over to the wardrobe, which is an efficient if rather cowardly way of avoiding Abel's eye. 'Not yet, Abel.'

'Men of his stamp dinnae want to be kept waiting. It's not mannerly, Mr Charles, and it's not sensible, not for a man in our line of work.'

Charles smiles, despite himself, at that 'our', and wonders for a moment how long it is since Abel worked a case – how long, indeed, since Maddox worked a case. He's seen the files in the office downstairs, and knows now that his great-uncle has been battling for his reason for far longer than Charles assumed that night only a few short weeks ago, when Abel had come looking for him and the two of them returned to this house to find Maddox flailing like a madman, and stinking in his own soil. And yet against all hope and medical opinion the master thief-taker has once or twice returned, and when he has, the edge and incision of his insights have made the madman seem like an obscene dream. It was the lucid, not the lunatic, Maddox who helped Charles solve his last case – that same Maddox who taught him everything he knows about the art and science of investigation, that same Maddox who both is, and is not, lying now in the room beneath them, marooned in an eerie, fretful immobility.

'You cannae bring him back by watching,' says Abel, softly. 'The doctor—'

'What does he know?' snaps Charles, his blue eyes flashing. 'He cannot even tell us what ails him, much less do anything useful to cure it.'

'Mebbe there is no cure, Mr Charles. Mebbe we will have tae let him go.'

Charles turns away, but Abel sees the lift of his chin and knows he is fighting back the tears. 'I know how much he means to 'ee, but you cannae spend every waking hour by his side. He wouldnae want it.'

'I should have been here. I should have done something.'

Abel sighs. He's suspected for some time that this might be at the bottom of it. 'It wouldnae hae made any difference, Mr Charles. The fit came upon him so quick – it would hae been the same whoever was by. And the reason you were nae here was because you were doing your job. That's what he'd hae wanted. Just as he'd want you to go call on that gentleman who left his card. For courtesy's sake, if naught else.'

'What's the use?' says Charles, with a shrug. 'It's probably just some paltry indoor case. Servants pinching the pastry-forks. And it's not as if we need the money.'

'Work is its own reward, as my old father used to say. And you need to get yerself away from this house for a few hours. Exercise yer mind. Even if it is does turn out to be naught more than pilfering.'

Charles takes a deep breath, then nods. 'All right. I'll go this morning.' He turns heavily and contemplates his small collection of shirts. 'I suppose I had better make myself look presentable. If I'm going calling on a baronet.'

On his way down the stairs half an hour later Charles pauses for a moment at the drawing-room door. The curtains have been opened and Abel is attempting to feed Maddox from a bowl of porridge. And we can see that the old man's face is drawn down on the left side, while the left hand and arm seem bent and unnaturally stiff. It will be obvious to you, now, what has happened, and there are doctors in London Charles could summon with knowledge enough to diagnose an apoplexy. But they will not be able to help him. Most of the porridge has already ended up on the napkin tied bib-wise under the old man's chin, and he is making small whimpers of distress at Abel's every attempt with the spoon. A month ago Maddox would have dashed it to the ground in fury and frustration, but now he has neither the will nor the capacity even to push the food away. With the mind he once had, and the dread and

8

deference he once commanded, there could hardly be a more bitter degradation. It's pitiful to watch – too pitiful for Charles – and he moves to close the door, but at that moment a thought strikes him and he turns back into the room.

'You did say, didn't you, Abel, that it was seeing that man's calling card that brought on my uncle's attack?'

Abel pauses in his spooning and looks up. 'Well, I cannae say exactly that's what it was.'

'But that was what the two of you were talking about, just before it happened?'

'Aye, so it was.'

'And the last word he said before he collapsed was a name – a woman's name?'

'Aye, Mr Charles. The last thing he said to me was "Mary". I thought he were talking about that woman he loved all those long years ago, before you were born. But you said you thought it could be someone else entirely.'

Charles takes the card out of his pocket and looks at it again. 'Yes,' he says quietly. 'I think it is.'

Charles's destination is Belgravia, which is a good stretch on a day like this, and he starts with every intention of walking, but after ten minutes of battling against the wind, his eyes squinting and streaming in the flying dust, he admits defeat and joins the queue for the omnibus. The early rush has subsided so he manages to get a seat, and sits with his shoulders hunched as the 'bus inches its way through the din of wagons, coaches, carts and hansoms pressed nose to tail along the Strand, and turns slowly into St Martin's Lane. This route is usually thronged with pedlars, beggars, ballad-singers and tinkers, but in weather like this only the boldest are braving the wind, both buyers and sellers. And as

Charles well knows from his time in the police, most of the city's street-sellers and costermongers live so hand to mouth that the edge of starvation is as close as three days' rain.

Half an hour later Charles steps down from the 'bus a mile and a world away, and starts through Belgravia's pristine stucco squares – a district so deep-rooted in the London landscape now that it's hard to believe these buildings date back only to the late 1820s: some of the houses Charles passes are even now not fully completed. But despite that fact, and the rather unsightly corners of builders' rubble and cast-off brick, these serene white houses are home already to the richest population in the world. And then as now, that kind of cash secures intangible assets as much as tangible ones, and the most valuable of them all in this rowdy, dirty town is privacy. Hence the eight-bar gates across the entrance to Chester Square, and the polite if somewhat pugnacious gatekeeper who insists on seeing the calling card left at Buckingham Street before allowing Charles to pass. A performance he has to go through a second time for the benefit of the butler who answers the door at number twenty-four.

'Are you expected?' the man says, glancing rather disdainfully at the (by now) rather dog-eared card, and clearly wondering if Charles has fished it out of a bin.

'Not, perhaps, this morning,' he replies, sardonic, 'but seeing as the card was accompanied by a request to call, I imagine my arrival will hardly come as a complete surprise.'

The butler frowns slightly. 'I will see if my master or my lady is at home.'

The door closes, and Charles stamps up and down for five minutes on the steps trying to keep warm, not much bothered that the noise must be perfectly audible from inside the house.

The door opens again, and the butler reappears.

'If you would come with me.'

Charles dutifully follows him along the hall and up the stairs. His eyes are, to all appearances, courteously averted, but his great-uncle has taught him well and he is extremely proficient at discerning a great deal from the seemingly trivial. Houses, animals and clothes often tell him more about the people who own them than those owners ever do (and we might reflect in passing how much we've already learned of Charles from his eccentric collection of specimens, his complete lack of interest in his personal appearance, and his care for his cat). As for this house, it is conventionally laid-out and conventionally furnished, in what the occupants no doubt consider to be good taste, but Charles, for one, considers it to be just a little too over-embellished, and a mite too ponderous. Exactly the same conclusions, as a matter of fact, as he drew from that small piece of cardboard two inches by three, which is all he's had to go on up till now. He can see likewise that the brightly coloured fabrics and upholstery in this house are actually of rather inferior quality, and the furniture probably second-hand. There seems, indeed, to be an intriguing tension between a desire for flamboyance and a reluctance to pay for it, and he wonders if perhaps those two sentiments are a reflection of the master and mistress of this house, and if so, which is which.

The butler opens the drawing-room door to let him in, then closes it quietly behind him. It is a blue room, this one, though the blues are not all quite the same tone, as if individual pieces have been bought from different sales. There are not the shelves of books Charles would have expected to find in a house owned by this family, and the cabinets at either side of the fireplace are congested instead with ornaments and china figurines, and here and there a porcelain-faced doll. The only books visible in the room are in two glass-fronted cases placed directly beneath a portrait, accorded pride of place between the long windows giving onto the square. Charles takes a pace or two towards it and finds himself face to face not with the man he has come to see, but with his father. Or, at least, with his likeness. Framed in over-ornate gold, the painting hangs above a pier-table, which, along with the books, holds an arrangement of wax lilies under a glass dome, and a candle in a silver chamberstick. The candle is lit, even in broad day, and someone has carefully pasted dark blue paper spangled with stars to the back of the bookcases. The overall effect is unsettlingly shrine-like, and far too queasily mawkish for Charles, but he's drawn to the portrait none the less. He's seen it before somewhere – no doubt reproduced as a frontispiece – but he looks at it now with a more professional interest. From a purely technical perspective the painting has little to recommend it, but it is the subject, not the style, that will make this one of the century's most recognized portraits. The dark jacket and the white shirt open at the neck; the unruly curls and the intense gaze; the pen held poised in the long, slender fingers. When this man died he was an exile and a pariah, 'an outcast from human society', denounced for his beliefs and reviled for his conduct, his works condemned and largely unread. And yet by the end of the century this image will have become an icon of all it means to be 'Romantic' – all it means to be a poet, and a genius, and an unacknowledged legislator of the world. An appropriate quotation that, because the man this portrait shows – as the inscription confirms – is none other than

12

Percy Bysshe Shelley
4th August 1792 – 8th July 1822
He has outsoared the shadow of our night:
Envy and calumny, and hate and pain,
And that unrest which men miscall delight,
Can touch him not and torture not again.

Charles moves closer, struck by the dates. The poet was not quite thirty, then, when he died, and this likeness must have been produced some time before that, but there is all the same an oddly childlike quality to the faint, almost girlish flush, and the pink bud of a mouth. And if he was not quite thirty in 1822, that means (as Charles quickly calculates), his son must be about that age now.

'They all do that.'

Charles swings round, too absorbed in the picture to have heard the encroaching steps. 'I'm sorry?'

The man before him is stout, rather paunchy, and a good three inches shorter than Charles. He has watery hangdog eyes, a beaky nose, and a sandy nondescript beard that is in need of a good trim. 'Nondescript' rather sums him up, in fact, since there is nothing remotely unusual or distinctive about him. So much so, indeed, that Charles initially assumes he must be some or other household retainer – a secretary or steward – but as the man starts talking it becomes obvious how wrong that assumption was.

'The painting. Everyone who comes here looks at it like that. Copy, of course. Real one's in the mater's room. But I'm told this ain't bad. Wouldn't know myself. Never did have an eye for art.'

He talks in the clipped, tight way so redolent of a public-school education, and for all that he looks nearer fifty than thirty there is still something of the overgrown

13

schoolboy about him. Part of it, no doubt, is down to his rather gawky awkwardness – something that most men in his position outgrow long before their majority, and which suggests to Charles that he was not always destined to hold the title his father never lived to inherit, and the money that title brought with it has come to him late, after years of stringency. Which may, now Charles thinks about it, go a long way to explaining the character of this house. Meanwhile, the man in question has wandered over to a table in the centre of the room, and begun to fiddle absent-mindedly with a scale model of a sailing-boat. Charles stares at it, and at him, for a brief, dumbfounded moment, for Shelley drowned aboard just such a vessel as that, and in all probability it was the unstable and extravagant design of that boat, and his failure to recognize it, and make allowances in the rigging of it, that drove him and the two men with him to their deaths. But that being the case, how can his widow and son bear such a reminder, every day, every time they enter this room? But here, yet again, his host wrong-foots him.

'A peach, isn't she?' he says, gesturing Charles to a chair. 'The *Eirene*. Had her namesake built for me at Mallaby's in Putney in 'forty-seven. Took her to Norway that year too. Lovely mover. Takes the wind like a swallow. Mater can't bear the sight of it. Can't blame her, I suppose. Always was a worrier. Specially about sailing.'

'Well,' stammers Charles, 'I suppose that's only to be expected.'

'Odd, though, ain't it? That a fellow should enjoy nothing more than pottering about in boats when his pater drowned in one. Never have been able to explain it.' He sets the boat back on its stand and comes over to the sopha opposite the one where Charles has taken a seat. He sits down rather

14

heavily and stares at Charles, rubbing his beard. He seems rather ill at ease, and keeps glancing at the door as if expecting someone else.

'Look here,' he says eventually, 'Maddox, is it? This is rather a rum do, and that's a fact.'

Charles waits, not knowing what encouragement is required. 'I am quite accustomed,' he ventures, after a moment or two, 'to dealing with matters of a sensitive nature. I know that a man in your position—'

Sir Percy waves his hand. 'Quite so, quite so. Not that. Not that at all. Thing is—'

And now the door does indeed open, and a woman enters the room with all the briskness of a career housekeeper. She is certainly dressed like one, in a sensible plain dress long past its first wearing and a pair of practical shoes, but Charles has wised up now and deduces – correctly – that this is the lady of the house, even if it is clear to him in an instant that she, too, was not born to the rank she now enjoys. And seeing that, he is on his feet at once, knowing from experience that a woman in such a situation will insist on her due recognition all the more ardently.

'My apologies, Percy,' she says, taking a seat beside her husband. 'Dear Madre is rather unwell this morning and couldn't bear to have me leave her.'

Sir Percy, meanwhile, looks visibly relieved at being released from a task that was clearly giving him a good deal of difficulty and, having made the introductions, sinks back into the sopha to take what Charles guesses to be his accustomed secondary position.

'Sir Percy has told you of our predicament?' she begins, looking Charles up and down with no apparent embarrassment. She is sitting as far forward on the sopha as her husband is behind. 'Perched' is the word that comes irresistibly to mind, and she does indeed look rather bird-like sitting there. Charles searches for a species and suppresses a superior smile as he settles on a squab. A rather unkind analogy, but undeniably apt for a woman so plump, grey, and pigeon-breasted and who is, to all appearances, bright-eyed without being particularly bright-minded. The look fits, certainly, but whether it will lead our young man dangerously to underestimate her intelligence, we shall have to wait and see.

'I was just getting to all that, my love,' murmurs her husband, 'when you came in.'

'Ah, well,' she says quickly, 'in that case, it may save time if I give you these notes I have prepared. They are, needless to say, completely confidential, and not to be divulged or copied without our express permission.'

Charles is taken aback, for the third time already in that house: this is quite definitely the first occasion that a client has ever prepared him a briefing in advance. He takes the papers she is holding out, but she gives him no more than a minute to start reading before speaking again.

'As you see, our dear Madre has been the subject of several previous incidents of the like shameful nature. Rogues and charlatans who have attempted to abuse her gentle nature, and exploit her absolute devotion to the Dear Departed for their own mercenary ends.'

Charles looks up from the paper, struck as much by her portentous tone as by what she says. Evidently both the poet and his wife are only to be spoken of in Capital Letters, and he knows now whose idea that shrine on the table was, and who – in this house – is the literal and metaphorical keeper of the flame. He clears his throat, 'These notes will be most useful as an *aide-memoire*, Lady Shelley, but perhaps you could start by giving me an account – in your own words –

16

of the "predicament" you mentioned. If you would be so good?'

Lady Shelley glances at her husband, then turns to Charles. 'Well,' she commences, 'you may know that in the early years of her marriage Madre spent a good deal of time travelling on the Continent, and also lived in a number of different houses in England. It was unfortunate therefore, but perhaps inevitable, that papers would sometimes go astray, or be left behind, and some of these have since fallen into unscrupulous hands.'

Charles nods, perceiving that some reaction is necessary, and she takes a breath and plunges on.

'In recent years, as the reputation of the Dear Departed has grown and the world is finally coming to appreciate the exalted quality of his Genius, certain individuals have come forward claiming to be in possession of those missing papers.'

This is all starting to sound suspiciously like a prepared speech and Charles wonders how many others of his calling have sat here and heard it.

'Some of these papers,' she continues, 'have proved to be genuine, and most of these Madre has purchased. Others have been the most infamous impostures.'

Charles glances down at the notes. 'I take it you are referring to the incident mentioned here – concerning George Byron?'

Lady Shelley snorts with disdain. 'He *called* himself that and claimed the descent, even if illegitimately, but believe me, he is no more Lord Byron's son than I am—' she looks around, seemingly in need of an even more outrageous and unbelievable comparison '—or *you* are.'

Charles is irrationally piqued by this observation, and there is perhaps just the slightest sharpness in his reply:

'Legitimate or not, it appears from these notes that the man did indeed possess some of Mrs Shelley's papers.'

Lady Shelley lifts her nose, as if troubled by a bad smell. 'Some were genuine, yes. We never did discover how that scoundrel laid hands upon them. But most of those he tried to sell poor dear Madre were outright forgeries.'

'I see,' says Charles. 'And the second case? The memoir?'

There is a sudden rattle as the wind hurls at the window and the candle burning beneath the portrait dips and wavers, throwing ghastly shadows up over the poet's face. Lady Shelley is on her feet in an instant, rushing to the table and holding her hand close about the flame until it straightens and gathers strength.

'The servants are under strict instructions,' she says, as she returns to the sopha. 'The candle is never to be allowed to die.'

'You were saying, Lady Shelley? About the memoir?'

Her face darkens, and she purses her thin lips. 'That was of a rather different order. A cousin of the Poet's, one Thomas Medwin, sought to make money from their slight connection when mere boys by publishing what he impudently termed a "Life". It was nothing but a base attempt at villainous extortion.'

Charles frowns. 'I'm not sure I follow – how could he use such a memoir to extract money?'

'By offering *not* to publish it, of course!' retorts Lady Shelley, somewhat shrilly. 'He told Madre she could prevent it appearing if she paid him two hundred and fifty pounds. Which she did not have, and would *not* have paid, even if she had.'

'So he was aware from the start that Mrs Shelley would not want such a memoir to appear?'

'That or any other. Madre has always maintained that if

the Poet's life is to be written she will do it herself. But now is not yet the time. The world is not yet ready.'

Charles is willing to wager this is another of Lady Shelley's prepared speeches, and her cheeks have now gone rather red. And he can understand why. There are aspects of Shelley's life that are far less palatable in 1850 than they would have been in the rather more broad-minded first quarter of the nineteenth century. Indeed, one would be hard put to come up with two notions more utterly repugnant to the strait-laced mid-Victorian bourgeoisie than Atheism and Free Love.

'So she tried to persuade this Medwin to forbear?'

'Quite so – in fact I believe "forbearance and reserve" were exactly her words. But the blackguard took no notice. Poor Madre was nearly frantic with worry, wondering what he might say.'

'Complete bounder,' mutters Sir Percy. 'Country's going to the dogs.'

Charles looks from one to the other. 'And the memoir itself, did it appear?'

Lady Shelley has regained her composure. 'Some three years ago. It was not, as it turned out, quite as detrimental to the fame of the Poet as Madre had feared, but it was still quite deplorably inaccurate on many points of moment, and seemingly written with the sole purpose of endowing the author with a significance in the Poet's life he most certainly did *not* possess.'

And how could she know that, wonders Charles, since she cannot possibly have ever met him? But he elects to let it pass. 'I believe you said there were other similar instances?'

Sir Percy shifts in his seat. 'Well, there was that Gatteschi fellow, but that was back in 'forty-five—'

His wife gives him a sharp glance, and a silent message

passes between them. This time Charles decides he will push, just a little, and see what results.

'Gatteschi?'

Lady Shelley takes out her handkerchief and waves it, as if to swat away such unpleasantness. 'It was rather distressing at the time, but nothing came of it in the end, God be thanked. Madre met him in Paris. Very handsome, very dashing, but *quite* without principles. Dear Madre has always been so trusting, and this dreadful man preyed upon it. He inveigled himself into her confidence and ended up in receipt of some letters relating to her past life that would apparently have had most unfortunate consequences if they had been made public.'

'Letters from Shelley?'

'No,' she says, flushing again. 'They were letters Madre had written to Gatteschi herself.'

How very interesting, thinks Charles. Why would she have unburdened herself of such damaging details to an all-but stranger? And what could she possibly have divulged that the world does not already know – and condemn?

'But as I said,' Lady Shelley continues, 'a dependable friend was happily on hand, and the police proved surprisingly efficient – for the French. All the papers were seized and safely destroyed. But the whole affair caused Madre the most dreadful torment. Thankfully she has me to protect her now. And I will absolutely *not* allow anything of the kind to happen again.'

Charles wonders if she realizes what a dim light this casts on the man she married – who should surely be the one to protect his widowed mother, if such a role is required – but if either of them is aware of it they give no sign. Perhaps Sir Percy is so used to hearing the like observations that he scarcely notices any more.

Husband and wife are both silent for a time, then he gives a feeble cough and she wipes her eyes. The mere thought of the Poet and his widow appears to raise Lady Shelley to a pitch of breathless emotion that her own husband has never succeeded in exciting. The Victorians have no word for 'groupie', but Charles is in the presence of one all the same. He waits a moment longer, having learned from his great-uncle what a weapon silence can be, and how swiftly most people will rush to fill it. But these two seem to be the exception.

'Am I to understand that you asked me to come here because something of the kind has indeed happened again?'

Lady Shelley looks up, and now her plain round face is suffused with indignation. 'It is infamous – quite *infamous*. It has come to our attention that a connection of Madre's from many years ago has returned unexpectedly to London, and may even now be hawking the Poet's private papers around London, in an attempt to sell them to the highest bidder.'

Charles notes that word 'connection'. It's the second time Lady Shelley has used it and it's clearly her own personal shorthand for all those she deems unworthy of the role in Shelley's life that Fate has so thoughtlessly allowed them to play. 'And by "connection", do you mean a friend, an admirer, perhaps a relative—'

'Most definitely *not* a relative,' she says quickly.

'And the papers this person claims to have – are they genuine?'

Again that exchange of looks between the two of them.

'Could be,' says Sir Percy, after a moment. 'Hard to tell without seeing 'em.'

'But if they *are* genuine,' persists Charles, 'I do not see that any criminal offence has been committed, and nor do I see

21

how the sale of them can be prevented. The memorabilia of prominent men will always find a ready buyer.'

'Oh, as to that,' says Lady Shelley, 'we are under no illusions. We are resigned to paying the price, however usurious. Securing Madre's peace of mind is our only concern.'

'In that case,' says Charles, making ready to stand, 'I would advise you to hire a lawyer, not a detective. I have no experience in such negotiations, and I do not see how I can assist you.'

'Oh, we have a lawyer,' says Lady Shelley, rather airily, 'but he cannot do what *you* could do.'

Charles looks at her, suddenly wary. 'And that is?'

Lady Shelley opens her mouth to reply, but Sir Percy must have caught something in Charles's tone, because he suddenly lumbers forward rather heavily in his seat. 'Look here, Maddox, I'm going to be honest with you. We're caught in a cleft stick as far as this rotten affair goes. Damned if we do, damned if we don't. And the poor mater isn't what she was. Headaches. Fainting. Partial paralysis on occasion. Dreadful business. Had doctor after doctor in to see her, but none of 'em can tell us what the trouble is. Last thing we want is this sordid to-do dragging on like last time, week after week, month after month. We'll take our medicine and pay the price, but what we need to know first is how much of this stuff there is. Don't want to buy a bunch of letters and then find there's more where that lot came from, and we're back to scratch and yet more to pay. You understand?'

Charles nods. He understands perfectly. Indeed, he's rather more sympathetic than they might assume, and not just because he's always considered blackmail one of the most loathsome of crimes. All unknowingly, Sir Percy has struck a painful chord: Charles, too, is facing the last decline

22

of someone he loves, and has found no doctor who can slow the fall.

'So,' he says eventually, 'you want me to be your spy.'

He had not meant it to sound so brutal, and Lady Shelley bridles, but her husband lays his hand on her arm.

'You can put it that way if you choose, Maddox. Way *we* see it is you'd be protecting me frail old mater from someone who's plagued the life out of her for years.'

It may not be poetic, but it seems heartfelt. Charles looks at them both, and makes a decision. 'Very well. I will see what can be done. But I make no promises. I think you are already informed of my fees?'

Sir Percy nods.

'In that case I will report back to you in a few days.'

They get to their feet, and Sir Percy shakes his hand. His skin is warm and slightly clammy to the touch, though the room is hardly overheated. Lady Shelley rings the bell, then goes to a small writing-desk in the corner of the room and takes out a slip of paper. 'This is the person,' she says, as she comes towards Charles.

A surname, and an address. A few moments later the butler appears, but as Charles gets to the door a thought occurs to him and he turns. 'One last thing, Sir Percy. Why did you choose me? There are many other detectives you might have consulted. Was it a recommendation?'

Sir Percy coughs. 'My wife was going through some of the mater's papers the other day and came upon a reference to your great-uncle. Seems he helped the grandpater with a minor legal matter some years ago. And when we heard that you'd taken over his business, we made the usual enquiries and so forth, and decided you would be as good as anyone.'

It's hardly a ringing endorsement, but that's not the reason Charles asked the question. 'When you say your grandfather, Sir Percy, was that on your mother's side, or your father's?'

Is there, perhaps, a moment's hesitation?

'Grandpapa Godwin,' answers Lady Shelley, stepping forward.

'I see,' replies Charles, noting again how she appropriates her husband's relations, and insinuates an intimacy with people she cannot conceivably have met. 'And yet it was the Shelley name I believe my uncle recognized.'

Sir Percy is standing now with his back to the window, a shadow cast before his face. 'Did he now, by Jove?' he says, with a slightly artificial jauntiness. 'And what did the old fellow have to say?'

Charles shakes his head. 'I have not been able to speak to him of it. He suffered a severe attack the day you called, and has not spoken since. I am assuming the two events were not connected. Unless, of course, you can tell me otherwise?'

There's an awkward silence. Then Lady Shelley comes towards Charles and accompanies him to the door. 'Well, if you do find any papers relating to Grandpapa, you must bring them to show us,' she says animatedly. 'We are – as you now know – avid collectors of all that concerns the Dear Departed.'

Charles gives no reply, but takes his leave once more and follows the butler downstairs and out into the cold and windy square.

The bruised clouds are purple with unfallen rain and the first icy drops are already in the air. Charles turns up his collar and quickens his pace. A small part of his brain is mulling how exactly he is going to do what he has just agreed to attempt, but most of it is contemplating that controversially ordinary man upstairs, and concluding with a private grin that those scientists who claim that character-istics can be passed from one generation to the next need

24

look no further than Chester Square to find the exception that proves the rule. For if talent, or intellect, or genius can really be bequeathed, what a prodigy this man should have been, who numbers among his immediate ancestors four of the greatest literary minds of the last two hundred years.

Back in the drawing room, meanwhile, the Shelleys are watching him as he makes his way along the square and disappears out of sight towards Eccleston Street.

'Well?' says Sir Percy, turning at last to his wife, all jauntiness gone. 'Don't strike me he knows anything, whatever you might have thought.'

'We cannot afford to be complacent,' Lady Shelley replies sharply, still looking down at the square. 'Not with so much at stake.'

A few yards away a beggar who has lost both hands has taken shelter under one of the elm trees and is sitting on the pavement cutting out figures with a pair of scissors held in his feet. A concertina of paper dolls is on the blanket in front of him, weighed down in the wind by ha'penny coins. Lady Shelley frowns and bangs on the window, gesturing peremptorily to the gate-keeper to come and move him off.

'Still think it could all be a terrific to-do about nothing,' mumbles Sir Percy. 'The mater never gave a hint about any of it when I was growing up.'

'How could she have done so without destroying the past for ever in your eyes? Without creating a monster in your mind that even her years of selfless devotion could not counter? It is no surprise to *me* that she has cast a veil of oblivion over those events, and spoken of them only in the bitter privacy of her private journal.'

'And there's no mistake – you're sure it's Harriet she spoke of?'

25

'*You*,' says his wife, with emphasis, 'have not been through their papers. *You* have not read how that wretched girl really met her death. Can you imagine what would ensue if such a document were to become known – such a scandal bruited abroad? *We* may know that woman's secret, but that will not prevent the vulgar world from casting her as an innocent and forsaken wife. After everything I have done to efface all trace of her.'

'But if you burned what you found—'

Her impatience now is flaming in her face. 'But how do we know what *else* there might be? What records that old meddler Maddox might have kept? For one thing, I assure you, is abundantly clear, and that is that *he* had a hand in it. Everything that happened that whole dreadful winter – *he* was involved. Think what that might mean – what more he might know that even we do not yet suspect – what he might say, should he choose to do so.'

Sir Percy shakes his head. 'From what I gathered, he's in no condition to say much at all—'

'But there may still be *papers*, Percy – papers he wrote at the time that would be far more credible, and far more damaging, than the ramblings now of a mad old man.'

'And you don't think it's a risk, hiring this nephew of his? Seemed pretty sharp-witted to me.'

'In that case,' she replies tartly, 'he should be more than capable of resolving our other, more immediate, problem. He is not to know that there is a second, and far more significant task we are using him to accomplish.'

She turns to the window and watches as the gatekeeper pulls the beggar roughly to his feet and manhandles him away. The paper dolls are scattering across the pavement in the wind.

'All the same, Jane,' her husband continues behind her,

'might it not be best just to let matters lie? After all, if nothing's come to light in all these years—'

'How many times must I say this?' she snaps. 'We cannot rely on that state of affairs continuing. If the old man shows no sign of ever recovering there will come a moment when this young fellow will take it upon himself to go through his effects. And who knows then what he may unearth – what papers he may discover that the old man has hidden? Far better that we anticipate such an event, and act now to counter it.'

Sir Percy shakes his head again, his ruddy cheeks suddenly pale. 'I'm still not happy about this, Jane, and as for what you suggested – strikes me as a pretty low way of carrying on. Rather *infra dig*, if you must know—'

She silences him with a glance and turns back once more to the window, her round, plain face suddenly hardened, hawkish. 'If we may contrive to avoid such a course, so much the better. But I tell you this – I will *not* have all I have striven for overturned, or see the labour of so many years laid waste.' Her eyes narrow and her voice drops so low she seems to be speaking only for her own hearing. 'I will not permit the spectre of that woman to return to haunt us, or allow everything this family has achieved to be ruined in her name.'

CHAPTER TWO

The Question

Back at Buckingham Street, Charles opens the door of the drawing room and stands there watching. He isn't really expecting any change, but his heart sinks nonetheless when he sees Maddox's head lolling to one side, and his body starting and flinching at the demons that beset him. The old man's mind wanders, still astray, his dreams darker than any wakened eyes behold. Charles hesitates in the doorway, fighting the urge to go straight back downstairs and ask Abel exactly what he thinks he's doing leaving Maddox here alone, but then there's a movement on the other side of the room and he realizes that he is not, in fact, alone. Molly is with him. She's been raking the hearth and making up the fire, but now she gets up from her knees and goes silently over to where Maddox is lying, wrapped in blankets in his favourite armchair. She pulls up another chair and sits down by his side, then takes one of his dry old hands in her own and reaches out gently to caress his rough grey hair. She does not speak – has never spoken since the day she was first employed in this house – but Charles watches mesmerized now as she starts to sing to Maddox in the low, keening hum he has heard once or twice before. Moment by moment, as the sound lifts and ebbs, the old man's restless body quietens to peace, and the fretfulness slowly smoothes from his face. It's the first time Charles has ever felt like an intruder in this room. He watches a moment more, then closes the door quietly behind him and goes back down to the front door, and a sudden shaft of sunlight that glows the street golden against the inky indigo sky.

Up at the Strand the traffic has come to a standstill and as Charles comes level with the road he can see at once why. Lumbering up from Holborn are three enormous pyramids, balanced somewhat precariously on a dray cart pulled by two labouring horses, and decorated from top to bottom with hieroglyphs, toothy crocodiles and enigmatic elongated cats. Four young men in loincloths are posted at each corner, passing down handbills inviting the discerning London public to present themselves at the Egyptian Hall, Piccadilly, there to peruse Mr Bonomi's Panorama of the Nile, a show unparalleled for its entertainment and edification, during the course of which they will traverse more than a thousand miles by river to the second cataract, and visit the temple of Abu Simbel by torchlight. And all for the paltry sum of a single shilling. Charles smiles at the proprietor's notion of ancient Egyptian garb (and not for the first time, since he saw this particular diorama a year ago when it opened and was actually rather impressed), then ducks behind the barrel-chested constable who is even now bearing down upon the Pharaoh's coachman, with instructions to move along there, move along.

Once safely on the opposite side of the street, Charles edges behind the crowd of excited onlookers, and attendant ragtag and snot-nose pickpockets, and slips up Bedford Street to Nattali & Bond, Purveyors of Second-hand Books, whence he emerges in due course with a parcel containing a set of Shelley's poetry. He'd wanted the Medwin memoir too, but Mr Bond had doubted many were printed, though he has promised (for a small inducement) to ask among his fellow booksellers and let Charles know if it can be found. The four volumes in Charles's parcel have gold-embossed spines and smooth marbled cardboard covers, but only the first seems to have seen any wear. An impression confirmed when Charles gets the books home and discovers that the pages in the other three have not even been cut. It's not a promising portent, and it's with a heavy heart that he sits down with volume one to begin *Queen Mab*. Only to put the book down again twenty minutes later, completely nonplussed. He has a vague memory that the poem was supposed to be a furious attack on everything from religion to meat-eating to the institution of marriage, and he had been looking forward to a spirited polemic. Only what he's found instead is a seemingly endless introduction peopled by spirits of quite another kind. Quite how Death and Sleep and the Fairy Queen can possibly be relevant to the task in hand Charles has absolutely no idea, which rather – in his opinion – defeats the whole object. And who is this 'Ianthe' Shelley talks of, with her dark blue eyes, who sleeps and may never waken? He picks the book up again, and turns, with some frustration, to the notes on the poem written by Mrs Shelley, which turn out to reveal rather more about her devotion to her husband's memory than they do about the meaning of what he wrote. Charles sits back, wondering for a moment about that very literary marriage, and what Shelley would have thought if he had lived to see his wife's fame out-star his own. Say, 'Shelley' in 1850 – or, indeed, in

30

2013 – and what will come to mind will not be *Queen Mab*, or *Adonaïs*, or even the *Ode to a Skylark*, but *Frankenstein*. Then as now, it is Mary who is celebrated, Mary who is recognized. She may do due obeisance before her husband's poetic genius, but it is her own hideous progeny that endures. Or, rather, the idea we image of it, for as Charles well knows – having sat through an excruciating burlesque version at the Adelphi Theatre only a year ago – it is the caricature dramatizations that have made the myth of the monster, not its creator's chilly, cerebral prose.

Charles is about to turn back to where he left off when the door opens and Abel appears, carrying a plate of mutton and potatoes. Charles has been so engrossed he's completely forgotten about lunch.

'Summat interesting in the end, was it, Mr Charles?' says Stornaway, putting the hot plate down a little gingerly on the desk. 'So there was nae threat to the pastry-forks after all?'

There's no disguising the I-told-you-so gleam in his eye and Charles has the good grace to return grin for grin. 'You can breathe again, Abel. The cutlery proved to be entirely unscathed. It was something rather more complicated than that, as it turned out.'

He hadn't realized how hungry he is and picks up the knife and fork and starts enthusiastically on the meat. Abel hovers in the door, transparently eager for elaboration. And, as it happens, Charles had been on the point of calling him up.

'Do you remember a case involving a William Godwin, Abel? Some sort of legal matter?'

'Lawyer, was he, Mr Charles?'

Charles makes a face; his recent experience of lawyers has not been a happy one. 'William Godwin, my dear Abel, was

31

as far from a lawyer as one could possibly imagine. He was a philosopher, and a celebrated one. And a writer of novels in his spare time, if you can credit such a shift from the sublime to the banal. And he was also my new client's grandfather, and it seems my uncle worked for him, too, years ago.'

Abel's spry old face now looks concerned. He's always prided himself on his memory, but having witnessed the drawn-out disintegration of a far finer mind than he ever had, he's now disproportionately disturbed by any failure in his own. 'When was this, Mr Charles?'

Charles shrugs. 'I'm not sure. Sir Percy didn't say.'

'Well,' says Abel slowly, 'I remember there was a period in 'sixteen when I were away from London for a time. It were when me old father died. And I were in Ireland on a case a year or so afore that. A smuggling ring, that one was.'

Charles smiles, seeing the remembrance of triumphs past in the old man's eyes. 'Would you mind going through the files for me, Abel, and seeing if you can find Godwin's name?'

Abel smiles now in his turn. It's not escaped his notice that there is a flush to his young master's cheeks that has not been there for more than a week. 'It'd be my pleasure, Mr Charles.'

When Charles takes his empty plate downstairs an hour later he finds Molly in the kitchen chopping vegetables for dinner. She looks up briefly when he comes in, then drops her eyes again. Her skin is so velvet dark that he cannot see if she is blushing, and even though he has rather an acute alertness to unspoken signals, he sees this as a technique to be employed as part of his job, and rarely applies it either to himself or his own relationships. Maddox is, perhaps, the

32

only exception, and his infirmity is now so overwhelming that it engulfs the minuscule space in his mind that Charles permits to trivial – for which read personal – preoccupations. As for this girl, he has a care for her, of a kind, but she has only shared his bed twice, and not at all in the days since his uncle's latest illness. Charles cannot decide if he is relieved or regretful – either that it started, or that it seems, just as suddenly, to have ceased.

Molly seems intent on her onions and her swede, and after a moment Charles puts down the dirty plate and leaves the way he came. He does not see, therefore, that as soon as he has gone the knife drops from her grasp and she turns away to the window, where she stands, her arms wrapped tight about herself, watching the streaming rain.

* * *

Two hours later Charles, too, is watching the rain, though in his case from the far more precarious shelter of a large beech tree, a few yards from the address in St John's Wood that Lady Shelley gave him. It's a square, white-fronted villa, two storeys high, with a small front garden and steps up to a creeper-covered porch on the raised ground floor. Such a house would set you back a good three million now (though this particular one has long been supplanted by a block of red-brick flats) but in 1850 this part of London had none of its twenty-first century cachet, being seen at best as prettily – or pettily – suburban, and at worst the haunt of the shameless and the sinful. George Eliot will soon be one of the most infamous examples, choosing St John's Wood to set up home with the still-married George Henry Lewes, and there are three self-styled 'ladies' keeping – or kept in – houses on this very street, where he who pays the rent is not the only man seen going discreetly in and out in the dark hours of the day. So it's with a certain piquant interest that Charles has set himself up with his newspaper just opposite Carlo Cottage, thankful that the wind has dropped, at least. No one has appeared so far, either at a window or at the door, and there is nothing to indicate the age or number of people in residence, though the slightly unkempt garden and small signs of wear and tear that only become obvious under careful scrutiny may have their own tale to tell.

Such surveillance is always the most tiresome aspect of his chosen profession, and the one to which Charles is least suited, being by nature both restless and impatient. So it is perhaps fortunate that he does not have much longer to wait before the door does indeed open, and a servant emerges onto the step. She's dressed for shopping, with a wicker basket over one arm, and stands a moment wrestling with a large black umbrella. But then there's a sudden shout from further down the street and Charles turns to see two young boys racing towards him through the puddles. There's no sign of a mother or a nursemaid, but these are clearly no urchins, even if their white stockings are now spattered to the knees with mud. They come hurtling towards Charles, whooping and yelling, and now the older is gaining yard by yard on the smaller boy, who turns to see where his brother is behind, slips, loses his footing and lands heavily on his face in a gutter choked with dead leaves and dog shit. Blood is running down the white stocking now, but Charles checks any urge he might have had to rush forward to the boy's assistance, which turns out to be the right decision – professionally speaking – because there's a quick movement at the window of the house opposite, and the door swings opens almost at once. Charles cannot see the figure now in the doorway, but an instruction has clearly been given, because the maid moves quickly down to the street and bends over the sobbing child, then takes his hand and leads both boys up the step and into the house. Which is food for thought, at least for Charles, who folds his paper and walks pensively away.

When we next see him it's on an altogether different street, in an altogether different part of London, but one where some of you may have followed him once before. A stretch of grim grey houses running along the back of the new Waterloo railway. Strident with the shriek of engines by day, and by night every bit as explicit as Soho once was in its display of naked human merchandise. When it comes to a reputation for sin, St John's Wood may have got it but it doesn't flaunt it, which is a subtlety you could never lay at any door in Granby Street. But at this hour the curtains are closed and the gas unlit, and there's no sign yet of the usual crush of bloods, idle browsers and men of the town. Charles makes his way to a small house towards the end of the street and goes round to knock on the door at the back. It's a while before there are sounds of life inside, but then again, its occupant works the night shift and it's not yet four. At length he hears the scrape of a bolt drawing back, and the door edges open an inch. The girl looks up at him, suspicious at first, until recognition dawns and the door opens a little more. Her face still bears the trace of last night's makeup, and he can see her nightgown under the blowsy white peignoir.

'Maddox, ain't it? What you doin' 'ere?'

'I should have come before. To tell you what happened.'

The girl crosses her arms. 'No need. It were all over the 'Aymarket in a coupla hours. You got 'im, dincha, like you promised? That bastard as done for our Liz?'

Charles shakes his head. 'Not the one directly responsible, I'm afraid – he was too clever for us. But the man who hired him will be made to pay. The police will see to that.'

The girl sniffs and considers him, but in the end she must have decided that his pledge has been redeemed, because the next time she speaks her voice has lost its bitter edge. 'You didn't needta come all this way to tell me that. Could 'ave sent that boy of yours wiv a message.'

'Yes, I could,' he says, though he's not at all sure he'd trust the cheery but rather feckless Billy anywhere near a place like Granby Street. 'But I have a job I need doing, and I think you could do it.'

The girl's eyes narrow. 'Want me to shag someone, do yer? Can't believe you'd fink of me if it were anyfing else.'

Charles's gaze is steady. 'No. It's nothing like that. I'm sorry, I don't know your name.'

'That's 'cause I never told yer. Me name is Nancy. Nancy Dyer.'

'Nancy, then. If you'll let me in I can explain.'

The room is as he remembered it, though broad day does it no favours. What had looked suggestive if rather shabby by lamplight now looks the latter only. The carpet is worn to the threads in places, and there's a scattering of coal dust across some of the walls. Cheap wine mingles cloyingly with the girl's thin scent. She hurries to remove her discarded underclothes from the bed, then balances against the back of one of the chairs, too tense, it seems, to sit down. 'So what is it, then?'

Charles looks round, then takes a seat at what he hopes will be a reassuring distance.

'Lizzie used to do jobs for me sometimes. Like getting information. Asking questions I couldn't ask. She was good at it, too.'

36

The girl's face is half disbelieving, half disdainful. 'So she were your snitch? When you was a rozzer?'

Charles shifts a little uneasily in his seat. 'We had an agreement – I only asked her if I was absolutely sure that what she was doing would help to right a wrong. And only if it involved powerful men who would otherwise never be caught. I swear to you, I never asked her to inform on her own, however terrible their crimes.'

'So only men like what 'ad her killed?'

'Exactly. Men like that. Men with all the weight of money and position to protect them.'

The girl raises an eyebrow. 'Bet she still 'ad to shag 'em. Best place to get a man to spill's always in bed.'

Charles blushes, despite himself. 'Sometimes, yes. But I always paid her well over her usual rate. And I was always nearby. I made sure she never got hurt.'

The girl makes a face. 'More'n I can say of my Arnie. 'E don't give a damn what 'appens to me. As long as I'm openin' me legs and earnin' 'im money to piss away on gin.'

Charles leans forwards. 'And in any case I don't want you to do that. Not this time – it's much simpler—'

There's a creak then, and Charles looks round to see a little girl standing in the doorway, her feet bare, her small face smudged from sleep, and a tattered doll gripped tight in one hand. She sways slightly, her eyes huge with uncertainty, and puts a finger into her mouth. Charles's heart catches in his chest. Remembering that same gesture, those same green eyes, that same golden head of curls. Remembering a girl child who'd clung as this one does, but to something that should have comforted her as no doll ever could – her older brother's hand. *His* hand. He can feel the warmth of her fingers even now – all these years later – as he unwound them one by one from his own and turned away, embarrassed to be seen with her and shamed as only a ten-year-old boy can be by a sister's tears. And that was when it happened. In the busy insignificant moment before his mother looked back from the other side of the street and saw her daughter gone. He couldn't have known – couldn't possibly have looked into the dark forward and abyss of time, and seen all the consequences of a moment of such childish carelessness. But that is his curse. Now and always. He cannot forgive himself because he cannot put it right. A sister missing, and a mother lost for ever to the madness of an irreparable grief.

Meanwhile this little girl has been eyeing him shyly, and now makes a tiny hesitant move in his direction. Charles flinches, despite himself, and as the little girl's face crumples into a wail Nancy rushes forward and scoops her child away. 'Come 'ere, sweet'eart,' she whispers. 'Don't think the gen'leman's used to the likes of you.'

'What's her name?' asks Charles, his throat taut.

'Lizbeth,' she says softly. 'For Liz. She were 'er god-mother. Well, unofficial, like. But I calls 'er Betsy.'

She's rocking the child gently to and fro, and only now catches sight of his face. 'Sorry, I know you cared about 'er too.'

Charles swallows. 'It's not that. Elizabeth is – was – my sister's name.'

The girl nods, as alert as Charles himself would have been to that shift in tense. They're silent for a moment, and then the little girl starts to fidget. Her mother gets to her feet. 'I'll give 'er somefing to eat and put 'er down, and then you can tell me what this is all about. It don't concern 'er after all.'

'Actually,' says Charles, slowly, 'I think you'll find it does.'

*

38

The rain has stopped by the time he leaves, and the first lights are coming on in the adjoining houses. As he walks back up towards Waterloo Road one of the curtains sweeps back and he can see into a narrow front room where three whores are preparing for evening business. A girl in a gauzy chemise and striped drawers is lacing another's corset, and a third has her foot upon a chair as she rolls a stocking up over her thigh. Charles slows, struck by a composition as perfect, in its way, as a Dutch master. They're oblivious to his observation, and despite the sordid nature of their trade there is laughter and – for now at least – there is affection in this tawdry little room. Charles watches a moment and then, as he starts to move slowly on his way, the girl in the chemise lifts her friend's ringlets gently away and kisses her lightly on her bare shoulder.

The windows of Buckingham Street, by contrast, unveil no intimacy, but Charles has scarcely opened the door when he is set upon by Abel, who has clearly been watching for his return and seizes Charles's arm excitedly. 'I think I found it, Mr Charles – the file, the one ye were looking for.'

Charles takes off his coat and heaps it on the hall table, as Billy emerges at the top of the kitchen stairs. 'Excellent work, Abel. I'll come up with you straight away. And hang this up, will you, Billy?'

As the two of them make their way up to the office, Billy picks up the coat and wipes the damp from the polished wood with his sleeve. Then he stands for a moment, his face in shadow, watching the two figures slowly ascend the stairs and round the corner out of sight.

The file is lying open on the desk, the oil lamp brought beside it. The writing is the poised and assertive hand of

Maddox in his prime, but that's not the first thing Charles notices. Unlike all the other case-books ranged on shelves in this office, this one has had a section removed. And not just one or two leaves either – thirty pages or more are gone near the end of the book, and even Maddox's account of the Ratcliffe Highway murders – perhaps the most notorious crime of the nineteenth century – merited only half as many as are missing here.

'It's the file for 1816, Mr Charles,' says Abel, breathlessly, as Charles goes over to the book and draws the lamp closer. 'I knew it mustae been when I were away. I'd've remembered it else.'

Charles barely registers the old man's relief that his memory has not betrayed him, so intently is he scanning the page before him. The paper is discoloured and the lines immediately after the missing section have been heavily inked through, but immediately below them Charles can make out the name *William Godwin, Esquire*, and underneath

For services rendered, the amount of 30/-

And then – rare indeed in these books, as Charles well knows – a single word, added in different ink at a later date: *Unpaid*.

Charles looks up. 'Does that mean anything to you, Abel?'

Abel looks blank. 'Nay, Mr Charles, I cannae say that it do. And I've never known the boss cut pages from his files either, that I can tell 'ee. Allus took pride in having everythin' noted and all the details in order.'

Charles nods, disquieted. Maddox was always punctilious to a fault as to what he revealed publicly of his clients' affairs, but made it a point of honour neither to prevaricate nor falsify in the privacy of his own records. Charles has read reports in those files that would, even now, change our view of many of his most celebrated contemporaries – cases involving prime ministers, captains of industry, peers of the realm. And yet all this material Maddox has allowed to remain intact, so why make such an extraordinary exception in this particular case? What was it about the work he had done for Godwin that made it so imperative to eradicate all trace of it?

'And he never let anyone see these books,' continues Abel. 'Except you, o' course. He allus intended ye would have 'em one day.'

Which is not, in the circumstances, an especially comforting thought. Charles looks again at where the pages have been cut out and runs his thumb down the paper. The edges are soft: whatever it was that Maddox removed, he had clearly done it some time ago. Charles opens the book and holds the page against the light, but the scored-through lines are still obscured.

'I tried that me'sen,' says Abel, with a sigh. 'I couldnae make out any of it.'

Charles puts the book down and gets to his feet. 'There may be a way,' he says, as he goes to the door and calls for Billy. 'It's a risk, with paper this old, but it might work.'

Five minutes later the boy is back down from his errand to the attic, carrying a wooden box, closed with a lock. It looks for all the world like a doctor's case, and when Charles opens the lid Abel can see a row of small glass bottles, each one carefully labelled.

'What might these be, Mr Charles?' says Abel, reaching to the nearest phial, only to have Charles quickly restrain his hand.

'Have a care, Abel. Some of these bottles contain acid. Or poison.'

Abel backs off at once, and eases his old body down slowly into the spare chair. Charles, meanwhile, has pulled on a pair of large leather gloves and poured a quantity of clear liquid into a small porcelain basin. This he dilutes with water, then applies to the ink with a stiff white feather. Slowly, carefully, stroke by stroke. His task done, he sits back, waits a moment as the chemicals bubble on the page, then takes a piece of cloth from the case and dabs the liquid away. Abel gets creaking to his feet, and comes to stand over Charles's shoulder. The acid has burned through here and there, and the words that remain have bleached to sepia brown. But they are legible, they are legible.

Charles is scarcely breathing, his heart beating hard, suddenly, in his ears. Ever since the day he returned to this house to find Sir Percy's card, and his uncle sunk in a stupor only death could deepen, he has wondered. Wondered how the mere sight of the Shelley name could have precipitated such a terrible seizure. But perhaps these words are the answer to that question, or at least the beginnings of one. For what Charles has here is not only an allegation of murder, but what amounts to a confession of complicity in Maddox's own hand. Was it the memory of another's guilt that came back to him with such horrifying force that day, or the consciousness of his own?

'Do you know what this means, Abel?'

But he already knows from his face that the old man is as disturbed by what they have just found as Charles is himself.

'Would Fraser know? Was he in London then?'

Abel nods slowly. 'He were. His memory isnae allus what it was, Mr Charles. But I could write and ask him.'

'Do that,' says Charles, thoughtfully, after a moment. 'And have a look, would you, for where these missing pages

42

.... allegation of murder, seeing it only as the

....rence of a justifiable anger and an insupportable grief.

.. ..w...... ...., I believe the accusation to be

mistaken only in the ...nity of the perpetrator. It was her death he...

...., even if no blow was struck, no poison

administered, no weapon ever wielded. Whatever part I myself

have played, whatever blame I must in future endure, I know now

where the true guilt lay. Ever since the appalling death of that other

innocent creature I have believed him accursed – fated to bring

death and ruination on all those unfortunate enough to come within

his sphere, whether by action, or by negligence, whether it is by

...., or not. But this time, I accept, I was wrong. ... .

a touch as mortal as a Medusa's gaze, and a heart as frozen as

as midwinter ice.

might be. Get Billy to help you. It's possible they may still
be somewhere in the house.'

* * *

By the time he leaves Buckingham Street the following
morning Charles has made a decision. He's not naïve, and
he understands the risks: he knows that what he has
discovered threatens to reveal something about his uncle's
past that the old man himself has done all in his power to
destroy. But he also knows – or suspects – that it's connected
in some way with Sir Percy Shelley's decision to employ

him, and he has no intention of colluding, even thirty years later, with the concealment of a murder. And all the less so if the victim was a woman or a child, for surely that must be what the words 'innocent creature' meant. Whatever task it was that Maddox undertook for William Godwin it was clearly no minor legal matter, whatever Sir Percy may have wished him to believe, and what Charles needs now is a rather more objective source of information than the philosopher's own grandson. Indeed, he's struggling to imagine how a man like Godwin ever came to need the services of a thief-taker in the first place, and if there are other people yet living who have the answer to that question, Charles has no idea how to go about finding them. But an account of Godwin's life might – just – hold a clue, and this it is that Charles is now in quest of. It's early – too early for Mr Bond (and as for Mr Nattali, he has been 'late' these five years and more), so Charles kills time with bread-and-butter and a mug of coffee from a stall on the Strand, and watches the fruit and vegetable carts heaving up towards Covent Garden, pursued by shabby urchins hopeful of a tumbling orange, but sharp enough to stay beyond the costers' whips.

The blinds of the bookshop are finally raised a quarter of an hour later, but Charles has to loiter another slow five minutes before the door opens to reveal the elegant, rather sardonic features of Archibald Bond. He is dressed, as always, in an impeccable ensemble of discreet greys, accompanied by a pair of white cotton gloves as immaculate as his stock. His hair is smoothed glassily against his head and there is an unobtrusive but unmistakable odour of pomade.

'Ah, Mr Maddox,' he says, with a careful smile, as he recognizes his client and holds the door open for him to enter, 'I am afraid I have no news for you as yet.'

Charles stares at him a moment, dumbfounded, but then remembers. The Medwin memoir. 'No,' he says, following Bond into the shop. 'It's not that. I'm after something else this time. A biography of William Godwin.'

Outside, the sky is bright with winter sun; inside, the shop looms dark with shelves from floor to ceiling. Motes float slowly in air heavy with the must of old books and dry paper. Bond straightens a pile of copies of the *Illustrated London News* that does not need straightening, then circles round to his accustomed place behind the counter. His assistant is halfway up the library steps at the back of the shop, eddying a duster along the tops of the volumes. He's worked here for as long as Charles can remember, and has hardly changed in all that time, having seemingly descended into a prematurely desiccated old age long before Charles was even born. There is a deep, disfigured hollow where one eye should have been, and the other wanders somewhat alarmingly, which may explain why Mr Bond prefers him to remain, as now, in the shadows. But he would not be without him: Sefton knows Bond's hoarded stock better even than his master, and will take but a moment to place a coarse and sinewy finger on any volume a customer may require.

'A biography of William Godwin,' Bond says now. 'I am not sure I can help you.'

'In that case,' replies Charles, somewhat curtly, 'I'm sure I can find another shop—'

Bond holds up a hand, 'You mistake me, Mr Maddox. I doubt my ability to assist you purely because I do not believe such a volume exists. I can offer you a very nice edition of *An Enquiry concerning Political Justice*, scarcely used, and a slightly foxed but otherwise serviceable copy of *Reflections on Education, Manners, and Literature*, but as to a memoir . . .' He spreads his hands, at a loss, and theatrically so.

Charles strikes the counter in frustration, sending dust into the air and a flicker of alarm across the proprietor's face.

'It is surprising, I grant you,' says Bond, in a placatory tone, 'given the undoubted status of the subject. I believe his daughter once planned to write just such a memoir, but as far as I am aware it has not yet appeared.'

Charles is about to turn away when Bond calls him back. 'After you left yesterday it was brought to my attention that we *are* in possession of one piece of Shelleyana that might interest you.'

Charles frowns – *Shelleyana?* – but he's intrigued all the same, and watches as Bond dips down behind the counter and reappears with a small book in his hand. It is undeniably a beautiful object – the leather a rich polished caramel, and the spine stamped in gold with a line of fleurs-de-lis.

Bond places it reverentially on the counter, opens it to the title page, then turns it to face Charles. The illustration is of a naked sleeping girl, her legs and lower torso enveloped in dark clouds, and hovering over her, a spirit holding a wand wreathed with leaves. And above the picture the title words

QUEEN MAB
by
Percy Bysshe Shelley

'A pirate edition, printed in 1829 by John Brooks of Oxford Street,' says Bond, smoothing a hand over the paper and lowering his voice as if in the presence of a holy relic. 'Exquisite, quite exquisite. And especially interesting for the collector in that it contains the dedication included in the original edition, but which the poet himself tried later to suppress. I believe he even went so far as to cut it from the copies of the poem he gave to his friends.'

Charles looks at him, then at the book, then reaches out to turn the page.

TO HARRIET * * * * *

Whose is the love that gleaming through the world
Wards off the poisonous arrow of its scorn?
    Whose is the warm and partial praise,
    Virtue's most sweet reward?

Beneath whose looks did my reviving soul
Riper in truth and virtuous daring grow?
    Whose eyes have I gazed fondly on,
    And loved mankind the more?

HARRIET! on thine: – thou wert my purer mind;
Thou wert the inspiration of my song;
    Thine are these early wilding flowers,
    Though garlanded by me.

Then press into thy breast this pledge of love,
And know, though time may change and years may roll,
    Each flow'ret gathered in my heart
    It consecrates to thine.

There is no such dedication in the edition of the poem Charles has back at Buckingham Street. He raises his eyes again to Bond. 'Who is this woman – do you know?'

Bond leans a little towards him. 'The poet's wife,' he says confidentially.

47

Charles frowns. 'But his wife's name was Mary.'

Bond smiles the knowing smile of the better-informed. 'Mr Maddox is speaking, I believe, of his *second* wife. The poet made his first foray into the marriage state with a Miss Harriet Westbrook. The same young woman who is referred to here.'

Charles's heart lurches a beat. 'And what happened to her?'

Again Bond spreads his white-gloved hands. 'That, I fear, I cannot tell you.'

There is a cough then, dry and circumspect, from the back of the shop. Sefton has descended silently from his steps and now beckons to his employer, shuffling all the while from one foot to the other. With a glance at Charles begging his indulgence, Bond retreats towards his assistant. Charles watches Bond confer briefly with the old man, and a moment later he comes forward again to Charles. 'Mr Sefton has – as always – an admirable memory. He recalls there was a Chancery case involving Mr Shelley, which caused something of a stir – he was challenged by his father-in-law, Mr Westbrook, for the custody of his children. A case it seems he eventually lost. One can only infer that the young woman herself had died some time before.'

Charles nods slowly. 'When was this?'

'Thirty years ago or more. I am afraid Mr Sefton could not be precise.'

'But it could have been as early as 1816?'

Bond frowns slightly. 'I suppose so, but why that year in particular?'

But Charles has already left the shop.

Now what, thinks Charles, as he strides back down Bedford Street, could possibly have induced any court in this kingdom to deprive an Englishman of the custody of his own legitimate children? A man, moreover, of wealth and family. What sin – what atrocious crime – could Shelley have committed to have merited such cruel and unusual treatment? That is the question, but for a man of Charles's resourcefulness the answer may not be so very far away. No further, indeed, than 136 The Strand, and the establishment of Messrs W. H. Smith & Son (a name you perhaps recognize). The reading room here may not be as imposing as the one Charles customarily uses at the British Museum, but the newspaper archives are extremely well stocked and the room is warm on a cold day, as the popularity of the seats nearest the fire attests. Charles makes his way to the racks of newspapers. He decides to start with the daily Court of Chancery reports for December 1816, and work forwards. And if he finds nothing, work backwards. But it's nowhere near as complicated as that, as it turns out. Within an hour he has found three references to the case in the *Morning Chronicle*, the most interesting being one dated 26th August 1817, which recounts that during the previous day's proceedings Sir Samuel Romilly, counsel for Mr Westbrook, had declared that his client objected to Shelley's guardianship of the children on two grounds: first, his dangerous and improper opinions on the subjects of religion and marriage; and second (and here Charles grips the paper a little tighter) that Shelley had openly co-habited with another woman while his first wife was still alive.

Charles copies down the paragraph, then spends a fruitless half-hour tracking further back for an announcement of Harriet Westbrook's death, but there is nothing. Which is strange, and perhaps suggestive. But if the dead elude him, the living may be easier to find, so he puts the newspapers back and turns to the 1818 poll books for Westminster, where he finds one John Westbrook Esquire, resident in Chapel Street, in the parish of St George, Hanover Square. And if Charles needs any further proof that he has found his man, Westbrook is listed as having cast his vote for the selfsame Sir Samuel Romilly who had taken his case to court. Charles does a quick mental calculation – Westbrook would be at least as old as Maddox now, if not older, so it's with little expectation of success that he pulls the current *London Post Office Directory* from the shelf. And, sure enough, there are no Westbrooks now in Chapel Street, so no possibility of questioning the family, even assuming they would agree to see him. There are directories for the rest of the country, of course, but Charles doesn't know if John Westbrook had a son, and other daughters might well have married and changed their names. He'd be looking for hatpins in a haystack half the size of England. He heaves the book back onto the shelf; basic police work has got him thus far, but there's little more he can hope to find here now. Moreover it's gone noon, and the reading room is starting to empty. He puts his notebook in his coat and makes his way back out to the Strand. But instead of turning left for Buckingham Street, and the comforts of a well-raked fire and Molly's steak pudding, he heads north. North to Bow Street, and the police station-house.

It was once Charles's daily destination, this tall, elegant building on the fringes of some of the most dangerous districts in the city. Three years he was based here, learning his trade, learning his London, and becoming – until he was dismissed for insubordination – a detective worthy enough to succeed even Maddox's exceptional example. And he still cannot quite suppress a little flutter of apprehension as he makes his way up the steps, even though his quarrel with Inspector Bucket seems finally to have been laid to rest, and the tentative beginning of a friendship has taken its place. The front office is empty now but for two drunken old men sitting slumped on the floor, and a small boy of five or six who is telling anyone who will listen that if they can show him Fleet Lane he can find his way home. The constable behind the desk seems too distracted by the howls and screeches echoing up from the cells below to take much notice of the boy, and Charles crouches down a moment to give the lad directions before taking a piece of paper from his pocket and handing it to the officer. The man looks sceptical at first, but then reads the name on the note. 'I'll see he gets it, sir.'

'Tell him I'll be in the White Hart.'

The pub is crowded, but then again, a pub this close to Covent Garden will always be crowded on market day. A nod to the landlord (another old acquaintance from his days in the Met) earns Charles a small but private booth at the back, and two glasses of beer, clanked down on the wooden table by a wearied waitress who scarcely looks at him. Charles orders pies and baked marrow, and settles back to wait. The patrons of this establishment are hardly what one might call select – indeed it was once the haunt of highwaymen and one of the staging posts from Newgate prison to the Tyburn tree (a possible origin, incidentally, of the phrase 'on the wagon', since condemned men were allowed off the cart for their last draught, but the hangman had to stay *in situ*, and sober). But on our particular December afternoon the bar is thronged by as many women as men, most smoking clay pipes, and all of them in various stages of drink-induced discontent. Charles observes quietly, and without interference, as the noise rises, and the disputes with it, until he spots the carrot head of his old colleague at the door, and stands to gesture to him. Sam Wheeler makes his way through a crowd that clearly knows his trade, for a path opens before him and the din dims a little until he has passed. There is no open animosity – no overt insult – but the wariness on their faces says 'rozzer' louder even than his tall hat, stock and uniform greatcoat.

There's a seat empty opposite Charles, but it doesn't surprise him that Sam elects to edge round the table to squeeze onto the bench by his side. No policeman with an ounce of nous would sit with his back to a pub full of rowdy costers, and Sam is way too wily for that.

He picks up his beer, then reaches into his pocket and puts Charles's note on the table in front of him.

'Well, I've looked, like you asked,' he says, wiping his mouth of froth, 'but I ain't turned up nothin'. There weren't no police files back then o' course, but we do 'ave some of the Runners' records and there's nothin' mentionin' the death of either an 'Arriet Shelley or an 'Arriet Westbrook. Not for 1816, and not for a year afore that neither.'

'And no unidentified victims matching her age?'

Sam looks sceptical. 'You really think a bloke like Shelley could have done away wiv 'is wife and managed to stash the body some'ow? Poet, weren't 'e? And a bleedin' nob to boot? Come off it, Chas, 'ow likely is that?'

'All the same – were there any young women whose bodies were never claimed?'

Sam sighs. 'Not as far as I could see. Though I didn't 'ave much time. I do 'ave work to do, yer know.'

Charles makes a rueful *moue*, which his friend knows is about as close to an apology as he's likely to get.

'That writin' you found that talked about a murder,' Sam continues, taking another swig of beer. 'You sure it was the Godwin job it were referrin' to?'

Charles starts to fiddle with the paper on the table, in part to hide his irritation. 'It was immediately above Godwin's name in the case-book. It had to refer to that investigation – what else could it be? And it's not just that. I'm convinced that's why the Shelleys hired me in the first place – I've asked around and there's no trace of those "enquiries" they claimed to have made about me. No, they didn't choose me because I'm good at what I do – they chose me because of *who I am*. Because there's something Maddox knows. And whatever it is, it was in those missing pages.'

Sam shrugs. 'Don't mean it 'as to be an actual murder, though, do it? I mean, people like that, they gets very 'ot and bovvered when the likes of us starts rummagin' about in their private affairs. That newspaper story you found about Shelley co-'abitin' wiv another woman – that ain't the sorta thing they'd want diggin' up. Not now.'

'And certainly not,' says Charles, drily, 'if they've been doing everything in their power to ensure it remains safely buried.'

'But even if they 'ave, it don't prove this 'Arriet was murdered. She coulda died in any one of an 'undred ways. Smallpox, typhoid, childbirth—'

'She was living apart from her husband.'

There is a silence. Charles glances up and sees Sam studying his bandaged hand.

'Look,' he says, pulling his hand under the table, 'I know what you're saying but I just don't believe it's as simple as that. And, more to the point, neither did Maddox.'

Sam eyes him carefully. ''E's still not well, then.'

Charles shakes his head. 'But you know as well as I do

that he would never have written those words if he wasn't absolutely sure of what he was saying. Even if he didn't have the proof necessary to make such an accusation in public.'

Sam nods. Even in 1850, Maddox is still remembered in the Metropolitan Police, and Sam needs no reminding of either his achievements or his much-merited reputation.

The waitress comes towards the table with two plates under tin lids and clatters them down. There is a delicious smell of meat and gravy and the two of them fall on the food like men half starved.

'I was thinkin',' says Sam, a minute later, his mouth full of pie, 'those words of your uncle's – he obviously weren't the only person as thought there'd been a murder. Someone 'ad obviously spoken to 'im about it and 'e didn't believe 'em – or at least not to start wiv.'

Charles raises an eyebrow. 'I had just about managed to get that far, Sam,' he says.

'No, what I mean is, 'as it occurred to you that that person might be the same one the Shelleys want you to spy on? I reckon this other person's showed 'em papers of 'is own – papers they 'ad no idea existed, and that's what's set the cat among the pigeons all of a sudden. I'm prepared to bet them Shelleys 'ad never even 'eard the name Maddox before that.'

Charles is staring at him now – staring like a man who has just had a revelation. As indeed he has. 'That's brilliant, Sam – *brilliant*. I've been wondering what the sudden urgency is in all this, why the Shelleys didn't try to track my uncle down years ago if they were so worried about what he might say, but if they've only just discovered he was involved that would explain everything. That has to be the answer – *has to be*.'

54

Sam grins. 'Glad to be of use.'

Charles picks up his fork, then lays it down again. 'One more favour, Sam. Can you have another look at the Runners' files for 1816? Not for Harriet this time, but for my uncle – see if there's any mention of his name, any suggestion of what he might have been doing back then.'

Sam wipes his mouth with his sleeve. 'Right you are. Now then, what do you say to pudding?'

CHAPTER THREE

A Wanderer

Back at Buckingham Street, time scarcely seems to have passed at all. It is as if the house is becalmed in a perpetual present tense: Molly is cooking, Billy is filling the coal scuttles, Abel is sitting at Maddox's side, and the old man himself is straying still, like a day-appearing dream, through the dim wildernesses of his closed and darkened mind. Charles climbs the stairs to the office, where he goes again through the case-books for the years before 1816 for any possible clue he might have overlooked. But there's nothing. Nothing, oddly, apart from another section mysteriously missing from late 1814, but there are no scored-through words there, either before or after the excised pages, and therefore no clue, now, as to what they once contained.

He is putting the files back on the shelf when he registers the sound of the door-bell downstairs, but assumes it's the butcher's boy until he looks up to see Billy standing at the office door. 'Female to see you, Mr Charles.'

Charles sighs. The lad is good with Maddox, and strong enough to lift him, which Abel clearly can no longer do, but the price to be paid in almost insubordination is inching higher by the day. 'What sort of word is that, Billy?'

Billy's cheek twitches, in the half-ghost of a half-wink. 'Well, Mr Charles, I wouldn't say as she were a "lady", if you take my meanin'. Though she's dressed a bit fancy for a "woman", I should say.'

Charles gets to his feet. 'Thank you, Billy. You may show her up here to the office. And perhaps you might consider giving the same degree of attention to the difference between a well-polished boot and a merely adequate one.'

But sarcasm is lost on Billy, who simply grins, and sidles back out of the room.

When the door opens a few moments later, he would hardly have recognized her. A neat dark blue dress, a white lace collar, and a bonnet demure enough for a Sunday-school teacher.

'Well,' he says, slightly lost for words, 'You look—'

'Respectable for once?' Nancy smiles. 'Weren't so 'ard. I 'ad all this stuff anyway. Used to be an 'ousemaid before I fell for Betsy and got chucked out on me ear. Comes in useful wiv blokes as wants to act out their little make-believe about doing the governess, and I aims to cater for all sorts. I can do the voice too, if I've a mind. Which is just as well, considerin'.'

Charles pulls out the only other seat in the room and offers it to her, his manners modulating unconsciously to match her dress. 'So what happened? Did it work?'

Nancy nods. 'Give that to yer – you knew exactly what rope to pull with that one.'

'So you took the child with you?'

Nancy smoothes her skirt. 'Went one better. Stuffed a pillow up me petticoat and pretended I were in the family way. And I made sure Betsy was 'ungry, so there I was

57

standing outside the 'ouse in the rain with a screaming child and me makin' as if to faint away. The maid were down to fetch me in a trice. Took me into the front parlour and sat me down, then whisked off to get Betsy a glass o' milk.'

'And? What happened then?'

'I 'ad a good look round the room like you said, but couldn't see nuffin' like a box of papers. Piles of books with words on 'em as must 'ave been foreign, and pictures too, though lots was stacked against the walls as if they'd just arrived – or was just goin'. But it were only a minute before the door opened and she were there.'

'The servant?'

'No, not 'er – the woman as owns the 'ouse. Well, not *owns* it, as it turned out. She's just rentin'.'

Charles frowns. 'Are you sure? There was no man there with her? No husband, or brother, or the like?'

Nancy shakes her head. 'Nah, not 'er. No weddin' ring, that's for certain. In fact I don't fink she 'as a lot of use for men. Got the feelin' she'd been let down once too often and decided she'd do better on 'er own. Lord knows I know 'ow she feels.'

Charles studies her a moment, his brain absorbing this new revelation. He'd assumed without even thinking about it that the resident of Carlo Cottage would be a man – he may be getting the measure of Lady Shelley now, but even by her standards it seems gratuitously discourteous to refer to a woman by her surname alone.

'She were right taken wiv Betsy, though,' continues Nancy. 'Took 'er on 'er knee and made that much fuss of 'er. Said she'd brought up fifteen kids not 'er own, poor cow. And I fink I 'ave it tough.'

'And you're absolutely sure it was the right house?' It's a stupid question, and the girl bridles, as if he's implying the stupidity is hers.

'Course I am! And, anyway, the maid used 'er name. Came in wiv a letter for 'er. Must 'ave been a bill because she looked right fretted by it. Put it to one side and said they could wait for their money. I didn't know what exactly she meant but it seemed clear enough she were a bit strapped. And that's when I got the idea.' She smiles at him, clearly delighted with herself. 'Can't you guess?'

Charles shakes his head, more than a little apprehensive.

'I said to 'er, did she know of anywhere that me brother could lodge for a week or so. Said 'e were comin' back from a trip abroad and needed a place to stay for a while till 'e could find a place of 'is own. And Lord above she swallered it! Said she 'ad two spare rooms upstairs and 'e'd be welcome to come and 'ave a look at 'em. Said she couldn't deny the cash'd come in 'andy. Asked a lot of questions, o' course – was me brother a respectable young man, what did 'e do for a livin', and suchlike. But I laid it on pretty fick, and she lapped it up. I said 'e was eddicated, but 'e was a painter, so 'e was good wiv 'is 'ands and 'appy to do little jobs about the 'ouse. She's only got the one maid and I could see there was a few bits and pieces needed doin', even in that room, so I knew as that'd go down well.'

She's still smiling, clearly waiting to be congratulated for her cleverness, but Charles is being uncharacteristically dense. 'I don't see how that helps us, Nancy. Who is this brother of yours?'

The girl laughs in loud delight. 'Why *you* are, o' course!'

He gapes at her. '*Me?*'

Nancy claps her hands. 'Genius, ain't it? Even if I do say so meself. Now you can get in there and ferret about to yer 'eart's content. Reckon I've earned the rest of that cash, and no mistake.'

Charles reaches automatically for his pocket, still trying to come to terms with what she's done. It is – on one level – a masterstroke and part of him is impressed, despite himself, with her presence of mind. And, as she says, there could be no better way than this to pursue his enquiries – both covert and overt, both the Shelleys' agenda and his own. Only a month ago he'd have packed his bag this very afternoon, but how can he leave now, with Maddox as he is?

Nancy has clearly divined his ambivalence and tries to catch his eye. 'I did all right, didn't I? I mean, gettin' you in there. Sorry about sayin' as you were a painter, but I 'ad to fink on me feet, and sittin' there wiv all those pictures it just came into me 'ead. And what wiv all 'em books bein' foreign, it seemed to me she'd 'ave a fellow feelin' for someone else as 'ad been travellin'.'

Charles smiles as he hands over the coins. 'You did a fine job, Nancy. Perhaps too good. It's going to be a bit difficult for me to be absent at the moment, that's all. My great-uncle is very unwell, and I don't like to leave him.'

'But you got all these people 'ere, ain'tcha? I mean, there's that boy, and the old fella. And the girl too – that black one. She's lookin' after Betsy for me downstairs. Wondered for a minute about 'er, to tell the truth – she seemed not quite all there, if you know what I mean – but Betsy seemed to take to 'er all right.'

'She can't speak,' says Charles, blushing; a reaction Nancy duly notes and files away for possible future use. 'Molly understands what you say, but she can't reply. That's what makes her seem – elusive. But that's all it is – the child will be perfectly safe with her.'

'Right, then,' says Nancy, getting to her feet. 'Best I be gettin' back.'

They stand facing each other for a moment. Then she sticks out her hand, as if she feels they need to seal the episode in some formal fashion. 'Nice doin' business wiv yer, Mr Maddox. 'Ope I can be of use again. Easiest money I've come by in a long time.'

He follows her out onto the landing and watches her go down the stairs, holding her skirt carefully as if she were indeed the lady she has been mimicking. Standing at the balustrade, he has a view down to the hall below and can see Molly on her knees on the floor playing with the child. Watching them, even for this tiny moment, he realizes with a jolt that he has defined the girl in his own mind not just in silence but in stillness, whether in the kitchen, on the street, or in his bed. But now she is crawling about on the tiles like a child herself, rolling a ball of twine backwards and forwards as Betsy shrieks in glee and runs about her trying to catch it. And for the first time since Charles has known her, Molly is smiling. A luminous, almost exultant smile that is all the more intense for being private, and unobserved. He must have moved then, or cast a shadow, because suddenly she looks up and they stare at each other for a frozen moment, and the look on his face takes all expression slowly from her own. Then Nancy catches her daughter up in her arms, the front door opens, and the two of them disappear down the steps into the windy street.

It takes Charles a good hour to convince himself that Nancy's plan is practicable, and the next task thereafter is to convince Abel of the same. Though there, to his surprise, he meets no resistance. Abel clearly feels that the household can cope quite well without him: 'Like I said, Mr Charles, the interests of yer clients must come first, and yer great-uncle would be proud of 'ee for thinking so.'

Charles has the good grace to flush at this – he hasn't told

Abel of his recent researches, or that he plans to defraud, or at the very least deceive, these particular clients, and the old man's honest openness puts him a little to shame. Only a little, though, because surely, he tells himself, Abel would understand. If he knew.

'I'll come back at least once a day,' he continues quickly, 'to make sure all is well. And you'll send for me at once, whatever the hour, if there's any change? Or if my uncle takes a turn for the worse?'

'Aye, I will. And you dinnae need to worry, Mr Charles. He and I managed on our own long enough, and now I hae Billy and the girl to help me. We'll fare well enough for a few days, never ye mind.'

Charles sighs. 'Very well. In that case I will endeavour to persuade the lady in question to take me on. At least for a week or so, until I can find out what I need. Though I don't mind telling you, Abel, the mere thought of being closeted in that tiny house with a sour old spinster is almost more than I can stomach.'

* * *

It's shortly after nine the following morning when Charles walks up the steps to Carlo Cottage and stops for a moment to take a breath before ringing the bell. He'd been worried he'd never pass muster as a painter, though Abel seems to think he will at least look the part (but if there's a veiled message there about the less than immaculate state of Charles's hair and wardrobe, it completely passes him by). The door is opened by the same servant he saw in the street when he was last here.

Charles touches his hat. 'My sister was here yesterday and suggested I might call.'

'Ah, yes, sir,' she says brightly. 'The mistress has been expecting you. Please come in.'

She shows Charles to the same parlour Nancy must have sat in, and he, too, is struck at once by the impromptu, provisional look of the place. It looks – in fact – rather as his own attic room did until only a week or so ago, though like Nancy he cannot yet decide if this is the impermanence of moving out, or moving in. He has no talent for languages, but it seems Nancy was right when she guessed that very few of the books here are in English – a number appear to be Russian or some other language that uses the same alphabet, while most of the rest look to be Italian. The prints and pictures certainly are – the two hanging above the fireplace are views of Florence, and there's a larger one propped against the far wall that shows the Bay of Naples and Vesuvius, a curl of smoke rising from the volcano's crater into a clear Campanian sky.

'Did you visit Italy? When you were travelling?'

No sour spinster ever sounded like this. A voice the colour of honey – a rich music of a voice that seems to bubble with suppressed amusement, and when Charles turns round the woman before him is a conflagration of all his preconceptions. Shorter and slighter than he is, with smooth olive skin and glossy black hair that shows no grey, though he guesses she must be – what – fifty? Even fifty-five? But it's the eyes that have him. So drowning dark, the iris and the pupil melt together, and so brilliantly intense he can meet her gaze only for a moment before he wants to look away. Only he can't. Something about those eyes holds him and will not let him free, and all he can do in the end is nod and look gauche, and be all too uncomfortably aware of it. The woman, meanwhile, seems to be perfectly accustomed to the effect she is having; she looks at him briefly,

63

her head on one side and that little ripple of amusement playing about her mouth, then offers him, with some panache, her hand.

'It is such a beautiful country, is it not? Claire Clairmont. Delighted to make your acquaintance.'

It is a name that may well be familiar to you, but it means nothing whatsoever to Charles. And he will not be alone, not in 1850, when the circumstances of Shelley's private life are still largely unknown, and will remain so in some respects, even into the twenty-first century. Meanwhile, and for one absurd moment, Charles is considering kissing those proffered fingers – and wondering immediately how many other men have thought or done the same.

'You will think me hopelessly frivolous,' she continues, shaking his hand. He can feel the barest pressure of her fingers through the bandage, but while she, for her part, cannot fail to notice it, she chooses to say nothing. 'But I omitted to ask your sister your name.'

'Charles,' he says, with a smile, completely disarmed and ripe to be wrong-footed, 'Charles Ma—' He stops, his cheeks blazing – how *could* he have been so stupid? 'Mab,' he finishes lamely, knowing even as he says it that he's merely compounded his mistake. 'Charles Mab.'

'Really?' she says, watching him quizzically, 'How very unusual. I'm not sure I have ever encountered a Mab before. At least, not in everyday life.' She smiles again, and motions him to a chair. 'And you are a painter, Mr Mab?'

Charles is by now so red about the face that there is little to do but flounder on and hope to retrieve himself. He nods.

'And what sort of painter would you say you are?'

He swallows; his throat is suddenly very dry. He can see the Bay of Naples behind her left shoulder. 'Seascapes,' he says, in desperation. 'Storms. Shipwrecks. That sort of thing.'

Her face darkens. 'I'm afraid I have no great love for the sea. And especially not in that character.'

Another blunder, he thinks, cursing. Shipwrecks – for God's sake! – when anything even vaguely reminiscent of Shelley is the very last thing he should be broaching, and certainly not now, barely half an hour into the house.

'But are you not now in a most difficult position?'

He stares at her: has she really found him out so soon? 'Well—'

'I mean,' she says gaily, 'London is hardly the best place to pursue such subject-matter, surely. I cannot recall much in the way of shipwrecks on the Thames. Though, admittedly, I have not lived here for many years.'

'You have spent time in Italy, Miss Clairmont?' He has to be careful now, having snared himself into choosing somewhere for his fictitious foreign escapade that he's never actually visited, but with luck and some sleight-of-hand he will have read enough over the years to weave a credible yarn. And a choice born of pure instinct may serve him well in one useful respect: from what he's gathered so far, it's a more than reasonable bet that this woman came across the Shelleys in Italy, probably in one of those loose-living Bohemian communities of English exiles that gather like summer swarms about Florence and Venice. Without being at all religious in any conventional sense, Charles has rather stern views – sterner, indeed, than you might have expected of him – and finds that sort of behaviour both idle and self-indulgent, and feasible only for the feckless few who have plenty of money they have never needed to earn. Though it seems the latter charge, at least, cannot be laid at this woman's door.

'The best part of my life was lived in Italy,' she says, settling back a little in her chair. 'But by that I mean the most precious, not the greater, portion. There was a time when I believed I had buried there everything I loved.'

There is a silence, and she pulls the shawl she is wearing a little closer about her. It seems worn, the shawl, and much older than the rest of her *ensemble*, which shows a fine disregard for the corseted constraints of London fashion. 'I feel the cold,' she explains, acknowledging his observation. 'Even after so long in the ruinous wastes of Russia, I still feel the cold.'

So the Russian books are not only evidence of an unusual flair for languages, but an even more unusual strength of character: few men Charles knows would contemplate travelling to so wild and far distant a place, and this woman seems to have done so all alone.

'You cannot imagine the contrast,' she continues, suppressing a shiver, 'from the golden heat and scented airs of Italy, to find yourself in such an icy, trackless desert. Mile after mile and not a single tree. I once travelled from St Petersburg to Moscow in the very depth of winter. Four hundred desolate unchanging miles by sled. Even with three layers of furs, the cold was unbearable. My eyelashes froze with my own tears.'

Charles is uncomfortably aware that their conversation has shifted – metaphorically as literally – a good long way in the wrong direction. 'I have heard St Petersburg is a magnificent city.'

'That is certainly the effect its builder intended,' she remarks drily. 'And, yes, there are palaces, and domes, and towers aplenty, all bright and new with paint and gilt, but it had to me the feel of Fairyland. As if a malicious witch might snap her fingers at any moment and the whole town would fly away. But that is perhaps more a reflection of my own melancholy temper at the time. Though it did bring me one connection I will always cherish.'

She smiles. Clearly she has a rather different view of the value of 'connections' than Lady Shelley.

'My first Russian pupil was in St Petersburg. She is now the Princess Czernicheff,' this with a flicker of pride, 'but she will always be merely "Betsy" to me. As I'm sure your Betsy will be to you.'

Thankfully Charles has now regained some presence of mind, and manages what he hopes is an appropriately avuncular smile.

'Your niece is an adorable child,' Miss Clairmont continues, a note of wistfulness stealing into her voice. 'Such beautiful eyes and such a stubborn little chin. And your sister seems to be in good health. She is fortunate indeed if she has avoided the sickness so often suffered in the first months of pregnancy.'

She wraps her arms once more about her, and looks away. Charles has rarely met anyone whose moods seem to vary so quickly, and he's not sure how best to proceed, but he is saved, in the end, by the appearance of the maid.

'Excuse me, madam, but the room is ready now. If the gentleman would like to see it.'

They both get to their feet, and Miss Clairmont gestures to the maid to take him up. 'I hope you will find the room is to your liking, Mr Mab, and that it proves suitable for a painter such as yourself.'

And if he had indeed been a painter, Charles is sure he would have found it eminently so. It's clean and empty, with a small single bed and light streaming in from the window. The view, when he goes to look at it, is over the little back garden – a garden, he notices, that's thick with dead black leaves and overrun with brambles.

When he goes back down to the sitting room he finds Miss

Clairmont standing at the fire, warming her hands. He contemplates her profile, struck again by the loveliness of her face and the voluptuousness of her figure. She's beautiful now; how exquisite she must once have been. He already suspected the Shelleys of deceiving him, and now he is sure: this woman before him is transparently incapable of persecuting anyone, and certainly not in the persistent and vicious manner Sir Percy was alleging. But if that much is obvious, much else remains obscure. How did she come by the Shelley papers she is said to own, and is it really possible – as Sam suggested – that she once went to Maddox with an allegation of murder, even though surely she couldn't have been much more than a girl at the time?

'Ah, Mr Mab,' she says then, smiling up into his thoughts. 'And what is your verdict?'

'It's a charming room, Miss Clairmont. If it is convenient to you, I would be happy to move in at once. I believe you told my sister the rent would be three shillings a week?'

It's at the top end of the market for such a room, in such a street, but Charles won't be paying.

Miss Clairmont once again offers her hand. 'We will expect you tomorrow. You will no doubt have all the trappings of your calling to bring along with you.'

Yet another thing Charles has overlooked, and he curses Nancy silently – if rather ungratefully: why couldn't she have said he was a writer, or a doctor, or something equally free from obvious professional baggage? 'I thought also . . .' he says, *faux*-tentative.

'Yes?'

'It seemed to me that your garden might benefit from a little attention. I would be delighted to spend a little of my leisure time putting things to rights.'

She smiles. 'I do not own the house, and feel a similar

68

degree of detachment from the garden. But if it would amuse you to dig about in the undergrowth, I for one will not prevent you.'

Back at Buckingham Street Charles pens a hasty note to the Shelleys, indicating that he has found a way of coming by the information they require, and requesting an advance to cover his rent and incidentals. Talent may not have descended down the Godwin line, but it seems meanness may well have done, and Charles has no intention of incurring expenses that may never be recouped. He sends Billy with the note to Chester Square, and indulges in a dry smile as he imagines Lady Shelley's outrage should she see such an unprepossessing youth polluting her exclusive enclave. He then looks in quickly on Maddox before going out again in search of some basic supplies. He remembers seeing a sign for a *Manufacturer of Materials for Artists* in High Holborn, and sets off in that direction, though the weather has taken a turn for the worse and it'll be no surprise to see snow by nightfall. By the time he gets to the shop he's starting to lose the feeling in his feet, and just wants to get this over with. After all, he needs only an easel, a few sheets of paper and some cheap paint. But when he pushes open the door and looks around the crowded shelves, it's clear it's not going to be anything like as simple as that. There are sketchbooks of every size and shape stacked alongside blocks of tracing paper, transfer paper, black lead paper, vellum paper and drawing boards; there are watercolours in shells, watercolours in boxes, tube and bladder oils, camel-hair and sable brushes, white Italian chalk, black French chalk, Swiss crayons, porte-crayons, indiarubber pens, and last but not least a fine selection of stumps (use – to Charles at least – unknown).

There is also, though, to Charles's relief, a solid and rather balding young man standing behind the counter, copying entries into a ledger. The sight of a paying customer so late in the day brings a happy flush to his sturdy cheeks, but it doesn't last very long. Charles rapidly proves to be one of that irritating class of clients who insist that they want one thing when it is patently obvious that what they really need is something altogether different. After five minutes' attempting to explain the relative merits of colours in cakes as against colours in powders, the shine on the young man's courtesy has worn off, and he's starting to look a little fatigued.

'Would sir not be better advised to consider something more adapted to, shall we say, his current level of experience? We have a number of very nice watercolour sets ideally suited to – *ahem* – a beginner.'

Charles glares at him. 'How many more times? I don't want the sort of stuff a beginner would use.'

'Well, if sir is intent on wasting his money—'

'*Sir* is quite happy to waste *other people's* money in this instance. So just put together whatever it is I need, and have it sent round to Buckingham Street before the day is out. Do I make myself clear?'

'Admirably, sir,' says the young man, who is now rather pink about the ears.

'One more thing sir may wish to consider,' he adds quietly, as Charles reaches the door. 'If – *theoretically speaking* – I was advising a client who wished, for reasons of his own, to *pass himself off* as a painter, I would probably recommend he acquired samples of his supposed work. It being natural that someone might wish to see it.'

Charles turns. 'And where, *theoretically speaking*, might you recommend he should obtain them?'

70

The young man drops his eyes once more to his ledger. 'I would suggest he tried Ackerman's. Of the Strand.'

Charles knows it, of course, it being so close to home, and something of a London institution, even if it's now long past its Regency heyday. By the time he gets there the gas has been lit in the windows and he can see a number of people browsing the racks of prints, and several well-chaperoned young ladies taking tea at the counter as they leaf through books of plates. Charles is interested in neither prints nor plates, of course, but it seems original works are just as easy to come by, and when he leaves the shop into heavy snow half an hour later he has a roll of paper under his arm and a small but suitable collection of maritime scenes ready for display.

The snow is falling, too, in Chester Square, whirling into eddies about the doorstep of number twenty-four and collecting on the area steps, where the pigeons know better than to dare to venture. Two floors above, Lady Shelley is sitting by the fire in her private drawing room, Charles's letter in her hand. There are two spots of colour on her cheeks, and a thinly triumphant smile on her lips.

'You see,' she says to her husband, who seems from his stance to have entered the room only a few moments ago, 'it is all as I told you it would be. We had only to wait, and an opportunity would present itself. And so it has. So it has.'

* * *

It's not yet eight when Charles returns to St John's Wood the following morning, an easel under his arm and a knapsack over one shoulder. As well as yesterday's purchases, the latter includes a few changes of clothes and another volume

71

from his collection of Shelley. The maid seems surprised to see him so early, but Charles wants to give himself plenty of time to arrange his new belongings before Miss Clairmont is likely to be up and about: he's already developed an extremely healthy respect for his new landlady's powers of discernment, and cannot afford any more *faux pas*. There are a few false starts, but within an hour or so the portfolio of drawings is lying as if nonchalantly against the chest of drawers, two or three shirts are hanging on the picture rail and an unfinished (and therefore extremely cheap) scene of the Cobb at Lyme Regis is mounted carefully on his new easel. He stands back with his hands on his hips, assessing the effect. It's getting there, there's no doubt of that, but something still doesn't ring quite true. It's all just a bit too – *new*. But that's a problem easily remedied. It's the work of a few minutes to sacrifice one of the shirts to a smeared and spattered authenticity, scuff the easel with a couple of well-aimed kicks, and dig out some of the cakes of water-colours into pools of rather muddy paint.

So, what now? The morning may have been an amusing distraction, but Charles has not lost sight of the real reason for his presence in this house. He closes the door carefully behind him and makes his way downstairs. There's a smell of cooking wafting up from the kitchen in the basement, and through the half-closed door he can see a small table laid in the dining room. But it is set only for one. Charles is clearly neither expected, nor welcome. He has no right to feel it as a snub, but after the warmth of his welcome yesterday it feels like one. He loiters for a few minutes in the hall, but when no one appears there is nothing to be done but retire to his room and resume his steady if rather ponderous progress through his volume of Shelley. The maid brings him dinner on a tray, and eventually, past midnight, he gets up to undress. And it's then that he hears it. Music coming from downstairs. Just a few bars, nothing more, and he wonders at first if he's imagined it.

He opens his door and goes out onto the landing, his ears straining against the silence. And there it is again. It is a woman's voice, and it is quite beautiful. Haunting, lingering, rising and falling, like a pure swell of unendurable grief. And when the sound sinks and dies for the last time, he can hear weeping. Weeping in the darkness, alone.

The following morning he wakes to hard winter sunlight and high clouds skidding across a blanched white sky. The sodden garden is suddenly dazzling, etch-edged with frost, and Charles is seized by an impulse to spend the morning outside, in the air, away from this cramped little room and the intricate density of Shelley's words. He dresses quickly, then goes down into the kitchen, where the maid is scrubbing the floor. She smiles at him, first shyly, and then with undisguised amusement, when he says he wants to work in the garden, but she gives him the key to a small outhouse where he will find mattocks and hoes and whatever else the previous tenants left behind. The air outside is freezing, and for the first hour or so he can barely feel his fingers, but by the time he has raked one border, and piled the rotting stems and leaves into a heap by the far wall he's worked up enough of a sweat to take his jacket off. He's just hanging it on the back of the bench when he turns to see the maid beckoning him from the house.

'Miss Clairmont was wondering if you'd like to join her for luncheon, sir.'

'Good Lord, is it that time already?' says Charles, with a grin, running his hand through his hair and smearing a good deal of mud on his forehead in the process. 'I would be delighted. Please tell her I will wash my hands and then join her in a few moments.'

The table has been set again in the dining room, but this time it is for two. The fire is lit, and a basin of soup stands ready on the sideboard, but of Miss Clairmont there is no sign. It's the first time he has been into this room and he looks round, taking the measure of the place. More books in crates and pictures stacked against the walls, but also a piano, a piano-stool draped in rich green brocade, and a mahogany sideboard. A sideboard that (as Charles quickly ascertains) conceals only what any such piece of furniture would be expected to hold. Having achieved that much, he goes over to look at the music propped open on the piano-stand, wondering if this was the song he heard the night before. It's a Mozart aria, the pages yellowing now, and annotated here and there in a rounded, flowing hand. And on the front cover, the faded inscription, 'To C—'. He's just turning the pages back to where he found them when the paper slips from his fingers and slides onto the floor under the piano. He curses under his breath and drops quickly to his knees, wondering what sort of figure he will cut if his landlady finds him poking about on all fours. He has to move the stool out of the way to reach the pages, and he can't at first understand why he's unable to shift it, but then he lifts the green brocade and sees his mistake. Or, rather, Miss Clairmont's subterfuge. Wedged between the stool's four legs is a small wooden trunk. A travelling trunk.

His heart is beating fast as he puts stool and music back carefully as he found them, and by the time his hostess comes through the door he is where he should be, behind his chair. Miss Clairmont's long black hair is down, and she's wearing a midnight blue gown that clings to her body

74

and cannot possibly have been either made or bought in England. She comes towards him in a rustle of silk on silk, and he can smell a dark musky scent on her skin.

'I thought you deserved some recompense for your pains,' she says, with a smile. 'That poor garden has indeed been brutally neglected.'

Charles is about to say how much he enjoyed the exercise (which is, in fact, true) but Miss Clairmont seems not to have expected a reply.

'And is it satisfactory, your garret?' she continues. 'Annie and I heard so much banging and scraping yesterday that we were quite sure you had embarked on a major renovation.'

Charles blushes. 'Well, I needed to get the best light. The right angle. You know how it is.'

Miss Clairmont takes her seat at the table, and rings a little silver bell. 'Well, I can *imagine*, certainly. I had my own portrait painted once, but I do not consider it a success. I'm sure the artist meant well, but she left me looking as if I had a raging toothache.'

'It can't have been easy to capture your likeness.'

Miss Clairmont laughs, a bright, delicious, open-mouthed laugh; he can see her white teeth and her red throat. 'I will take that as a compliment, Mr Mab, even if you did not intend it so!' she says, as she unfolds her napkin. 'Pray have the gallantry not to disillusion me – it's a very long time since I have received such flattery from so charming a young man.'

The maid comes in to serve the soup – and save Charles, incidentally, from any further reckless praise. The broth, as it turns out, is rather too watery, and the cutlets that follow rather too tough, but Charles is far too captivated by his companion to notice very much. It is, indeed – and despite the food – quite the most enjoyable meal he's had in a long

75

time. Miss Clairmont is enchanting company – well read, well travelled and well informed, moving easily from an animated discussion on British politics to diverting and self-deprecating tales of life in her 'ice cave'.

'You would not believe the chaos and confusion that reigns in even the most aristocratic Russian households, Mr Mab,' she tells him, as the maid collects the dishes, and places a coffee pot and cups in the centre of the table. 'I once counted some twenty children running about in the same house, and all of them more or less under my care. I cannot *quite* be sure of the number, because frankly you never could be certain who was actually in residence from one hour to the next. What with the legitimate offspring, the foundlings and orphans, and the ramshackle tribe of cousins, half-cousins, old maids and idiot aunts, you can picture to yourself the constant racket and quarrelling I had to contend with. Truly, Mr Mab, it was like living in an everlasting state of Saturnalia.'

'It must have taken courage to journey to such a far-off place on your own.'

A shadow crosses her face. 'I believed I had no alternative. I thought that in Russia I might be able to forget all the disasters that had blighted my youth – all the misery I met with in Italy. But the more I fled the more they haunted me, and the wounds have now carved themselves so deep in my heart I do not think I will ever be free of them.'

She is being – he suspects – deliberately mysterious, though an unkinder word might be manipulative: Charles defies anyone to hear such an intriguing overture without wishing to know the rest, but he's prepared to bet that all such questions will be met only with silence and with-drawal. But he's willing to play that game, if she is. After all, he has enquiries of his own to pursue.

'I am sorry to hear that you were unhappy in Italy. That a country we both love should have caused you such pain.'

'I do not blame the *landscape*, Mr Mab,' she says sullenly.

'Speaking for myself, I always found the Italians most hospitable – somewhat wily, yes, and not the cleanest—'

Her face hardens, but she does not reply.

'I'm sorry,' says Charles, after a pause. 'I should not have pressed you.'

She nods quickly, then lifts her cup and takes a sip. The silence spreads and softens, and a sudden wave of her scent sifts oddly with the bitter aroma of the thick black coffee, so unlike any Charles has ever tasted. He wonders if he should take his leave – if he has offended her – but just as he is on the point of rising she begins to speak again, though her voice is so low, and her eyes so distant, that her words seem for herself alone.

'I lingered in Italy for almost five years, always hoping for some change for the better, but none ever came. On the day I left it seemed the very skies shared my grief as the coach ploughed on in the pouring rain, and I could scarce even bring myself to look out of the window at the trees and mountains I had once so loved. Every hill we came to, I made myself get out and wade up through the mud and the mist in a desperate attempt to numb my heart by fatiguing my body. When I wrote my journal that night – stiff in a chair in a dire hovel – I swore I would never take up my pen again, if it was only to record such desolate, impossible misery.'

The maid comes in and replaces the empty coffee pot with another, then stirs the fire, bobs to her unseeing mistress and closes the door.

'Many times since I have wondered,' Miss Clairmont continues softly, 'how my life might have been different had

I chosen another path. But I have always been a hopeless idealist when it comes to love. *Tutto, o niente.'*

'I'm sorry?'

She raises one eyebrow, the flicker of a smile returning to her lips, '*Everything, or nothing.* And you, a traveller in Italy, ask me that? I would have thought you might have picked up a little of the language, having spent so much time there.'

Charles turns to pour himself more coffee. 'I travelled with two companions. One spoke Italian so well I never had any need to learn it.'

Miss Clairmont smiles wryly. 'I had a similar experience myself, many years ago. Only in that case *I* was the one to be taken along to make a third, merely as interpreter. *Or so I was told.* Sometimes it seems to me that my whole life has been spent in the thankless and unacknowledged service of others. One of those same two people once had the insolence to tell me that I bring down all my sorrows on my *own* head, by following too much the devices and desires of my own heart – I, who have always been forced to do everything my heart abhors!'

A note of querulous self-pity has now crept into her voice, and deep lines have appeared on either side of her mouth, dragging her face down into petulance and middle age. And now Charles is wondering whether those sudden shifts in mood, which he dismissed at first as mere caprice, might indicate something more profound, and possibly disturbing, about this woman. Her manners are entrancing, without question, but the character that lies beneath them is beginning to seem far more complex. Not just unpredictable, but even – perhaps – perilous.

He clears his throat. 'The life of a governess is, I'm sure, always a hard one. Especially for one so young, and so far from home.'

She sighs, and he sees, with some shame, that there are tears in her eyes.

'*That* I was resigned to, though I confess it was a long and bitter struggle to reconcile myself to the life I was forced to live. No, it has not been work that has exhausted me. Not work, but love.'

She gets up suddenly and moves to the window, where she stands with her back to him, gazing out over the withered garden, and into the past.

'When my mother was ill she and I lived together in a room scarcely bigger than this. There was space only for one bed, so I slept on the sopha, every night for more than a year. And still I had to labour every daylight hour to keep us from starving. In all that time, I had no respite. Others who might have helped – who *should* have helped – merely turned their backs, saying such a life would be hell itself. And so it was. So it was.'

There is grief in her voice now, and a deep, unbearable, long-silent resentment.

'Six days in seven I endured two hours in a creeping, stinking omnibus to teach Italian to a spoiled, stupid girl, and all I had to return to was the remnants of a filthy meal, and a mother who scarcely knew me. Who would go out when I was gone and wander the streets half dressed, not knowing who she was or where, and handing money I had slaved for to chance-met strangers and passers-by.'

She hangs that proud head of hers now, and leans heavily against the window. Charles takes a step forward, torn between pity and a terrible recognition. 'What did the doctors say? Could they not help you?'

She raises her head a little, but does not turn. 'They claimed she was suffering from nervous fever. An "excess of function in her nerve centres", or some such words. By

79

the end she could scarcely keep still – day and night she would writhe and mutter and pull at her clothes. She had no rest – and gave me none. You cannot possibly comprehend what that is like.'

'I do,' he says quietly. 'More than you know. My great-uncle is suffering from a very similar malaise. We are doing what we can to care for him, but that seems all too pitifully little. But we are hopeful. We are hopeful.'

Miss Clairmont turns, and he can see compassion in those luminous eyes. 'I am sorry, Mr Mab. Truly. I fear it is a malady that does not retrace its steps.'

Charles swallows, and nods.

'If you will forgive me,' she says, 'I have letters I must write.'

Charles bows and moves aside to let her past, and as she draws level with him she puts a hand on his arm. He feels the warmth of her skin for the briefest second, and then she is gone.

Charles knows better than to try to investigate the trunk in the broad light of day, and by the time he leaves that afternoon for Buckingham Street the light is growing dim, and the sky has turned the sickly yellow-grey of imminent thunder. The fire has burned low in the drawing room, and the wind whips in the chimney as Charles settles down at his uncle's side with a glass of brandy. Abel is asleep on the other side of the fire, and Maddox sitting quietly, his hands twitching now and again, his head moving slightly erratically as he looks about the room. Charles takes one of his cool dry hands into his own. The left hand, the lifeless hand.

'How are you, Uncle?'

He says it in no expectation of a reply, but sees, with surprise, that the old man seems to respond. Or perhaps it is just a coincidence. He edges a little closer, and on the other side of the room Abel sniffles suddenly in his doze, then settles back once more against his cushions.

'I am sorry I have been away so much recently, Uncle. I have been on a case.'

Again that tiny movement.

'Indeed, I believe you worked once for the same family. Many years ago. The name of Godwin?'

And now he is sure. There is something in the old man's face that is an answer to his words. Charles moves forward in his seat. 'You remember the case?'

A jerk of the head and Maddox's eyes swivel past Charles's face. Charles looks round but there is no one there – no one and nothing, except the little side table that bears the remains of his great-uncle's lunch, and his case-book for 1816. Abel must have brought it up to look at it. Charles reaches quickly for the book and places it gently on Maddox's lap. 'Were you looking at this, Uncle? Is that what you meant?'

The old man eyes him narrowly, then looks down at the book.

'Is there something about this that you remember?'

Again Maddox is staring at him, but as one gnarled hand reaches slowly for the book, a coal slips with a rush of sparks onto the hearth and Charles has to race to stop the rug catching light. And when he turns back to the old man he has lurched up with a strange stifled cry, his eyes stark open, his feet tangling in the bedding as he tries to get from the chair.

'Now what's to do here, Mr Charles?' exclaims Abel, starting from his sleep, his face drawn in alarm.

'He was trying to tell me something, Abel – something about the case.'

81

Abel looks at him askance, clearly unconvinced, but conditioned by a lifetime in service to hold his tongue. Maddox, meanwhile, is belying anything Charles might now contend by sagging sideways in his great-nephew's arms, his head lolling to one side and a ribbon of spittle hanging from his mouth.

'Or mebbe it was just the thunder that was frettin' him,' suggests Abel, as the two of them steady Maddox slowly back in his seat, and Charles lifts the pillows so he can sit upright. 'That storm's not afar off now.'

Maddox stares at the two of them suspiciously, then cowers back in his chair, his hands before his face as if warding off a blow. Perhaps the most distressing aspect of his decline in the last few months had been his own awareness of it – fitful, yes, but all too frequent. The strange sleep that has since descended on him has, if nothing else, saved him from that, but if the veil is now to be lifted, might that not prove more killing than the kindness of quietude?

But all the same it is progress, of a kind. As Charles keeps repeating to himself while he sits with his own dinner and watches Maddox manage far more food – and brandy – than Abel says he has taken in the best part of a week. All things considered, Charles's heart is as light as it has been for days as he stands in the hall making ready for the journey back across town.

'Are you sure about this, Mr Charles?' worries Abel, as they look out at a night sky electric with flashes of silent lightning. 'It's no weather for wandering about outside when ye've a warm bed here.'

'I won't be wandering, Abel. I'm going straight up to the Strand to hail a hansom. All you need concern yourself about is my uncle. I can look after myself well enough. It will seem odd if I do not return on such an inclement night and, besides, there's something I need to do. Something that may mean I will not have to stay there at all for very much longer.'

'Well, if you're sure, Mr Charles,' says Abel, clearly unconvinced. 'At least let me go up and have Molly fetch 'ee down a greatcoat. The boss has a good heavy one he winnae miss.'

'Very well,' says Charles, with a smile. 'I suppose that wouldn't be a bad idea.'

But five minutes pass with no sign of the coat, and a drumbeat of heavy raindrops is starting to patter on the pavement. Charles grows irritated; he goes to the bottom of the stairs and calls up, 'Is there a problem, Abel?'

A moment later Abel appears on the landing, looking flustered. 'My apologies, Mr Charles. Heaven knows where that Molly has got to – Billy says she was sick this mornin', but she made yer uncle's dinner right enough.'

Charles heads for the door. 'It really doesn't matter. I can do just as well without it. Send for me if you need me, but otherwise I will be back tomorrow afternoon.'

The rain is pounding the street now, and Charles races up to the Strand through a wash of flooded gutters and wheel ruts. His feet are soaked with mud and running dung long before he gets to the top, but otherwise his luck is with him and he finds a cab within a few minutes. He calls out the address to the driver and settles down into the damp leather seat, watching the rain glittering in the jets of gas outside those few shops still open. And if the West End is empty of people, St John's Wood is even more so, and there are no lamps in the windows at Carlo Cottage when Charles swings down from the cab and rushes up the steps to his new – and second – front door. He stands in the hall, waiting for his breathing to ease, and listening for sounds of wakefulness above. But there is nothing. A crackle of forked lightning pulses blue across the walls and the thunder breaks hard overhead, but still there is no sign or movement upstairs.

Charles moves quickly and silently to the dining room, where he kneels down by the piano stool and lifts the brocade away. He tries the lid of the trunk, but it is – as he expected – locked. No matter. He reaches into his pocket and extracts a ring of keys he keeps for moments such as this, confident that he will have one to fit such a common-place piece of luggage. But ten minutes later and all dozen keys tried, he is forced to accept that – like everything else, it seems, in this house – the trunk may not be quite as ordinary as he initially supposed. He turns it in his hands, examining the lid, the hinges. He's been lucky once already tonight, and his luck holds again now: some time in the past, on one of its many journeys, this trunk has been dented or damaged by water – the wood is warped at the back and the lid doesn't fit quite true. And when Charles bends down to look more closely he can see the edge of a sheaf of paper inside. And it happens he has just the tool for that too: a small pair of snipe-nose pliers that are a relic of that short time he spent training to be a doctor, before he gave it up to become a policeman, and which he kept, unlike much else from that time, because he thought they might prove useful. As they have in the past, and as they do now. He steadies himself against the trunk with one hand and slowly inserts the pliers with the other, holding them horizontal at first, then twisting them a slow half-turn once the pointed ends are inside the trunk. It's a delicate job he has now, but he's always had steady hands, and he closes the pliers carefully about the edge of the sheets, and starts to edge them out, inch by cautious inch. There's a moment when they catch on something and he hears the sound of tearing, but what he eventually pulls free are six or seven sheets of smooth handwritten paper. There is no title, no heading, and the pages are clearly only part of a much longer piece, but none of that matters. Because Charles has only to read a dozen lines to see the one word he's been seeking all this time.

Shelley.

He looks up, startled, as a rush of lightning catches him floodlit in his guilt and the thunder breaks again over his head, but when an even deeper darkness descends, and still no one stands accusing in the doorway to indict him, he gets up and makes his way quietly up the stairs to his room, where he lights the little lamp by his bed and begins to read.

CHAPTER FOUR

Love, Hope, Desire and Fear

... should think, and in any case I cared not. All that mattered was to see him, whether by arrangement or by sleight. He came not to the first rendezvous I appointed, and I wish now that I could have persuaded my weak heart against seeking refuge, like some panting helpless hare, in the lair of a lynx that was intent only on devouring it. He wrote later that the whole *affaire* was my own doing – that he defied any man to play the Stoic to an eighteen-year-old girl who came prancing to his bed at all hours of the night – that I pursued him, after that first encounter in London, and scrambled myself eight hundred miles across Europe with no other aim but to repeat it. And I cannot deny it. I wish only that I could have divined, like the Cumaean Sibyl, that the price of my few brief moments of happy passion was to be a lifetime of loss, and penitence, and sorrow. How could I have known, that night in Geneva, as I looked down from my room and saw his coach rolling slowly to the door, that my dark Fate had by then been sealed, and the seed already planted that would bear such beautiful, and yet such terrible fruit?

*

Receiving no answer to my note, I made sure to be on the terrace in the morning, where I sat, as if absorbed in my book, watching all the while the movement of the boats on the lake. The water sparkled jewel-like in the sun and it seemed – then – a happy portent that the air was clear, and the white peak of Mont Blanc could be seen rising majestic above the purple mountains and the winnowing clouds. The air was fragrant with spring flowers, and the vineyards on the farther shore vivid with the young green of new leaves. So sweet a day! It was an hour or more before I caught sight of the vessel I sought. No other man could match his strength of profile, his proud and erect carriage, and even so far away I could not but recognize him. Polidori was attempting to bring them about, splashing ineffectually as the boat swung in the shallows, and showing himself thereby, at least to my eye, no better an oarsman than he was to prove a doctor. Though at that moment I blessed his ineptitude, for it gave me the few minutes I required to ensure that by the time they were nearing land, we – Shelley and Mary and I – were all walking, as if by happy accident, on the shore.

So many have asked about that moment – that first encounter between the two finest Poets of the age – and I have read accounts of it that have made me smile, secretly, in the privacy of my heart. I confess now that the reality was but a poor match for the expectation; it was, in truth, a meeting characterized by awkwardness on all sides. Mary had not been told, then, of my secret, and knowing that he was deceiving her rendered Shelley distracted and ill-at-ease, and despite all his loud disdain for rank and money, he was quite overawed to find those detested qualities incarnated in such vigorous and celebrated flesh. And Byron did indeed draw every eye, standing there, up to his knees in the water, his deformed foot thereby concealed – as he was ever eager to do – and a red scarf tied turban-wise about his hair. I could see guests gathering on the hotel terrace and whispering behind their hands, and I guessed what they were saying – people of that sort love nothing more than to titillate themselves with gossip about subjects they profess to deplore, and Byron did not only live, as he boasted, a hundred years' life in the space of twenty-five, but supplied meat enough for a century's scandal in half as many months.

Poor Shelley, by contrast, always loathed all such impertinent public scrutiny, and writhed so inwardly under it that no doubt his ignorant observers considered him more than a little peculiar – it was not merely his strange clothes and wild hair that set them muttering, but the shrieks of demoniacal laughter he gave out whenever Byron said anything in the least entertaining or, indeed, anything at all. As for his lordship, I could see from the lift of his lip that he found it difficult to reconcile the dazzling works he had read with an author who appeared little more than an ungainly youth. For my part, I said little, being content merely to wait and to watch, for Shelley's encounter with Byron was not the only such first meeting I wished to observe: my lord had never till then been introduced to the celebrated 'Mrs Shelley'; not, of course, that she had any right to be called so – not then. There she stood, with those bright eyes of hers, and that famous hair falling in gauzy wavings about her shoulders and lifting in the wind off the lake. I had predicted he would fall in love with her – everyone else did, and why should he be any different, he who knew how to value a lineage such as hers? I had told him in London that it would not concern me, that I would merely redouble my efforts to stand well in her esteem, but I had not meant it. I did not wish to share him – not at all, if truth be told, and certainly not with *her*, the step-sister who has been no sister to me. I had paid the price of a *folie à trois*, I was determined I would never be drawn into the yet more furious maelstrom of a *folie à quatre*. But to judge of their first handshake, I deemed I had little to fear. He did not appear to think Mary so very extraordinary, and indeed I have been told since, by others, that my Albé never thought her anything but vulgar and, moreover (though how he knew this I cannot say), a great and infamous liar. I sigh as I write his name, for I called him Albé then, in gentle play on the initials 'LB'. It is my fate, and my curse, that when I think of him now those letters stand only for 'loathsome brute'.

My first aim in contriving this meeting between the four of us had been to secure an invitation to dine, and thereby foster what would appear to others to be an acquaintance born of chance, however studiously I had in fact contrived it. But in this first step I only half succeeded, for within a few minutes Byron rather pointedly offered a place at his table to Shelley alone, then made a hasty bow to myself and Mary, before stamping off back towards the boat.

His rooms at the Angleterre were, of course, far more luxurious than ours, and while we women were banished to a meagre dinner in our far-off eyrie, his lordship regaled his guests with roast pork and turbot, and several bottles of fine claret. I say 'guests', because Polidori too attended, and seemingly made a vile and malicious insinuation about Shelley's keeping *two wives* – a remark Shelley unluckily let slip to me some days thereafter, whence my violent dislike of the man commenced. But by then all was in train. We would all of us breakfast together as soon as Byron rose – which was never much before noon – and in the afternoons he and Shelley would post about the lake in their little rented boat, Shelley at the oars, and Byron singing what he claimed were Albanian songs, though they sounded like no music I have ever played, and involved such strange cacophonous guttural noises that families in nearby parties dispersed before them like so many frightened chickens. Which may, of course, have been exactly his intention. Mary and I, meanwhile, read Latin and Italian in the heat of the day, and walked about in the garden with little William as the sun began to set, looking at the rabbits and the insects and the beady-eyed lizards warming themselves on the hot stone wall. It could not last, of course – we were attracting too much unsavoury attention, and our rooms were, in any case, far too expensive, so we all agreed, the five of us (for Polidori *would* intrude), that it would be politic to remove to quarters more secluded. Though nothing we did, it seemed, could stop the prying eyes, and we discovered later that the wretched little hotel proprietor was renting telescopes to his guests so they could spy on us from the terrace and work themselves into a frenzied indignation thinking they had spied female underclothes displayed for all to see, when it was, in truth, nothing but Byron's blameless tablecloths left out in the sun to dry.

But I am running ahead of my story. After much discussion and disagreement, we eventually lighted on two properties side by side on the southern edge of the lake, which were acceptable both to Byron's pretensions, and our own party's rather more modest pockets. Byron accordingly leased the Villa Diodati, and we took a charming little house close by at Montalègre, which Shelley adored because it had a little harbour of its own where he could moor the boat he had by then persuaded Byron to buy. It was scarcely ten minutes from one door to the other – I know it, because I walked it every day. In the morning, with Shelley and Mary to breakfast, or to my desk in the library where I was fair-copying *Childe Harold*; in the afternoons, to dine; and later, in the darkness, to Byron's bed. Always in the darkness, because it was impossible otherwise to avoid Polidori, who would appear like an evil genius whenever I attempted to get my Albé alone. The man seemed always to require the urgent use of some article kept only in the room we were in, and on each such occasion that face of his he clearly thought so handsome was contorted by the most scornful of sneers. But he kept that sneer, needless to say, for me alone and was careful never to betray any such insolence to his aristocratic employer. Indeed, his presence became so intrusive I began to wonder if he had not been placed there as a spy by Lady Byron, or some other member of her unspeakable family; I could not have guessed he had been paid for his snooping by his lordship's own publisher.

And so I would creep, when all in both houses were abed, along that narrow path through the vineyard, with the glow-worms winking in the thickets and the dew settling on the new-mown grass, to the Diodati. Would I could say that the positions were reversed, and that it was Byron who came to me, mad with love, limping through the summer moonlight, but it was not so. Shelley once told me there were two Claires – one gentle and cheerful; the other nervous, reserved, melancholy. Certain it is that my greatest weakness has always been that I am as easily swayed by the one I love as the reed is by the wind; and it was no less a weakness to have told Albé so. I would fain say Byron seduced me with sweet words – that he wrote poetry to me, as he did to others – but he did not. I pursued him in the wild hope that love would come and that passion would endure, but it did not. I gave myself to him, as other women had and other women would, but it was not for me, as it was for them. *I* was no society lady, able to shield her sin under the mask of marriage. *I* believed – I had been *taught* to believe – that love is *free*. That to promise for ever to love the same person was no less absurd than to promise to adhere to the same creed. And that *was* my creed. I went to Byron in that spirit, and I thought he received me as a believer in the same pure ideal. How could I have known, scarcely eighteen, that men such as he use this vicious doctrine to slake their carnal

91

appetites, and inflict more pain and cruelty than can ever have been caused by the supposed tyranny of the institution of marriage they claim to despise?

By the mid days of June, the pattern of that summer of 1816 was set. Byron and Shelley became as brother Poets, finding every day another common passion, another shared pursuit. And I think we were all of us a little giddy with such a richness of thought, and talk, and laughter, and mutual delight. I remember one blissful evening when we drifted about the lake long after nightfall, trailing our hands either side of the boat as we gazed down into the limpid water, and then up at the bright dome above our heads, where one by one the stars glimmered, then gathered light in the darkening sky. It was the last clear night for two weeks; by morning a battalion of grey clouds had rolled down from the Jura, and a fierce wind was raging across the surface of the water. Even Shelley could not contemplate boating in such weather, and Byron was far too lazy – or craven – to try. And so it was that we spent almost a fortnight closeted together around the fireplace in the Diodati drawing room, as the rain beat against the long windows and the mists rolled up from the lake, tossing ideas about between us like so many brightly coloured balls, and telling each other tales. Tales from literature, tales from history, and tales – sometimes – of our own lives. I remember Shelley recounting to Byron one night how he and Mary had met, and as I listened to his words I turned to Mary and saw her face, so closed and white in the flickering firelight, knowing – as she did – what a lie it all was. She did not look up – did not, or could not, meet my eye – but I wondered, then, if she had started to believe what it suited them both to tell the credulous world. A world she has so blinded to her narrowness of heart and meanness of conduct that all it can see is the shining beauty of her mind.

*

Not that she cared much to display it, that summer. She rarely spoke, those long evenings, but sat pale in the shadows, watching and listening and – no doubt – judging. As I look back at that fortnight now it seems to me that the room was charged with a web of unspoken feeling – a tangle of electric connections much like those currents Shelley and Polidori debated of one night, that they said might one day unlock the door of life and bring the dead back to vital warmth. Connections unseen, but irresistible, and as explosive in their expression as they were erratic in their effects. Mine with Byron, a bright secret within a darker one; Poldori's with Mary, pursued by him, unsought by her; Shelley's with Byron, as ardent and infatuated as Byron's ever was with himself; and mine with Mary, the most ambivalent and enduring of them all – already so then, and how much more so now.

I do not remember, now, what first led us to talk of ghosts. No one could have known what would eventually come of it, and in any case it was entirely natural that our thoughts should tend in such a morbid direction, with the unquiet shadows cast by the guttering candles, and the wind howling about the walls like a banshee. I do recollect Byron coming down one night with a book of old German horror stories, and taking great delight in declaiming them to us in a loud and lurid voice. I recall one of a skull that was restored to life to accuse its murderer, another of two sisters so alike that they could scarce be told apart, and a third of a phantom cursed to kill each new heir to its line with a kiss. I shuddered as I watched Byron's eyes seek out mine as he spoke of the hideous wraith bending over the crib, and my heart misgave me as I saw him, in my imagination, perform the same foul rite, and breathe the same cold poison onto his own infant's brow. Shelley, by then, was in a state of the most excited animation, talking – babbling even – of how he had tried to raise ghosts when a boy and had once sat up all night in a charnel-house, reciting

93

from a book of spells and hoping to see a ghastly spectre rise from the heaps of dry old bones. It sounded childish, spoken in that shrill, high-pitched tone that always came upon him in agitation, and I could see the sardonic sneer once again on the doctor's face. And yet Polidori would soon observe with his own eyes that it was no passing juvenile fit that Shelley spoke of, but an ever-present terror that could reduce him, without warning, to a pitiful abject hysteria, or to night after night of sleep-walking from which he would awake hours later with no recollection of where he had been or what it was he had done.

Byron then cast down his book with a theatrical gesture, declaring the thing to be contemptible trash and that surely our combined intellects could concoct a horror story worth the name. Better still, cried Shelley, let us each devise our own tale, and contend with one another to harrow up our souls and set our eyeballs starting from their spheres! His own eyes were hardly less frenzied at that moment and I could see Mary's look of apprehension – she was concerned, always, to avoid any circumstance that might provoke a renewed attack, but Shelley was not to be gainsaid. He sought his notebook out at once, saying he had an idea for a story based on his own early life. Again I saw Mary's look, again I saw the shadow of disquiet cross her face, but she said not a word. Polidori announced he would set aside the play he had been writing (which I was not alone in dismissing as utterly worthless), and that he already had an idea for a story concerning a woman with a skull instead of a face. Shelley squealed with laughter at this, saying that he could furnish him with the perfect model, an artful, ugly, hermaphroditical beast of a woman, who had once made his life an utter misery. And then his face darkened with thought, or memory, and he cast himself into a chair by the fire, declaring that the most profound horror was to be found not in the artificial apparatus of the macabre, but in the terrible depths

94

of even the truest-intentioned human heart. I can recall moments, he continued, his voice dropping to a whisper, when I have looked upon my own being with unutterable abhorrence, and started from my own company as if it were that of a fiend, seeking anything rather than a continued communion with *self*.

Mary went to him then, and spoke to him softly, putting her hand to his forehead and looking into his eyes. I could see she was telling him that the idea was ill-advised, that no good could come of it, but she could not dissuade him. Byron, meanwhile, had stretched himself full length on the *chaise-longue* and was dictating at great speed to Polidori, who was endeavouring to capture it all in his leather-bound notebook. As for me, I had tried my hand at writing once before, and Shelley had been kind enough to encourage me and tell me I had a talent worth nurturing, and I saw no reason therefore why I should not make an attempt at a ghost tale of my own. Mary did her best to discourage me, but I had long since shaken off the conviction so studiously borne in upon me as a child – and not least by *her* – that it was fruitless, in our family, even to put pen to paper unless one could produce a work of such originality as would cast all other books into the shade. I could not refrain from an inward smile when I saw that she, indeed, seemed not a little fretful at having no immediate idea of her own to hand, but a question or two she subsequently asked Polidori about the discussion we had had of galvanism and electricity led me to believe that she was considering this as the basis of her tale. Though her tone appeared careless when she thanked him for his reply, I saw her go at once upstairs, to where she had stowed her writing-desk. The selfsame desk she would later leave, so disastrously, in that odious Maddocks's care.

But to return to my story. We slept at the Diodati that night, as so often that fortnight, and when Byron made his appearance at luncheon the following day Shelley was already far advanced in his tale, his hair disordered and flecks of ink spattered on his hands. Mary sought to induce him to join us at table, but he shook her arm roughly away, and for the rest of the afternoon he sat there, his desk placed to face down towards the water, writing with one hand and with the other conveying currants and pieces of stale bread to his mouth from the pocket of his long grey coat. As the hours wore on the weather worsened, and we felt in the air the sulphurous onset of thunder. We had seen storms in the region before, most especially in our journey across the Alps, when we cowered together against the cold through a desolate white landscape of overhanging precipices and huge, menacing trees, but that night at the Diodati was the worst we had yet endured. With the descent of darkness the wind swelled to a roar, and the flashes of lightning leaping from peak to peak lit up streaks of clouds racing across the angry sky, and the bowl of the lake seething like an alchemical crucible. As hour after hour passed it was clear that this vast collision of the elements was stimulating Shelley's nerves to an almost painful pitch, while Byron, by contrast, was evidently aroused in quite another manner. So much so, indeed, that he and I adjourned discreetly to his room after dinner, leaving the others variously preoccupied about their books.

When I descended again the clock in the hall was striking half after eleven, and the storm was at its very height. Byron was as always invigorated by the act of love, and had begun talking once more, and with renewed enthusiasm, of holding our own *phantasmagoria.* Let us extinguish all the lights, he declared, and demand the dead to appear and speak to us, for what do we have to fear? I am no murderer, even if my wife's family seem to think me capable of even blacker and more shameful transgressions. I dread no revenant come to punish *me*. Indeed? I replied archly. No father of a ruined daughter, or shamed and cuckolded husband determined to seek you out? No Commendatore hell-bent on revenge? He eyed me oddly then and, throwing on his dressing-gown, resumed his desk. I bobbed a mocking curtsy to his turned back, and betook myself back down to the saloon, where I joined the rest as unobtrusively as I was able, though not of course without attracting the customary look of impudent scorn from Polidori. And then as the hour of twelve struck, the drawing-room doors were thrown open with a splintering crack and a figure stood in the blue-white glare of a bolt of lightning, both arms outstretched, and draped in a black cloak and hood that reached down over his face. It was as if a monster from a Gothic novel had come that moment to life, or returned, a vampire glistering with the clammy dew of hell, from among the mouldering dead. I saw Shelley start aghast from his chair, even as a smile of ironic amusement slid across Polidori's face. He knew, as I did, that this was exactly the sort of cruel jest Byron delighted most to play – had he not taunted me, only a few nights before, with dark insinuations that he was the father of his own sister's child? My own nerves might withstand this latest prank, but I feared for Shelley, in his high-wrought state, after so many days caged up in such constraint. And for a moment – the briefest moment – I wondered if Mary too had not believed it, for in the dazzle of the lightning I had glimpsed her face, and seen there not just horror but something that I should almost have called ecstasy.

But all this passed in an instant, for then Byron threw back his hood and laughed, declaring loudly that it was the night of all others for tales of the supernatural, and even if we had no spells at our command, we should be more than capable of reducing our audience to a cold sweat of terror merely with our words – those of us, at least, whose works could make any valid claim to lasting fame (this, no doubt, directed at Polidori). And so – as he finished with a sweep of his black-swathed arm – we will now, at the midnight hour, read aloud what we have written. Mary began at once to protest, saying she had nothing to share, and I saw the doctor look quickly at her, as he made a few notes in that infernal pocket-book of his. Shelley, by contrast, seemed recovered from his alarm. Indeed, he appeared of all of us the most eager to begin. He went to close the shutters himself as the servants made up the fire and extinguished the lamps. I wondered what Byron could have to offer, knowing how little of his energy he had dedicated that day to his pen, but he had, it transpired, quite other ideas. As the room darkened we took our seats again about the fire, and the flames threw grotesque dancing shadows across the walls, transforming each of us in our turn from mortal to monster. Polidori, attentive but detached, ever the observer; Mary, folding her hands on her lap in seeming demureness, her real feelings betrayed only by the dead whiteness about her lips; and Shelley, passing strange, his eyelids drawn back as if in pain, and his breath coming fast and shallow. As I had seen him once before, on that other day of horrors which he and I endured. That day of which I have already spoken, and dread to speak of again.

Byron took his place in the centre of the circle, planted his feet apart and raised his arm, pointing slowly to each of us, one by one. All struggled to hold his stare but I – for what reason should I be abashed before him? And then he began, in sonorous tones, to recite. Not a piece of his own, but *Christabel*. Coleridge's *Christabel*. And much as I have always hated it, I could not but agree that it was a fine choice for such a night, that gruesome tale of a serpent-witch taking the shape of a lost and innocent girl. We sat there, silent and motionless, as Byron's voice mingled with the lashing of the rain against the glass and the boom of the thunder, close and far, and the room became by degrees ever more icy. The fire had risen to a blaze but seemed powerless to dispel the chill, which felt, at that moment, and in that strange and heightened atmosphere, the very ice of death. On and on he intoned, and as he approached the moment when the enchantress begins to disrobe, I could see Shelley becoming painfully restless, his hand at his side and his chest heaving with the effort for calm.

> Beneath the lamp the lady bowed,
> And slowly rolled her eyes around;
> Then drawing in her breath aloud,
> Like one that shuddered, she unbound
> The cincture from beneath her breast:
> Her silken robe, and inner vest,
> Dropped to her feet, and full in view,
> Behold! her bosom and half her side –
> Hideous, deformed, and pale of hue –

At that moment one of the shutters crashed open against the wall and Shelley staggered to his feet with a shriek of such anguish one might have thought his living heart was being torn from his breast. No – no! he cried, and ran sobbing and stumbling from the room. Mary rose at once, but Polidori prevented her and, consigning her to Byron's care, seized the nearest candle and followed Shelley's steps. Mary was by this time crying bitterly in his lordship's arms and, not wishing to play the role of spectator where I was accustomed to that of principal, I made my way out into the hall. I thought only at first of getting a little air and dispelling the poisonous atmosphere of the saloon, but I heard at once the low sound of voices and perceived that Shelley had taken refuge in the breakfast room. There was a little closet next to that chamber, and as the lightning flooded again through the windows and the thunder clove the air above me as if to sunder the very mountains, I pushed open the door and slid into the dark space.

I do not think, to this day, that they knew I was there. Neither ever said so, and both, now, are long dead – one by water, the other by his own hand. And certain it is that they gave no sign then. Silent still, I inched the connecting door open and saw Shelley lying on a couch on the far side of the room, his face and shirt soaking wet. It was clear at once that Polidori had thrown water in his face to quiet him, and I could see now that he was holding a cloth to Shelley's face and adjuring him to breathe deeply. I nearly gave myself away at that moment, so furious was I to see him administering ether to a man in such a febrile and nervous state. Did he not know what consequences it might have? His intention, no doubt, was to induce lethargy, but I had seen ether used before and knew it had the power to provoke a state of even greater agitation. I could scarce keep my place for the next few moments, but Shelley seemed to demonstrate none of the ill effects I apprehended. Indeed, he appeared instead to slide slowly into a curious intermediate state; his body lulled to something like repose, but his tongue excited to a flood of bizarre and nonsensical chatter in which half-memories merged with true fears, and long-told lies struggled towards the light. He owned the truth, for the first time in my hearing, of Harriet and all that dire affair, but the next instant he was jabbering incoherently of a demon with his own face, and a nameless persecutor who refused to come to blows, which matched with nothing I knew – then or since – of his history. And then my blood ran frozen as he described in heaving gasps how, as Byron was speaking, he had looked towards Mary and seen standing in her place the monstrous figure of a woman with her breasts uncovered, and eyes staring at him where her nipples should have been. He stammered that this horrifying vision had taken hold of his mind, and when Byron spoke then of the witch, and her deformed arm and bosom, the picture had come to his mind of a young girl he had known many years before, whose face still haunted his waking days, and would not let him rest. This, he whispered then, his eyes widening, was the story he was writing – this was the tale that would awaken those who read it to terror, and a sick fear of what lurked unseen in their own souls.

I heard the door to the drawing room open then, and Byron calling my name, and I slipped away.

I was not the only one of us to sleep badly that night, and when I ventured downstairs in the grey light of daybreak, I found Mary alone. She started when she saw me, like a guilty thing surprised. She has said, since, that it was this very morning that she announced to the assembled company that she had *thought of a story*. It is a lie: no such declaration was ever made, then or on any other day that summer. She was not at her desk writing that morning, when I discovered her, but on her hands and knees before the dying fire, feeding page after page into the flames – pages covered not with her own handwriting but with Shelley's. She answered, when pressed, and with some irritation, that the story he had begun was making him ill – that she had found him sleep-walking again, and he had complained to her that his senses had been brought to a state of such unnatural excitement that the very blades of grass and boughs of the trees had presented themselves to his eye with microscopical distinctiveness. Her *duty*, she said, with much emphasis on the word, was to prevent further such mischief, and thus it was that she had taken it upon herself to destroy what he had written and ensure that his Genius and his gift were spent on subjects worthy of them, and not on some childish make-believe fit only for the nursery. I looked at her

101

somewhat scornfully at this, tempted to enquire whether it was *he* or *she* who would decide what would be deemed thus 'worthy', but I refrained. Though I did wonder, afterwards, at her insistence that the tale was mere fabrication, and bore no relation to the truth. I myself had heard Shelley claim it was sprung from memory, but perhaps she knew, from her own knowledge of his past, that he had once again been subject to one of those concatenations of fact and phantasy that had plagued him ever since I had known him, and which left him so often doubtful of what was real, and what imagined.

And what, I said aloud then, will he find to occupy him now, seeing as you have taken it upon yourself to burn his tale? That, Mary replied, was no concern of mine. Then she stirred the ashen ghosts of Shelley's story with the poker, watched the flames lift for a moment, and turned on her heel and departed.

I obtained an answer to my question, all the same, even if it was some days before it became clear to me. For the story which has established her fame, and made her almost as celebrated as the man she married, the story that began – I concede – as her conception became in the weeks and months that followed no longer hers but Shelley's. She has admitted – for how could she pretend otherwise? – that he assisted her with it, that they walked and talked often together as the tale came into being, and that he made many changes to the manuscript, but I know it was more, far more than that. I saw her writing to his dictation – saw him correcting her fair copies and making revisions, both in Geneva and later, once we had returned to England. Why else would he have sent it to publishers under his own name? Why else should this book alone bear the mark of genius, and everything she produced thereafter lack any spark of original thought? And why else would it treat – so painfully and so terrifyingly –

of one who considers himself an outcast from society, abhorred and despised, a pursuer become the object of pursuit, tormented for ever by the abominable crime he believes that he has committed?

CHAPTER FIVE

The Sepulchre of Memory

Charles puts the manuscript down, his mind reeling. He is not sure what he expected to find – but it was not his uncle's name. He knew Maddox had worked for Godwin, but cannot imagine any reason why that should have involved taking charge of his daughter's possessions, only to find himself condemned as odious for his pains. And what of the murder – if murder there ever was? With Maddox's words ringing in his brain, Charles came here looking for a victim – looking for *Harriet* – and he has indeed found her, but what he has *not* found is her killer. Or not, at least, according to this manuscript. Yes, there is mention of Harriet, and of the lies Shelley and Mary told, but there is none of the horror – the natural revulsion – a young woman like Claire would surely have let slip had she known that 'the truth of all that dire affair' was that Shelley had killed his own wife. And this is no timid, shrinking girl. Horror and revulsion are here in full measure, but they stem from other events entirely – from Shelley's fear of some dead memory or long-past dream, and from her own recollection of a terror

104

once endured at his side, unchangingly preserved and buried there.

But if questions about Harriet remain, Charles has, at least, an answer to the mystery of Claire and how she came to be so intimate with the Shelleys. This woman is Mary Shelley's step-sister. And now Charles thinks about it, he does seem to recall that William Godwin married again after Mary Wollstonecraft's death, and if he had a second wife it's perfectly possible he also had step-children. But that's an answer that leaves Charles all the more contemptuous of Lady Shelley and her husband, for even if Claire and Mary were not sisters in the literal sense of the term, it's the most mean-spirited of casuistries to deny any 'relation' between them at all. But if there is a woman alive capable of such small-mindedness, Lady Shelley is surely that woman. And it does, undeniably, explain her fear of Claire. Her terror of what Claire might reveal, were her papers known. Because there is another revelation, even in these few short pages – a revelation Charles could never have foreseen, and which would break on the unsuspecting world with all the force of a thunderbolt. If what he's just read is to be trusted, Claire Clairmont is the only person left alive other than Mary Shelley herself who knows the truth about the authorship of *Frankenstein*. And it is only too obvious to Charles why Lady Shelley and her husband would want to keep that truth concealed – whatever price might have to be paid, and whatever unforgivable literary betrayal might ensue.

Charles sits back against the bed, thinking of Claire – thinking how very young she must have been when these events took place. How young, and how beautiful. Beautiful enough, it seems, to have been the mistress of no less a lover than Lord Byron. And perhaps not merely that. Charles looks back at all those allusions to seeds planted, and secrets yet hidden, and wonders if that summer spawned more than a monstrous fictional progeny. Did Claire Clairmont bear Lord Byron a child? It would explain her wistful fondness for infants not her own, and her mysterious hints about what had befallen her in Italy. And if there was a child, where is it now? Is that what she meant when she said she had buried all she loved there? He closes his eyes, imagining the atmosphere in that house by the lake all those years ago, the darkened room, the stifling thunder, the shadows leering across the walls. The very air they breathed taut with sex and intelligence and possibility, and bitter with betrayals yet to come. Love and hope; desire and fear. And Claire – and Claire—

Two hours later, Charles starts awake to a grey dawn sifting through the thin curtains, and the sound of the maid in the kitchen downstairs. He curses silently – there's no chance now of getting the papers back unseen, so he tucks them inside his copy of Shelley, wraps that in a cloth and hides it in turn at the bottom of his box of paints. Then he washes hastily in the icy water on the washstand, and slips quietly downstairs and out of the house.

As he strides back down towards town, the air and the exercise clear his mind a little, and he starts to form a new theory that might fit the facts. Could William Godwin have hired his uncle in connection with the Chancery case for the custody of Harriet's children? The dates tally, and Sir Percy's reference to a 'minor legal matter' may have had more truth in it than Charles was initially prepared to allow him, and his wish to downplay such a scandalous episode only too understandable in the circumstances. Charles can easily see Godwin turning to a man like Maddox if he was looking for evidence to exonerate Shelley or discredit the

Westbrooks. It's a stretch, but it might even explain why Maddox took charge of Mary's writing-desk, if there were documents he believed might be helpful – or indeed *un*helpful, if they became known. Though none of that, of course, explains the allegation of murder. Which is why, despite his instinctive antipathy to everything his clients stand for, Charles now has every intention of doing exactly what the Shelleys have paid him to do – or, at least, appearing to. For the moment; until he has found out what he wants to know. Even though that puts himself and Claire on very different sides. Even though (as I'm sure you will have noticed) he has singularly failed to maintain a proper professional distance from this woman he may yet have to outmanoeuvre – this woman who is no longer 'Miss Clairmont' to him, but 'Claire', despite the fact that he has seen only too clearly that she cannot be wholly trusted or even, perhaps, believed.

By the time he turns into the Strand the rain has started to come down in a thin miserly trickle that runs freezing down the back of his neck. The only signs of life are the breakfast street-sellers hauling their stalls into their accustomed pitches, and the odd gaunt-ribbed dog nosing about for scraps in the gutters. Charles doesn't expect much more activity at his uncle's house either, not at this time of day, but he does assume the fires will be lit and the curtains drawn. So when he opens the door to a cold and darkened house, he knows that something is wrong. He stands in the hall, wondering what to do next, until he hears sounds coming up the back stairs. Strange, muffled, lurching sounds that resemble nothing Charles can at once identify. Curious rather than really alarmed, he makes his way down to the kitchen, but the sounds, whatever they are, are not coming from there. The room is empty, and the range is cold. And then he hears the noise again and knows suddenly what it is. In the scullery, behind the half-closed door, someone is retching into the metal pail, choking the noise off each time with a stifling hand. Charles frowns grimly. That'll teach Billy to spend his evening off drinking bad beer with the coster-boys. Perhaps next time he might be more sensible. He turns to go and almost collides with Abel, who is shuffling down the stairs, grumbling about stoves unlit, breakfasts uncooked and water still unboiled.

'Mr Charles,' he says, anxiety flickering across his face, 'we werenae expecting you so early. Will you be wanting your breakfast?'

Charles shakes his head. 'No, Abel, or at least not yet. When you bring up my uncle's I will have something then. We can only hope that Molly will be better soon – we clearly cannot rely on *Billy* in the mornings.'

He's raised his voice a little now, thinking it would do no harm for the lad to hear himself found thus wanting. Abel is looking at him a little oddly, but Charles doesn't care: Billy needs taking more firmly in hand, and when this case is over and he is back in the house on a permanent basis, he'll do just that. He puts his hand on the old man's shoulder, as if to emphasize that he is not to blame. It's only now that he notices there is a note addressed to him on the table. In Sam's handwriting. Charles reads it, then slips upstairs to the drawing room. Maddox is still asleep, and after watching a few moments, Charles closes the door gently and goes back downstairs and out into the street.

New Cut, Lambeth, Sam's note said, and as Charles soon discovers, it is market day. Not just fruit, vegetables and flowers, like its rather older and more respectable equivalent to the north at Covent Garden, but a full half-mile of pans and pitchers, saucepans and shirt-buttons, cakes and crumpets, pickled whelks and plum duffs, kettles and caddies, shoes and sheets and sealing-wax, and cabbages and string, and just about every other random article and eatable a Victorian household might ever have need of. The market proper doesn't start till evening falls, but the sellers are already setting up, and some stalls are being minded by alert, sly-faced boys, who've been paid a few pennies to watch the stock. Charles's destination is at the far end towards Waterloo Road, and turns out to be a large shop-front with paint flaking off the door and bars on the glass. But this place clearly hasn't functioned as a shop for some time: there are coloured lamps strung above the entrance, and the glass is layered with posters of vaudeville attractions, featuring actors, singers and musicians in dramatic, languishing or suggestive attitudes, as required. A large grey rat is nosing about in the rubbish that's collected about the entrance.

A few moments later Sam arrives, wheezing a little, a long coat concealing his uniform and his pockets full of apples. Charles grins – some things never change.

'Well,' he says, as Sam draws near. 'What is it? Have you found something?'

'I 'ad a look at them records, like you said, and sure enough there was somefing towards the end of 1816 as might be what yer lookin' for. It were all a bit cryptic, though, and it were 'ard to work out exactly what'd 'appened, so I 'ad a quick word with Inspector Bucket and 'e put me on to a geezer as was working in Bow Street then and might remember. And 'e said to give you 'is complimums too, by the way. The inspector.'

Charles nods. 'So who is this man? And what on earth are we doing here, of all places?'

''E works in 'ere,' answers Sam, cocking his head in the direction of the door. ''E's the doorkeeper of the New Cut penny gaff.'

Sam pushes open the door and Charles follows him down a long, narrow and unlit corridor. The air is rank with sweat and stale beer. After two turnings, left then right, they end up finally in the lobby of a small theatre, which has been squeezed into the cramped space available by taking out the floor between the ground and first storeys. A gallery of seats has been perched on planks between the joists, and the boards already sag with the weight; and up above their heads there are still scraps of floral paper clinging here and there to what must once have been bedroom walls. An old woman is slowly sweeping up scraps of paper, bottles, meat bones and empty twists of tobacco along the line of benches near the orchestra pit, and on the stage an Italian-looking man with a little pointed beard is playing the piano to accompany two men dressed as women, who are sashaying about the boards singing, dressed in spangles, feathers and bright yellow wigs. Charles has been to penny gaffs before, so he should know what to expect, but even he is taken aback at the explicit obscenity, both of word and gesture. At the back of the theatre a line of little coster-boys greets every indecency with whistles and cheers. The ticket booth is empty at this time of day, but Sam soon lights on a dirty, scowling lad and dispatches him looking for the man they have come to see.

'Don't judge 'im by this place,' cautions Sam, under his breath. 'Seems 'e ain't any other way to earn 'is bread. Bucket said 'e were a formidable Runner back in 'is day. Bit of a lesson for all of us there, wouldn't yer say?'

Charles looks across the theatre and realizes that there's a man now moving towards them between the rows of seats. His dress is as gaudy as his place of work – bright red cravat, embroidered waistcoat, blue velveteen trousers – but his skin is sallow and his eyes red-rimmed and dull. He must be twenty years younger than Maddox, but it's clear this old Runner has not had the famed thief-taker's easy existence. There is an old pride, still, in his erect back, but once or twice he misses his footing and Charles can see, now, the tremor in his hands.

'Name's Finch,' whispers Sam. 'Started at Bow Street in 'fifteen. Doin' errands mostly, to start wiv, as far as I could make out. But Bucket swears 'e's reliable, and even though 'e's partial to a drop, 'is mind ain't gone.'

Sam flushes then, aware of his blunder, but Charles just shakes his head. 'Don't worry, Sam, I know what you mean.'

'Two tickets for tonight, is it, young sirs?' says the man, chirpily, as he comes a little unsteadily towards them. 'Twopence for the good seats, right at the front. It's *The Blood-Stained Bride* tonight, and by popular demand Miss Meredith has extended her engagement with us for a week to appear once more in the role of Emily. Lovely gruesome murder, that one, and afterwards there'll be all the usual complement of music and dancing. Lots of pretty ladies here, gents, and not averse to showing a bit of leg to fine young gentlemen like you.'

'We're not here for the show,' says Charles, somewhat frostily. Even three feet away he can smell the gin on the man's breath. 'I want to ask you about something that happened when you were at Bow Street. Back in 1816.'

The man's face closes. The jaunty all-but-wink disappears, as if it had never been. 'That's a long time ago—' he begins warily. But Charles has forestalled him. He takes a sovereign from his pocket and lays it on the counter of the ticket booth.

Finch glances down, then back at Charles. 'I were only a boy back then. I don't know what I can tell you.'

'It 'appened that winter,' says Sam. 'I've 'ad a gander at the files, and there were a mention of an incident 'andled by Mr Maddox, and 'ow Sir Nathaniel was satisfied matters 'ad been dealt wiv in the right 'n' proper way.'

'Mr *Charles* Maddox?' says Finch. 'Is that who you mean?'

'This young man 'ere,' says Sam, leaning forward and dropping his voice, 'is 'is great-nephew. Taken over 'is business, as you might say.'

'In that case,' says Finch, standing stiffly now and holding out his hand, 'I'd be honoured to offer you my assistance. I never worked with your uncle, sir, but I knew his reputation.'

Charles bows and, after a moment's hesitation, shakes his hand. 'Do you recall the episode Sam mentioned?'

The man sits down heavily at the booth, then looks up again at Charles. 'It must have been that young woman, sir. I don't think I've thought of her from that day to this. But it must be her.'

'What young woman?' says Charles, quickly. 'What was her name?'

Finch shrugs. 'That I never knew. They buried her as Smith, though I don't know if it was her real name. Not likely, I should say. Not much more than twenty, that I do remember. And of good family, they said, though I never saw the corpse myself. Should have been our case – all the lads said so – but the guv'nor told us Mr Maddox had it all in hand, and had requested discretion. Words of that kind.'

Charles and Sam exchange a glance.

'And how did she die?' asks Charles, quietly.

'She drowned, sir. They found her body one winter morning, floating in the Serpentine.'

*

112

'Don't you see?' says Charles, excitedly, as the two of them walk back up Waterloo Road ten minutes later. 'It *has* to be Harriet Shelley. The right date, the right age, and she *drowned*, Sam. Don't you remember what Maddox said – *"No poison administered, no blow struck, no weapon wielded"*? Of all the deaths she could have died, only drowning matches the murder Maddox talked of.'

'Sorry, Chas,' says Sam, shaking his head, 'I just ain't buyin' it. I just don't fink a gent like Shelley coulda killed 'is wife and got away wiv it. It just ain't plausible.'

'Come on, Sam! You know as well as I do he could have made it look like suicide.'

Sam extracts an apple from his pocket and takes a bite. 'And yer really fink yer uncle wouldn't't've noticed?' he says, spitting juice down his jacket. 'Of all the Runners and 'takers in London, 'e'd have known the signs. There wouldn't't've been no pulling the wool over 'is eyes.'

Charles purses his mouth and looks away.

'And yer can't even be sure it really was 'er. Not absolutely.'

'Then who the hell else was it?' snaps Charles. 'My uncle had no other case at that time – nothing that explains how he came to have the death of a young woman on his hands, and doing everything in his power to cover it up.'

But Sam's shaking his head again. 'It weren't coverin' up if it were suicide. Just a way of keepin' it outa the papers – and that'd also explain why 'er name was changed. You can see why someone'd ask 'im to do that. 'E'd done that sorta fing for clients before.'

Charles nods slowly. 'So he had, Sam. But there's one fact that doesn't explain. Why in God's name was *Godwin* involved? He and his family were the Westbrooks' sworn enemies. Why should he lift a finger to help them, or spend

money protecting a woman his own daughter had supplanted long before?'

But to that question, Sam has no answer.

* * *

Carlo Cottage seems destitute of all life when Charles strides
up the steps later that afternoon and slides his key into the
lock. There are the remains of a fire in the drawing room,
but the embers are dying inwards into ashen ghosts and
there is no sign of the maid coming to replenish the coals.
He hesitates in the hallway, wondering whether this might
not be an ideal opportunity to replace what he has taken. He
was going to wait till nightfall, but then the other occupants
of the house will be present, even if sleeping, and now it
seems there may be no one about to hear. Decisive, once the
decision is made, he goes quickly upstairs to collect the
papers, then comes back down and strides across the room
to the piano-stool, where he removes the drapery, and
lumbers the trunk round so that he can slide the papers back
inside. Which is when he hears the minutest of tiny sounds
behind him, and raises his eyes to see—

Claire.

'And what do you think you are doing?'

'I – I—' Charles stammers, his face ablaze.

She comes towards him, in that rustle of silk, that breath
of dark scent.

'Shall I,' she says, taking a seat opposite him and
arranging her skirts serenely about her, 'save you the
embarrassment of concocting a story that you and I both
know will be nothing but lies from start to finish?'

He looks into her eyes – those eyes so black, so brilliant – and cannot read what he sees there. Fury? Compassion? Even, perhaps, and strangest of all, satisfaction? And then he hangs his head and turns away.

'Well,' she says, and now that he cannot see her face she permits full rein to the smile she has been doing her best to repress. 'If you are not prepared to speak, it seems the task must fall to me. It is only a theory, of course, but I think that what I just interrupted was an attempt on your part to return some papers of mine to where you found them. I think, moreover, that you have made notes about those papers so that you might report back what you have discovered to your master. Or,' and here she raises an eyebrow, 'perhaps *mistress* would be a more appropriate word. Tell me, how long is it that you have been in the pay of the odious Lady Shelley?'

It's not a word he would have expected from one woman about another, however unconventional the speaker, and his reaction is evident in his face.

'Oh, you no doubt think my language excessive. You would not, had you suffered at her hands as I have done all these years.' And then, seeing his expression change, 'But perhaps they have told you *I* am the one who persecutes *them*.' She laughs then. 'Well, you must make up your own mind whom to believe. But is not your very presence here the strongest possible evidence against them? *I*, after all, have not installed an informer within the hallowed portals of Chester Square.'

He's looking at her now – staring in what would otherwise be the most discourteous manner from a gentleman to a lady. But then again, Claire is like no lady Charles has ever met, and he can hardly call himself a gentleman. Not now that she has discovered what he's been doing. 'But how—'

She laughs again. 'Do you really think I did not guess why you were here? My dear Mr – *Mab*, is it still? I recognized you the moment I saw you. You had been skulking across the street from here for more than an hour in the rain not two days earlier. I grant you were moderately successful in concealing yourself, but anyone who has lived the life I have lived, and kept the secrets I have kept, becomes more than usually alert to such insistent observation. I confess I was momentarily dismayed to have found your delightful "sister" to be nothing but a fraud, but it has so often been my fate to find those on whom I bestow my affections to be totally unworthy of them that it scarcely distresses me any more.'

Her voice has taken on the petulant tone Charles has heard in it before, but he is hardly in any position to refute her.

'And besides,' she continues, the amusement returning as quickly as it had gone, 'if *I* had pried into *your* things as *you* have pried into *mine*, I should have discovered that your supposed portfolio of artworks is nothing but a mismatched muddle, clearly executed by a host of different – and indeed *in*different – hands. Whatever you are, you are certainly no painter, Mr *Maddox*.'

And now she really does have him. He gapes, utterly confounded – even if he's been stupid enough to give the game away, there's nothing, surely, that can have given his *name* away. How on earth—?

She is watching him with that mysterious smile, her head slightly tilted, a lock of hair twisting around one finger. 'You resemble him, you know,' she says softly, after a moment. 'Very much. He was such a handsome man.'

'Who?' he says, his voice barely more than a whisper.

'Your namesake. The first Charles Maddox. Your – it must be grandfather, I think?'

116

Charles shakes his head, blizzarded by this stupefying turn of events. 'Great-uncle. He never married.'

Claire sighs. 'What a terrible waste. Heavens, it must be more than thirty years ago now that we met,' she says, then stops and looks at him, her face suddenly still. 'But, of course, you know that. No doubt you have spoken to him, and heard every last detail from his own lips.'

She drops her gaze now, but not before Charles has seen fear flicker across her eyes – it's so fleeting he scarcely registers it at a conscious level, but it is enough. Call it intuition, or interrogator's instinct, but when he opens his mouth to answer, what he tells her is a lie: 'My uncle is not well enough to talk of the past, Miss Clairmont, but, yes, I have read his files. I know what happened.'

And now he is certain. Her body betrays her disquiet in signs so slight as to be almost imperceptible – the tiniest tension in her fingers, the momentary quiver about her mouth – but Charles, if anyone, can read the mind's construction in the frame. Something took place, all those years ago, that Maddox witnessed and she does not want known. Something far more dangerous than mere scandal, since this is a woman who has spent her life flouting social convention, without a care for the consequences. Whatever it was, it made Maddox privy to a secret she believes Charles, too, has now discovered. And it is a secret that gives him power over her. Or would do, if only Charles knew what it was – knew what was in those missing pages he's claiming to have read. And that will be doubly difficult to discover now, without revealing his pretence and ceding his advantage. They are silent for a moment, she breathing a little fast, a little shallow; he conscious only of his own quandary. Because this is not the first time Charles has been rather too clever for his own good, and it won't be the last either.

'And so,' she says at last, lifting her eyes to meet his, '*I* have exposed *you*, only to be exposed myself, in my turn. I am not wholly surprised. You seem to take after your great-uncle in more than your mere appearance.' She pauses. 'Your move, Mr Maddox.'

And as he gazes at her now he sees a challenge in those beautiful eyes. A look far too direct and forthright for a Victorian lady, and proof once more – if proof were necessary – how little such common proprieties mean to this woman, and how far the long journey of her life has taken her from the mass of her contemporaries. Charles, too, aspires to the unconventional – would like to think himself as disdainful as she is of what others think, and what others expect, and it is this that decides him now, even though it will make him doubly deceitful – both to her and to the Shelleys – and there will be no possibility of retraction, once the offer has been made.

'I propose that we might be of use to one another, Miss Clairmont. There are things I want to know, which I cannot ask my uncle in his present state of health, but which I believe you can tell me. And by way of exchange—'

'By way of exchange?'

'By way of exchange, I will endeavour to help you in this current – matter.'

She looks at him a moment, then smiles. 'A deal with the devil. And never was Beelzebub more beguiling. Very well, Mr Maddox, I will agree. Though on one condition. Like the *djinn* in Scheherazade's tale, I will give you what you seek, but thrice only. You may ask me three questions, and I will give you your answers. But that is all. There must be some limit, even to the truth. What say you – is that not fair?'

Charles hesitates, wondering uneasily if he has not played

118

into her hands, and given her – all unwitting – the better of the bargain. But it is too late now. He nods. 'That is fair.'

'And you in your turn will take up my cause? Act as my champion?'

He smiles drily. 'Within reason, Miss Clairmont. There must be some limit, even to knight-errantry.'

She raises an arched brow. *'Touché.'*

Claire rises now and goes to ring the bell, then returns to her seat with a shiver, gathering about her the same worn old shawl he saw her wear before. Charles gets to his feet and does what he can to build up the fire.

'Since we have so much to discuss,' she says, as the maid appears in the doorway and is dispatched to the kitchen for coffee, 'I think we might both benefit from a little refreshment.' She arranges her skirts once more. 'So, what is it that you wish to ask me?'

As he was raking the fire he was racking his mind. Three questions, three answers. Three opportunities, and three alone, to obtain the information he wants. But how is he to extract the facts without betraying the real extent of his ignorance?

He takes a seat on the sopha opposite her and pulls his notebook from his pocket. There is nowhere to go now but forwards. 'There is a reference, in those papers of yours I read, to my great-uncle.'

She looks at him for a moment, clearly a little perplexed, but then her face clears. 'Oh, you mean that horrible man *Maddocks*? That was someone else entirely. We rented a house from him in Marlow in 1817, and left various things in his charge. After we left for Italy the loathsome little man sold some of them, and attempted to hold us to ransom for the rest.'

119

'I see,' says Charles, wondering if his most promising theory has just shattered into pieces. 'So the name was merely a strange coincidence?'

Claire sighs. 'The coincidence is stranger even than that – Shelley had already encountered a man named Maddocks once before, when he was living in Wales, at a place called Tremadoc. Such odd recurrences of names happened to him so often that I think he genuinely came to believe there was some purpose in it – some larger design. That he could somehow contrive to change the past by repeating it. Or if not alter it, redeem it.'

Charles frowns. 'I am not sure I understand you.'

'It is not easy to explain – not to someone who never knew him.' She takes a deep breath. 'When he was seventeen Shelley fell in love with one of his cousins. A beautiful girl, by all accounts, called Harriet Grove. He wanted to marry her, but her family put a stop to it – apparently they discovered some letters he had written to her which they considered alarming. I do know he was wretchedly miserable for a while, and when he met Harriet Westbrook some part of him must have thought her name was a sign that he could reclaim his first love – or exorcize it. I believe he married her in that hope, but it brought nothing but calamity on them both. And it was the same when he met Mary. Harriet once claimed that the only hold Mary ever had over Shelley was her name. It was such an odd thing to say I have never forgotten it.'

'But surely she must have meant her surname – that Shelley was drawn to her as a daughter of William Godwin, of Mary Wollstonecraft—'

'No,' replies Claire, with an insistence that surprises him. 'It was *not* that – or at least, not that alone. It was the name "Mary". When I asked Shelley about it years later, he merely laughed and changed the subject. As – I note – *you* have just done, Mr Maddox. Your second question?'

Charles waits, prolonging the silence. Then, 'When I read my uncle's files I found one thing I did not expect and cannot explain. It is an allegation of murder.'

He is watching her now, just as she is watching him, alert to every movement, every sign.

'Where did you find this?' she says eventually, her face blank of all emotion.

'At the end of the report on the work he did for William Godwin. There is damage to the paper and some words are missing, so I cannot be sure what he meant. But it must be connected to that case. There is no other explanation.'

Her face is still, frozen; her mouth opens, but no words come.

'I can – I think – answer your riddle,' she says at last. 'What did your uncle say – exactly?'

'There was mention of justifiable anger and insupportable grief, that no blow was struck, and no poison administered—'

'Harriet,' she says suddenly. 'He was talking of Harriet.'

Charles sits forward in his chair, feeling the electric tingle of adrenalin fizzing in his brain – he was right, he was *right*. 'You are telling me that Harriet Shelley was *murdered*—'

But she is already shaking her head. 'No, Mr Maddox, she was not. It was suicide. There is no question of that. That poor silly girl destroyed herself, and Shelley could never rid himself of the conviction that he was to blame. But he was not *responsible*, Mr Maddox, not in any actual or criminal fashion. Although,' she continues bitterly, 'that did not stop those vile Westbrooks alleging so. Harriet's sister, Eliza, in particular, made all sorts of disgusting accusations, despite the fact that Shelley was more than a hundred miles

121

away when Harriet died, and had not seen her for months.'

'And you know all of this to be true – you were there yourself.'

'No,' she retorts, picking now at the fringes of her shawl, 'I was not. I will not mince matters, Mr Maddox, and in any case you are doubtless very well aware that I was, at that time, expecting a child. I remained in Bath all that winter, because I did not wish my mother and Godwin to discover the truth.'

'Then how can you be sure—'

'Really, Mr Maddox,' she snaps. 'Do you not think that if there had been the slightest evidence of murder the West-brooks would have pressed for immediate prosecution? No, despite all their foul insinuations, even they were forced to acknowledge that Harriet had left a letter confessing that she took her life by her own hand – her own choice. And in any case, what would Shelley have stood to gain by such a crime? He had no need to rid himself of his wife: he had already done so years before.'

Charles sighs. So this is the sad truth of 'all that dire affair': Harriet Shelley died alone, and of despair. Shelley seduced her, married her, and then he cast her off. Leaving her with two children and the prospect of living out her years reliant on her family's charity; half a lifetime in a shadow existence, neither maid nor married, widow nor wife. No wonder her father was so desperate to gain guardianship of her children, and no wonder Sir Percy and his wife are now equally desperate to keep her fate forgotten, and unknown.

Claire looks across at him, and there is something brittle about her mouth that suddenly jars. The accusations Shelley endured may have been unfounded, even malicious, but at their heart was the shocking suicide of a mere girl, married at sixteen, a mother at seventeen, and dead at scarcely twenty-one. But the only expression on Claire's face now is one of exasperated resentment. Has she, Charles wonders, become so preoccupied by pity for her own past that she has no compassion left for anyone else, not even those who have been dealt a harder hand than hers?

'I may not have been in London,' she continues, 'but I *do* know that Eliza Westbrook was . . .' she pauses '. . . a very *forceful* woman, and I am not at all surprised that she attempted to persuade your uncle to support her despicable allegations, and lend credence to her claims. She would, no doubt, have seen him as a most useful ally. That, I am sure, is your explanation.'

Charles thinks back to what remains of Maddox's words, and has to concede that her interpretation does indeed fit the facts, as far as he can discern them. His uncle could have been approached by Miss Westbrook, and investigated the circumstances of Harriet's drowning on her behalf, only to conclude, in the end, that despite Shelley's despicable behaviour, the man was not guilty of any crime. Did the passage not end, explicitly, '*I was wrong*'?

Claire, meanwhile, has folded her hands in her lap, 'I do not pretend to understand the logic behind your questions, Mr Maddox, but you have only one of them remaining.'

Charles watches her a moment. She is staring into the fire, her hands twisting the fringes of her shawl. If he were a poker player (which he is not) the question he is about to ask would be his wild card. One whose value he cannot guess until after he has played it.

'What happened that day,' he says slowly, 'the day of horrors you talked of? The day that terrified you so much you dreaded to speak of it again?'

She gasps, '*As if you do not know!*' Then she puts a hand to her lips, and seems to press them, trembling, closed.

'May I remind you, Miss Clairmont,' he says, seeing the flush now across her cheeks, 'that you promised to tell me the truth. That our agreement was made on that basis. There was something, wasn't there – you hint as much – something Shelley had done, something his wife knew—'

She flashes a look at him now.

'—something that has prevented her all these years from writing her own account of his life?'

'His *wife*,' she whispers fiercely, her eyes glittering with tears, 'has betrayed him. When I think of what Shelley endured at her hands—'

'Then what is it that impedes her – what had he done?'

'He had done *nothing*,' she snaps, looking at him in sudden defiance, her colour high. '*Nothing*, I tell you. No one knew him better than I, and I swear to you that no man had a higher moral sense than he – no man a finer understanding of the distinction between right and wrong.'

'Even though you wrote yourself that he was tortured by a belief that he had committed some appalling crime? That he had a sick fear of what lurked unseen in his own soul?'

She lifts her chin. 'Even so. You should not believe everything you have read, Mr Maddox, even in *your own uncle's files*.'

'Then *tell me*, Miss Clairmont – tell me what I should believe. *Tell me what it is you know.*'

He watches, scarcely breathing, willing her to continue, willing her to say more. But she does not. And when at last she speaks again her face is pale. 'You have had your three questions, Mr Maddox, and I have answered you. If there is no other way to do justice to the dead than by reliving the agonies of the past, then I will do it, but it will be done in

124

my own way, and at a time of *my* choosing, and certainly not at *your* behest.'

She gets up quickly and goes to the window, then stands there, holding the shawl about her, staring into the drear and listless day.

Charles wonders if she has dismissed him – if this strange audience has now concluded, but then there is a knock on the door and the maid enters with the coffee. She sets the tray down on the table by the fire, then leaves the room, though not – it must be said – without a curious sidelong glance at her mistress. A moment later Claire turns from the window, and Charles wonders if it is tears he can see on her cheeks. She moves in silence to the table and busies herself about the saucers and the spoons, but by the time she approaches him, the hand that holds the cup is steady, and as she bends to give it to him a skein of her hair slips over her shoulder and brushes against his cheek. Then she returns to her chair, and takes a sip of her coffee, before setting the cup carefully down and smoothing the silk of her dress.

'I have fulfilled my part of our bargain. Now it is your turn.'

Charles sits back slowly in his seat. 'What is it you want me to do?'

She smiles thinly. 'The Shelleys have told you, no doubt, that they wish you merely to discover what papers I possess, but I fear you will find your role as *spy* slipping only too easily into that of *thief*. For that woman will stop at nothing to protect the fragile artifice she has been constructing all these years. Indeed, one might almost believe *her* to be the daughter, and poor Percy merely the son-in-law, so closely does she cosset her *dear Madre*.'

She pauses then, but Charles has wit enough not to be

drawn – not this time – and in any case her words are slightly too histrionic, slightly too rehearsed. He sits back a little further, wary that even such a tiny movement might betray the direction of his thought.

'I fear poor Percy comes a *very* poor third in *that* marriage,' she continues. 'If marriage you can call it. From what I can gather, Lady Shelley spends so much time beset by mysterious illnesses that she scarcely has time – or inclination – to perform her wifely duties. Is it any wonder she has produced no heir? Not that *that* is any great loss. She may lord it over the rest of us as if she were born in ermine, but I have it on good authority that her parents' marriage will not bear too close a scrutiny. May not – indeed – even merit the term *marriage* at all.'

Charles shifts uncomfortably in his chair. This is beginning to sound like the curdled invective of the sour old spinster he had once – mistakenly – assumed her to be. Something of which sentiment she must have sensed, for the very next moment she has executed one of those volte-faces that he has seen so many times now, but which still catch him unprepared.

'You must forgive me, Mr Maddox,' she says, with a light laugh. 'All these years of living for myself alone have made me, no doubt, nothing but an eccentric and resentful old maid.'

He flushes, as if she had overheard his mind. 'Surely not—'

'There is no need to flatter me,' she interrupts. 'Not any more. I have always been rather a good hater, and now I have food enough to feed that faculty for the rest of my life. I cannot forgive that woman for what she has done to me, but it is what she has done to *Shelley* that is truly unpardonable. In the few short weeks I have been in London, it has

126

come to my knowledge – I will not trouble you how – that Jane Shelley has not only been destroying papers, but has colluded in the creation of outright forgeries – forgeries designed to eradicate facts she considers "inconvenient", and ensure that hers is the only version of Shelley's life the future will ever see.'

Charles stares at her. 'And Shelley's widow is conniving at these forgeries?'

'Mary?' she says with disdain. 'Her *own* fame is all that matters to *her* now – her own spotless and perfect reputation. Not content with poisoning the last months of Shelley's life with her coldness and reserve, she now forsakes even his memory. She was brought up, Mr Maddox, to believe herself the world's darling – "the lovely gaze where every eye doth dwell" – and from the first day I met her she has been intent on retaining that position, at whatever cost to those around her. At whatever cost to Shelley. At whatever cost to *me*. Mary has been the ruination of my every happiness. All the mistakes of my life – the most terrible mistakes – were made because of her.'

She had talked of hatred, and there is no other word for what Charles sees now on her face. A hatred that has wound its roots tight about her heart and seems, at this moment, to be an almost physical pain. He thinks back to her account of that summer in Geneva, and the tension between the step-sisters, palpable even under its veneer of politeness – even if the cause of it was never openly revealed. Has there always been such antipathy between them, all the long and lonely years they have lived apart?

'One thing I have learned,' she says softly, as if in answer to his question, 'and learned the hardest way, is that love and enmity may exist side by side – may become, in time, almost indistinguishable. That one may be bound to another

127

person by ties too deep and fierce for tenderness – ties the breaking of which will rend your heart more than any common notion we have of love.'

It is a truth that Charles, too, has learned. Indeed, all he has ever known of love is pain. The loss of a sister, the absence of a mother, the coldness of a distant father, the awful decline of the great-uncle who became that father's substitute; all the relationships life gave him have failed him so totally, small wonder that he resists adding voluntarily to their number.

There is a silence.

'I still do not know,' Charles says eventually, 'how I can assist you. What I am to do.'

She looks up. 'You are to tell them the truth – or that part of it I choose they should know. Go to Chester Square and tell Sir Percy and his vulgar little wife that I have exposed their infamous scheme for the imposture it is. Tell them that I despise them from the very depths of my being, but that I am ill, and I am tired, and I want such peace as the world can still afford. So I am prepared to consider selling them my papers. All of them. Provided that the negotiations may be conducted solely through you.'

She looks at him but he shakes his head, finding himself saying exactly what he had said in Lady Shelley's drawing room, though for rather different reasons: 'But I have no experience in such things. You need a lawyer – with so much money at stake.'

'It's not about money – I don't want their money. I want them to believe that I am so heartsick of the past that I want nothing more to do with it. I know from bitter experience that they will not trust *me*, but if *you* tell them that, they will believe it. And by the time they discover the truth it will be too late.'

Charles frowns. 'Too late?'

She smiles at him, an artful, knowing smile. 'Surely you have understood by now. I have no intention of selling them a single page – a single line. All I ask you to obtain for me is time – the time I need to complete my book, so that the full truth of our lives may finally be told. The time I need to ensure that there will be nothing whatsoever they can do to prevent its publication.'

'You intend to *publish* what you have written? Is that wise – will it not expose you to—'

'Scandal and ignominy?' she finishes archly. 'I have weathered many a worse storm. For the last thirty years I have hidden myself away – shunned the light, like some wretched creature of the underworld – and the price I have paid has been to see those two women appoint themselves sole guardians of the truth about Shelley's life. But now that scoundrel Medwin has written of me in his memoir, and ripped away the protecting veil I had wrapped about my name, I have nothing left to lose. I do not want my memory to be as sunk in oblivion as my life has been. I have trodden this life with neither guide nor companion, and before I leave it I want to write the story I have never dared to tell.'

She is weeping now, and Charles resists an impulse to move to comfort her – tells himself consciously to resist it, and cannot understand how he finds himself on his knees before her chair, his arms about her shoulders, and her body racking his with wrenching sobs. The scent of her is so strong now that it threatens to overwhelm him, and when he turns his face he can feel the softness of her hair against his lips. She must be – *is* – old enough to be his mother, but that doesn't seem to matter, doesn't stop him feeling the stir

129

of response in his own body. He gets hastily to his feet, his cheeks scarlet, and sees first bewilderment, then comprehension in her eyes.

'Forgive me,' she says again, looking down, only this time there is no playfulness in her voice, merely regret. 'Forgive me.'

'There is nothing to forgive,' he says, his voice rough. Something has changed between them – something fragile as yet, but as unmistakable as that dark scent of hers, which he can smell now on his own skin.

She, for her part, watches his averted and self-conscious face, then rises and goes over to the piano-stool, where she takes a small key from a pocket in her dress, pulls aside the brocade and opens the trunk. Charles glances up as the lid creaks open and is amazed at what he sees – he should have guessed by now how much material she might have accumulated, but he is astonished, all the same, at the sheer quantity of papers inside the trunk. Some neatly bound in faded ribbons, others cast in loose and careless. It seems chaotic, but there must be some order to it, for it takes Claire only a moment to find what she is looking for.

'I know,' she says, turning to him, a paper in her hand, 'that what I have told you strains belief. I have asked you to take a great deal on my word alone, and you are wondering, even now, if that word can be trusted.'

He starts to reply, but she prevents him: 'That was not a test, Mr Maddox, merely an observation. I had not intended to show you this – I had not intended to show you anything, after you took it upon yourself to take by stealth what you could not obtain by any honest means. But I have changed my mind.'

She looks down now, at the letter she is holding, and her fingers close tight about it, as if clinging to the past. 'Shelley wrote this to me three months before he died. I did not know, then, what misery was about to befall me. Or that with his death there would be nothing left for me but dying.'

'But surely,' says Charles, 'surely you still had your child.'

She raises her face slowly to his, her features suddenly haggard, her eyes gaunt with a living grief. 'You do not know? But, then, how could you? By the time this letter reached me, my darling was dead.'

CHAPTER SIX

The Recollection

*La Signora Clairmont
presso al Professore Bojti
Piazza dei Pitti
Firenze*

Pisa, Monday 3rd April 1822

My best and loveliest girl,

I write on an evening as beautiful and as bright as your fair face, my love. Do you remember, last summer, when I wrote of the view from this very chamber – of the setting sun, and the sleeping swallows, and the bats flitting fast in the twilight purple air? Oh, that such a time might be reclaimed, if only for a moment, for it has been a day of tempests without doors, and violence within. But now the rain and wind have passed, and a momentary peace restored, so I have taken up my pen and surrounded myself, as with a magic circle, by thoughts of you. We have lived so long, you and I, our thrilling silent life – our life of outward coolness and inner fire – that you will wonder, I dare say, at such a beginning. So much care we have observed, when we have taken up our pens, and so many stratagems employed in disguise, that it is with a kind of wild exhilaration that I write nakedly now, with no such subterfuge. You will scold me for my recklessness – I who have always counselled you to hold your heart in check, and curb the impulses of your passionate nature. But it is so. After what has passed this day I must relieve my heart in words.

My side torments me and my exhausted mind agitates the prison it inhabits. I have scarce been able to see, these two days and more, and my eyes and appetite are still weak. But not so my resolution. I determined this morning to wait no longer – to tell her at once of my decision, and of my promise. It has been six weeks and more since we have shared a chamber, and she has always, as you know, been averse to early rising, but I was surprised this morning, all the same, to find her still abed at noon. But a moment's observation told me all the tale. I have seen her in the like condition too many times not to know the meaning of that wanness in her face, that lankness in her hair. She saw me then, and raised herself in the bed, calling me a beast and a brute, and all manner of vile names for forcing her once more to endure the unutterable pain of bringing a child into the world, only to have it die, once again, in her arms. She could not forgive me, she said in wild fury, for three children dead – there could be no natural, no happy conclusion to this new pregnancy and she would curse this for a hateful day as long as she lived. She turned her face, then, to the wall, saying that we had lived eight years together and if all the events of those years were blotted out and erased, only then might she have a chance for happiness.

I went to the bed then and knelt down beside her, saying I had never wished her woe, and would do all in my power to ease her pain, and that if she wished it, I would take up my old idea of an expedition to the East, where I might enter into an entirely new sphere of life. That I knew not how far this was practicable, given the state of my finances, but that I could talk again with Medwin and see what he might be able to lend me, and what might therefore be done. But I scarce finished my sentence when she turned to me with a laugh that chilled my very soul. Do you think to take *her* with you? she cried. Do you think to abandon me here, pregnant with *your* child, as you once abandoned that little fool Harriet? Do you hope *I* will destroy myself as she did, and you will be free once more from a wife you have tired of? No, she said, her features distorted by loathing, you will not rid yourself of me so easily. You and I are bound together for ever. You know it, and you know the reason for it – it is a bond that you can never sever.

And how could I *not* know it – how could *you* not know it? You were with us when my William fell ill, when my daughters died – you will remember her raging at me, saying the misery I had caused her rendered her milk tainted, and poisoned the babes even as they took suck at her breast. But all this you know. You have understood, for longer even than I, the fateful consequences of that perilous state of mind that has again overwhelmed her, and that black melancholia she considers her mother's most terrible legacy, which no doctor has ever relieved. Did I not beg you to put off a visit to your own beloved child for fear of leaving her alone, lest she should be driven by despair to some fatal end? And as I write those words I recall again that day, that dreadful December day in Skinner Street, after I learned of Harriet's death. I was haunted then by memories of her, and the ghosts of those old remembrances seemed to make some reproach to which I had no reply. Mary, of all people, knew of those feelings – knew of those terrible associations – and the recollection of that room now is shadowed for ever by the picture that comes always to my mind. Her face as she sat there, in the corner chair, listening quietly as always, as I told Godwin again and again of my

134

opposition, on philosophical grounds, to matrimony, and my wish to accord what respect I still could to Harriet's memory, and delay our marriage by a year. And then she rose, and came towards me, mouse-like in appearance as she always contrived, but a tiger's ferocity looking from her eyes. Of course you are free to do as you like, she said, placing one hand on my shoulder and the other on her belly, and I am free to act as *I* like, and I have to tell you that if you do not marry me I will not live – I will destroy myself *and my child with me.*

And the same look I saw then, I see now. Just as I saw it when Clara died and she laid all the blame of it at my door. Day after day, in violent hysterics and words of poisonous retribution, saying that she would never forgive me for caring more for you and your child than I did for her and ours. It was for me, she said, to put right the terrible wrong I had done her, it was for me to replace the child she had lost. Whatever that scoundrel of a servant has since alleged – whatever lies have been told, or Byron believed – that is the real and only reason we adopted Elena in Naples. I found that sweet babe and brought her to the house because Mary begged me to. Such a tiny child she was, my Elena, with her bright green eyes, and curls of golden yellow hair. How could any woman look on that child – hold it in her arms – and feel no motherly affection? How could she prove so deaf to its cries, so blind to its needs, as to refuse to give it nourishment? But by then the deed was done, and all the papers lodged in our names. And when Mary insisted we depart the city at once, I could see no way but to leave the child behind. In all that has happened – all that I regret and would wish undone – of this alone my heart cannot acquit me. And when the letter from the orphanage came telling me Elena was dead, I felt as if the destruction that consumes me were as an atmosphere that wraps and infects everything I touch. I can never speak openly of why I acted as I did, and the world, in consequence, damns me for a liar and a brute. Mary has always insisted that it was our own maid who spread the rumour – that it was all Elise's doing – and I cannot prove it to be otherwise. But the suspicion will not lie quiet that she, in some way, was the source. How else could the Hoppners have come to hear of it? Why else should they have thought Elena was *your* child – yours and mine? Why else would they claim that I had given you violent medicines to procure an abortion, and only brought that poor babe to the house when those vile methods did not work? That, of all those hideous accusations, is the worst. You know, better than anyone, that I could never commit the unutterable crime of destroying any living creature, far less an innocent infant. And never – O never – could I harm a child of *yours*. A child of *mine*.

I have clung too long to the feigned hope that we might come to a new understanding, Mary and I. That we might make amends together for those dark and dreadful deaths, and free ourselves from the curse of repeating the past. I had thought the woman who had for parents William Godwin and Mary Wollstonecraft would applaud me in my ambition to forge a new connection based on the principles those very parents had expounded. Mary had always told me so – she had fled with me in the beginning promising so. Would that I had known, before we left London together for France that first time, that for all those high protestations she would become to me so jealous a chained foe. Would that I had not been blinded by her lineage and her name to what was hidden in her heart. But it is her curse, and my own, that a person possessing such excellent powers as hers should be so incapable of applying those capacities to domestic life.

But in truth the blame is mine – all mine. When first we met I saw only her high soul, and the wildness and sublimity of her feelings. I saw only the brilliant daughter of brilliant parents, I saw only passion in her gestures and looks, and boasted, even, of her capacity for indignation and hatred, seeing only – then – the most flattering proof of the strength of her attachment. It was intoxicating to be loved so, after the meek, submissive embraces of my poor little Harriet, mesmerizing to have such a girl hang on my every word and throw herself with complete abandon into my arms. I remember the moment she declared herself mine – how she roused a fervour in my blood that still could not match the fever in her own. How against all reason – all prudence – she drew me down to her as she lay upon the very turf of her mother's grave – the heat of the day, the smell of the summer grass, the heaving of her heart, and the seize of her lips as they strained into mine. And not a hundred yards away, idling in the sunlight and shade of that ancient willow, you, my dearest Claire. At the very moment of ardour I heard your voice. Singing.

Even while I write, my burning cheeks are wet.
Alas, that the torn heart can bleed, but not forget!

And later – after the Rubicon had been passed and the way back barred – how could I bear to hear what you tried so hard to tell me? How could I see your warnings as anything but what *she* insisted they were – lies and wicked fabrications sprung only from a black and vindictive envy? She did confess to have suffered 'girlish troubles', but attributed all to a step-mother's resentment, and a father's carelessness. What loving father, she said, would have sent so young a girl away from home for so long? Surely only one who had been influenced by a sullen second wife to disregard the lovelier and more gifted child of the first. She did not tell me, then, that it was always *she* who initiated those furious quarrels that discomposed the entire house. She did not tell me, then, that the doctor summoned to examine her came not to see the skin disorder of her arm but because your mother and Godwin apprehended a far more dreadful evil. No, your words, and yours alone, can account for all this.

What a different journey we might have trod, you and I, had I seen *you* that first time I called at Skinner Street, when Godwin told me both his daughter and step-daughter were away from home, but he would, in due course, allow himself the 'not inconsiderable pleasure' of introducing me to all the young ladies of the family. You will smile sadly and shake your head at my mimicry, but my rash promise to solace his declining years has haunted me from the day I made it. I have mortgaged my own future and my boy's and still I cannot slake his insatiable demands, still he writes for money – always, always for more money.

You, my dearest girl, have always understood me – have poured balm on my weary aged soul, have sustained me in all my illness, and encouraged me in all my work. Why else – even in the high throes of a hectic passion – would I have insisted you came with us when we fled to France? When I told Mary what I proposed she seemed at first to accept my decision, only to call me back a moment later and declare – with the suddenly frozen face I have so miserably come to know – that you could make yourself useful as our interpreter, and that she would tell you so. You will say I was naïve – that I should have perceived at once what lay behind those words – but I believed her when she talked of love as free, of the passion between us as a thing of purity, far above the dreary exclusiveness of modern morals. It took but the travel of a single day to tear the scales from my eyes, and show me that *her* understanding of our relation condemned you to cold oblivion just as surely as the narrowest and most oppressive contract of marriage. And for all the love she professed to my face, and in my arms, there was rancour even then in her heart. I did not wish to see it – might never have known it had you not found her, pen in hand, at work on that story. A story she had written of you; a story she entitled 'Hate'. A story I consigned to the flames the day we set foot back in England.

These last months here we have become to one another an ever-present torment. She feels no more compunction in torturing me than she does in torturing herself, as if we have indeed become one flesh, bound in an accursed and everlasting union of the living and the desired-dead. I have been ashamed before our friends – by her manners, her sulkiness, her shrill and carping tongue. I have seen the green distortion of jealousy in her face whenever your name is spoken, and heard the things she has said of you when she thinks I am not by. Leave her, you will say, leave her and come to me. But what might she accuse me of, in the vehemence of her revenge, if ever I forsake her as I did my poor Harriet? And when I think now of that pitiful child who did not a thing amiss but love me – when I think of what I was induced to say – the letters I was forced to write after I left her – the words dictated to me – accusing her of mean and despicable selfishness when she was so close to her confinement – I recall it now and the blood runs icy in my veins. Well might Harriet have cried that I had become a vampyre – that I behaved to her little better than a beast.

The terror of regret has tainted my whole life, like the spectre of an unquiet dream come back to blacken the cheerful morn. Thoughts of the past pursue me like a treacherous likeness of myself – a hideous daemon that bodies forth all that is cruel and depraved and disgusting in the dark depth of my inmost soul. I wonder sometimes if it is not, after all, a real persecutor, but my own self from which I flee – some hideous excrescence of my own mind. You tell me it is nothing but bad dreams – that no one haunts me, no one shadows my steps – but I tell you, I have seen

139

him, even here. Even in Italy I have seen him, ever on the far edge of my sight, never fully revealed, never fully perceived. It is as if in a mirror I catch the echo of my own face, my own eyes dulled as if underwater. My own eyes those of a man already dead.

Forgive me, my love, for such a long and broken letter. I have never written thus before, and I will not do so again. But now, for these few moments, I can ease my heart by opening it to you. How much more it would relieve me to see you – to place my head on your soft bosom, and feel the gentle breathing of your heart. I know that you have your own pain – that you are anxious for your darling Allegra, and trust not Byron to have the care of her a father owes. But I fear you have no other choice but to trust to time and change on his part. Who knows what may happen in the space of a few short months? And what words may achieve, I will attempt. Anything that might diminish your pain, I would do it. I cannot endure the thought of your lonely unheard tears – I would put up with any anguish if I might thereby ease a moment of yours. I know *she* does not agree with me on this – she thinks my care an interference, and nothing of our concern. But she is right in this respect, if none other: you cannot take the child. Byron would not allow it – and a rash attempt to remove her, such as you have lately contemplated, would have the direst consequences, and not the least for you, my dearest girl. I know you fear the convent is in an unwholesome district, subject every summer to malarious airs, but I can only beg you to remember that when I last saw Allegra there, she was in good health and fine spirits. Taller than when you saw her last, of that there can be no doubt, but in every other way recognizable at once as the babe you once held against your breast – her eyes the same deep violet blue, her hair as darkly lustrous, her little face just as lovely, her little chin just as determined. Still vivacious, still mischievous, still – O how beautifully – *your* child.

Six have I had, of my own, and one alone is left to me. Two torn from my heart by the vile judgment of a tyrannical court, and three consigned for ever to the cold earth's iron embrace. And now there is to be another. A child I do not want – did not expect – indeed can hardly account for, so rarely have I shared her bed. Jane Williams took me aside some days ago and wondered aloud, in that way she has, that one might almost believe that rough and piratical fellow Edward Trelawny were Mary's lover, so intimate they seem, but if the child be his she will not tell me so. It is mine, she says, mine begotten, and mine to sustain. The fruit of another accursed Spring. Like all those other Springs that have led not to renewal but only to death and grief.

And there I lay, within a chaste cold bed:
Alas, I then was nor alive nor dead.

I must close, my dearest girl. I hear her step and I dare not be found at my pen – dare not give her any new excuse to raise her hand to me. Hold fast, my dear girl, and all may yet be well. She says she has had a presentiment that this pregnancy will come not to term, and though I swear by all I hold true that I do not wish for such an end, if her premonition proves correct, it will be the last summer I spend with her as my wife. I will find a way, dear girl. Make no plans for Vienna until we may speak together of this. All may yet be well. Know that I love you, and all may be well.

Goodbye, my dearest love. Do not forget – be sure to burn this letter, and directly.

S

141

CHAPTER SEVEN

Mary

The fire is dying low now, the embers preying upon themselves. It is not a comfortable image, and Charles gets up and walks to the window for light and air, his mind sombre with mute rage. Claire gave him this letter – this letter never burned, much read, and stained here and there with tears – because she deemed it proof: proof of Shelley's love for her. But to Charles the proof – the evidence – in this letter is not of love, but of death. A woman threatening suicide in terrible revenge. Three innocent children dying before their time, and a fourth discarded because she did not suit. And, yes, of course children died, no one knows that better than Charles – in the first quarter of the nineteenth century almost a third of babies were dead before the age of five – but for the Shelleys to lose three of their children, one after the other, argues that something more disturbing than mere misfortune was at work. Even a mother's constant care was not enough, it seems, to counter that grand, self-centred disregard that characterized so much else about Shelley's life. For despite all his shrill self-justification, this is a man who clearly believed that one dead infant could readily be

142

replaced by another, however randomly chosen, and that maternal affection might transfer as casually as cast-off baby clothes.

And where did Shelley find the little girl he brought home? Did he discover her in that Naples orphanage, or did he perhaps see a baby left a moment in some crowded marketplace, and decide it would have a better life brought up as his own? Take it with him there and then, and give it to his desperate and grieving wife as a substitute for the child she claimed he killed, only to see that mother's face curdle to a mask of scorn. A sudden surge of nausea almost overwhelms Charles as he remembers his own sister – another golden-haired and green-eyed child – who was snatched in the street and never again found. Left perhaps to die, like this little girl, because she failed to find favour, no more real to those who took her than a puppy, or a porcelain doll.

You may think Charles is deducing a great deal here from very little, and extrapolating far too much from the pain of his own past, but you might change your mind if you knew (as Charles does not) that Shelley never made any attempt to see his first two children after the custody case, even though the 'tyrannical court' accorded him that right; that he once took up a child he found wandering, and it was only the merest chance the parents discovered her again; or if you had heard, as I have, a story still told all these years later by some Oxford city guides, of the day when Shelley switched two babies in the high street and walked serenely on, hilarious at his own joke, not caring whether the exchange was ever noticed, or if the changelings were ever returned to their rightful mothers' arms.

Charles can picture now, and only too clearly, the bizarre and claustrophobic atmosphere in which this strange *ménage* played itself out – the looking-glass world Shelley built for himself, and then could not escape. Well might Claire have called it a *folie à trois*, for there is something tinged with madness in all these echoes and half-reflections, these endless repeating patterns, and the incessant giddying sense of having constantly to reassess what is real, and what is feigned. The two women drawing him always in opposite directions – one dark, one fair; one passionate, one chill; one always eager, one forever aloof. And what is Charles to make of the man at the heart of the maze – this man who is at once pitiful and pernicious, at once tender and terrifying? Because for all his talk of love and freedom, the fact remains that Shelley left his young and pregnant wife to take two teenage girls on a mad scramble across Europe, which rendered both of them social outcasts – one expecting an illegitimate child, and the other unlikely ever to make a conventional marriage. And yes, Shelley could have argued that brought up by Godwin as those girls had been, they would neither of them have cared about such conventions, but Charles suspects that whatever the philosopher may have preached about sexual liberation and the equality of the sexes, he would have recoiled in horror at his own daughter putting those precepts into practice in such a flagrant and irrevocable manner. Indeed, is there not a hint of that in this very letter? There would have been no need for Shelley to argue the case for the postponement of his marriage to Mary after Harriet's death if Godwin had not been strenuously pressing for just such a ceremony, and at once. And is not Shelley's attempt to place all the blame for his ill-treatment of his first wife to the account of the second a little discreditable? Was he really so weak – so easily manipulated? Charles sighs, thinking of Claire, remembering the tears in her eyes as she handed him this letter – this letter she has kept all these years as a pledge of love. And it can indeed be read as such, but it can also be read as a shameful attempt to defend an eight-year status quo that brought her nothing but pain, and stole from her whatever life and love she might still have found. The deeper Charles reaches into Shelley's past the darker it becomes. Well might Maddox accuse him of bringing death and ruination to everyone about him; well might he conclude the poet's was a midwinter heart.

Charles turns back to the room, wondering, for the first time and with sudden misgiving, whether he has been drawn into the same mirror world of deceit and subterfuge that had his uncle seeing murder where there was only suicide. A world as phantasmagoric as one of Shelley's own nightmare visions, bearing all the appearance of daylight reality, but which is nothing more than the writhings of an overwrought imagination. It is time to draw a line; time to regain some detachment, some objectivity. He goes to ring the bell, and the door opens almost at once.

'May I speak to your mistress, Annie?'

'She's indisposed, sir. She said to give you this.'

My part of our bargain has been fulfilled; I expect you now to honour yours. You will not be received in this house again until you have done so. I am not well – indeed I have been ill for many years – and I need repose. You have already occasioned me quite enough suffering.

C. C.

Both content and style sit rather oddly with the confident, flowing hand, and the bloom of health he saw in her face not much more than an hour ago. Nor does Charles quite concur that what he has caused Claire so far can really be

145

called suffering. Inconvenience, yes, even irritation, but she's turned the situation so smartly to her advantage he could almost believe she contrived it. Like all her sudden shifts of mood, it is disconcerting, and all the more so now.

The maid meanwhile is waiting. 'Was there a message, sir? Madam said—'

'Yes, yes. You may tell her that I will do as she asks. As we agreed.'

She bobs. 'And Madam said you were to give me a letter, sir. Most particular she was.'

Charles takes it from the table where he left it and sees the maid smooth the pages and place them carefully, once again, in the trunk.

'Will you be requiring dinner, sir?'

'No, Annie. Indeed, I am not sure when I will next be here. I shall go upstairs and collect a few things. In case I should need them.'

'Very well, sir. I will inform Madam.'

Out on the street the rain is falling finely, and the day failing in a gathering fog. It's too late for Chester Square now, even had Charles a mind to go there. By the time he turns into Buckingham Street the mist has thickened to a heavy brown haze, and it's only when he's a few short yards from the house that he sees someone standing on the doorstep. Someone a little shorter than he is, a little thinner – someone who moves now into the light cast by the upstairs windows. Charles quickens his pace, a flicker of unease catching at his heart. 'Sam?' he calls. 'Sam?'

Wheeler starts at the sound of his voice, then comes towards him through the fog. 'It's all right, Chas. Nothing to concern yerself about. Old Stornaway got a bit carried away, that's all.'

146

'Carried away about what?' demands Charles, gripping Sam's arm. 'What's happening? What are you doing here?'

'Seems Abel went up to check on yer uncle earlier this afternoon and found 'im lyin' on the floor, and a lot of books and papers strewn about the place—'

'What do you mean *on the floor*? Is he hurt?'

He makes to push past Sam into the house, but the constable holds him back. 'Easy, Chas. Like I said, it's all right now. He's got a coupla bumps 'n' cuts but the doctor's been and no 'arm's done.'

'The *doctor's* been – and no one thought to send for me?'

'Well, Abel probably weren't thinkin' that clearly. And Bow Street's a lot closer than St John's Wood.'

'But why you? Why the police?'

Sam gives a shrug. ''E 'ad some wild idea the 'ouse'd been broken into.'

'And has it?'

'No sign. And that boy of yours swears all the doors was locked.'

'And nothing's been taken – nothing's missing?'

Sam shakes his head. 'I got Abel to 'ave a look, after we'd got 'im calmed down. 'E were a bit shame-faced by then. Realized 'e'd got everyone panicked over nothin'. Looks to me like yer uncle might 'ave woken up when no one was by and tried to take a look at the books by Abel's chair. Only 'e's a bit unsteady, and managed to trip over the blanket or some such, and in the process knocked a whole loada stuff flyin'. Seems the simplest explanation anyway.'

Charles looks at him, remembering seeing his uncle struggle to his feet in exactly that way. He might well have done something similar again. The question is, what on earth was Abel doing leaving him alone?

'Thank you, Sam,' he says eventually. 'For coming.'

147

Sam smiles. 'You're welcome. You know as I'd always do it.'

They shake hands and Sam strides up towards the Strand, whistling quietly under his breath. Charles, meanwhile, is making his way up the stairs, two at a time. Whatever happened before, the room's been put to rights now, and Abel is sitting in a chair on the far side of the fireplace, a blanket drawn over his knees. He looks pale, and paler still when he sees Charles. 'I were only gone a little while, Mr Charles,' he starts. 'I were lookin' at those old files again, in case there were anythin' I'd missed, and I just left yer uncle a minute to go upstairs. I only sat down for a moment – I cannae think how I came to fall asleep, it's not like me at all—'

Something Charles cannot but accede, which in his current mood makes him only more suspicious. He says nothing to Abel, but goes over instead to his uncle and kneels down beside him. There's a graze on his forehead that's darkening to a bruise, but otherwise he seems unscathed. But as Charles reaches to touch the injury gently the old man opens his eyes and utters a strangled cry, throwing up his hands to shield his face. There are scratches on both palms. Charles frowns, and whispers soothingly to him, before turning to Abel. 'Where are the books Sam said were on the floor? The ones my uncle was supposed to be reaching for?'

Abel glances across to the table by the fire. 'Well,' he begins hesitantly.

Charles gets up and goes to the pile. Half a dozen case-books are stacked together, but it's the one on the top that he picks up. It's the 1816 file – the file that started this whole affair. Only now the leather binding is scorched, and the edges of the pages blackened. Charles's heart is hammering as he opens the book and turns to where Maddox's notes on the Godwin case had been – where the allegation of murder had been. But the paper is so charred now that it crumbles away in his hands. There is nothing left; the words Charles deciphered are gone, the name obliterated. There is nothing to show the accusation was ever made. 'What happened to this book?' he says quietly.

'It were on the fire, Mr Charles, when I came in. The boss were lying on the floor, and the book were on the fire. Billy pulled it free, but by then the flames had already took hold.'

'And was that why you thought someone had been in here?'

Abel flushes. 'Well, it seemed a mite coincidental, Mr Charles. That it shouldae been that book, of all of 'em, when ye're workin' on the same case. But young Mr Wheeler checked everythin' downstairs, and he's convinced no one couldae got in. So I have tae assume the boss dropped the book by mistake. He were sitting in that chair by the hearth, and I left it on the table next him when I went upstairs. I suppose I can see how it mightae happened.'

Charles looks at Abel, and then at the armchair. He, too, can see how it might have happened, but he, like Abel, is wary of coincidence, and more apt to see design than accident in such apparent happenstance. But if someone did indeed throw the book on the fire deliberately, is an unseen intruder more or less disquieting than the possibility that his uncle tried to burn the book himself? Has he, in fact, already tried to do that once before – that time during the storm? Charles had thought, then, that his uncle wanted to tell him something about the case, but perhaps it was the book *itself* he was after – the *book* he wanted to destroy. Has the old man been watching and listening all this time, trapped in his own silence, terrified of what Charles might discover, and what might be disclosed about his own past? But even that makes no sense, because if Harriet's death was indeed suicide and not murder, what can there be in that for him to fear?

Charles sits down by his uncle and takes his mottled hand in his own. The old man's pulse flutters like a pinioned bird. His eyes are open, but there is no recognition, no response.

'Have you heard from Fraser yet?' Charles asks, without lifting his gaze from Maddox's face. 'Does he remember the Godwin case?'

'I've not heard from him, Mr Charles. I'll be sure to tell 'ee if I do.'

Billy arrives with more tea, and Abel sets him bustling about Maddox. Tucking blankets, straightening pillows.

'Where were you, Billy,' says Charles, 'when this happened?'

Billy flashes him a glance. 'Down in the scullery, Mr Charles. 'Avin' another go at those boots o' yours. Like you asked. I 'eard Mr Stornaway cryin' out and came up sharp.'

'And Molly?'

Billy moves round behind the chair to pour the tea. 'Don't know, Mr Charles. At the market maybe. I didn't see 'er.'

'But neither of you left the door open, even for a moment – or saw someone loitering outside you didn't recognize?'

'No, not me,' he says, coming back with the tea. 'Don't know about Molly. Best you ask 'er that yerself, Mr Charles. Sure you'd get more outa 'er than me, if you take my meanin'.'

Perhaps it's his tone, perhaps it's something about the look on his round pink face, but Charles is suddenly seized by an overwhelming urge to strike him. Which he suppresses, but only just. 'By the way, Billy,' he says sharply, 'I thought I'd warned you weeks ago about getting drunk with the coster-boys.'

Billy's face flushes an even deeper red. 'I know, Mr Charles. I 'eard you the first time. I ain't done it since.'

'Don't lie to me, Billy. I know you were out again with them the other night. I won't have it – do you hear me? Coming back at all hours roaring, and throwing up in the kitchen.'

Billy opens his eyes wide in outraged innocence – or a very practised impersonation thereof. 'You must be mistaken, Mr Charles. Weren't me, and that's a fact.'

But Charles has caught the boy out once too often already. 'If I find out you've lied to me again—'

'But I'm not lyin', Mr Charles. Cross me 'eart and 'ope to die. It weren't me, I tell yer – and if you really want to know—'

'I've had enough of your impertinence, Billy. If it happens again you will be dismissed, and without pay. You will not get a second chance. Am I making myself clear?'

The boy drops his eyes, and mumbles, 'Yes, Mr Charles.'

'Very well. Now bring me paper and an envelope from the office. I have a note I want you to take to Chester Square.'

Billy nods again, and is curtly dismissed, but when he gets to the door he sees that Charles has already turned his back. The boy watches him a moment, playing with some coins in his trouser pocket, and the expression in his eyes now is one of unambiguous contempt. The contempt the cunning have always had for those who fancy themselves fine intellectuals, but fail to see the facts right in front of their faces.

* * *

151

The following morning Charles wakes at last from a dream of drowning to find Thunder perched squarely on his chest and peering down at him with that quizzical look any cat-owner will recognize at once. Charles heaves him off – not an easy task, given Thunder's size – and goes to the washstand. A bad night's sleep has left him with a headache and dark shadows under his eyes. Worse, he now faces the prospect of an audience with Lady Shelley.

He is kept waiting at Chester Square, as before, but this time there is another factor at work, of which he is entirely unaware. The mistress of the house is standing at a second-floor window, watching as Charles scuffs his heels on the pavement, and rubs his hands together against the cold. The room behind her is, at first sight at least, the mirror image of the drawing room below that we have already seen. The same long windows, the same washy sunlight filtering through the long muslin curtains, the same portrait, hanging in exactly the same place. But this time, the painting is the original, not a copy, and there is no candle on the table below and no fake wax lilies, only a plain white vase bearing stems of green leaves crowned with clusters of tiny pink flowers; the air is filled with an irresistible sweet fragrance. It's like a room from a totally different house. Refinement, taste, restraint; elegant furniture and shelf upon shelf of books. And books that have been placed here to be read, not looked at, for the volumes are stacked haphazardly, with gaps where some have been taken out and not yet replaced. In the far corner there is a small curtained bed, in which the poet's widow is sitting, looking towards the light, and her husband's face.

Were you in that room, your first thought, I'm sure, would be how very frail she is. How child-like. The woman who casts so long a shadow over this story, and has left such a monstrous and misshapen creation in her name, is so fragile in the flesh she makes all those around her seem clumsy and inept. Most obviously her own son, who is at this moment lighting his pipe rather cack-handedly with a spill lit from the fire. And as we approach the bed, we can see that this woman must once have been every bit as beautiful as her step-sister, although the quality of that beauty could hardly be more different. Everything about Claire so rich and dramatic – her complexion, her hair, her figure, her choice of clothes; Mary, by contrast, all pale delicacy, her skin white, her eyes grey, her bed-jacket a quiet cloud-coloured silk. And that famous hair of hers, silvered now but showing still some red gleams of burnished gold.

'It is exactly as Percy has explained, Madre,' says Lady Shelley, turning now from the window. 'We have been given an absolute and categorical assurance that no records of that dreadful winter remain. The pages in question are missing, and a thorough search of the house has produced nothing. Doubtless the old fellow destroyed them years ago and is in no state now to reveal what they contained.'

The woman on the bed looks from her son to his wife, but does not speak, though perhaps her thin fingers grip a little tighter about the counterpane.

'So you have nothing to fear,' continues the younger woman, seeing the gesture, and mistaking, I suspect, what it means. She goes briskly to the bed and sits down beside it, then takes her mother-in-law's hand in her own. 'There will be no revelations about Harriet. Either about how she met her death, or all the sordid circumstances that attended it. We are safe; *you* are safe.'

Mary Shelley looks at her, then past her to the portrait hanging on the wall. Sir Percy, meanwhile, seems distinctly uncomfortable, and fidgets uneasily with his pipe. His wife casts a glance of irritation in his direction, then turns again to her mother-in-law.

'Dear Jane,' the older woman says eventually, her voice thick as if she has not spoken in many days. 'Always so concerned for me, always so energetic to protect my interests.'

Lady Shelley smiles indulgently, and pats the hand that lies inert in her own.

'And yet,' Mrs Shelley continues, slowly but deliberately, as if each word were a burden to her, but must still be spoken, 'I could wish you had thought to consult me before embarking on such an undertaking. I should have advised against revealing so much to anyone, or putting ourselves at the mercy of a man of that low sort.'

'Well, I did say as much to Jane—' begins Sir Percy.

'And you know,' his mother continues, cutting across him, 'as well as I, that Claire cannot be trusted. It has always been dangerous to afford her so susceptible an audience as this young man must have been. I fear I can imagine only too easily what lies she will have told him of our childhood, and of Switzerland, and all that came after.'

Jane Shelley opens her mouth to speak, but Mary forestalls her, shaking her head, but awkwardly, as though the movement gave her pain. '*That*, my dear Jane, I have endured before. My concern, now, is what *else* she may have said to this young man – what she may have shown him.'

'I thought the Clairmont woman was in Bath that winter,' says Lady Shelley, clearly nonplussed. 'What could she possibly know about Harriet?'

Mary Shelley takes her hand from her daughter-in-law's grasp and places it momentarily against her forehead.

'Are you unwell, Madre?' says Lady Shelley, anxiously.

'No, my dear,' she says at last. 'A momentary faintness, that is all. I am inured to it now.'

She looks at the two of them, and when she speaks again, it seems that she has forgotten the train of the conversation. 'Do you know – did your informant say – if any other records have been discovered in that house concerning Shelley – concerning myself?'

The baronet and his wife exchange a glance. 'I was not aware,' Lady Shelley begins, 'that you had had any other dealings with that Maddox fellow.'

Mary Shelley flushes slightly. '"Dealings" is altogether too grand a word. It was – a minor matter relating to the time Shelley spent in Wales before he and I met.'

Sir Percy frowns. 'You mean that queer incident in Tremadoc in 'thirteen?'

Her tone is light now, dismissive: 'Nothing came of it. Indeed, I doubt so trivial a matter even merited the effort of its documentation. And, as you say, had any such papers come to light, no doubt you would have been told.'

There is a knock then, and the butler appears. 'Mr Charles Maddox is at the door, madam.'

'Thank you, Emerson,' says Lady Shelley, getting rather inelegantly to her feet. 'You may show him up to the drawing room.'

'What will you say to him?' asks Mary Shelley, looking up at the younger woman's sturdy form bending over her.

'You do not need to worry yourself about that, Madre. We have no more use for that arrogant young upstart. I will listen to what he has to tell me, thank him for his efforts, and inform him that we have decided not to pursue the matter of Miss Clairmont's papers after all. He has been more than amply paid for his time. Let that be an end to it.'

'And you think,' says Sir Percy, 'he'll let it go as pat as that?'

She smiles complacently. 'What other choice does he have? Come, Percy, let us leave dear Madre to rest.'

The room is silent after they have gone, and the woman in the bed does not move. But it is not the immobility of repose. Her face is drawn with anxiety now, and the hand once again tugs at the counterpane. After a moment she turns, with some difficulty, to the small travelling-desk that has been placed carefully within reach on the bed, with a rigidity discernible now, on her left side, that calls to mind the stiffness Maddox also suffers. Her travelling-desk is smaller and more graceful than Claire's trunk, but this rosewood box has clearly seen the same long years of journeying, the same restless moving from place to place. And as she lifts the lid we can see a large bundle of letters, tied with satin and neatly stacked, here and there a petal pressed between them. And next to them a copy of Keats's poems, so badly water-stained the title is barely legible, that they discovered in Shelley's pocket when his rotten and half-eaten body was thrown back by the sea. Mary Shelley gazes a moment at the book, then reaches to the bundle of letters, and places it carefully on her lap. They are all, the letters, written in the same hand. All but one. And that lies folded at the bottom of the box, without ribbon, and without remembrance.

She was, they tell us, famous for her reserve, so practised at concealing her emotions that even those closest to her condemned her freezing coldness, and perhaps that accounts for the oddly blank expression we see now on her face, as she reads the letter she has hidden from all the world. Or perhaps Leigh Hunt was right, and she was indeed 'a torrent of fire under a Hecla snow'. All we can

156

know for sure is that she reaches now for the bell-rope, and when the bright and freckle-faced maid arrives a few moments later she is dispatched downstairs for paper and ink.

'And be sure, Alice, not to trouble Lady Shelley, or my son.'

* * *

Charles, meanwhile, has followed the butler up the stairs to the blue drawing room, where all is as it was before. The knick-knacks, the case of books, the candle still steadily burning. Charles goes over to the portrait again, struck, this time, by the choice of epigraph beneath it. No praise for the sublime Genius of the Poet, such as he would surely have expected Lady Shelley to select, but a reference that is at best ambivalent to envy and calumny and hate and pain, and an unrest that was at once a torture and delight, but can touch the Poet now no more. Was it, Charles wonders, his widow who chose these words?

'Good morning, Mr Maddox.'

It is Lady Shelley. Wearing – surely – the same plain grey dress. As well as a look of some self-satisfaction on her rather masculine face. She takes a seat, but does not motion him to do the same.

'Well, what have you to say?'

Treating him like any other hired hand is – of course – trivial in itself, but the discourtesy rankles and Charles finds himself replying with equal impoliteness: 'What have *you* to say, Lady Shelley?'

She is clearly not used to being spoken to in such a manner, and recoils in distaste. 'I do not take your meaning.'

'You omitted to tell me, when we met, that the person who was allegedly persecuting you is a lady—'

157

'Hardly a *lady*, and hardly *allegedly*.'

Charles ignores the interruption. '—and if not your relation, most certainly your husband's.'

She stiffens. 'There is absolutely no blood between them. She is no relation of his, or of Madre's.'

'I believe most reasonable people would take my side of that particular question, Lady Shelley. But we shall let that go by, for the moment. Whatever the truth of it, Miss Clairmont has clearly been very poorly treated – by Lord Byron, by Mrs Shelley, and by Shelley himself, while he lived.'

There are deep spots of colour now, on her cheeks, and a look of mocking scorn on her face. 'Oh, *I* see – I see it *all* now. You have been taken in, just like everyone else. The woman should have been on the stage, so artfully does she play herself. Claire the martyr, Claire the poor put-upon, Claire the brave innocent betrayed by the world. And I thought you an *intelligent* man.'

Charles bridles. 'I am not so easily deceived, Lady Shelley.'

'Ha!' She snorts. 'You are a *man*, are you not? And therefore as much prey to her devious wiles as every other sorry member of your sex.'

Such a disdainful dismissal of the entire gender does not augur well for the serenity of the Shelley marriage, but Charles had guessed that much already, even before Claire's waspish observations.

Lady Shelley draws herself up in her chair. 'That woman loves nothing better than to cast herself as a forlorn victim, abandoned and deceived. You are a fool if you believe a single word that falls from her lips. You know nothing of her – nothing whatsoever.'

'I am a good judge of character, Lady Shelley.'

'If you believe *that*, you will be even more pathetically vulnerable to her ploys. Let me see,' she says, folding her hands firmly on her lap. 'I am guessing, of course, but I imagine that, despite your obvious enthusiasm for your new acquaintance, you have already been taken unawares, on more than one occasion, by an unexpected, not to say capricious, change of mind.'

'Well, that's hardly—'

'Moreover, I surmise that there has been at least *one* instance when you have found yourself – rather to your surprise – giving her comfort of a physical, not to say *intimate* nature. Can you contradict me?'

Charles's cheeks now are the ones to burn. He turns away, ill at ease.

Lady Shelley, meanwhile, smiles a thin, superior little smile. 'I last saw Miss Clairmont more than a year ago at our place in Sussex. Her niece had been staying with us – at *her* request, I may say – and had become engaged during that visit to a very presentable young man. It was quite the whirlwind romance – they had each been disappointed in love, and found a natural, not to say touching, comfort in one another. All was going along very nicely until the morning Miss Clairmont was expected, when poor Madre burst into my room gasping, "Don't go, dear – don't leave me alone with her. She has been the bane of my life since I was two years old." I had been preparing at that moment to go up to town, expressly to avoid any danger of encountering that woman, but seeing Madre so distressed there was no longer any question of my departure. And it is just as well I stayed, for Miss Clairmont took violently against the engagement from the first moment she heard of it – she had not been in the house half an hour when her poor niece came rushing up to my room, and flung herself sobbing at

159

my feet, crying, "Save me! Save me from my aunt – she is kneeling on the floor of the drawing room cursing me!" I was not going to permit that sort of behaviour in *my* house, so I locked dear Madre in her room at once for her own safety, and went down to Miss Clairmont myself. I found her, I am sorry to say, in a state of complete frenzy – sobbing and shrieking and throwing off the most horrid accusations against us all, accusing her niece of ingratitude, and Madre and myself of inducing her niece to treat her parents like the dirt under her feet. And various other vile things not fit to be repeated. I decided there and then that I had no choice but to say – and in Miss Clairmont's hearing – that I was sending for the doctor to administer a drug to her. That worked the trick, may I tell you. She became quieter at once and ordered the carriage that very minute. We have never – any of us – seen her again, though I am told she does not scruple to abuse us behind our backs, even if she can no longer do so to our faces.'

She slips a sideways glance at Charles, who is still turned away.

'It is merely one example,' she continues, 'albeit an extreme one, of what my Lord Byron used to refer to as her "Bedlam behaviour". We have all seen it, over the years. The Clairmont blood brings nothing but misery, and that woman is a curse and a plague to all about her. And as much of a charlatan, may I say, as that mother of hers. Who was, I can tell you for a fact, not even married to her father, whoever *he* was.'

But this last is one step too far. Charles swings round to her, his face furious. 'Have you heard the old saying, Lady Shelley, about those who live in glasshouses and how inadvisable it is for such persons to start casting stones?'

She is not triumphant now: the rage he sees in her eyes is

more than a match for his own. Had the door not opened at that moment there is no telling what either might have said. Sir Percy glances from one to the other, and sees that his wife's solid bosom is heaving with indignation. 'Thought I ought to look in. I could hear the rumpus from the morning room. Jane?'

'It seems,' Lady Shelley says with difficulty, 'that Mr Maddox is tempted to believe the lies and *fabrications*,' this with a venomous glare at Charles, 'of Miss *Clairmont*. He seems, indeed, ready to credit that *we* are the persecutors in all this – we and our dear Madre.'

Sir Percy takes a step or two further into the room. 'Have to say, Maddox, that that would be most unwise. Tricky customer, that one. Could lead you a long way down a very wrong road. Very wrong road.'

'Tell him,' urges Lady Shelley grimly. 'Tell him about your sister. Tell him what happened to Clara.'

Sir Percy shakes his head. 'Not sure we really want – I mean, private family business and all that.'

'*Tell him*, Percy.'

He takes his pipe from his waistcoat pocket. As much to have something to do as anything else, it seems, for he makes no attempt to light it. 'Back in 'eighteen when the mater and pater were on the Continent, this Clairmont woman took it into her head there was some problem with that child of hers. Some gossip she'd been told about Byron claiming he was going to make her his mistress when she was old enough. Complete rot, clearly, his own daughter and so forth, but the Clairmont woman worked herself into a state of first-class hysterics and left the pater no choice but to go trooping off with her halfway across Italy. Seems his lordship agreed to let her see the child, but only if the pater and mater were in attendance. Only trouble was, pater had omitted to mention he'd left the mater back in Bagni di Lucca. Filthy hot summer, five-day journey, baby sick and small boy in tow – dreadful prospect for a woman alone. Got there eventually to find the pater completely taken up with the Clairmont woman and her brat. Baby, meanwhile, was getting no better and local quack worse than useless. Mater eventually insisted they take it to a reputable fellow in Venice, but by the time they got there, doctor couldn't be found, despite Pater's best efforts. Fits, dysentery. Quite hopeless. Died at the inn, in Mater's arms.'

Silence descends. Sir Percy's clipped monotonous delivery only heightens the utter horror that must have overwhelmed Mary Shelley that long last day, with no help at hand for hours ahead. Charles knows now, and only too well, what betrayal it was that poisoned the Shelley marriage, and why Mary blamed her husband for her baby's death. And not just her husband but her step-sister, whom she must have seen as equally culpable, equally selfish. Charles promised he would be Claire's champion – would do all in his power to assist her with these people – but he has never disliked or distrusted her more than he does at this moment.

He takes a deep breath. If it is to be done, 'twere best it were done quickly. 'I will be brief, Sir Percy. I imagine we would both prefer that this matter is concluded as swiftly as possible.'

He sees Lady Shelley bristle at the 'both' that so pointedly excludes her, but she says nothing.

'During the time I was resident at St John's Wood I was able to ascertain that Miss Clairmont does, as you suspected, possess a considerable quantity of Shelley papers. But, given her *relation* to your mother, that can hardly come as any great surprise.'

Sir Percy's flush deepens, and he swallows uneasily. 'Go on.'

'It might have been helpful, when I was last here, if you had seen fit to inform me who exactly she is. But no matter. The facts are these. Miss Clairmont discovered me one night examining those papers, and accused me at once of being in your employ. There followed what I suppose you might term a frank exchange of views, but by the end of it we had come to an understanding.'

'Which was?'

'She asked me to tell you that she is willing to sell the papers.' Which is, of course, strictly true, as far as it goes, but given the rather sanctimonious statements he has just made, he's taking at best a rather oblique position here as regards the truth, the whole truth, and nothing but the truth.

Sir Percy turns away, so that Charles can no longer see his face, 'All of 'em?'

'Everything she has,' replies Charles. 'She says she wishes to be free of the past.'

Sir Percy nods. His back is inexpressive.

'But there was one condition. She asked me to negotiate with you on her behalf.'

Sir Percy's head lifts. 'And you agreed?'

'I did.'

Lady Shelley lumbers to her feet. 'I think we have heard all we need to hear. We will consider Miss Clairmont's proposal, and inform you in due course of our decision. In the meantime I expect you to return whatever monies advanced to you that have not yet been spent, less an appropriate fee for the time expended. Good day to you.'

It is with an obscure intuition of defeat that Charles follows the butler back down the stairs. Double agency has always been a dangerous game, and he has the distinct impression the Shelleys have been playing with a completely different end in view, and one they seem – he is not sure how – to have achieved. It's a conviction that lasts halfway across the square, and it's only when he reaches Eccleston Street and pauses to cross the road that he realizes he's being followed. By a girl. Her hand clasped to her head to keep her cap in place, and her apron billowing about her in the wind as she runs towards him calling his name.

'Mr Maddox?' she says, half out of breath as she catches up with him. 'I have a letter for you, from my mistress.'

Charles takes the paper she holds towards him. 'This is from Lady Shelley?' he says with some irritation – surely the damn woman cannot be claiming her money back already.

'No, sir. From *Mrs* Shelley. She said I was to give you this. But only after you had left the house.'

Charles looks at her, then at the letter. 'Thank you,' he says, tucking it into his breast pocket.

'And she says if you have a reply to address it to me. All her letters are opened, you see.'

'Very well—'

'Alice. Alice Parfitt.' She bobs a curtsy and is gone.

He'd intended to walk back, but changes his mind now, and waits for the omnibus. It's relatively empty, at this time of day, and he makes his way to the back, past three thickset women with baskets of vegetables, and a muttering old man with an ulcerous face and a grey coat patched at the elbows. And once he finds a seat where he won't be overlooked he takes the letter out and opens it. The writing is unsteady, and the ink faint, with here and there a darker word, as if the pen had been gripped more tightly.

Mr Maddox,

I do not know you, but I met your great-uncle, once or twice, many years ago. I doubt very much he will remember me – his must, after all, have been a more than usually crowded and eventful life. But I remember him and I recall, even now, his acuity of mind, and was saddened indeed to learn of his recent infirmity. And yet there is a part of me that almost envies him – there have been times when I would willingly have exchanged the anguish of consciousness for such a blessed insensibility – times when I have yearned for even the possibility of forgetting. But I digress, and this is not, in any case, a letter of condolence.

My son has only now informed me that he engaged your assistance in the matter of Miss Clairmont's papers; this, of course, you know. But he has also confessed that one part of his reason for hiring you for this task was that he might, thereby, discover whether any records still remained in your uncle's possession, relating to the task he undertook for my father in the winter of 1816. Had Percy spoken first to me, I should have urged him to plainer dealing, and I am writing to you now, if not to excuse his deceit, then at least to explain it.

After my husband died, I supported myself and my one remaining child for many years by my own efforts, and as both a dutiful and a loving son Percy feels a special obligation to provide for me now, in his turn. His wife, likewise, has always been especially protective, and particularly wary of any matter that might threaten to injure either my reputation, or that of my husband. So you will understand, I hope, when I tell you that their interest in your uncle's lost papers was motivated only by this natural, indeed laudable, concern. It was entirely by chance that Mr Maddox happened to be working for my father at the very time my husband's first wife met with her tragic end, and your uncle became, thereby, cognizant of certain facts and events, quite inconsequential in themselves, but which we, of course, would wish to remain

165

private to ourselves alone. Having met your uncle even so very briefly, I am convinced that, were he able to speak for himself in this matter, he would respect that wish — nay, see it as his obligation, as a distinguished practitioner of his trade, to keep all such matters confidential. This conviction I have, in turn, communicated to my son. I have likewise assured him that since you are the only heir Mr Maddox has ever had, and the successor now, to his business concerns, you may also — surely — be relied upon to adhere to the same honourable code.

I would wish that this is all I had to ask you, but I must touch now on a far more delicate subject. I found your great-uncle to be a man of both judgement and discretion, and I am about to pay you the compliment of assuming that you share his personal qualities, as well as his professional principles. I must speak now, and with that understanding between us, of Miss Clairmont and my husband, much as I would wish to avoid so repugnant a matter. But having spent as much time in her company as I am told you have, I would have you know the truth. No doubt she has given you a most persuasive account of her own history, and has painted me as a monstrous and unfeeling wife, forgetful, now, even of what is due to my husband's memory. Do not mistake me — I care not what she says of me, for my own reputation matters very little. But I <u>do</u> care what she says — or might publish — of Shelley. I know there have been allegations, more than once, that Miss Clairmont was his mistress, but I tell you, Mr Maddox, as I have told others before you, that it is all a wicked lie. He <u>never</u> had an improper connection with her, and I find it unbearably painful that he should still — after all these years — stand thus slandered. I cannot say for a certainty whence such accusations have sprung, but you have met her, and talked with her, and I am sure you will have perceived that vein of phantasy and <u>mélodrame</u> that is so peculiarly her own. I recognize it, because I too have struggled to see beyond the belligerent and often hysterical woman Miss Clairmont is now, to the timid and trusting girl she was when first we met. A girl who has been

166

striving all her life for love, and never found it. I have ever tried to do my duty by her, but even when we were children I often wondered if there were not some deficiency – some fatal lack that led her to ape me in all I did. All I had, <u>she</u> wanted. My clothes, the way I arranged my hair, even – and to my horror – my Shelley. I dreamed – after his declaration of love, after our decision to elope – of freedom and escape, and found to my dismay she was bound to me even more inextricably than before. I do not know, even now, how she persuaded him to take her with us, for we needed no interpreter, and wanted no companion. All I know is that I came down the stairs that summer dawn and found her there, her trunk packed, her cloak about her, and the strangest of strange expressions on her face, threatening to wake the whole house there and then if I did not agree to her coming.

There followed the most wondrous six weeks I have ever experienced. The excitement of being away from England – of being together, and in love. Our first sight of the Alps, their icy summits darting white pinnacles into the clear blue sky. Not even our miserable lack of money could diminish my happiness, and yet even then I knew – at sixteen I knew – that it was not appropriate – not <u>healthy</u> – for her to pursue Shelley as she did. It was not right that she should challenge him to bathe with her naked in a pool by the open roadside. It was not fitting that she should ask to share our bed, even if there was indeed – as she claimed – an infestation of rats. When Shelley and I were alone, we two, all was well; when she was there, chaos and wretchedness were always the consequence. But Shelley was, from the first, utterly blameless in this. You may say that he was older – that he should have insisted she conduct herself more prudently – but you never knew him. You do not understand that in so many things he was still a child himself – he loved nothing better than to sail paper boats on the Serpentine, or roll billiard balls about on the carpet with our son William. Children were always his chosen playmates and confidants – indeed, he used to say every true follower of Plato must be a lover of children, for they are our masters and instructors in philosophy. He loved children almost as much as he loathed oppression in any form, and thus it was that he once attempted to kidnap his sisters from their school, claiming they were being ill-treated. And his attentiveness to Miss Clairmont sprang from that same purity of sentiment. She was _always_, in his eyes, that same child he first met at my father's house. The same plump, vivacious, rather demanding _child_. Sadly in need of the love and attention her mother never gave her, and deserving, therefore, of all his kindness. Whatever she supposes now – whatever she designed _then_ – his own mind was never sullied by it. My marriage, Mr Maddox, from first to last, was a thing of passion. A thing of love that had no end but death. And when he set out, at the end, on that journey that was to snatch him for ever from my arms, the last letter he wrote was not to her, but to me – to his 'best and ever dearest Mary'.

I seek not to needlessly blacken Miss Clairmont's name in saying such things, nor raise my own character by cheapening hers. Nor would I attempt to gloss over my own failings as a wife – whatever invective she has cast upon me, I richly deserve. Indeed, I cannot recall a single moment of the last months of my husband's life without a feeling of revulsion. All I could think of that last terrible summer was how to get my son away from that barren and accursed place, and when I returned to Shelley's papers to prepare my edition of his work, it shook me to my very soul. After so long an interval to read his words again – it was as if I was compelled to taste every last drop of a fathomless well of bitter waters, to know the anguish he was in and to be forced to acknowledge that I myself had occasioned that pain by my rages, my coldness, my ceaseless demands. That, no doubt, is the story Miss Clairmont tells, but it is not the only truth of that terrible time. For no outsider, however closely placed, can know the real state of affairs between two people bound together in so near a tie. You are young, Mr Maddox, and are not yet prey to the past. I hope you are never compelled to discover that love – love given and received – can be the greatest agony, as well as the most terrible joy. Despite all we endured together – despite the loss, one by one, of three sweet children – he remained, to the last, true only to me.

It is all too often the fate of men of genius to run too far ahead of their own times, and Shelley was no exception. His ethereal soul was not suited to this rude cold world. If his head ever erred, his heart did not, and I can fearlessly avow that – judged impartially – his character would stand in finer and brighter light than that of any of his contemporaries. That is why I have striven so hard and so long to protect him, and to prevent the publication of any history of his life that I myself know to be false, and would succeed only in tainting his remembrance. Whatever you have read – whether penned by that mischief-maker Thomas Medwin, or by <u>any other hand</u> – no account has ever been given at all approaching reality in its details, either as regards himself, or those of us who shared his life. I wished once to write such an account myself, but my father-in-law threatened to withdraw even the meagre allowance he condescended to make me, should such a volume ever appear. And now he is dead I am too old, and too ill, to take up my pen. All those years with Shelley, my idea of heaven was a life without Miss Clairmont – she haunted me then in the flesh, and she haunts me now, in absence, like a punishment divinely ordained for some dreadful sin I have committed all unknowing, and for which, even now, I am still atoning. For the one fear that darkens my last days is that the task which is now beyond my strength will be assumed, when I am gone, by her – she who will claim <u>she</u> knew him best, she who will usurp, in the eyes of the world, the position that I alone held in his heart. And so I beg you, with the humility of a widow, and the desperation of a woman who knows her days will be not long, to exercise with her whatever influence you may have. There will be others, no doubt, in the years to come, less intelligent and more unscrupulous than you, who will endeavour to *obtain those papers she hoards for their own ends, and by then what power I still possess will be long consigned to dust. That same dust that already consumes my husband, and all but one of my own sweet babes. Better far that she should allow the dead to sleep in peace – and commit what still remains behind to silence and forgetting.*

M. W. S.

Charles lowers the pages slowly, and stares out of the 'bus window. They are passing along Oxford Street, and a small crowd has gathered around a man with a dancing bear on a chain. The animal has a spiked collar about its neck and two small girls are making it lift its feet by poking it in turns with pointed sticks as a gnarled old man plays a barrel-organ, and a boy with no shoes collects ha'pennies in a cap. As the 'bus draws level there is a moment when Charles stares directly into the animal's hollow and lifeless eyes. And then they jolt forward and Charles turns away, uncomfortably aware that some might say his own position is not so very different. Propelled first this way and then that, believing one woman, then the other, and convinced now that neither of them can be trusted.

He has not even met Mary Shelley, and yet he knows she is lying. For there is one fact he possesses that she cannot possibly suspect. It was not three sweet children the Shelleys lost but four. Three of their own, and the one they adopted. But of little Elena there is no mention here. She, it seems, has long been consigned not just to dust, but to oblivion, and will find no place in any version of the poet's life that either his wife or daughter-in-law will permit to appear. But if Charles questions Mary's veracity, he does not for a moment question her intelligence. Claire may have talked in the language of chess, but this woman is a strategist worthy of the game. Hers is so polished, so adroit a performance he suspects it has been played many times before, and not least with all those would-be biographers who have been so zealous over·the years for the naked and unforgiving truth. All those other men whose intelligence has no doubt been flattered, and honour praised. For is not chess a game, in the end, of sacrifice? Of knowing how much to forfeit for a greater end? In divulging her son's inept deception, Mary Shelley has told Charles only what he suspected long before: it was a pawn she surrendered, nothing more. There must be a far more important piece in play here, if he could but discover it.

Charles sits back, thinking about deceit. He was once, as a little boy, an avid collector, not just of objects but of words – odd derivations, curious coinages, collective nouns. Names for groups of animals fascinated him especially, and he was always entranced to add a new one to the list in his little notebook. The more bizarre they were, the more he coveted them, whether ostentations of peacocks, murmurations of starlings, or murders (prophetic, this one) of crows. But one such name he could not fathom, and he remembers, now, going one morning to his father in his study and asking why it should be a 'deceit' of lapwings? What had such pretty birds done to be so condemned? His father had taken off his spectacles with a sigh, and turned laboriously to the small boy tugging at his coat. It is an erroneous etymology, he explained, sternly instructive. The word was not originally *deceit*, it had become corrupted, over the centuries, from *desert*. But why, Charles persisted, excited to have claimed so much of his father's attention, why *that* name? Because parent lapwings will abandon their nest to lead predators astray, protecting their young in the very act of appearing to forsake them. And is that not, thinks Charles

171

now, exactly the 'deceit' Mary Shelley has just committed? Confronted by a potential enemy, she diverges in the opposite direction, away from whatever secret she is safeguarding and into the impenetrable thickets of her past relationship with Claire. Only Charles has a hunch it is not her offspring that Mary is protecting – not this time. Because why else would she insist that Charles reply through her maid? Whatever it is she is concealing now, it does not concern her son – indeed, he must be completely ignorant of it, because otherwise there would have been no need for such a ploy. There is nothing in this letter, at least on the face of it, that necessitates that Charles reply at all, and yet she was so concerned that any response should be placed into her own hands alone that she sent the maid running after him to say so. Charles looks at the pages again. There is something here – something planted in plain sight like a snare in the grass. Something that, if he knew her secret, he might feel obliged to contradict, or contend. Like Claire, this woman fears what Charles might know; the question now is whether it is the same secret that both women share. Is there, in fact, some collusion of concealment between these two step-sisters? Could there be a pact of silence that endures even now, despite their bitter enmity, and all their years of dark distrust?

As the 'bus bumps over the cobblestones towards Regent Street Charles turns again to the letter and reads it once more. Slowly, sentence by sentence, subjecting every phrase to a casuistical scrutiny. And it's then, of course, that he notices it. Something that exposes a failing far closer to home than the secrets of the Shelley past. For there, on the first page, she talks of his uncle's records as *lost*. Charles hadn't noticed it the first time, but now the word howls at him. How could this woman possibly know his uncle's records are missing? Charles has been scrupulous never to say so – not to the Shelleys, and not to Claire. No, thinks Charles, his jaw setting in a grim line, he knows exactly how Mary Shelley came by this knowledge, and by the time he gets to Buckingham Street his mind is spilling with a blistering rage.

'*Billy*,' he bellows, crashing the door open so hard it shudders on its hinges. 'Get your sorry arse up here *at once*.'

There is silence for a moment, then the boy appears slowly round the corner of the kitchen stairs. 'Mr Charles?'

But Charles already has him by the throat and against the wall. 'How dare you, you treacherous little shit? How much did they pay you? A few shillings? After we took you in and gave you a job.'

'What yer talkin' about?' stammers Billy, his face purple. 'I ain't done nuffin'.'

'Don't *lie* to me,' yells Charles, ramming him back hard. 'I know what you did – you told them, didn't you, about the pages missing from that book? It was you who threw it on the fire – they paid you to destroy it. They paid you to have it burned.'

'What the 'ell would I know about some bloody book? I can't even bloody *read*.'

'You were *there* – that day I deciphered the words. You'd have known what it looked like—'

'I don't know what yer bloody talkin' about,' wails the boy. 'Yer '*urtin*' me!'

But as Charles tightens his grip he feels a hand now on his own shoulder, shaking him, trying to pull him away. 'It werenae the boy, Mr Charles. It werenae Billy.'

It's Abel, his eyes watery in his withered face.

'What the hell are you talking about, Abel?'

'It werenae the boy, Mr Charles, it were me. I'm right sorry for it. All I can say is I didnae know.'

Charles slowly loosens his hold and the boy squirms away and out of arm's reach. There's a livid red mark on his neck, and he's breathing with difficulty.

'See? *Told yer* – yer always accusin' me and it ain't never my fault – like the other day—'

'I suggest you *shut up*, Billy,' says Charles, quietly, still staring at the old man. 'And I suggest *you*, Abel, tell me the truth.'

'It were one of those days ye were away, Mr Charles. That gentleman called again—'

'Sir Percy Shelley?'

The old man swallows, then nods. 'The one as left the card. 'E came 'ere lookin' for 'ee and I said as ye were away. And then he said had ye had any luck wi' findin' the records and I – well . . .'

'Yes?'

Abel swallows again. 'I told him what we found. That the pages were missin'. I'm sorry. I thought as 'e was yer client ye wouldnae mind. I thought,' he shakes his head sadly, 'as I might be helpin'.'

Charles stares at him, shamed now, and remembering that he had told Abel nothing of his suspicions of the Shelleys, given him no instructions as to silence, and therefore can hardly blame him now. He takes a deep breath – and a step in the old man's direction. 'What exactly did you tell him, Abel?'

'Just that the pages in the 'sixteen file had been taken out a long time back. That we'd looked for 'em but couldnae find 'em anywhere.'

'Nothing about the words I uncovered?'

Abel shakes his head. 'No, Mr Charles. And I swear t'ye I didnae put the book on the fire. That were yer uncle, like as I told 'ee.'

Charles nods, 'Very well,' then turns to Billy: 'I'm sure you have some task or other to do downstairs. See you get on with it.'

The boy leers a glance at him, then hobbles back down to the kitchen, rubbing his neck theatrically. Charles watches him go, then makes for the stairs, only to have Abel catch at his coat as he goes past.

'It's a'right, Mr Charles? I havenae done aught wrong?'

Charles pauses a moment, then touches him lightly on the arm. 'It's all right, Abel. Now, if you'll forgive me, I have work to do.'

His pace quickens as he goes up the stairs, leaving the old man standing watching him, his face troubled and pale.

Charles's heart is still beating rather too fast as he closes the attic door behind him and leans against it. Some remorse he has on Abel's account, but as for Billy – Billy has got away with far more than he's been punished for in this house, and Charles has no compunction in levelling the scale, even if the boy didn't happen to deserve his chastisement this time. He pulls off his coat and sits down heavily on the bed, the pages of Mary Shelley's letter on the quilt in front of him. He reads it again, and then for a fourth time, but the real mystery hidden here still eludes him. As he folds it up and puts it back in his pocket he realizes that in his fury at Billy he has hurt his injured hand and goes over to the washstand to find a new dressing. Only the roll of bandage is not where he left it. He stands a moment looking round the attic, and it strikes him that should Maddox have thought to hide those missing pages in this room he would have been spoiled for choice. He could have secreted them under the velvet lining in the box that displays Charles's coins, or in the scabbard of the battered and jewel-less Persian scimitar. And there is, besides, a secret drawer only

175

Charles knows of at the base of his case of chemical compounds. But of course the papers cannot actually be anywhere in this room – Maddox has not been up to this floor since Charles moved in, and if those pages do still exist they were removed and hidden long ago. Almost certainly before that tour of Italy whence Maddox returned, some months since, a changed and much older man. Charles wonders for the first time whether he should have asked Abel more about that trip – he knows hardly anything about it – either where they went, or why Maddox made such an enormous effort, at such an advanced age, to undertake his first and only venture beyond his native shores. For while it's become clear to Charles that his great-uncle has been in a slow decline for far longer than anyone guessed, it's equally clear that it was only after his return from Italy that he began to suffer the terrifying attacks of violence and madness that led Charles to move into the Buckingham Street house. A house he has now inhabited, incidentally, for several weeks without ever coming across any secret hiding-place – neither door inexplicably locked nor cupboard mysteriously sealed. The only part of the house, in fact, Charles has *not* treated as if it were his own has been the drawing room, which is now more than ever his uncle's personal province. Indeed, few of the other rooms were even being used before Charles moved in and hired Billy and the girl; as Maddox aged, his territory retreated, and there are still bedchambers on the second floor that Molly has not yet wakened from their damp, dust-sheeted slumber. Those rooms Charles knows Abel searched, but did he have the temerity to intrude upon his master's private domain? And yet isn't the drawing room by far the most likely hiding-place?

Ever since he was a boy Charles has tried to follow

Maddox's methods and emulate Maddox's rigour of thought, and what success he has seen has stemmed from that source, both in the Detective police, and in the months since he set up in business on his own. How many times, over the years, has he heard Maddox say those selfsame words? *There is no problem, however intractable, that cannot be resolved by the steady application of logic and observation.* Logic, thus far, has not availed him; perhaps observation may prove more instructive. Charles sits down on the bed again and closes his eyes. It's a technique he's used before – a way of refining his perceptions, and eliminating the extraneous. Allowing his mind free play. If he went down to the drawing room now all his senses would be assailed: the smell of the fire, the sound of the clock ticking, his uncle shifting fretfully in his sleep. Here, in the darkness behind his eyes, there are no distractions.

And so he stands now, in imagination, in the centre of that elegant room downstairs, turning slowly about, exploring the space as if for the first time, yard by yard, inch by inch, as though it had become some Renaissance theatre of memory, each object to be considered not just for itself but as a sign of something else – as a place of potential concealment. It is, as far as he can tell, exactly the same room it was when he was a boy: the same books, the same busts of the philosophers, the same picture of the gardens at the Villa d'Este hung between the two long windows. The books are too obvious for a hiding-place, and the busts are solid stone, as Charles remembers only too well from trying to lift one as a child, but perhaps the painting is a possibility – there could be a space, perhaps, between the canvas and the frame. But the picture is a favourite of Maddox's, and Charles doubts his uncle would have risked doing it damage. Charles loved that picture as a boy – the avenue of dark cypresses, the *enfilade* of retreating statues, the figures half seen in the shadows, and there in the centre, on the crown of the rise, the villa glimpsed between the trees, so imposing and so sinister, and so unlike any other house he had ever seen. Every time he was taken to visit his great-uncle he was drawn to it again, to the colours and the soft *sfumato* and the story the picture seemed to suggest. A story, incidentally, that he once tried to write down, hesitantly at first, but with a slowly growing confidence, only to have his father demand what he had been doing all day, and dismiss his efforts as nothing but an idle and childish indulgence, unworthy of his time. You, I suspect, will think that a pity, and find it significant that Charles never attempted to write anything like it again, and scarcely even remembers the incident any more. You may also think it a shame that he is considering the painting now not as a story, or a work of art, but solely and exclusively as a physical object – a piece of evidence that may or may not have something to reveal. And what he can see in his mind now is how the stipple of the brushwork catches in a shaft of sunlight cast slant-wise across the canvas. And then, suddenly, he knows. Knows as a scientist knows, and he is, of course – among many other things – a scientist. Because, hung where it is, that painting is never touched by direct sun; the only light it ever sees is *reflected onto* it, from the mirror above the mantelpiece on the opposite wall. A mirror, Charles recalls with a tingle of excitement, which has always seemed rather elaborate for such a classically austere room. And now he remembers a dull afternoon years before, when Maddox forced a much younger and more fidgety Charles to stand before that mirror, showing him the carving and the rich detail, and telling him that the proper name for that style of frame was – not baroque, but something else. Charles racks his brain, searching for the precise word. It began with an *r* – rococo? No, not that – but something similar. Not rococo but *rocaille*. And when Charles's hopeless incompetence in French left him staring blankly, none the wiser, Maddox had pointed out the abundance of tumbling conches and serrated scallops and asked him what they looked like.

'Shells, Uncle Maddox. Like the one I found on the beach at Filey last summer, only bigger. Much bigger.'

So what might the word '*rocaille*' mean?

A frown, then, tentatively, 'Shelley?'

Charles had never understood why Maddox roared with such delighted laughter at that.

But he does now.

A minute later Charles is racing down the stairs and into the drawing room, scarcely noticing Molly on the steps on the landing, whisking away the cobwebs with a long feather duster. 'Abel!' he calls. 'Where are you, Abel?'

'Whatever's to do, Mr Charles?' says Abel, as Charles clatters into the drawing room to find the old man sitting by his master's sleeping form. 'I dinnae want to waken him.'

Charles comes to a halt, breathing heavily. 'I think I may know where those missing pages are,' he says, more softly now. 'They've been here all the time – hidden somehow in that mirror.'

Abel looks at the mirror, then back to Charles, transparently sceptical. 'Whatever makes 'ee think so?'

'I'll explain later. Can you help me? I want to see what's behind it.'

Charles lifts one of the hard-backed chairs in front of the mantelpiece, and Abel steadies it as he climbs up and reaches for the heavy frame. He'd assumed it was hung like a picture, but finds, to his chagrin, that it won't come away. 'Is the damn thing nailed down, Abel?' he says, catching sight of his own shadowed, angry eyes in the tarnished mirrored glass.

'I cannae tell ye, Mr Charles,' says Abel, from below. 'It werenae me as fixed it. The boss had a carpenter come in special to do it. But that were years ago now.'

But even as he's speaking Charles has shifted onto tiptoe and realized that the mirror is set at a slight angle from the wall. So slight as to be almost imperceptible from the floor, but wide enough at the top, as he can now see, to allow the insertion of what looks like some sort of thin silver tube. It's a stretch, but Charles is just tall enough to reach in and draw it out. The metal surface is rusted here and there, but otherwise it seems intact, and it must have been made – surely – for the purpose, so perfectly does it fit its narrow niche. Even in the rush of discovery a part of Charles's mind notes how much trouble his uncle has gone to, and how much, therefore, must have been at stake. But all that is for later. Now he just wants to *know*. He turns the tube upside down and shakes it gently, then watches – with that *frisson* the detective, the journalist and the academic researcher all share – as a sheaf of yellowing paper uncoils slowly into his waiting hand.

CHAPTER EIGHT

Harriet

3rd January 1817

Investigations in the Matter of Mrs Harriet Shelley
Conducted at the Behest of William Godwin, Esquire,
Skinner-street, Holborn

There follows in these pages my final report in this all too bitter case, which has been the occasion of so much grief, and for which I have paid so great a price. Would that I had never accepted it; would that I had kept to my determination to forswear all dealings again with aught of that name – a name my hand trembles to write, and that I struggle even now to hear, far less utter. But my pledge to one, and the duty I believed I owed to another, induced me, against my reason, against my judgement, against my*self*, to concede. I believed that I might by a slight endurance on my part help secure to them a lasting happiness. I could not know then it would be so fatal a cure.

Remarkable as it may appear, given all that has gone before, I had not met Godwin until he requested me to call at his house in the third week of September last. But if I knew the name, I knew, likewise, the reputation and the work, as any man must who reads widely, and has an active mind, though I state at once that I disagree profoundly with the argument of *Political Justice*, and condemn utterly the influence it has had, having seen with my own eyes the pernicious consequences. It was indeed those pernicious consequences, which I have steeled myself with so much anguish to relate, that led me initially to refuse the meeting out of hand. But when Godwin wrote again, insisting that I alone possessed such intellectual powers as he had need of, and that I had been warmly recommended by several great men of his acquaintance (whom he obligingly enumerated), I confess my pride was flattered, much as my curiosity was piqued. And thinking, wrongly as it transpired, that the individual I reviled was no longer in England, I judged I risked little in agreeing at least to a preliminary meeting. How mistaken – how disastrously mistaken – I was in this will become only too clear in the pages that follow.

But all of this was, as yet, in the future. As I made my way to Skinner-street that morning I was anticipating, with some degree of apprehension I confess, an introduction to a distinguished philosopher, a fine thinker, an exacting intelligence. What I encountered in his stead was a short, balding, solid little man, with a long, thin nose, and a very disagreeable wife. And even had I not my own sources of information as to the perilous state of the gentleman's finances, I should have seen at once that the bookshop of which he had become the proprietor was a failing concern: ill managed, ill situated, and the shelves half empty. I wondered at first, and for a moment, that any man of business could employ such a timid and self-effacing assistant behind his counter, only to find that the young woman in question was none other than the elder daughter of Mr Godwin's first wife, a Miss Fanny Imlay. A modest, gentle, well-meaning creature, to judge of first impressions, though it was evident, from words Godwin let

182

drop later, and – may I say – in the young woman's presence, that he adjudged Miss Imlay considerably inferior in capacity to his own daughter by that same lady. That he considered the latter to be singularly bold and active of mind, and almost invincible in everything she undertook, while the former, though sober and observing, was too much given to indolence; that he thought his own daughter very pretty, while Fanny could at best be termed 'not unprepossessing'. I glanced more than once at the aforementioned young woman during this exposition, and it was evident to me that she was only too accustomed to hearing her own talents thus denigrated in comparison with her younger sister's. I say this, not only in condemnation, however well deserved, but in anticipation of what is to come, for I believe such behaviour on Godwin's part – such arrant thoughtlessness – played its own part in the tragedy that was so soon to unfold. For my own part, and from such limited observations as I was able to make, I considered the young lady to be virtuous, gentle and kind; qualities, in my opinion, to be both admired and fostered in woman, even if they were neither valued nor encouraged by her celebrated mother, with her infamous concern only for the rights and freedoms of her sex. That Miss Fanny resembled that lady as little in looks as she did in temperament I could see for myself, by reference to a very fine portrait of Mrs Wollstonecraft Godwin which hung over the fireplace. Such a fine portrait, and so centrally displayed, that any subsequent wife might have found it irksome; that the second Mrs Godwin did so, and profoundly, was obvious to me at once, as was the fact that her husband seemed not in the slightest aware of it.

The said Mrs Godwin busied herself, firstly, in providing refreshment, or rather in instructing Miss Imlay to do so; she then took a seat beside her husband, and proposed to lay before me the facts of the case. I was, I admit, disconcerted. I have, on occasion, encountered women of insight and intelligence in the course of my profession – women able to follow the principles of logic and observation that I have always expounded – but I did not expect to find one in Mrs Godwin. Appearances were decidedly against her, but I gradually divined that her coarse features, prominent bosom and rather extraordinary green-tinted spectacles concealed a mind of considerable cunning, even if she could boast neither education nor understanding, in the strict meaning of those terms. I had wondered, on my first introduction to her, and recalling what I had heard of her from others, that she had induced a man such as Godwin to take her to wife, but the more I knew of her, the more I discerned how the feat might have been accomplished.

The lady in question was, at first, most insistent that the matter be handled with the utmost discretion, but I made bold to remind her that her husband had already been given assurances as to that by clients I had served, and that they might rely, therefore, on its continuance now. Thus reassured, she proceeded at length to relate the circumstances as they then stood. It was evident as she spoke that she, at least, had no notion of the events I have already related here, although it was impossible to discern from his impassive expression whether her husband was in a state of the like ignorance. And so it was that I was forced to endure a long account of the adulterous liaison between Mr Godwin's daughter and the man who had debauched her – a man my interlocutress abused in one breath and exalted the next as 'the son of a baronet, you know, with the most enormous fortune'. She told me likewise, as I already knew, that her own daughter had departed England in their company, and had still been of their party in their late excursion to Switzerland. What I did *not* know, until that moment, was that there were rumours Shelley might be contemplating a return to his former and still lawful marital abode. I will say at once that I was neither shocked nor surprised at this, and with good

184

reason: given what I had witnessed I knew no conduct, however base, was too vile for such a scoundrel.

But the woman in my presence now knew nothing of this; and it took, moreover, no preternatural or superhuman insight to discern that if there was indeed such talk of Shelley's intentions it had been considerably amplified, in the Godwins' minds, by the consequences for their own two selves of any such decision. Mrs Godwin was careful, in my hearing, to express only a parent's proper concern for the invidious position in which Miss Godwin would find herself, should such an event occur, but I was convinced in my own mind that the extraordinarily precarious nature of the Skinner-street establishment was an even more urgent anxiety. Doubtless they were unaware that I already knew what lavish promises Shelley had made to assist Godwin with loans, and that most if not all of these had still not yet been paid. I knew, too, that Shelley had been evading apprehension by the bailiffs in the weeks before his last precipitate departure for the Continent.

I asked then, feigning ignorance, but interested as to the reply I should receive, if either Mr or Mrs Godwin had spoken in person to Shelley as to his plans in relation to his wife. A look passed between them at this, and Mrs Godwin answered, somewhat pink about the cheeks, that all direct communication had ceased the day the poet first left London in company with the two young women, some two years previously. 'Mr Godwin has forbade him the house,' she said, 'and quite right too, after such a scandalous and disgraceful betrayal. He swore he would stop seeing Mary, you know. He stood there, on exactly the spot where you're standing now and swore the affair was over and there would be no more clandestine meetings and midnight assignations and secret messages going to and fro. And the next we hear he's upped and gone with her, and tricked my Clairy into going with them.'

Mr Godwin had, his wife continued, maintained an uninterrupted correspondence with 'the delinquent' but only in relation to 'certain monetary matters', which I took to be the aforementioned pecuniary advances. It was only much later, and too late, that I was to learn that Fanny had acted as intermediary between the two hostile parties after Shelley's return to London, representing each to the other as best she might, and taking to herself – it seemed to me – all the woeful consequences of that bitter and fractious exchange.

I observed with mounting irritation Mr Godwin's rather supercilious expression throughout his wife's narration. Despite my abhorrence of Shelley, and my utter repugnance for both his conduct and his principles, I was very much tempted to enquire how the philosopher Godwin reconciled his own public condemnations of the institution of marriage with his continued ostracism of a man who appeared to have followed those precepts only too assiduously. Nor did I venture my own opinion as to the justice – moral or indeed political – of importuning such an individual for money while refusing to afford him even the time of day. Mrs Godwin, meanwhile, had become increasingly testy, saying that the current state of affairs was most trying and unsatisfactory, and had rendered it difficult, nay, almost impossible, to obtain the information they required as to Shelley's wider intentions.

That, in short, was to be my undertaking.

I had already, as I have related, forsworn any further contact with a man I considered to be both a felon and a blackguard, and I had no intention of becoming embroiled once again in circumstances that could only lead, I knew, to further misery and regret. I rejoined at once, therefore, that this was not at all my customary class of investigation, and I would seek out another man in my line of work who would be better placed to assist them; whereupon Mrs Godwin began to talk in the most graphic terms of her step-daughter's distress at the dreadful possibility of abandonment by a man into whose protection she had so recklessly thrown herself.

'And there's her little William to consider,' she said, taking out her handkerchief. 'Such a darling little boy, not nine months old, and the brightest, most sweet-natured, trusting wee creature. If only you could see him, Mr Maddox, I am sure you would relent.'

And so – with the greatest misgivings – I did.

Mr Godwin then spoke for the first time, supplying me with various practical details, and giving me thus the distinct impression that the less seemly facts were far beneath his lofty notice, and that he left such unpleasantness for his wife to manage. His daughter and Mrs Godwin's were both, he said, at that moment resident in Bath, while Shelley had been seen in town more than once, in consequence, he believed, of a charge undertaken on behalf of the Lord Byron, to deliver a manuscript to his publishers, which his lordship had entrusted to Shelley in Switzerland. It was possible, he continued, that Shelley had visited his wife in the course of one of these expeditions, but Godwin was unaware whether the lady in question was still residing at her father's house.

Mrs Godwin became most voluble at this point, venturing the loud opinion that Harriet Shelley was not, in fact, a 'lady', but a tavern-keeper's daughter, who was no match for the son of a baronet for all her fancy ways, and she had, moreover and as everyone knew, tricked him into that marriage out of pity, and that anyone with the slightest knowledge of the affair knew for a fact that he had never loved her nor she him. Godwin became understandably uneasy at this indecorous, not to say uncouth, outburst but, while carefully qualifying the coarser aspects of his wife's assertions, claimed he could only, in truth, confirm that Mrs Shelley was a very foolish, if a very beautiful girl, and he himself had witnessed her on more than one occasion making unconsidered statements on subjects about which she evidently knew next to nothing.

'I cannot deny,' he continued, shaking his long, bony head, 'that my daughter is by far the more apt helpmeet for a man of such undoubted abilities, despite the unfortunate, not to say untoward, manner in which the connection between them came about. The partner of such a man should be one of a philosophical and intellectual cast of mind; Mrs Shelley, self-evidently, is neither.'

Miss Fanny became somewhat *distrait* upon hearing Mrs Shelley spoken of in such terms, and began to weep rather piteously, insisting that Harriet was a sweet girl – that she spoke very nicely, and dressed very neatly, and never had an unkind word for anyone. That the only harm she had done Shelley was to love him, and to have been too young and innocent to know what such a love could mean. I wondered at that, at the time – wondered at what a girl like her could know of love, and at the flush on her cheeks as she spoke the poet's name. It was the intuition of a moment only, but I ask myself now what might have been prevented had I acted upon it. But how could I, a stranger unknown to her, offer the comfort and counsel that is a mother's part? The lady that Fate had decreed should play that maternal role seemed entirely unaware of what I had perceived, retorting only, and rather unkindly, that 'Harriet always could wrap poor silly Fanny round her little finger'; an observation that served only to distress the girl the more. Mrs Godwin then pursed her lips together and announced that it would be better if Fanny retired to her own chamber, before leading her smartly from the room, as if for all the world she were a child of eight, not a young woman of some two and twenty years. I, meanwhile, had seen enough, and made ready at once to depart, saying I would as requested do whatever was in my power to ascertain the current whereabouts of the absent Mrs Shelley.

Godwin had given me an address in Marchmont-street, and I arranged at once to have the premises observed against Shelley's return. I had seen him, several times, with my own eyes, but the description I gave to the man I set to watch clearly had the air, to him, of the most ludicrous caricature. But when the same man returned some days later he told me he had indeed seen one who matched exactly the person I described: his hair wild, his eyes hectic, his back stooped; flushed and giggling like a girl, and clad in a rag-bag of untidy clothes that would have looked more fitting on a boy of twelve. My man had followed the poet to a chop-house where he met with a group of friends, but Shelley supped only on pieces of bread dipped in a bowl of milk, along with what appeared to be a pocketful of baker's currants, some of which he proceeded to propel surreptitiously at other unsuspecting customers. At one moment during the repast one of his companions must have made some remark that aroused his interest, for my man described how all at once he threw his hands in the air, shrieked aloud, and cast himself violently back in his chair. The latter then over-toppled under his weight, leaving the poet prostrate on the ground, where he lay shouting and stamping his feet for some minutes, until his hapless friends made it their business to right him.

I had wondered, when first I met him, if there might be a history of lunacy in the family; indeed, I had advised once before that William Lawrence be consulted – that Shelley was clearly in need of the expert medical attendance that a practitioner such as he

189

could offer, but I met with no success. And when I raised the subject with the Godwins I encountered only suspicion and denial. I am no expert in such matters, I confess, but I have, albeit rarely, seen instances of such behaviour in others and I have never known it lead to a wholesome or a healthful life. I acknowledge that many such individuals exercise a peculiar and enduring charm – that many can appear, for large tracts of time, to be no different, in all important respects, from the mass of their fellow men, but this is only the most painful and treacherous illusion. Such people are always, in the end, a bane and a curse to those about them; the fact that they themselves cannot perceive it renders the damage they do only the more deadly.

But to return to the business. My man followed Shelley back to his lodgings, but he ventured nowhere further, either to his wife or elsewhere, and took the coach from London the next morning.

In the course of the succeeding week I had enquiries made as to the whereabouts of Mrs Shelley. It appeared, at first, that she was indeed still resident at her father's house in Chapel-street but living there in a state of the most retired seclusion and never seen abroad, though the nursemaid was often to be observed out walking with the two children. But in the days that followed we discovered that she had, in fact, departed the Westbrook house some weeks before, and no one knew of her present where-abouts. It was then, and most unexpectedly, that I received my second summons to Skinner-street. A summons written in alarm and sent in agitation, and one occasioned not, this time, by selfishness and greed, but by what would prove to be only the first of a sequence of unspeakable catastrophes.

In this case, if not in the other, I do not accuse myself. I do not know what more I could have done, beyond advocating that kindness and care as seemed to have been so sadly wanting, but I doubt very much that my words would have been heeded. Long experience has taught me that my fellow beings are never blinder than to the consequences of their own conduct, and never more obdurate than in accepting the need for a change therein.

The facts, in short, were these. That very morning, after several days of deep melancholy – a melancholy only deepened, it appeared, by letters received from Bath – Fanny Imlay had disappeared from the house. I found, indeed, the whole establishment in uproar – maids dispatched hither and thither in random and ineffectual enquiries, and the youngest Godwin child, a rather fearful-looking boy of some thirteen years, crying aloud for his sister and trailing about the house, unregarded, it seemed, by anyone in it. Godwin himself I found hunched over his writing-desk, taciturn and morose. As well he might be. What does it say of any father that all three of the young women consigned to his care had now gone to such extraordinary lengths to escape from it? Though the blame, in my opinion, should not be his alone. I shudder to imagine the life Fanny led in that household, under Godwin's careless tutelage and his wife's bad-tempered demands. Five children there had been living there, and none of them sharing the same two parents; she, poor girl, the only one with neither mother nor father present, and the one most in need of the support and affection only a true parent can give.

If Godwin had become more silent in the face of such a calamity, his wife appeared even more strident, if such a thing were possible. Poor silly Fanny, she repeated incessantly, was always falling into such fits of dejection at the slightest provocation, and without the slightest cause. 'You mark my words, William,' she said to her husband. 'It will just be another attempt to put herself forward and have people notice her. That girl never did know how to conduct herself properly – but what do you expect with an adventurer like Imlay for a father? It will all be just another billow in a ladle, just you see. I'll wager even now she is thinking better of it, and is on her way home with her tail between her legs. And she'll have a piece of my mind when she gets here, make no mistake about that.'

This vulgar tirade seemed at length to rouse the philosopher from his broodings, and he reminded his wife, with a certain terseness, that she might have done better to keep the secret of Fanny's parentage from her, or at the very least informed her of it in a rather more delicate manner. I was forced to conclude from this that even if the circumstances of the young woman's birth were widely known outside the family, Fanny herself had not known until recently of her own illegitimacy. I could see how sorely this might have affected her, and began to feel a degree of concern far in excess of what Mrs Godwin clearly believed either necessary or appropriate. And this concern was only augmented when Godwin took me aside to inform me that Fanny had, only a few days previously, been sadly disappointed in a long-held ambition to join her mother's maiden sisters at their school in Dublin, and assume a career there as a teacher. Mrs Godwin then interjected loudly that *that* was all *Mary*'s fault, not Fanny's, and how could you blame them? However reluctant I was to find myself in agreement with Mrs Godwin on any point of note, I had to concur that it was in all likelihood the public scandal occasioned by Miss Godwin's elopement that had caused the ladies in question to decide against offering such a position to a young woman living in the same household, albeit their own niece. But the fact that Fanny was in no way to blame for this change in her prospects cannot have afforded her much consolation in the loss of them, left, as she must have believed, without any possibility of making a life for herself independent of her family. Godwin begged me then for my counsel, and I gave it as my opinion that, in the absence of other likely friends or relations, there seemed only two places that the young woman might have fled: to her half-sister and step-sister in Bath, or to the aforementioned aunts in Dublin, and I thought it likely that Dublin would be her preference of the two., My advice, therefore, was that I should send one of my most trusted men to Bath, but I would go myself to Swansea, that being by far her likeliest port of departure for Ireland. I wrote out a description of Miss Imlay, and asked Mrs Godwin to ascertain the likely contents of her travelling case. How much more grave my concerns became when that lady returned downstairs to report Fanny had taken with her only a small reticule, and the clothes she was wearing. 'And that watch that Mary bought for her in Swisserland,' she said. 'Make sure to mention that. Expensive, that was.'

Not two hours later I had boarded the coach bound for Swansea, taking with me George Fraser, having chosen him for the task above my other assistants, given his previous acquaintance with the two young women then in Bath. It was a slow and miserable journey, the weather wet and the horses over their fetlocks in mud, and having deposited Fraser at his destination, I arrived eventually at my own late in the afternoon of October 9th. A hard wind was blowing off the sea, and I wanted nothing more than a hot bath and an honest dinner, but disdaining both I made at once for the house of an acquaintance, a man in the employ of the port authorities. I have known and trusted him a dozen years or more, and many a time has he furnished me with vital information as to the arrivals and departures on the Irish packets. I have lost the reckoning of the criminals who have been thus apprehended, and the stolen property restored thereby. But this time, alas, we were both of us doomed to a terrible failure. There had been but one crossing that day, the wind being so foul, and there had been no young lady answering Miss Imlay's description aboard. Having extracted a promise for vigilance and dispatch I repaired to a small ill-favoured inn, where I ordered such a repast as the sour and slatternly landlady could offer, and retired as soon as I might to my bed, exhausted, dispirited and uneasy.

I did not know, then, that Godwin had received a letter from Fanny that very day, a letter that talked so wildly of a departure from which she hoped never to return that it had him starting immediately after her. I did not know — and it will haunt me to my dying day — that scarcely an hour after I had left the noisy and stinking tap-room at the Mackworth Arms there came a knock at the outer door and an enquiry, in low and trembling tones, whether there might be a room available for a respectable lady travelling unaccompanied. A small room only was required, and for that night alone. She would be gone, she said, by morning.

I wonder now, with pain, how she spent those last hours. How many times she put the bottle of laudanum to her lips before she had the courage to take the fatal dose. How sadly her thoughts must have returned to the mother she barely knew, who had tried, she too, to put an end to a life that had become to her unbearable. I wonder likewise if any circumstance might have prevented it. A kind word unlooked-for; a knock of concern at the door; a letter in a much-loved hand. But no help came. By the time a thin sun was rising over the bleak iron sea, I awoke to commotion and alarm in the corridor outside and arose in a terrified haste, my heart misgiving me and a terrible certainty weighing upon my heart like lead.

The maid it was who found her. The maid who needed only one glance at the young woman on the bed to know that something was dreadfully amiss. She was lying, fully clothed, above the counterpane, in one hand her sister's last gift, and in the other a single sheet of crumpled paper. I know all this, because I saw it. Before the doctor came, and the constable, and the idly and offensively curious, I thrust the maid from the room and slammed the door behind her. Then I went to the bedside and placed my hand against the pale forehead, and saw with a heart that faltered that on her eyelashes there still lingered tears. And then I took the paper from her cold and rigid fingers and read the words she had left for us to find.

I have long determined that the best thing I could do was to put an end to the existence of a being whose birth was unfortunate, and whose life has only been a series of pain to those persons who have hurt their health in endeavouring to promote her welfare. Perhaps to hear of my death will give you pain, but you will soon have the blessing of forgetting that such a creature ever existed as

Fanny Imlay

My duty – my professional duty – was clear. This note must remain, and the constable must see it. But I had a higher duty, or so I thought then. Not to her family, who, I feared, would be only too ready to commence their forgetting, but to the young woman herself. I knew what scandal and gossip would be whipped up by the very mention of her name, and what vile speculation would dog her to her grave, if it were bruited abroad that one connected so closely with the Godwin family had died here by her own hand, desolate and alone. Hearing footsteps on the stair I knew I had no time, and I made a decision I have never since regretted, not for one moment: I took the letter and tore the name away, then stepped quickly to the hearth and consigned the scrap of paper to the fire.

It was little enough, by way of a service, and not as decisive as I had hoped, for I discovered later that she had her mother's initials sewn into her stays, and I fear that the prying of a callous posterity will uncover the secret I was striving so desperately to keep. But for then, and I hope for some little time yet, it was enough – enough to keep her poor wounded name from the speculations of the newspapers, and cast the kindness of concealment about her last hours. And even if I had failed her living, I had the power to protect her dead. Swansea is a small town, and word of such an untoward incident promulgates only too quickly, but I was relentless. No effort was spared, no payment unmade, and by nightfall on the third day I had ensured that the inquest verdict was given merely as an unexplained death, and there would be none of those references to insanity or self-destruction as would have seen her corpse treated with indignity and disrespect.

My tasks of that first day completed, and a letter sent to Godwin to inform him, in the sparest terms, of his step-daughter's fate, I was sitting down at last to a cold and unsavoury dinner when the inn door flung open and I saw to my horror a face I recognized. He looked as ghastly as a man half dead, his face white, his coat stained with mud, and his cheeks blotched, as I now noted, with tears.

Shelley.

He was beginning to stammer some incoherent words to the terrified landlady, when he cast his eyes towards me and started backwards as if in terror. 'Maddox!' he cried, his voice failing. 'You come upon me like an Orestes – have I escaped the clutches of the relentless villain who pursues my every step only to find myself trapped once more, and beyond all expectation, in your stern and pitiless glare?'

  'If it is that same fellow to which you refer—' I began, when he interrupted me, a fire in his eyes.

'How vile you are to doubt me!' he cried, setting the wizened locals at the hearth pointing and whispering. 'I saw him – that creature – only yesterday. He was *there* – there I tell you – staring at me as I boarded the coach for Bristol – I went looking for her there – she wrote to me from there—'

And it was only at that instant, I think, that he realized I was not, after all, some dark excrescence of his own troubled mind – that I was real, and my presence was no coincidence, but compelled by the same dire misfortune that had brought him hither.

'But tell me not,' he gasped, 'that she – that you—'

I saw his look of terrible pain, I saw the flicker of a last and desperate hope, but my heart was frozen iron in my breast. And so I told him everything that had happened, everything I had done, every last and dreadful detail. Without mercy, without kindness, without sparing.

Anyone else would have pitied him then. Had I not known what this man had done, I too might have pitied him. But I did not. I held the knife, I knew the wound, and I twisted the blade with all the savagery in my power.

'I saw her,' he stammered at length. 'Two days ago. She wrote to me asking me to meet her off the London coach. She said – she *promised* – that she was on her way to Dublin. That her aunts had relented – that she looked forward to happiness at last. But her voice was quivering as she said the words—' His voice broke then, and he buried his head in his hands, weeping uncontrollably that he had not known, that she had never said, not expressly, and that the whole world was not wide enough to contain his misery. Not now.

I was on the point of berating him yet further – of telling him what heedless hurt he caused to all the women unfortunate enough to encounter him, all those other young women he induced to love him, be he aware of it or not – when he suddenly gave out a piercing cry and fell to the ground, his body racked by fearful spasms. The landlady was upon us in an instant, terrified at the sight, but I had seen those fits of his before; I knew they always supervened at some moment of sudden shock or high-wrought feeling, and never led to the fatal consequences the landlady clearly apprehended. I likewise suspected – though I have voiced the thought only once, and to no avail – that Shelley was not above simulating such attacks, as a means to divert attention from whatever culpability might otherwise have attached itself, at those moments, to him. I instructed the landlady, therefore, that he should merely be put to bed in one of the rooms upstairs and the doctor sent for in due course, should the symptoms not abate.

I myself was too exhausted to attempt anything further that night, and charged the landlady not to wake me unless in case of emergency, or should a message come from the coroner. Imagine my irritation, then, when there was a loud knock at my chamber before first light. I arose wearily and opened the door, and found the maid holding a note in what I knew to be Shelley's hand.

I can do no more for her. All that could be done, you have done; and I have received this last hour, a letter from Godwin urging my return to Bath. He begs me not to disturb the silent dead – to comply with her own last wish for obscurity, and avoid at all costs any risk that his wife and remaining children might be exposed to the horror of the public papers. Should I remain for the obsequies, that risk must only be augmented, and I will, therefore, depart this very morning – this very hour – and return to my Mary, knowing that even if her family will not be present to see poor Fanny committed to the earth, that you, at least, will undertake that sad duty in our stead.

P. B. S.

I write out these words from memory; the note itself I cast into the fire in disgust, within a moment of reading it.

Of that interment, I wish not to speak. The rain driving in off the sea, the black-suited clergyman racing through the service that he might return to the comfort of his own fat fireside, and the bodies, three of them, sewn into their rough sacks, heaved one by one into the tainted pit of a pauper's grave. I did not even know which one was hers.

A vile journey I endured home, with none of the comforts of my own private carriage, the public coach crowded, and the heavy wheels jarring and jolting on the dirty road. Fraser, I knew, had already returned to London, so I spent all that long expanse of hours cast in my own thoughts, and debating whether I could, in conscience, continue with Godwin's commission, given the base opinion I now entertained of he who had hired me. I understood his terror of the press, I had sympathy with his wish to avoid further needless scandal, but I could not – and do not – forgive him for having abandoned that poor child to be buried alone and nameless, and with no one who loved her by. I have discovered since that he and his wife contrived to conduct themselves so calmly – so coldly indeed – in the face of this tragedy that not one person in their household had the smallest apprehension of the truth; I have discovered likewise that they continue, even now, to give out all manner of spurious accounts to explain the young woman's supposed absence, and even after so many weeks have passed one of her step-brothers still has not the slightest notion of her death.

I returned at last, dirty and hungry, to my own house. Perhaps it was the sad fate of poor Fanny Imlay, or the fruit of too much solitary introspection, but I found myself, that night, overwhelmed by a sudden foreboding. I told myself my fears were irrational, but I could not rid myself of them, knowing as I did that no one had suffered more at Shelley's hands than his wife, and that she, even more than Fanny, had seen her young life blighted for ever by his brutish selfishness. Late as it was, therefore, I summoned Jacob Todd, the man I had set to ingratiate himself with one of the serving-maids at the Westbrook house in Chapel-street, in the hope we might come thereby by news of Mrs Shelley, and yet in all that time he had discovered nothing. Todd confessed, at length, that he had recently seen Mrs Shelley's sister leave the house for several hours together, but had not followed her, being – I suspected, though he denied it – too engrossed by the object of his feigned affections, to attend to the task he had been engaged to pursue. I berated him then, and cruelly, accusing him of a careless and indefensible breach that might have consequences far beyond any he was competent to conceive. Once I had sent him from the room and dismissed him from my service, I instructed Fraser to watch the movements of Miss Eliza Westbrook. I had been told by my informants that she and Harriet enjoyed a remarkable intimacy, given that there were some thirteen years between them, and I knew the elder sister had, indeed, lived for some months with the Shelleys when first they married. That this state of affairs had degenerated into bitter recriminations, even before the poet's desertion of his wife, did not surprise me; that Miss Westbrook was among the most zealous in her family to punish the reprobate, and disgrace him publicly, surprised me even less. But all that concerned me for the moment was that Eliza, if anyone, would know where her sister had fled.

In the week that followed I received, almost daily, supplications from Godwin to augment the account I had sent him from Swansea with whatever further information I had now at my disposal; supplications I steadfastly refused to gratify with even the briefest of replies. I cared not for his feelings, judging he possessed very few; I did care, and very much, about Mrs Shelley, where she might be, and what circumstances had driven her to such a reckless course of action. I feared the worst, and those fears were brought to a greater and more painful intensity when Fraser brought me word that the Westbrooks had hired a young man, one William Alder by name, to drag the ponds in the area of Hyde-park nearest the house. My distress on hearing of this was extreme, but Fraser soon established that nothing had been found. It was some time before I was to receive further news, and I attempted to engross my mind with other pressing cases recently neglected, until one morning in November I was woken by Fraser pounding on my door an hour before breakfast and calling to me, hot-faced and out of breath, that Miss Westbrook had dressed the children herself before the rest of the household was awake, and taken them to an address near Hans-place, Brompton.

'And I know as why she chose it,' he said, in his deep, slow tones, as we waited for the carriage to be brought round. 'That fellow Alder has lodgings in the same house. Seems likely he might have found a room for her there. And that husband of hers has been there too.'

'Are you certain?' I enquired, my attention aroused.

'The landlady's daughter described him to the life. Said she'd seen him two or three times since the young woman moved in, the latest only last week.'

I glanced at him, wondering, not for the first time, at the facility he displayed in obtaining information from women; the fair sex seemed to find him unaccountably appealing, despite his shaven head, broken nose, and less than engaging manner. I had employed him for quite other reasons, and in that role he had never failed: many a man had had cause to regret lying to me, after enduring the undivided attentions of George Fraser. He had a talent for persuasion of the physical kind, and I never scrupled to employ that talent in a just cause, but it appeared I had underestimated other, more intangible capacities, which have since proved almost as valuable on occasion.

'You must be mistaken,' I began. 'I have had a lad watching the Marchmont-street lodgings from the first, and he insists that Shelley has not returned to town.'

'That's as may be, guv,' he replied slowly, transparently sceptical. 'But I don't see as how anyone could mistake Shelley. Never seen such an odd-looking cove, and that's a fact.'

I could not disagree, and indeed it chimed oddly with an experience I had had of my own, some three or four months earlier, of which Fraser could not be aware, when I had thought I glimpsed Shelley walking ahead of me in the Strand, even though I knew to my certain knowledge he was not then in England.

The carriage arriving at that moment, we spoke of this no more, and less than half an hour later the coachman set us down outside the lodging-house, where I made myself known to the lady proprietor of the establishment and asked if I might go up to Mrs Shelley's rooms. She could not be unaware of the richness of my equipage, and she was now eyeing my attire with an interest that was evident to me, despite her attempts to disguise it. It cannot have been often that she welcomed gentlemen so handsomely accoutred.

'Mrs Shelley, sir?' she said, looking – or feigning – ignorance. 'We have no lady by that name here.'

'A lady of below middle height,' intervened Fraser, who had the advantage of me as to her appearance. 'Rather plump than trim as far as her figure goes. Quite a beauty once, I should say.'

'Ah,' said the landlady, with a look I could not at once decipher, 'you must mean Mrs *Smith*. Do you bring word from her husband? She is hoping to see him every day.'

'But did he not—' began Fraser, but I replaced a restraining hand on his arm, and requested he return to the carriage and await me there; I did not wish that all the information at my disposal should so quickly be revealed.

'I am, as you so cleverly surmised, a fr—' But my tongue stumbled against the word, and I could not utter it. 'A business connection of her husband's. It has but recently come to my knowledge that his wife has been reduced to the painful circumstances in which she now finds herself, and I wish to do all in my power to assist her.'

That last, in any event, was the absolute truth.

'Well,' sniffed the woman, folding her arms, and looking up and down at my fine marcella waistcoat. 'You can begin by assisting *me* with the *money*. A month's rent she owes me, and that's a fact.'

I smiled in what I hoped was a gracious manner, and proceeded to take my pocket-book from my coat and count out the coins, one by one. Her acquiescence, if not her confidence, thus purchased, she informed me that the young lady's room was 'at the top – the last you get to,' and left me to find my own way up.

As I climbed the narrow stairs and smelt the damp seeping from the walls, I knew what I would in all likelihood find: a tiny room cramped under the eaves, with but a small window and the whole place no doubt reeking. And when I reached the last landing I could see at once that some, at least, of my assumptions were correct. I knocked sharply and heard a few moments later the sound of a bolt drawing back and a light but weary female voice saying, 'If it's about the rent—' as the door swung open. 'Oh,' she said then, drawing back and frowning, 'I took you for Mrs Thomas.'

I had wondered at Fraser's remark that Mrs Shelley must 'once' have been a beauty, for I could not believe she was much more than twenty, but I understood his observation now. The woman who stood before me looked at least a dozen years more, with none of the freshness and bloom of youth the calendar surely owed her. Her brown hair was lank, her eyes lustreless, and if her figure did indeed incline to *enbonpoint*, her face was gaunt and her skin dull.

'Who are you?' she said, holding the door close, and pulling her shawl about her. 'What do you want?'

'It is, indeed, about the rent, or at least in one respect,' I replied, as I proceeded to inform her that I had just had the honour to assist her with that particular obligation.

The smile that greeted this information was enough to show me how lovely she must once have been. It illuminated her whole face, lifting the lines from her eyes, and setting the ghost of a flush on her thin cheeks.

'Do you come from Shelley?' she said, with a gasp. 'Is he well – does he want to see the children?'

How I cursed the man then, in my soul; to have abandoned this young woman so callously, depriving her of the protection she had every right to expect, and leaving her suspended in a pitiable state that was neither marriage nor widowhood. 'I regret,' I began, 'that I have no commission from him. But what I may do for you, you may rely upon.' I handed her then my card and saw at once she knew the name.

'Maddox,' she said slowly. 'I believe I have heard of you. Did you not assist Shelley in the matter of Tremadoc, a year or so past? I saw him so rarely at that time, and things were not well between us . . .'

Her voice trailed off then, and I saw her put her hand to her eyes. 'I did attempt to be of assistance,' I continued, affecting, out of delicacy, not to notice her gesture, 'but I am afraid I found neither testimony nor evidence to corroborate your husband's assertions.'

'You might have had mine,' she replied, a little tartly, 'had you asked. I could have confirmed every word. I witnessed it all. The

204

shots of the gun, the damage to the wainscoting, the cries of revenge. It was truly terrifying.' She pulled her shawl once again about her. 'No one knows the truth of that night but Shelley and I. Neither what happened, nor why.'

It was a curious thing to say, in the circumstances, and I was about to question her further when there came a sound from within, and as she turned back into the room I saw a little girl, perhaps three years old, sitting on the threadbare chair near the fire. She seemed a delightful child, her hair golden, her eyes as blue as her father's, and her rosy cheeks plump and dimpled; whatever hardships her mother might now be enduring, it was clear this child was well fed and nurtured. She whimpered again, then, and I saw that her doll had fallen to the floor and I stepped forward at once, forestalling her mother, and restored the plaything to the child's lap.

'What a pretty string of blue beads you are wearing,' I remarked, not knowing what else to say, and never having had experience of talking to children.

'They were her father's gift,' said Mrs Shelley. 'He hung them from the hood of her cradle, the day she was born, and now she cannot bear to be parted from them.'

'What is her name?'

'Ianthe,' she replied. 'Ianthe Eliza.'

'It is a pretty name. And an unusual one. From Ovid – the *Metamorphoses*.' I was about to relate the story, but recalling that it is, after all, rather a disconcerting one, I thought better of it.

Mrs Shelley, for her part, smiled sadly. 'I know nothing of such things. All I know is that Bysshe was most insistent on the name. He wished her to be called Ianthe Mary, but I have never liked the latter, and I insisted in my turn on Eliza, for my sister. And I am thankful now that I did. How could I have borne to have my little girl share *her* name? To be reminded every day of *her* and what she did, and the ruin she has made of my life, as if I do not have memories enough to torment me?'

Again, I thought bitterly, again Shelley evades all blame, again his conduct is excused, and the women he has ruined torture them*selves* in their desperate endeavour to exonerate him.

'*She* is culpable, not he,' said Mrs Shelley, seeing my look, and guessing perhaps my thought. 'We were happy, he and I, before he met her. We had our darling daughter and another coming, and all was well, before he became infatuated with that horrid old man William Godwin. And then *she* seduced him with all her wild talk and taking him day after day to her mother's grave, till at last she told him she was overcome with passion for him, and gave herself to him, then and there, on the very gravestone her mother lay beneath. It is not right, Mr Maddox, it is not *right*.'

By now she was weeping piteously, and as I saw her search blindly for a handkerchief I offered my own. And as she took it, and as the shawl slipped a moment from her grasp, I saw. I saw her secret, and I knew what it was that had driven her from her father's house.

'You are with child?' I asked gently.

She flashed me a look then, though whether of anger, fear, or shame, I could not tell. 'Please go now. I do not wish you to be here when my sister returns.'

'But surely there is more I can do to assist you – does your husband even know of your condition?'

'No!' she cried, her eyes wild. 'And he must not be told of it! *Never!*'

'But he must discharge his duty!' I exclaimed, my mind in fury. 'Not merely towards your existing children, but towards this one. To have behaved so despicably – to have continued to exercise all the rights of a husband while presenting himself in that character to another woman – another woman who has already borne him two children—'

'You do not understand,' she wept. 'He is not to blame – I have not seen him – not since – not since long before—'

But I knew she was lying: I was certain Shelley had visited her there, just as he had, all too probably, visited her at Chapel-street prior to his departure for Geneva, and the miserable predicament in which she now found herself was the only too obvious result. I was on the point of remonstrating with her once more, despite her tears, when the door flew open and a woman strode into the room, holding a small boy by the hand. He ran at once to his sister's chair where he climbed up beside her, and proceeded to watch us in that quiet, circumspect way children acquire who have known little but disturbance in their lives, and wish not to add to the sum of it. The young woman in question – though I use the adjective out of courtesy, rather than exactness – turned at once to me. The first impression I gained of her was of a height and an appearance utterly at odds with her sister's; from a distance she might well have been deemed handsome, with her abundant black hair and pale complexion, but standing as I was, within a few feet of her, I could see that her skin was seamed with the smallpox and of a dead white, and her hair, of which she was evidently very proud, coarse and wiry.

'Who are you, sir?' she demanded. 'My sister is not nearly well enough to receive casual visitors.'

'Please, Eliza,' whispered Mrs Shelley, going at once to her side. 'Mr Maddox was offering to help me. Perhaps he might be able, if he knew—'

'*I* can give you all the assistance you need,' replied Miss Westbrook, firmly, leading her resolutely to the bed. 'You need no one but me, Harriet,' she said, as she settled her gently against the pillows. 'You have never needed anyone but me, and now that that villain has gone, we may be together once more, and for ever.'

Seeing her then, bent over her sister's prone body, her hand to her cheek, and her eyes full of a burning tenderness, I wondered.

Wondered if Mrs Shelley might have sought more than concealment in fleeing her father's house; wondered, indeed, whether the story she once told Shelley of her yearning to escape a domestic oppression might have had nothing to do with a supposed parental tyranny, but have been, instead, a naïve and girlish attempt to describe a domination of a far subtler nature, and from which, it seemed to me, she had never truly escaped.

At that moment Miss Westbrook seemed to recall my presence, for she straightened up, marched swiftly to the door and held it open. There was no mistaking the gesture, just as there was no mistaking the look that flickered across Mrs Shelley's face as I stepped briefly towards her and made my bow. 'You know where you may find me, Mrs Shelley,' I said gravely, contriving to leave a fold of banknotes on the table by the bed. 'I am at your service, and will remain so.'

'Mr Maddox?' said Miss Westbrook as I drew level with her in the doorway. 'Do not call again. We need no interference from strangers. However seemingly benevolent.'

I had, needless to say, no intention of acceding to this demand, but recognizing that it was useless to attempt to see Mrs Shelley again in her sister's presence, I judged it best to wait until the morrow, and call upon her again then. But, other urgent business calling me from town, I was not able to make good on this intention. The first I knew, therefore, of what had occurred was when I was summoned from my breakfast on Sunday to see 'a lady'. A most insistent lady, the housemaid informed me, and not to be gainsaid, despite the day and the early hour. I did not stay to don my coat, but went down at once. It was not – as I hoped – Mrs Shelley but Miss Westbrook I found awaiting me there. I had scarce opened the office door when she fell upon me with fevered eyes, gripping my arms and commanding me in ragged tones to reveal what I had done with her sister.

'I have done nothing with her, madam,' I countered stoutly, pushing her, somewhat indelicately, from me.

'You *must* know!' she cried. 'I know all about you – going to her lodgings claiming to be her friend and all the while in the pocket of that odious man. And do not seek to deny it – I saw the note she left – she found out, you know, what the two of you were conspiring—'

At this moment George Fraser came to the door with a look of enquiry on his weather-beaten features, attracted, no doubt, by the sound of raised voices. I assured him that all was well, and requested he ring the bell and have the maid bring coffee. I then turned back once more to my interlocutress. The interruption had done little to calm her fury: her sallow cheeks were red and her bosom heaving with suppressed emotion.

'Perhaps,' I said, indicating a chair, 'you would have the goodness to explain what you mean, Miss Westbrook, and then I will attempt to be of assistance to you. The discovery of persons absconded, kidnapped or otherwise missing being one of the services I am pleased to offer.'

If such words sound sardonic now, I fear they were indeed so; at the time I thought only that poor Mrs Shelley had endured her sister's suffocating affections long enough, and had sought, for a few days at least, to elude them. I knew furthermore that she now had money, and might have secured herself a room in a far more salubrious establishment than Hans-place. Miss Westbrook, meanwhile, glared at me with near palpable hatred, and for a moment I thought she was on the point of hurling abuse in my face and storming from the room, but I have encountered such as her before and I continued coolly to hold her gaze. A few moments later she dropped her eyes and sat, almost meekly, in the chair I had proffered. I likewise took a seat, and composed myself upon it. 'Now, Miss Westbrook, perhaps we might advance a little. You say your sister is no longer at her lodgings?'

209

'She has not been seen since taking an early dinner yesterday,' she replied forlornly. 'Mrs Thomas said she had become ever more despondent and gloomy since Thursday last, saying little and keeping largely to her bed. That was when *you* called, Maddox – this is all *your* fault—'

I held up my hand. 'There is no evidence whatsoever to support that assertion, Miss Westbrook, and I am not accustomed to let such unfounded accusations go by unchallenged. Now, you spoke of a note?'

She nodded, and extracted a sheet of paper from her reticule.

Is it not enough that I should be pursued by those dreadful letters, but that they should harry me now in person? That man – that Maddox – is in Godwin's pay – he is Godwin's creature. The mischief that man has made is not to be told & now he wants nothing more than to get me out of the way so he can marry his daughter off to my husband. Money, money, money is all he thinks on & my Bysshe it is who has paid the price. He is no longer the man I loved – a cruel imposter has taken his place. I know now there is no joy in this unhappy world; I can only pray there is another where those that have endured as much suffering as I will at last find peace.

Do not think to follow—

'To what letters does she refer?' I said, my voice suddenly hoarse.

'Do not feign ignorance,' Miss Westbrook hissed. 'You know very well that she has received letter after letter, each one viler than the last, telling her that no one regards her, that it would be better for all if she were to put an end to a life that is a torment to her, and which renders her nothing but a burden to all those unfortunate enough to be associated with her.'

'And whence do these letters come?' I asked, my throat dry, though I knew the answer; knew and feared it.

'From *Bath*,' she replied. 'From *Bath*. As well you know.'

I got up from my chair then, and walked to the window, remembering that it was just such a letter, from that same place, that had cast poor Fanny Imlay into the last melancholy that had driven her to a pauper's grave. Remembering that, and cursing myself in equal measure that Harriet Shelley had discovered – I knew not how – that I remained, in theory if not in fact, employed by the one man she seemed most to fear.

I turned then and strode to the door, and called down to Fraser to have the carriage brought round at once. Then I faced my interlocutress and took a deep breath. 'You are correct in one respect, Miss Westbrook. I *was* – I stress the word – recently commissioned by Mr Godwin to discover the whereabouts of your sister.' She gasped then and half rose to her feet, but I interrupted her, 'Please hear me out. I said I *was* employed. By the time I paid that call on your sister I no longer considered myself to be so. The concern I expressed for her situation was genuine, and sincere. And I give you my word that I have told him nothing of her being at Hans-place. If he has knowledge of that address he has not had it from me.'

I confess I feared a tirade then – a rain of fists or a fit of hysterics – but I was wrong. She merely slipped slowly back into the chair and began to weep. Great gasping sobs that seemed to tear her very frame apart.

'What am I to do?' she wailed. 'I cannot bear the thought of life without her. If she has harmed herself – if she has left me—'

I moved quickly towards her then, and helped her to her feet. 'As I stated before, Miss Westbrook, I am skilled in recovering those who are absent, from whatever cause. Indeed, there is no man in London better placed than I to find your sister. But I need your help. You knew her best, and it is vital, therefore, that you recruit your spirits as well as you may and assist me, for her quick discovery may depend on something that you alone know, even if you are not at present aware of it.'

She nodded then and endeavoured to still her tears. Fraser, meanwhile, appeared at the door with my coat over one arm and my hat in his hand, saying the carriage awaited us downstairs.

*

Hans-place was much as I remembered it, as was Mrs Shelley's room, though it seemed, if anything, smaller and more cramped without her. I asked Miss Westbrook to look over her possessions, lest there should be some clue only she might perceive, but I did not need her assistance to conclude that her sister had taken but few clothes with her. Her personal effects likewise remained, meagre as they were, and her small writing-case was found to contain a number of letters sent her by Shelley, though none of these were from Bath, and all – as far as I could tell – must have been written nearly two years before, in the first few weeks after he had abandoned her. I felt my face grow hot with indignation as I read the unutterably careless and self-regarding words he had penned to her, telling the woman about to bear him a child that she had never filled his heart with an all-sufficing passion, and accusing her one moment of mean and despicable selfishness, and demanding the next that she send him clean stockings. There were no other papers aside from this, and certainly nothing that might explain how Mrs Shelley had come to know of my connection with Godwin. Nor could her sister enlighten me further in this respect. But then a thought occurred to me. I persuaded Miss Westbrook – with some difficulty, I confess – to stay for me in the carriage, and had Fraser summon William Alder from his room on the floor below. It being the Sabbath, I judged we would find him at home, and no doubt still abed, and it was indeed only a few minutes later that I heard the sound of two men ascending the stairs.

*

Alder revealed himself to be a young man of some self-assurance, with rather fine features for one of his class and an abler tongue than most such. Fraser showed him into the room, and then stood with his back against the door. I think it must have been at that moment that Alder sensed things were not all they may have seemed.

He looked to me, to Fraser, and then to me once more. 'What's afoot, gentlemen?'

I affected to be absorbed in the letters on the table. 'We wished to ask you some questions about Mrs *Smith*.'

'She's a'right, ain't she? I was worried when I didn't see 'er last night.'

'As well you might be. Mrs *Shelley* has disappeared,' I said, turning slowly to face him, 'and there is a very great deal of evidence to suggest that *you*, Alder, may have had a hand in it.'

'*Me?*' he spluttered. 'I only tried to 'elp 'er! She needed somewhere to stay for a while and I knew there was a room free 'ere. What she did after that, I ain't got a clue – honest to God.'

'You have worked at her father's house, I believe?'

He nodded. 'As a plumber. That's 'ow I earns me bread.'

'And hence Mr Westbrook asked you to assist him in the dragging of the Hyde-park ponds?'

He was red-faced now, and merely nodded once more.

'And you did not think to spare yourself the trouble, and Mr Westbrook both the expense and the undoubted distress of such a proceeding, by informing him that his daughter was all the time resident here?'

'She made me promise, on me ma's life, not to say nothin'. Weren't my place to interfere, were it?' he finished sullenly.

'And was it *your place*, Alder,' I said, moving towards him as he retreated uneasily, 'to meddle in my business, and carry stories of that business to Mrs Shelley – stories, may I inform you, that have proved to be completely erroneous, and as a result may have contributed directly to this latest disappearance?'

His face was white now. 'Don't know what you're talkin' about, guv. Honest.'

'I should be careful how I bandied such a word, Alder. It may return to haunt you in the most unpleasant fashion.'

Alder had by now backed within a foot of Fraser, who took hold suddenly of his arm, twisting it hard behind his back.

''Ere – leave me alone – I ain't done nothin' – I swear.'

'On your mother's life?' I said, raising an eyebrow. 'I should not be so rash, in your position, for I have my own means of finding out people, and Fraser here is not the sort of caller most elderly ladies would wish to find at the door, in the dark, when they are in the house alone.'

'All right, all right,' he rasped, his features contorted in pain. 'I'll tell yer.'

I nodded to Fraser, who loosened his grip, but did not release it.

'I was workin' at the Chapel-street 'ouse again a few weeks back, when I 'eard one of the maids say she 'ad a new fancy-man. Only she weren't too sure of 'im 'cause 'e seemed more interested in what was goin' on in the 'ouse than 'e was in 'er. That got me thinkin' so when I saw 'im later I took it into me 'ead to follow 'im along. And 'e led me straight back to your place. Nice crib that, though yer gutters needs replacin'. That's 'ow I knew it were you when you came 'ere. Would've recognized that carriage anywhere, never mind round 'ere.'

'I see,' I said, keeping my expression impassive, but impressed, despite myself. 'And how did you discover the connection to Mr Godwin?'

He shrugged. 'That were just luck. I was just about to 'ook it when I saw another fellow come to the door, so I sidled a bit closer and made as if to tie me boot. Then I 'eard 'im say 'e 'ad an urgent message from Mr Godwin for Mr Maddox. That's 'ow I knew your name, and 'is name, and after you left 'ere I went up and told 'er, and all the blood drained from 'er face. I knew then as you were bad news.'

His tone was defiant now, as if daring me to contradict him. Fraser caught my eye and I nodded.

I took up my hat. 'I will await you in the carriage, Fraser. See that Mr Alder here is left in no doubt as to the very great unwisdom of daring to cross me. But do him no permanent damage. Once he has learned his lesson, I intend to offer him a position. In my employ.'

As indeed I did. Alder proved, in fact, invaluable in the following days, spurred no doubt as much by the prospect of a very much more lucrative occupation, as by feelings of personal culpability in relation to Mrs Shelley. I set him to maintain a watch on Hans-place, and obtain what intelligence he could from the occupants; a task facilitated, no doubt, by the *affaire* he was already conducting with the maidservant, one Mary Jones. He likewise told me everything he knew as to Mrs Shelley's movements in the previous weeks, but of her present where-abouts and future intentions, he could offer no insight. I was not, at first, deterred by this, having a just estimation both of my own talents and the means at my disposal, but as the days lengthened into weeks I became both dispirited and ever more apprehensive. My men could discover no trace of her, neither at the most likely lodging-houses, nor at any of the London coach depots. I endeavoured, more than once, and with increasing insistence, to persuade Miss Westbrook to inform her father of what she knew, but I could not prevail. I fear that her failure to reveal her sister's first place of refuge coloured her judgement in this, and led her to shrink from what I can only concur would be a justified rebuke.

*

November had passed and December commenced before I received any word of Mrs Shelley. I was at dinner in Downing-street, whence I had been invited to offer my advice as to the apprehension of the miscreants responsible for the late disturbances in Spa-fields, when the waiter slipped me a message in Fraser's hand: *Alder has seen her – Chapel-street.* I made my excuses immediately and hurried down to the waiting carriage. The night was dark and the fog so heavy we could not move at any pace through the crowded streets, and I half despaired of arriving in time, but the carriage eventually drew to a halt a few yards from the Westbrook residence, and Alder stepped forward to open the door.

'Saw 'er by chance, guv. I were in two minds whether to try to talk to 'er but thought it best to send for you instead.'

I glanced at him; there was still the ghost of a bruise along his jaw and I could well understand that he wished to run no risk of further intimacy with George Fraser.

'She's been 'ere 'alf an hour and more. Just walkin' up and down. Cryin' I think she is, and talkin' to 'erself. Once or twice I saw 'er approach the door but then seem to think better of it.'

'And you have not informed Miss Westbrook, or anyone else in the house?'

He shook his head. 'No, guv. I judged as I'd leave that to you.'

I nodded, and turned to look down the street. A little distance ahead of me, I could see a figure walking away from me slowly in the mist; even at that distance I knew from her gait that it was a woman, and one much advanced in pregnancy. I could, as I intimated to Alder, have gone quietly to the door and summoned Miss Westbrook, but I did not see a way of doing so without alerting the whole household, and I judged likewise that had Mrs Shelley wished to see her sister she had had ample time already to do so. By that judgement I stand, but I cannot acquit myself of not perceiving the degree of alarm my own appearance would

216

engender. I knew she feared Godwin, but I did not comprehend the full extent of that fear, or the terror she might conceive at the merest glimpse of a man she believed to be hounding her at his behest. I should have deduced this, but I did not; I should have sent Alder in my place, knowing that she had deemed him her friend, but to my everlasting regret, I did not.

Ordering Alder instead to remain by the carriage, I started down the pavement towards her. The fog thickened suddenly and I hastened my step, but the heavy air so absorbed all sound that I was almost upon her before she heard my approach. She turned then and I saw her face – a face at once stricken with panic.

'*You – you,*' she stammered, clutching her shawl tighter about her.

'Do not distress yourself,' I said. 'I wish only to assist you.'

'You said that before,' she whispered, taking a pace backwards, 'and then I discovered you are working for him – for *them.*'

'I work for no one, I give you my word.'

'I do not believe you – why else would you—'

'Because I have had dealings with your husband in the past, and I know the cruelty – the wanton, careless cruelty – of which he is capable.'

'No, no – you misjudge him – it is *her* – if it were not for her he might return to me – we might be happy again.'

I stepped forward then and gripped her hand. 'Do not think it – do not *wish* it. The last time I saw your husband it was in the same house where a young woman had destroyed herself – destroyed herself out of love of *him*, a love he allowed, even encouraged, but had no more thought of returning than he does of returning to *you.*'

I spoke it out of a desire to free her – I spoke it because my greatest fear was that he might indeed seek to return to her, and I wished her to have the strength to refuse him. I knew my intentions to be honourable, but I did not allow sufficiently for the effect such words must have had upon a woman – upon a spirit so distraught, a heart so sorely wounded. I had accused him – and justly – of cruelty, but I stand accused in my own mind of no less a crime.

'*No, no,*' she cried again, wrenching her fingers from my grasp. 'It is all a lie, all a wicked, wicked lie.'

And she turned from me and ran, stumbling, blinded by the tears that were streaming from her eyes. I hesitated a moment – a cursed moment – then set off after her, calling her name, but we were hard by the entrance to the park, and by the time I reached it she had disappeared into the darkness. I remained there for some moments more, then spent more precious minutes retracing my steps to the carriage, where I ordered Alder, somewhat breathlessly, to muster as many men as we had and conduct a search of both the park and the streets around.

They found nothing – then. I was still awake at three the following morning when Fraser returned to say there was no sight or trace of her. My relief at these words was profound, but all too short-lived. This was Saturday; it was Tuesday morning that I received the note from Alder that destroyed all my hopes. He begged my presence without delay at the sign of the Fox and Bull in Knights-bridge. They had brought a woman's remains to the inn, he said, through the old gate leading into the park whence all those found drowned were always conveyed. He said no more, but I knew; knew he would not have summoned me so unless he was certain beyond all possibility of doubt.

And so it was for the second time in as many months I stood before the body of a young woman ruined by love of that man, confronting the piteous waste of a death that could have been prevented – a death, in this case, that I seemed only to have hastened. I blamed Shelley – blamed him bitterly – but I knew I merited my own share of censure.

The water had been cruel. Her body was bloated, the rank cloth clinging to the swollen form of her dead child, and her sweet face mottled with the taint of rottenness. These are not, I know, the words of a practitioner of my art, but my feelings were not the feelings of a professional man. Indeed, had one of my subordinates displayed such a weakness in the face of death I should have cashiered him at once and without reprieve. And knowing that, I strove to regain my self-command and assess the corpse not as a man who had known her, but with the dispassionate and appraising eye of the detective, scrutinizing the cadaver for signs of violence, and seeking to determine how long it had been immersed. But grim indeed was that examination. I could see no obvious wound – no marks I might have feared about her neck – and I was forced to conclude, with infinite sorrow, that she had indeed ended her own existence. A jewelled ring remained on her finger, and there was a small purse in her pocket, which contained, I discovered, a single sheet of paper, badly spoiled, and barely legible. The ring I left; the paper I removed, and without the slightest compunction.

I have it now, and copy it here. It is a dark tale this paper tells, a tale of death, and grief, and guilt; some part of it I believe I comprehend, but it holds secrets that even now remain obscure to me, and shrouded in mystery.

As for myself, I had protected one young woman from public scandal and ignominy; I now faced the same distasteful task once more. It was harder, in the gossip of the metropolis, to achieve my end, but I knew the coroner, John Gell, and the editor of *The Times* was in my debt. I likewise persuaded Sir Nathaniel Conant, the chief magistrate at Bow-street, to allow me free rein, though

This – this is not to be forgot –

He met himself, walking in the garden

His grief remained – let it
remain – untold—

Then hear thy chosen own, too late,
His heart most worthy of thy hate
For pale with anguish is his cheek
His breath comes fast, his eyes are dim,
In mercy let him not endure
The misery of a fatal cure

without thee, can I tell my woes?
And with thee, can I speak my grief?

Shall I wakes then those horrors anew
That swelled in my desperate brain
When to death's darkened portals I flew
And sought misery's relief to my pain?'

Fiends would relent
Knew they the snares that there for memory lay

Ianthe will remain with you always

Dear lovely child—

That stream so swift that rushes along
Has oft been dyed by the murder's song;
It oft has heard the exulting wave
Of one who oft the murdered braved.

He bears a load which nothing can remove
A killing, withering weight

See that fair form that he can save.
Her garments are tattered, her bosom so bare?
She shrieks from the yawning watery grave.
And, shivering, around her enwraps dark hair.

O thou, whose radiant eyes and beamy smile
Yet even a sweeter somewhat indexing—
Have known full many an hour of mine to guile
Which else would only bitter memories bring

The breath of night like death did flow
Beneath the sinking moon.
The wintry hedge was black,
The green grass was not seen,
Thine eyes glowed in the glare
Of the moon's dying light,
As a fen-fire's beam
On a sluggish stream
Gleams dimly – so the moon shone there,
And it yellowed the strings of thy tangled hair

Would I were as sinless fair and young
As innocent of sorrow & shame
As those who in thy cold embraces sleep
Ere misery has made my living corpse
Too bitter food for thee

The moon made thy lips pale, beloved;
The wind made thy bosom chill;
The night did shed
On thy dear head
Its frozen dew, and thou didst lie
Where the bitter breath of the naked sky
Might visit thee at will,

It is not true – the past may come again –

The waters
close and leave
no trace

Full many a mind with radiant genius fraught
Is taught the dark scowl of misery to bear;
How many a great soul has often sought
To stem the sad torrent of wild despair

not without profound misgivings, knowing he trusted me, and I had never before abused that trust. I then instructed William Alder to take up residence at the Fox and Bull, so as to be on hand to give witness at the inquest, and ensure that Mary Jones gave the name of the deceased as Harriet Smith, and provided only such further evidence as was strictly necessary. The jury sat barely a quarter of an hour before returning, as I had ensured, a verdict of 'Found Dead in the Serpentine River'. The body I then caused to be taken to the Paddington cemetery and buried there under her assumed *alias*.

A second pauper's grave, a second desolate and windswept interment, the only persons present the minister, myself and Miss Westbrook, her face heavily veiled, scarce able to support herself in the wretchedness of her grief.

'We will have our revenge, my love,' she whispered hoarsely, falling to her knees in the mud as the body was lowered into the grave. 'Papa will institute a process in Chancery for custody of the children, and expose that man to the world as a profligate and an atheist. All who know him will abhor and shun him for the murderer he is.'

'I must, I fear, bear some responsibility myself,' I began, assisting her to her feet as the sexton turned the first soil upon the pit. 'I am very much afraid that our last meeting only served to distress your sister further, and that had I acted differently—'

But she was already shaking her head. 'If you are to blame, then so am I. I was away from the house on Saturday and did not receive this until I returned.'

She put her hand into her reticule and drew from it a letter. 'She must have left it at the door and waited in the street, hoping – expecting – that I would come out to her. And I did not. I can hardly bear to think what must have passed through her mind. She must have thought I no longer loved her – that I did not care . . .'

I had no great regard for Miss Westbrook, but I did pity her then. I pressed her hand. 'She would not have believed so.'

She shook her head once more and put her handkerchief to her eyes as she watched me read her sister's last words. A letter she copied for me later, at my request, and sent to me at Buckingham-street. A letter that tore my heart; a letter no man could peruse without seeing – in the tears that stained it, in the very orthography – the most afflicting proof of the depths of her despair.

Sat. Eve.

When you read this let'. I shall be no more an inhabitant of this miserable world. do not regret the loss of one who could never be anything but a source of vexation & misery to you all belonging to me. Too wretched to exert myself lowered in the opinion of everyone why should I drag on a miserable existence embittered by past recollections & not one ray of hope to rest on for the future. The remembrance of all your kindness which I have so unworthily repaid has often made my heart ache. I know that you will forgive me because it is not in your nature to be unkind or severe to any. dear amiable woman that I have never left you oh! that I had always taken your advice. I might have lived long & happy but weak & unsteady have rushed on my own destruction I have not written to Bysshe. oh no what would it avail my wishes or my prayers would not be attended to by him & yet should he see this perhaps he might grant my last request to let Ianthe remain with you always dear lovely child, with you she will enjoy much happiness with him none. My dear Bysshe let me conjure you by the remembrance of our days of happiness to grant my last wish – do not take your innocent child from Eliza who has been more than I have, who has watched over her with such unceasing care. – Do not refuse my last request – I never could refuse you & if you had never left me I might have lived but as it is, I freely forgive you & may you enjoy that happiness which you have deprived me of. There is your beautiful boy. oh! be careful of him & his love may prove one day a rich reward. As you form his infant mind so you will reap the fruits hereafter Now comes the sad task of saying farewell – oh I must be quick. God bless & watch over you all. You dear Bysshe. & you dear Eliza. May all happiness attend ye both is the last wish of her who loved ye more than all others. My children I dare not trust myself there. They are too young to regret me & ye will be kind to them for their own sakes more than for mine. My parents do not regret me. I was unworthy your love & care. Be happy all of you. so shall my spirit find rest & forgiveness. God bless you all is the last prayer of the unfortunate Harriet S—

There was a silence then, as I folded the paper and handed it back to Miss Westbrook, with a bow of thanks. I knew now that her sister's last desperate act was not the decision of the moment: that even if I might have prevented it, I alone was not its cause.

My lamp burns low now, and I will hasten to relate what remains to be told. I will set down my final acts in this case, in the hope that it will be the last time I need involve myself with a family that has been to me such a source of anguish, and that has induced me, three times now, to contravene the professional code I have always upheld, and conduct myself in defiance not only of the law, but of my own most steadfast principles.

Today is the third of January; four days since I presented myself at Skinner-street, that I might hand Godwin my bill. I could have sent one of my men, it is true, but knowing the parlous state of his pocket-book I deemed it prudent to deliver it in person. Few can deny me, faced with such a demand. I fully expected a family in mourning, it being still less than three months since the death of Miss Fanny Imlay, but I found instead a dwelling *en fête*. Flowers in the windows, wine on the table, and the most complacent smile on the face of Mrs Godwin when she opened the door. A smile that, I saw, faded somewhat at the sight of me.

'Oh, it's you,' she said haughtily. 'Was Mr Godwin expecting you?'

'No,' I replied. 'And it seems I call at an inopportune time. You are celebrating?'

'Indeed we are,' said Godwin, coming to the door and gesturing me to enter. I had never seen a smile on his face before, but he seemed now brimming with satisfaction, and so eager to share it that even I was to be considered a sufficient audience. 'We are endeavouring to forget preceding sorrows, and to enjoy the flattering prospects which have now presented themselves. My daughter is to enter the married state on the morrow, and will become thereby the wife of the eldest son of a baronet, Sir Timothy Shelley, of Field-place, in the county of Sussex. She will thus acquire a not insignificant status and character in society, even though she was, hitherto, a girl without a penny of fortune. You can imagine how great a relief this has brought to my and Mrs Godwin's minds.'

There was a slight commotion, then, in the adjoining room – a commotion of laughter and excited talk. I glimpsed a maid, holding in her arms a little boy – a boy with soft curls and a round, gentle face – and a moment later I found myself in the presence of the affianced couple. He, nervous, agitated, and when he saw me, red-faced; she – she I could not read. The room fell silent and I allowed that silence, permitted it to distend to the point of eloquence.

'I gather,' I said at last, addressing myself to Shelley, 'that I am to wish you joy. Not only in the acquisition of another wife, but in your restoration to Mr Godwin's good graces.'

Shelley laughed then, that silly, girlish, dreadful laugh of his, and an even deeper flush overspread his features. 'Ha – Maddox! Pat you come like the evil fairy at the feast! But the thought is apt, for tomorrow's ceremony does indeed seem magical in its effects – indeed you would not believe—'

Mrs Godwin simpered at this, but I saw Miss Godwin's hand at his arm, her motion of restraint.

'Could you not have waited?' I said then, my gaze encompassing the whole company and coming to rest, at last, on the two of them. 'If the self-inflicted death of a *sister* were not deemed sombre enough, surely the suicide of a *wife* requires the lapse of more than a mere month before the mourning blacks are flung aside, and the funeral baked meats furnish forth the marriage table. But since not one of you here deigned to attend either interment, perhaps you do not deem yourselves bound by such trifling conventions, any more than you seem to consider it necessary to observe even the rudiments of common decency.'

Shelley was by now white to the lips, his face drawn in a mask of peculiar affliction.

'And are you, none of you, in the slightest concerned that there are now two young children who have lost their mother, having already, it seems, been abandoned by their *father*?'

'Oh, as to that,' said Miss Godwin, airily, 'the Westbrooks will no doubt provide.'

'I repeat,' I said, unflinching, 'could you not have waited?'

'I wanted,' stammered Shelley then, 'I did propose that we should – that it might be more seemly—'

Miss Godwin turned at once with a look of dismay to her father, and he it was who stepped forward now in intervention. 'I do not consider, sir, that we owe Harriet *Westbrook* any undue consideration. I have it on unquestionable authority that she violated her marriage vows long before Mr Shelley left England with my daughter. The lady has, moreover, lately been consorting with any number of men, including a reprobate Irish scapegrace and a captain in the Indian Army, and finally stooped so low as to descend the steps of prostitution, and live openly with a low fellow by the name of Smith.'

I looked at him, scarce crediting his words. 'How did you discover this?' I demanded. 'You know as well as I that I conducted the most thorough and comprehensive investigation as to the whereabouts of Mrs Shelley, and no such information ever came to my hearing. She may have called herself Smith, but she did so merely in an attempt to conceal her real name – and no doubt to protect *you* from scandal, much thanks she seems now to have merited thereby.'

She it was who stepped forward then, and what I heard in her voice froze my soul. 'My father was given these facts by a man who had been in *your* service. He said *you* had sought to suppress it, but that we deserved to know the truth. The whole abhorrent truth.'

'Todd?' I said, hardly believing the evidence of my own senses. '*Jacob Todd* came to you with this?'

'He said, likewise, that it was common knowledge that she had drowned herself the day she left Hans-place – that the corpse was so badly decomposed that it could not possibly have been in the water but a few days.'

'That, Miss Godwin, I can refute from my own experience, for I saw the body with my own eyes. Indeed, I spoke to Mrs Shelley myself a full month after the date to which you refer. The same night, in fact, that she penned her last letter – her last letter, sir,' this to Shelley, who had the good grace to hang his head, 'to *you*.

'I do not doubt,' I continued, 'that were I to enquire more closely into the rest of Todd's assertions I should find them no more reliable than the first. What evidence has he given you for the existence of this Smith, this Irishman, this captain in the Indian Army?'

They glanced at one another then, and I saw fear pass between their eyes.

'I see,' I said, nodding. 'It is as I expected. The man has obtained money from you – or the promise of it – by relaying information which is at best unsubstantiated gossip, and at worst slanderous lies. And you have all believed him because this was what you *wished* to believe. For a philosopher, Mr Godwin, you show a scant regard indeed for the truth.'

My blow hit home, I could see that at once. And having the advantage, I pressed it. 'As for you, sir,' I said, turning again to Shelley and seeing the look of terror in his eyes. I knew what he had done and I should never have connived in the concealment of it. But it was too late now. What evidence I had once had was lost, and they would all of them deny it. All that remained to me was to make his own fear his punishment, and that I did, and without remorse. 'You, sir, bear the greatest blame in this sad affair. *As you have in others, no less iniquitous.* Was it not enough to have abandoned her in the first instance, on the point of bringing an infant of yours into this world, but you had to compound that cruelty by getting her once again with child? A child begotten in dishonour and the most shameful secrecy?'

'No – *no!*' cried Miss Godwin, starting forward.

'Was it not enough, Mr Shelley,' I continued, unyielding, 'to have abused her thus in person, but that you should harangue her by letter into the bargain, and harass her to a dreadful and untimely death?'

Shelley gaped at me, stammered some unintelligible words, then turned and staggered to the wall, one hand at his side, panting and retching.

'How dare you accuse Shelley so abominably?' Miss Godwin exclaimed. 'That woman was always harping on suicide, long before they were even married. It was a – a *monomania* with her. You may ask anyone – they all heard her talk of it. She tried

227

to kill herself more than once when she was still at school, and spoke of self-murder perfectly serenely even before complete strangers.'

'Did it not occur to you,' I replied, endeavouring to keep my temper, 'that such talk was nothing but a sign of profound self-doubt? A doubt her husband, if anyone—'

'No,' she countered obdurately. 'If it was a sign of anything it was of a mental weakness – a fatal insufficiency that was always going to lead to the same dire end. Indeed, beyond the mere shock of such an event having befallen a being once so nearly connected with Shelley, there is little to regret. Sooner or later she was bound to put an end to a life that was a torment to her, and which rendered her, let us be frank, nothing but a burden to all those unfortunate enough to be associated with her.'

It was my turn, now, for silence; my turn to realize that I had been acting on assumptions based on a wholly inadequate understanding, and drawing conclusions from evidence that was not only partial, but treacherous.

'Did you enjoy, Miss Godwin,' I began slowly, 'your stay in Bath? You must have had a good deal to see, a good deal to write of in your correspondence—'

It was her turn, now, to flush. Her chin lifted and I saw defiance in her eyes. Defiance, and something else too, that I dared not define, dared not probe. Something that recalled to me, suddenly, and with a cold rush of sickness, what her father had said of her utter implacability in any matter upon which she had set her heart – her all but invincibility whenever something she coveted was at stake.

And as I sit here now, I remember that look of hers, and I cast my mind back to everything that passed between us, and I wonder. I wonder for the first time, if what I was told is true, or if I have been all these months deceived. I think of him, most especially, and I wonder if I have made the direst and most appalling mistake—

CHAPTER NINE

The Past

Charles puts the pages down. Slowly, as if the revelations contained in them have rendered the very paper unstable. He knows, now, why Maddox might have wanted this to lie buried all these changeful years; it is not just that he blamed himself, in part, for Harriet's death. His judgement, his rectitude, his character are all cast into question by this account. That he should have removed evidence, concealed the identities of not one but two suicides, and suborned two inquests – even a professional reputation such as he enjoyed would have been shaken by such a disclosure. And Charles knows, too, the real reason why the Shelleys were so desperate to discover whether his uncle had kept any records of the Godwin case; why they have always been so insistent that the only version of Shelley's past should be their own. There are facts here, ghastly whispers here, that would change everything, were they known; revelations with the power to shatter in pieces the image they have so carefully constructed of the ethereal and otherworldly poet, and his devoted and brilliant wife. For Harriet's death was no simple suicide, even if no court in the land could ever have convicted her killer, and only ghosts may take revenge for it. She might have taken the final fatal step herself, but she was driven to it, pregnant by the man who had already once abandoned her, and hounded by bitter and vindictive letters from the woman who had taken her place. A woman who knew her weakness and ruthlessly exploited it, even if 'no blow was struck, no poison administered, no weapon ever wielded'. It was not Shelley Maddox had accused of killing Harriet – not Shelley he thought had a midwinter heart, but his *wife*. Charles thinks back to the letter Mary Shelley wrote to him and remembers, with a lurch much like the one his uncle described, how she had dismissed a rival as prey to 'some deficiency – some fatal lack'. Only it was *Claire* she had spoken of then, not Harriet. Is this, he thinks, how that woman orders and controls her world – by labelling anyone who dares oppose her as mentally deranged?

From the start, this case has duped him, an endlessly receding hall of mirrors in which nothing can be believed, and no deduction trusted. But now, at last, he knows. Or rather he knows what it is he does *not* know. The puzzle has always had a piece missing, but he sees now the shape of that space – he understands, finally, what he is looking for. It is all here, threaded through his uncle's words, and Charles understands at last, why not one but *two* sets of pages have been cut from Maddox's files, and why the other missing section has still not yet been found. Because Maddox did not meet Shelley in 1816, as Charles has always assumed and the two women led him to believe, but in *1814*, when he undertook that still-mysterious 'matter of Tremadoc'. Whatever it was, it left Maddox with such a loathing of Shelley he could scarcely speak his name, and in

231

possession of a secret that the women, even now, are terrified he might reveal. A secret that, if Charles pursues it, will surely damage the dead as much as it might injure the living. Something even Sir Percy does not guess at, for why else would his mother seek to shield him from it? Perhaps Charles was wrong and, like the deceitful lapwing, Mary Shelley is protecting her offspring after all.

Charles's own lamp has burned low now, and the glowering clouds are darkening the December day before its time. The door edges open and Thunder pads in purposefully. A scatter of snowflakes is melting slowly on his prickled fur. Charles watches the cat leap gracefully onto the bed and pace about for a few moments before selecting a place on the pillow and folding himself neatly into a curl of black fur, tucking in his tail and closing his eyes. Charles gets up and stretches, and goes to ring the bell. He has no carriage at his disposal, and no team of men at his command, but all he needs, for the moment at least, is Abel Stornaway. Though as he puts his hand to the bell-rope it occurs to him that it might be kinder to go down the two flights of stairs, rather than expect the old man to heave his weary body up to the attic.

Abel looks up as Charles enters the drawing room and takes a seat by his great-uncle's chair. Maddox is, as so often these days, suspended between sleep and waking, his eyelids fluttering at unseen dreams, but is it Charles's imagination, or is his face less taut, his mouth less drawn? He touches Maddox's hand and feels the fingers move in response, and turns, a question in his eyes, to Abel.

'Aye,' says the old man. 'Ah've seen it me'sen. He seems a little closer these last few days. We may yet have him back, Mr Charles, we may yet.'

'I read those papers,' says Charles. 'I need to talk to George Fraser.'

Abel nods slowly. 'Do you want me to come wi' ye?'

'No,' says Charles. 'That won't be necessary. Just write his address down for me. I'll go first thing in the morning.'

'I should leave it till Thursday, Mr Charles. If I were ye.'

'What in Heaven's name are you talking about, Abel?'

'Have ye taken no account of the date, Mr Charles? Tomorrow is the twenty-fift'.'

Charles opens his mouth to reply, then stops short with a smile. 'Why, so it is. Not that it makes—'

But he's interrupted then by the sound of knocking at the street door. A sharp knocking, not heavy but rapid and repeated.

Charles looks at Abel but the old man shrugs his ignorance, so he gets up and goes out onto the landing. Downstairs, at the door, he can see Billy talking to a woman – a woman with a shawl pulled up under her eyes in the swirling snow. *Claire*, is Charles's first thought – a thought edged with guilt; but no, the shape is too slight, the clothes too poor. And then he hears words rising towards him and knows at once who it is.

'Look will yer just go and ask 'im?' she's saying, her voice hoarse with the cold. ''Cause I ain't about to take no for an answer from a pafetic little whippersnapper like you.'

'Now look 'ere,' Billy begins, but Charles is already at the step and pushing him aside. 'Nancy,' he says. 'What on earth are you doing here?'

She looks at him as if unsure where to start but then a gust of wind pulls the shawl from her fingers and in the moment before she jerks it back up again he sees the vicious black bruise that swells half her face, a bruise with ugly sharp edges and a line of blood where something has slit the skin.

'What in God's name happened to you?'

'Arnie – that's what 'appened to me. 'Ad one too many and took 'is belt to me. As per bleedin' usual. But this time it weren't just me – this time 'e raised 'is 'and to Betsy. 'E ain't ever done that before and 'e won't ever get the bleedin' chance to do it again. I told 'im – not if I've got anythin' to do wiv it.'

As she turns and hoists the child to her hip Charles realizes she has been there all along, clinging hidden among her mother's skirts. Her thin little face is almost translucent with cold.

'I packed me bag and left,' Nancy continues. 'Just like that. Only I don't 'ave nowhere to go. Walked about for a coupla hours and then I thought o' you. It'd only be for a few days – promise. And Betsy won't be no trouble – she's quiet and—'

Charles reaches out and puts a hand on her shoulder, feeling the trembling tension in her thin frame, and understanding now, if not before, just how desperate she is. And how determined not to let him see it. To ask, yes, but not to plead.

'Like I said, it'd only be a few days—'

'You're welcome to stay, Nancy. I'm sure you'll want a place of your own as soon as you can find one. But there's room here until you do.'

Billy turns to Charles, his eyes round with alarm. 'Surely you're not – I mean – the likes of 'er—'

Charles does not look at him. 'It seems Miss Dyer has a more just appreciation of the way this house is run than you do, Billy. I'm the one who makes the decisions here. So will you please take her and the little girl down to the kitchen and ask Molly to put some milk on the stove to warm, and make up a spare bed in her room.'

The look of raw, gasping relief on Nancy's face now is too painful to see, and he covers his own embarrassment by refusing to meet her eyes and turning instead to Billy. 'And when you've done that, you can go up to the butcher's on the Strand and fetch a goose, assuming he has any left at this late hour. And call at Nattali & Bond in Bedford Street and see if they have the book I requested.'

It'll be a cold and heavy task, up the hill and with the pavements icy, but Billy could do with the chastening.

When the three of them have gone downstairs he closes the door and starts back up to where Abel has all this time been watching.

'That were a generous thing you did then, Mr Charles. Not sure as what the boss wouldae said, in yer place, but it took a kind heart to do it, and that's a fact.'

'Well, if Billy should be proved right and we wake to find the house ransacked and all our valuables gone, I shall blame you,' replies Charles.

'Me?' says the old man, his eyes widening.

Charles smiles. 'It was you who reminded me what day it is. How could I turn a mother and child away on Christmas Eve?'

By noon the following morning the house is redolent with roasting goose, the dining room has been opened for the first time since Charles came to live here, and when he goes down to the kitchen he finds Nancy hard at work shining the silver. She's wearing the same sober blue dress she wore to St John's Wood, and he wonders if both the clothes and the polishing are designed to remind him how useful she can be. But, to be fair, it's probably the only dress she has that's fit to be seen in a household like this one. He does have a moment's anxiety, seeing her with his uncle's best canteen laid out on the table before her, but her smile first disarms and then shames him.

'Found all this moulderin' away in that great coffin of a sideboard upstairs.' She grins, taking up the polishing cloth. 'Looked as if it could do with an outin'. Why 'ave such nice stuff and never use it?'

Seeing Molly's eyes flicker warily upon her now Charles has a quick pang of remorse. In all the flurry of the last few hours he has not thought to tell her why Nancy is suddenly in the house; the girl may well be thinking she's about to be discharged. She certainly looks flustered, her gestures clumsy, and her dark skin beaded with sweat as she wrestles the goose in its dish. Nancy, by contrast, is moving about the kitchen as if she's lived there half her life, and Charles can easily see why Molly might think she is harbouring her successor, not only in her kitchen, but in her room. He backs off to the door, telling himself she's too busy now – that he'll find a moment, later, to explain.

Up in the office he unpacks the parcel Billy collected from the bookseller: *The Life of Percy Bysshe Shelley, by Thomas Medwin. In two volumes. London, 1847.* Charles is impatient, now, to press forward with the case, but hardly expects to find very much truth in this no doubt superficial and sycophantic account by the poet's own cousin. But he couldn't be more wrong. Not that the usefulness of these books has anything to do with the quality of the writing. There are whole tracts that do not mention Shelley at all, as well as great slabs of copy that have been unashamedly lifted from a series of articles in the *New Monthly Magazine*, written by a 'Mr Hogg', a name Charles certainly does not recognize. But bad as it is as a piece of literature, the memoir turns out to be rather better as a piece of evidence, for no biography Charles has ever read has painted such a perplexing, not to say unsettling, picture of its subject. So much so, in fact, that he soon starts to wonder if it's deliberate – if there isn't something else Medwin is trying to tell him under cover of all these disquieting details. Something Mrs Shelley, perhaps, persuaded him to omit. She, after all, wanted this memoir suppressed altogether, and she's quoted here in the preface as insisting that it is *not the time to tell the truth* of her husband's *errors of action*. And Medwin is not alone, it seems, in raising profound questions about Shelley's life, and then refusing point-blank to provide any answers: the extracts from Hogg, too, query whether Shelley ever felt the need for 'repentance', yet offer no explanation why such repentance might have been necessary, or what the poet had done to require it. What is it, thinks Charles, that everyone who knew Shelley seems so zealous to hide, or to excuse?

If he had a more modern vocabulary at his disposal Charles would be thinking now of manic depression, or bipolar disorder, and who can say, at this distance of time, if that diagnosis might not have more than a grain of truth in it? Anyone reading a biography of Shelley now will be hard put not to conclude that he suffered from some sort of personality disorder – the symptoms are all there: awkward and erratic in social situations, compulsively obsessed with repetitive patterns and daily routines, and subject to fits of uncontrollable violence when faced with the slightest opposition or constraint; one moment narcissistic, the next morbidly disgusted by his own bodily functions. I am, of course, talking in terms Charles would never have used, but it is striking how consistently Shelley's friends and associates described these aspects of his character, even if they lack all the nuances of modern psychiatric terminology. 'Mad Shelley', they called him at Eton, where he once impaled a fellow pupil's hand to a desk with a fork. There was a demon in him, they said, a demon that hounded and pursued him, down the nights and down the days, through all the labyrinthine ways of his own tortured mind. A good part of this Charles is able to glean even from Medwin's highly inaccurate account, but what he also discovers, rather to his surprise, is some fellow feeling for this strange, tortured child with his ungainly stooping stance and excruciating high-pitched voice. Taken for a youth of seventeen when he was at least ten years older, as gauche and untidy as a boy half his age, and fixated to a degree any modern reader will find disquieting with the company of very young girls (two of whom he tried, once, to purchase, though this Medwin either does not know or chooses not to say). One of these qualities Charles, of course, shares, having an equal disdain for the state of his own wardrobe, and he cannot but be impressed by the brilliance of this young man's intellect, by the range and depth of his scientific interests – from the phenomenon of combustion, to the uses of chemistry, the powers of electricity, and the latent mysteries of nature. Charles calls himself a scientist – takes pride in such a term – but his room does not, even now, boast an electrical machine, an air-pump, and a solar microscope, as Shelley's did when he was just eighteen, though even at that age Charles would never have used such apparatus so recklessly he left everything in the room burned or stained, or been so careless with his chemicals that he swallowed arsenic by mistake.

One other thing they appear to share – and Charles reads the passage with the jolt of one who always thought himself unique – is what we would now call a photographic memory. It has always been, for Charles, quite extraordinarily useful, but as so often for Shelley, a great gift seems to have been as much a bane as a blessing. Medwin claims Shelley was able to call up places, words, and figures at will – and what poet would not envy him that? – but that same image-making aptitude brought with it nightmare dreams and waking visions that bore all the appearance of reality and left him unsure of the truth of his own past. Indeed, there is much in Medwin's memoir that cannot adequately be explained in any other way. Like that strange recurring vision of a winter landscape, a scene that excited such fearful emotions that Shelley ran from it panic-stricken, to the refuge of friends:

> *I have beheld scenes, with the intimate and unaccountable connexion of which with the obscure parts of my own nature, I have been irresistibly impressed ... The most remarkable event of this nature which ever occurred to me happened five years ago at Oxford. I was walking with a friend, in the neighbourhood of that city, engaged in earnest and interesting conversation. We suddenly turned the corner of a lane, and the view, which its high banks and hedges had concealed, presented itself. The view consisted of a windmill, standing in one among many plashy meadows, inclosed with stone walls; the irregular and broken ground, between the wall and the road on which we stood; a long low hill behind the windmill, and a grey covering of uniform cloud spread over the evening sky. It was that season when the last leaf had just fallen from the scant and stunted ash ... The effect which it produced on me was not such as could have been expected. I suddenly remembered to have seen that exact scene in some dream of long—*
>
> *Here I was obliged to leave off overcome by thrilling horror—*

'Mr Maddox!'

Charles looks up with a start.

It's Nancy, standing deferentially in the doorway, 'I came

to ask,' she says, 'if you'd mind 'elping Mr Stornaway and the lad fetch your uncle into the dining room.'

Charles notes that 'Mr' and approves, even if a cynic would no doubt condemn it as merely self-serving civility. He gets to his feet, hearing Billy now, on the landing, whistling a Christmas song, and finds himself suddenly wishing there were chestnuts in the house, or holly they might hang. Which is all the more surprising when I tell you that he has always hated Christmas in the past – after his sister was taken it became the darkest and most desolate time of the year, his father silent and Charles watching helplessly as his mother retreated in terror from a season celebrating the joy of a coming child, her pain at the loss of one never waning with time.

'And I hope you don't mind me sayin''—' The girl's voice breaks in on his memory. She hesitates, wiping her hands a mite nervously on her apron.

'What is it?'

'That girl – Molly – it ain't my place, I know, but I couldn't 'elp noticin'. You do know, don't yer, that she—'

'Thank you,' he interrupts, a mite tersely, 'but I have it in hand. There is no need for you to concern yourself about that.'

'Well, if you're sure . . .' She is eyeing him rather doubtfully.

'Perfectly,' he replies firmly. 'Now, did you not say I am required elsewhere?'

Half an hour later they are sitting, he, Abel and Maddox, around a table that can seat twelve with ease, and has seen peers and prime ministers in its time, and even once, so rumour has it, a head that bore a crown. The man who hosted those far-off ceremonials is scarcely recognizable now, but all the same Charles is struck by the difference in Maddox today. The old man's eyes seem more alert, his hand less rigid. He's even managing to feed himself, albeit rather messily, and with a constant undertone of occasionally intelligible mutterings. Charles wonders if it is merely the change of scene that has worked such an alteration and whether, if that's the case, they should make more of an effort to move him about the house; whether, indeed, he should look into the purchase of a wheeled chair and take him outside in the open air for the first time in months. But for now they repair once more to the drawing room, where Nancy stokes the fire and pours the port before closing the door softly behind her and leaving the three men alone.

Abel is soon snoring and his uncle nodding, and it's not long before Charles, too, sits back and closes his eyes, lulled by the crackling of the fire and the spreading warmth of wine. The only other Christmas he spent in this house was the last before they lost Elizabeth. He can remember her now in this very room, round-eyed with rapture at the candles and the yew tree Maddox had brought in specially. It was the first Christmas tree she had ever seen, and Charles can still remember the look on her little face at the toys and bags of sweets and dried fruits Maddox had hung among its branches. She would be eighteen now, but however hard he tries, Charles can never bring her forward in time and imagine the young woman she would have become; she is frozen for ever on the day she was taken, in her bright flowered dress, her small face smudged with tears. Charles is thinking of her now – seeing her now – so absorbed in the past that when he hears her name spoken he cannot tell if it is real, or merely an echo of his own long yearning.

'Elizabeth.'

241

He opens his eyes to see a tiny girl hesitating in the doorway, her doll swinging from one hand. She is so like, so hauntingly similar, that Charles wonders for a wild moment if his boyhood prayer has been answered and he has been given his impossible second chance. It is the impression of an instant only: his mind – his intellect – tells him this is not Elizabeth, but that does not stop his heart turning over as she comes racing towards Maddox and holds up her arms to be kissed.

'Where have you been, little one?' says Maddox, softly, an old hand reaching gently to her golden curls. 'We have all been looking for you.'

She smiles and puts a finger in her mouth, twinkling and mischievous. There's a little smear of treacle across her cheek, and Maddox smiles in his turn. 'It looks to me as if Cook has been spoiling you again,' he says, pretending to be stern. Charles knows now it was his uncle's voice he heard, and he watches in pain as the old man takes the little girl on his lap, a little girl who is not the one he takes her for, but has, all unknowing, done the one thing none of the people in this house have yet managed to do and unlocked the darkness enveloping his mind.

There's a movement now in the doorway and Charles sees Nancy, her hand on the knob and her face drawn with anxiety. 'Betsy – what did I tell yer about not troublin' the gen'lemen?'

But Charles has already held a finger to his lips, and as the silence falls they watch the little girl curl against the old man's arm and his gentle movement to and fro as he rocks the two of them sweetly asleep.

* * *

When Charles comes down the following morning Betsy is sitting on the floor in the drawing room, playing with her doll and chattering away happily to Maddox – who is managing, slowly, to make some sort of reply. Charles smiles at him and gets, for the first time in weeks, something like a smile in return. Abel arrives now, with the breakfast tray and the newspaper, and Charles leaves the three of them together and goes downstairs. There's no one in the kitchen so he has his roll and coffee alone, reminding himself that he has still not spoken to Molly, then goes back up the stairs to the front door and a heavy fall of snow. He spots a green Atlas omnibus lumbering heavily along the Strand just as he gets to the top of the street, and a breathless rush through people and freezing puddles gets him to the 'bus stop just in time, though it leaves him with cold muddy splashes right up to his knees. Charles ventures south of the river only marginally more often than the modern London cabbie, and it's a good long time since he's had any need to visit Walworth. Here and there little rows of cottages give some clue to the village it once was, but almost all the green has gone and the later dwellings push thickly together in slum congestion. But it was Maddox who bought Fraser his house, and Charles knows he would never have consigned his old assistant to anything other than a comfortable retirement. So when he finds the address he is not surprised to discover that the little house in Victory Place is a model of its kind. Not quite as large as his erstwhile master's, but solid, three-storeyed, and backing onto Locks Fields. A generous gift from a generous man.

When Charles knocks at the door it's opened by a tiny maid in a large white cap who seems terrified at the mere sight of him and scampers off back into the house before he has even opened his mouth. Charles waits, watching two boys playing ball in the street and doing his best to avoid the attentions of a little grey dog, which can clearly smell cat on his trousers. He can't recall ever meeting Mrs Fraser, and remembers only how astonished everyone was when Fraser announced that he planned to get married. He'd always been something of a success with the ladies, and had seemed perfectly comfortable with his bachelor existence until one last street fight had left him half dead and half blind, and the woman Maddox brought in to nurse him was quickly offered a rather more all-embracing role. In every sense. And she it must be who comes to the door now. Younger than Charles would have guessed, a little grey, but with a broad smile and alert, kindly brown eyes.

Charles offers her his card but she waves it away with a smile, 'I would have known you anywhere – you look just like him. Do you want to see George? He claims he's reading but he's doing no such thing – been dozing over that fire for the past two hours to my certain knowledge. Come in – it will do him good to see you.'

Charles is rather disconcerted by the cordiality of his reception: he's professionally inured to engendering suspicion and distrust, and this is hardly a social call. But he can hardly explain that on the doorstep. He follows the round and bustling form of Mrs Fraser down the hall and into the snug sitting room at the back, a room furnished in a very female taste, with an abundance of frilled cushions, sentimental prints, ornamental lamps and china curios. All this knick-knackery should remind him of the Shelley house, but there is a warmth here, both literal and metaphorical, that quashes the comparison before it even forms. Fraser is indeed exactly where his wife described him, his newspaper slipping slowly from his lap, his shaven head thrown back against the chair and his mouth open in a gentle snore. The only discordant note – the only thing Charles had not remembered – is the black eye-patch.

Mrs Fraser goes over to him and touches him lightly on the arm. 'Someone to see you, George. It's young Mr Maddox.'

She smiles at Charles as George Fraser snorts himself awake, and rubs his nose with the back of his arm. 'I'll have Lily make tea,' she says brightly, and leaves the two of them alone.

Charles watches Fraser pick up his paper, fold it neatly, and place it on the little table beside him. 'So, what brings you to these parts?' Fraser says slowly, meeting Charles's gaze at last. If his wife is welcoming, he is decidedly wary. He knows Walworth is not in Charles's way anywhere, and there must be something he is wanting.

'I've been working on a case. For Sir Percy Shelley.'

He waits. There should be a flicker in the other man's eyes at this, but he was trained well, and by one of the best.

'It seems,' Charles continues, circumspect in his turn, 'that it's related to an old case of my great-uncle's. Back in 'sixteen. I think you were involved.'

'Mebbe,' says Fraser, turning to poke a fire that clearly does not need it. 'Can't say it comes immediately to mind.'

Charles doesn't believe a word of it, and he's not about to take equivocation for an answer. He takes the pages he found from his coat and holds them out. 'I know what happened, Fraser. I know what he did, and what you did. I'm not here about that. I'm here because I want to know what happened before – why Maddox became involved with those people in the first place. I want to know what I *haven't* found – what's in the pages from 1814 that my uncle has destroyed.'

Fraser looks at him, then leans forward and takes the papers. He reads the first few lines, turns to the end and raises his eyes, at last, to Charles's face. 'Did he give these to you?'

Charles shakes his head. 'He's too ill – he had some sort of attack a few weeks ago. He can't really talk, can scarcely move. I found those papers behind the mirror.'

Fraser nods, though whether that indicates he knew of the hiding-place Charles cannot be sure.

'The Shelleys lied to me from the start,' Charles continues. 'I think they only hired me because they wanted to know what Maddox might say, what records he might still have. What I've found here is damaging enough, but I think there's something else – something connected with Tremadoc?'

Fraser looks at him steadily. 'It started there, yes.'

Charles seizes the pages and turns them, stabbing at one phrase, then another. 'Look at this – *no conduct, however base, was too vile for such a scoundrel – a man I considered both a felon and a blackguard – what evidence I had once had was lost, and they would all of them deny it*. But you know, don't you? You know what Shelley had done.'

Fraser studies him for a long moment, then gestures towards the sopha. 'I allus knew that this day might come. Though I thought as he'd be dead when it did, and safe from the consequences.'

'There can be no consequences now, surely, not all these years later.'

'Not as to the law, perhaps. But that's not what he'd be afeared of. What he'd fear now is *you*. What you would think on him. On what he did.'

Charles swallows. 'I've come so far now – I just need to know the truth. After all, he may never – it may never—'

Fraser nods slowly. 'Why don't you take that seat there? We'll wait, shall we, for that tea? And then I'll tell you what I know.'

And as they sit, uneasy in the silence, looking towards the door, it is time for me, in my turn, to tell you what I know. What I know, what I suspect, and what I imagine.

PART TWO

1814

CHAPTER TEN

Autumn

It is October. A chill rain is falling, and the warm sun is wan. Outside a huddle of small lodging-houses hard by the Pancras workhouse a young woman stands in a doorway and looks up into the shrouded sky, wondering if she will brave the day. She is, what, sixteen? Seventeen? But despite her youth there is something about her that suggests she is not used to living in such a down-at-heel district. Either that or she believes this is merely a passing difficulty and the world will right itself soon enough, and deliver her a local habitation more suited to her name. And what, might you ask, is that name? Watch patiently a moment more and you will see the dark woollen shawl about her head slip and a skein of bright red-gold hair escape wildly into the wind, and you will know at once who this is. It is little more than two weeks since she returned from the dazzle of the Alps, and a dream of love, to the grim London day-to-dayness of mud and making-do. And bitter recriminations: even now, the man who will eventually become her husband is sitting in their cramped room on the second floor composing yet

251

another letter to his wife. A letter full of icy philosophy and hot self-justification. There are rumours too, as this girl well knows, that the bailiffs may have discovered their dwelling-place, but it is not that particular pursuit that concerns her now. She tucks her hair back into her shawl and makes her way down towards London. It's a good step she has before her, especially on such a day, but she is used to walking. Did they not walk for four solid days south from Paris? Thirty long, slow miles a day through a landscape scathed by conflict, and in an atmosphere between the three of them that festered scarcely less. The memory sets a grim line now across her brow, and yet in a dozen years from now she will write of that journey as a golden time, the acting-out of a novel, a romance made real. I suspect this is only the first of many such contradictions we may observe, only one of many such self-deceits, but for the moment, at least, we will let it pass.

We move now to Buckingham Street, and the quiet of that first-floor room where Maddox permits entrance only by invitation. He is sitting there, intent on his pen, covering the pages of his current case-book at a measured pace, pausing only occasionally to consult a much smaller notebook he carries always about his person. The fire is lit, and a pot of coffee sits at his elbow. His coat has been hung carefully on the back of the door, and he is wearing a fine embroidered silk waistcoat, which is only one of many such fashionable items his closet boasts: his is a very lucrative calling, and clothes have always been rather a weakness. There is no sound now but the rhythm of the pen across the paper, and the ticking of the clock above the fireplace. And then, suddenly, the bell downstairs. A sound both expected and unexpected in this house: unexpected because Maddox has no appointments today; expected because it is the nature of his occupation to have visitors unannounced. He lifts his head a moment, hearing the door opening and voices downstairs, and notes in passing that one of them appears to be a young woman's, before calmly resuming his task.

You might find this a little odd – that a man who has built so much success on the principles of logic and observation should not seek to apply the latter to a caller who is clearly both unanticipated and, surely, unusual, both in her gender and her age. And indeed I should have loved to describe him, Holmes-like, watching as she made her way down the street five minutes before, and deducing every detail of her character and history in a single appraising gaze. And had he done so, what might he have seen? Confidence and purpose, first and foremost, for there was no hesitation in this girl's step, no last-minute equivocation at the door, and there is a lift to her head that is rare among women, and rarer still in one so young, and alone. He would have noticed, too – having an eye for dress in others as well as a partiality for it in himself – that under her long dark shawl there is a striking, colourful and (for London) very unusual tartan dress, and thereafter drawn various preliminary conclusions (all correct) about not only the independence of her taste but some of her likely recent travels. But this is Buckingham Street, not Baker Street, and Maddox has no convenient sidekick to impress, nor any inclination to waste his valuable hours idling at the window.

Though that is not to say that he does not ready himself to conduct just such an assessment when a knock comes to his office door. But when George Fraser shows his caller into the room and Maddox rises to meet his visitor he sees only one thing.

Her face.

*

The eyes, the broad clear brow, the small, careful mouth. It is – and yet it cannot be—

'Mary?' he stammers, as the door closes and the girl puts back her shawl. And then the bright hair spills about her shoulders and the likeness fades. Fades, but does not die, not entirely, for the impression of that impression will linger in his mind and colour his behaviour long after his conscious intelligence has dismissed it as nothing but a curious coincidence.

'So you were given my name?' she says then, somewhat nonplussed.

'No,' he flounders, unaccustomed to beginning a professional consultation in so inauspicious a manner. 'It was – a misunderstanding. Nothing more.'

He gestures to a chair, but she shakes her head. 'I am told, sir, that you are the most competent thief-taker in London. That if any man can discover the truth of a mystery, that man is you.'

Maddox glances at her, more coolly now, and elects to take a chair himself. 'Immodest though it may be to admit it, I do indeed believe that to be so, Miss—?'

'Godwin. Mary Wollstonecraft Godwin.'

She pronounces the names as if they were honorifics. Which, in a manner, they are. Badges of an intellectual lineage such as few can boast. That proud set of the head explains itself now. She, meanwhile, has been observing his reaction and noted the recognition in his eyes. She cannot have expected an uncouth man, not living in this house, in this street, but it seems she may not have envisaged such a well-informed one.

'I imagine,' she continues, a little less confidently, 'that the mysteries you resolve are of many different classes. That in one case it might be the identity of a killer, whereas in another a matter as minor as the recovery of a stolen watch.'

Maddox puts his fingers together, intrigued as to where this may lead. She is circling the room now, just as she appears to be circling the subject.

'And some, I presume, fall easily into no recognized category – may even defy rational explanation.'

'Such as, Miss Godwin?'

She flushes slightly, a flicker of blood under her pale skin. 'Such as, for example, if one found oneself haunted – persecuted, even – by an individual, or individuals, without any – who have no—' She falters, and her face reddens again.

'You are the subject of such a persecution, Miss Godwin? Or perhaps your father. I understand his views are deemed by some—'

But she is shaking her head. 'No, not my father, my – that is – my—'

Her hand flutters – the left hand that bears no ring – and comes to rest at her belly. It is the smallest of gestures, and at least half unconscious, but Maddox is well versed in the reading of such signs, and beneath her protecting hand he can see now the tiny, almost imperceptible curve of a three- or four-months child.

There is a silence, and then she appears to come to a decision. 'Do you know the name of Percy Bysshe Shelley?' she says, her chin lifting.

Maddox nods. 'I have heard it.' Not in any positive context, it must be said, but he elects not to say so.

'He is a poet,' she continues, 'perhaps the finest our age will ever see. But the greatness of his soul is matched by an almost equal infirmity of body. His health is weak, and he is prey to the most violent and fearful spasms of the nerves.

255

And were that not trial enough, he has been subjected to the most wicked and contemptible pursuit by a villain who will not even show his face. We thought a six-weeks absence from England would bring it finally to an end, but it has started again only this week – only yesterday.'

She turns away from him now, and leans her hand on the back of a chair. It's clear she will not allow herself the relief of tears, and Maddox respects her attempt at dignity by offering neither salts nor handkerchief, though he has both about him. 'I am sure,' he begins, 'that you did not come here for sympathy, but for assistance. Assistance founded on rigour of thought and prior experience of handling like cases. And therefore I will tell you at once that the likelihood of apprehending such a man will depend in large part on his motivation in undertaking such a course of action.'

'What do you mean?' she says, turning back to face him.

'From what you have said, there has been no attempt at extortion in this case – no endeavour to obtain monies by offering to desist. This leaves only two possibilities. The culprit is either a wronged man seeking revenge, or an evil one intent merely on inflicting harm.'

He expects her to respond at once to this – indeed, he formed his words with just such a test in mind – but to his surprise she merely reddens again and turns away.

'A man in quest of what he deems to be a righteous vengeance,' he continues, 'will persist until he achieves it, whatever the difficulties that may lie in his way. A mere mischief-maker has not that motive, and his persecution will not, therefore, endure. You may think that such a point is mere casuistry, but I am sure a very little thought will reveal to you the significance of such a distinction. For the former may be traced by the meticulous application of logic, whereas the latter may never be traced, his choice of victim being determined, in many such cases, by mere caprice. Hence,' he concludes, 'I raise the point with you now. Because I assume that is why you are here, Miss Godwin – to ask my assistance in identifying this man?'

She faces him once more, her self-command reclaimed. 'Mr Shelley has many enemies. A man of his genius, who passionately opposes religious and political oppression in all its forms, and has the courage to speak out against such acts of tyranny, will always find himself impugned by bigots, and cast forth as a criminal by those unable to appreciate the sublime truth of his opinions.'

Maddox nods slowly. 'I am afraid I can only concur. But I have found, in long years of conducting this profession, that even the most extreme invective the newspapers can express translates but rarely into such a campaign of harassment as you have described. What explanation does Mr Shelley himself offer for these attacks?'

'He believes they are the work of a quarry-owner named Robert Leeson. Shelley encountered him nearly two years since when he was living in Wales. At Tremadoc.'

She sighs. 'It is a complex story, and my own knowledge of it is limited, but I do know that Shelley became entangled in a scheme to build a new sea-wall and drain the land behind. He believed the work would be to the benefit of the common people living thereabouts, but became incensed when he saw this Leeson brutalizing the labourers. Relations between the two of them worsened, and there was, in the end, the most dreadful assault one night, which all but cost Shelley his life. He left the house the next day without staying even to pack. But that being the case I do not see why the man should still pursue him now, so many months later, and so many miles away. It defies reason.'

'I am inclined to agree. I do not have sufficient facts at my disposal for a categorical assertion, but it would appear to be most unlikely. And you can think of no other instance – no event in the past or action on Mr Shelley's part – that might have prompted some other individual to pursue a retribution of so personal a nature?'

She shakes her head. 'I know of nothing.'

And he believes her. There is no one better skilled at discerning the involuntary movements by which the body of a liar betrays the lie, but Maddox sees none of them now. She is holding his gaze with a remarkable steadiness. And so, he thinks, she does not yet comprehend what lies at the root of this, but she knows it is no random act of gratuitous malice. Maddox wonders, for a moment, how well she really knows this man she speaks of – this man to whom she has dedicated her life, and for whom she must have risked both private censure and public ostracism.

'What form, Miss Godwin, do these incidents of persecution customarily take? Have there been other menaces of physical violence? A threatening correspondence?'

'Not the latter, I think,' she says. 'But I can speak with certainty only of the most recent occurrences, since our return from France. Thrice now Shelley says he has seen the same man in the street, but each time he attempts to accost him the man has gone – it is, Shelley says, like the fiend of a distempered dream that haunts him, leading him forth into a teeming darkness.'

'I see,' says Maddox, tempted to smile but recalling that the man is, after all, a poet. 'And you have not seen this man yourself?'

'No – neither Claire nor I have had sight of him. And she has been out abroad with Shelley far oftener than I.' If there is the faintest hint of bitterness here, she must have heard it in her own voice for she moves quickly to erase it. 'Claire is my step-sister. She lodges with us at present, and as I have often been ill of late, it is only reasonable that Shelley should take his afternoon walks with her.'

'I am sure,' says Maddox, but he is not deceived. Any more than he is yet convinced that this alleged persecution is anything other than a mental phenomenon, the delirium of an overheated fancy.

'I know what you are thinking,' she says suddenly, looking sternly upon him. 'You are thinking that Shelley has imagined it all – that none of it is real. I concede his nerves have been somewhat overwrought of late, that he has not been – entirely himself, but I can assure you, I have seen him after he has returned from these encounters, and I tell you no man could look so under the influence of mere phantasy. He can scarcely breathe – writhes upon the floor, his eyes frantic and his forehead beaded with sweat.'

Which is not, in itself, sufficient to persuade Maddox, who knows only too well that physical symptoms are not always the consequence of a physical cause. But he chooses not to pursue the point; at least, not yet.

'I suspect, all things considered,' he says instead, 'that I should talk of these matters with Mr Shelley myself. Information from a third party – however well intentioned or, indeed, intelligent – is never the best way to obtain and analyse evidence.'

She is caught now, he can see that, and one of his suppositions is confirmed: this visit of hers has been taken on her own initiative, and in secret.

'That is,' he continues steadily, 'if you are indeed decided to commission my services. Have you been informed as to my rates?'

She flushes again. 'I have – that is, that man—'

'George Fraser. One of my close assistants. He will keep

an account and render a copy to you each week for payment. I trust you are in a position to honour such a debt? My time is valuable and I do not care to waste it on clients who cannot pay.'

It was, perhaps, a little condescending, and he sees at once that she will not brook such disdain. 'Mr Shelley, sir, is the son of a baronet. He has ample means at his disposal.'

'I am very glad to hear it. You may, then, expect a call from me in two days.'

'You could come tomorrow, if you wish. We will be at home.'

Maddox shakes his head, and goes to the bell. 'I regret I have other business that will claim my attention tomorrow. But I will call promptly on Saturday morning.'

He has, in fact, no plans of a definite nature to absorb his Friday, but he makes a point of conducting an investigation of his clients before embarking upon any such investigation on their behalf. And there is something about this case that is already making him uneasy. He cannot define what it is, but it is there, and he has learned that such intuitions are not to be despised.

Fraser appearing now at the door, Maddox makes a bow. 'Good day to you, Miss Godwin.'

* * *

Friday dawns clear and bright, and begins with a breakfast of chocolate and hot rolls, followed by a brisk walk up the Strand to Bow Street. So it will surprise you, I think, that when we next find Maddox he is not in consultation with his former colleagues among the Runners but seated in a stiff gilt chair in an extremely imposing panelled room in Whitehall, in the company of the home secretary. Also in attendance we have a short man in a dour and anonymous suit of black, who gives his name as Sir Henry Pearson, and has before him a large pile of notes and correspondence. Opening pleasantries have clearly been conducted, and it is time to attend to business.

'Here is the first reference to the individual in question,' begins Sir Henry, scanning the papers. 'It appears in a report describing a meeting of revolutionary subversives in Dublin in February of the year 'twelve. A certain "young boy" seems to have made quite an impact, speaking for over an hour on the crimes supposedly committed by the corrupt English Crown upon the Irish. A people, incidentally, the same young man was shortly to describe as a "mass of animated filth".'

The words are sardonic, but the tone curiously flat. He turns a page. 'I also have a copy of a pamphlet by the aforementioned boy, and an incendiary letter written by the same to the *Dublin Weekly Examiner*. It appears this young radical was showing all the signs of becoming a veritable thorn in our sides, but only six weeks after his arrival in Ireland he decamped on a sudden to Wales, sending ahead of him a large box of frankly treasonable material, which, thanks to chance and a signal failure to pay adequate postage, we intercepted at Holyhead. I believe, my lord,' he says, looking up over his spectacles at the home secretary, 'that this was the first time the name Shelley came to your attention.'

'Indeed,' says Lord Sidmouth. He is a parched, thin-cheeked man with sallow skin and narrow, rather simian eyes. 'I determined, upon advisement, and in consideration of his legal minority, that no prosecution should be put immediately in train, but that the subject should be monitored for further evidence of seditious intent.'

261

'An agent was accordingly assigned,' resumes Sir Henry, 'to gather intelligence as to this Shelley's associates, and intercept his correspondence. However, it seems he may have become aware of this surveillance, since he soon moved once more, this time south to Lynmouth, where his party attracted considerable attention on arrival, due to the large number of heavy wooden chests in his possession, and the vast number of letters he dispatched about the country. Our agent was here able to observe his insurrectionary activities at first hand, since Shelley elected to convey his inflammatory messages either by launching them upon the sea in bottles and toy boats, or floating them into the air by means of . . .' He stops a moment, and scans the page again, as if distrusting his own eyes. '. . . *fire balloons*.'

He coughs; a small sound, but one he manages to endow with a whole world of disdain. 'Other such material was posted about the countryside on trees and farm buildings, though this particular task – whether from guile or indolence – he consigned to his luckless servant, who was promptly arrested and fined. The sum of two hundred pounds being clearly far beyond the foolish man's purse, he was committed to a six-months imprisonment. The true purpose of this proceeding was, as you will no doubt have guessed, to smoke Shelley from his lair, but contrary to all expectation – and his own sanctimonious rhetoric as to the necessity of assisting the "opprest and poor" – he refused to pay his servant's fine and fled the district, leaving his unlucky underling to languish out his sentence in the Barnstaple gaol. Further enquiries were instructed by your lordship,' this with a nod to Sidmouth, 'but, due to an unpardonable lapse on the part of our then agent in the town, we lost all trace of him. Indeed, it was not until the unfortunate servant was finally freed that we were able to gain any intelligence as to Shelley's whereabouts, for the man was dull-witted enough to lead us straight to his master, who was then residing at a house called . . .' he turns the pages and looks closer '. . . *Tan-yr-allt*, if my pronunciation is correct, in Tremadoc, on the coast of north Wales.'

There is a silence as a servant appears at the door with a message for the home secretary, who makes his excuses ('a matter of State'), bows and departs. The servant is dispatched for coffee, and returns a few moments later with a silver tray. As the coffee is poured, we might take advantage of the pause and consider what we have heard. That so inconsequential figure as the nineteen-year-old Shelley should have provoked so comprehensive an intelligence operation sounds, at first, incomprehensible, but you must remember that this is a time of riots, and machine-breaking, and the threat of invasion. A time of all-too-recent revolution in Europe, and the simmering suggestion of it still in England. A time when new ideas are suppressed as ruthlessly as insurrections, and those – like Shelley – who choose to publish them might well find themselves damned for it, if not hanged. You must remember, too, that even if Shelley's political effusions appear preposterously impractical and incoherent now, they would certainly not have seemed so at the time.

Maddox, meanwhile, has made a few notes in his book, and waits until the door closes behind the departing servant to turn to Sir Henry. 'As to the matter of Tremadoc,' he begins, but Sir Henry holds up a hand.

'We will come to that in its due place. I think you would find it instructive to hear what else our agents were able to discover as to the previous history and character of this man Shelley.'

Maddox bows; he is familiar with the ways of men of Sir

Henry's calling, and indulging his pomposity is a small price to pay for the quality of information he is able to bestow. 'I would be most obliged.'

'Enquiries were put on foot in his native Sussex, as in Oxford, whence he had been expelled after but two terms, on a charge of atheism.'

Maddox raises an eyebrow, but makes no comment.

'It is not, I have to say, a very pretty tale they had to tell,' continues Sir Henry. 'It seems Shelley is of an extremely excitable temper, and has been subject since boyhood to violent paroxysms of anger, most especially when contradicted or opposed. Conversely, as you might say, he has suffered repeated and extended periods of somnambulism. One acquaintance related a tale of his being discovered in Leicester Square at five o'clock one morning, dirty and dishevelled, and unable to give any account of how he got there. He will likewise – and this may prove to be significant – construct elaborate stories that bear all the appearance of truth, and which he himself appears to believe, but which are utter fabrications from first to last. This curious mania of his may lie behind an accusation of adultery directed at his own mother, and an oft-expressed conviction that his father wished to have him committed to a madhouse as a child; though on the latter count it seems there was indeed a period of some weeks during which he was kept under lock and key away from the rest of the household, which might suggest a genuine lunatic episode. Whatever the truth of it, had I been Sir Timothy I might well have considered such an expedient. The boy was not yet thirteen when he attempted to blow up his school with gunpowder, while his vacation pursuits appear to have included setting fire to the house, and torturing the family cat. He even,' he concludes drily, 'composed a poem on the subject.'

Maddox looks up. It's not the first time a man he is investigating has exhibited such characteristics as a child; indeed, it has struck him more than once how many murderers begin their descent into crime with the ill-treatment of animals, and the setting of fires. But Shelley, surely, is not a murderer. He writes a few words in his book, aware that the room has fallen silent.

'There is also a note here,' Sir Henry clears his throat circumspectly, 'questioning whether this Shelley might be of the sodomitical persuasion. Seems an unusually large pro-portion of his acquaintances describe him as "feminine". "A girl in boy's clothes," one is said to have remarked.' He closes the file and sits back in his chair, which creaks discreetly.

There is a pause before Maddox, too, sits back in his chair. 'Given what you have said,' he says slowly, 'might it be fair to assume that if Mr Shelley believes he is being pursued by a nameless persecutor, he might not, in this particular case, be prey to fanciful illusion, but has merely detected the presence of one of your own informants?'

'An interesting theory. I presume your use of the present indicative was deliberate?'

Maddox nods. 'He believes this pursuit continues even now – indeed claims to have seen the man he fears at least twice since returning to London only two weeks ago.'

'In that case I would suggest you are dealing with a case of pronounced and persistent *paranoea*. We have not actively pursued him since he departed Lynmouth, and my agents played no part whatsoever in the incident in Wales.'

Maddox looks up. 'What can you tell me of that?'

'Much of what you have been told is true, though the interpretation put upon it hardly objective. There were some locally who claimed the whole episode was an hallucination;

265

others said it was more likely a hoax put about by Shelley himself to afford him an excuse to withdraw from what was always a most ill-advised scheme. Our own view is that the incident was more likely to have been staged by Leeson and his associates to drive the Shelleys from the district. One shot, at least, Shelley himself fired, that much is certain; it is far less clear if he was fired upon first. Or, indeed, at all.'

He turns to the coffee pot and refills his cup. 'You are aware that something similar was said to have occurred in Cumberland some months before? It seems that there, too, Shelley contrived to infuriate a remarkably large number of people in a remarkably small amount of time, and woke one night to a knock on the door and a fist in his eye. He was forced to leave the neighbourhood. I presume you perceive the pattern?'

Maddox nods. How could he not?

'His lordship instructed me to give you whatever assistance might be within my power,' says Sir Henry, gathering up his papers and sending, thereby, a clear signal that the interview is at an end. 'I shall conclude, therefore, with a piece of advice. Be wary, and careful. Wary of a man who seems to bring ill-fortune to all those who encounter him, and careful of your pocket-book: he has debts halfway across England, and seems to feel no compunction, moral or otherwise, at defrauding even those small shopkeepers and tradesmen who can ill afford the loss.'

Maddox has already drawn rather the same conclusions, but accepts the counsel with good grace. Ten minutes later he is on the street once more, walking slowly and thoughtfully back up towards the Strand. It's rarely he receives such a decisive indication that a client bodes nothing but ill, and yet he cannot rid himself of the image of the girl – not just that face, which is the mirror of one he once loved, but the intelligence and the courage that make this new Mary so like the one he lost. It should not be necessary to remind a man of his experience that this resemblance may be traitorous – that even if the qualities he perceives are true, there may be others that he cannot possibly yet discern, and which may undermine what he wants so much to see. It should not be necessary, but it seems it is, and there is no one to do it.

The following morning we find him in his carriage, sitting back against the cushions as it toils up the Gray's Inn Lane, with an expression on his face that suggests a night of little sleep and much uncertainty. Fraser has to check the address twice at Pancras, so unlikely does it seem that the son of a baronet should be lodging so meanly, and they are kept waiting a good five minutes in the drizzle before there is any sign of life at number five Church Terrace. And the person who does eventually open the door is, to say the least, unprepossessing.

'Want that Shelley, do yer?' she says, her pink hands on her fat hips. 'Second floor. An' if you've come offerin' 'im somewhere else to stay don't let me stop yer. Folks are already startin' to talk – two women 'e's got up there and all sorts of noises at all times of the night, if you take my meanin'.'

Her puffy face manages to exhibit an almost equal quantity of prurience and prudery; it is not a pleasant combination. Fraser follows Maddox up to the top of the house, and there, again, they wait. All sorts of noises indeed, for sound and fury rages now behind the door. Then, as they listen, a woman's high-pitched wail is suddenly cut off, and there is a clattering thud as something strikes the near wall.

Maddox nods to Fraser to knock again, more insistently this time. 'You there – open up!'

Footsteps this time, and low, urgent voices, then, finally, the door inches open. It's Mary Godwin. Her white cheeks are flushed, and behind her, in the room, there is the sound of weeping.

'Mr Maddox,' she says, 'I am afraid you have had a wasted journey. Mr Shelley is unwell – Claire is unwell – we cannot receive you today.'

'I could not help noticing – the noise.'

She waves a hand. 'Oh, that was nothing. Merely Claire having one of her silly nightmares. She will be quite well soon enough if left to herself. I am sorry that you—'

She was holding the door to, but now it suddenly flings open. 'Maddocks? *Maddocks?* Does the villain pursue me even here?'

The man – boy – before them now is quite possibly the oddest-looking creature Maddox has ever seen. Taller than he expected, but stooping and round-shouldered, his chest hollow, his lips as soft as a girl's, and his hair sticking from his head in a tangle of rough, dirty spikes.

Maddox hears Fraser stifle a laugh, and there is indeed something ludicrous about this boy – ludicrous but beautiful, too, even if it's impossible to light on a single feature that merits the word. Aside, perhaps, from his eyes, which stare back at them now with a violet blue intensity.

'Mr Shelley,' says Maddox, with a slight bow. 'I do not believe we have been introduced.'

The boy stares at him a moment, then lets out a howl of wild, hysterical laughter that screeches in Maddox's ears like a fingernail on a plate. The boy throws back his head, and cries, '*Maddocks! Maddocks! Maddocks!*' until Mary Godwin places her hand on his arm in an attempt to calm him.

It's a practised gesture, and that fact alone is silently suggestive. 'You are mistaken, my love,' she says, with careful composure. 'As you can see, this is quite another gentleman.'

'Ha!' he cries. 'So what brings him creeping about here under the alias of my enemy?'

'I do not creep, sir,' says Maddox stiffly. 'And my name is my own.'

Mary Godwin turns to him. 'The scheme at Tremadoc was set on foot by a man called William Maddocks. He was also the magistrate who investigated the attack on Mr Shelley. You can understand why he should have been startled by the mention of the name.'

If it is meant as an apology it is meagre, to say the least. Shelley, meanwhile, scarcely seems to have heard. 'Magistrate? *Magistrate?* William Maddocks could not adjudicate on the proper division of a bread roll. The enquiries he made were infamously inadequate – he meant from the start that the perpetrator of that atrocious assassination should escape, and slither back to the protection of his degenerate paymaster.'

'That, my love,' the girl says quickly, forcing him round to look at her, 'is what our visitor has come to discuss. Mr *Charles* Maddox will be able to discover the truth of it. He will give you the evidence you need to challenge this Leeson and put an end to his villainous persecution for ever.'

Maddox is about to protest but a look from her swiftly silences him.

'Enquiries of this kind are Mr Maddox's calling,' she continues to Shelley. 'It is why I went to see him. To ask him to help us. That he might identify this man who pursues you, that we might put it behind us and begin again, together. I meant to have told you of this before but there has been so much – these last few days have been so very—'

She stops, and Maddox notices again the sound of weeping in the room beyond. Softer now, but still there.

'I think you were correct in your initial assumption, Miss Godwin,' he says. 'The moment does not appear to be opportune. Perhaps it would be better if I were to call again another day.'

'No!' she cries, her eyes widening, then quickly, more calmly, 'Now that you are here, and Shelley knows that you are ready to assist him, it will be the matter of a few minutes to give you the information you require.' She turns to Shelley, a plea in her eyes, and after a moment he puts a hand gently to her cheek.

'Very well,' he whispers, kissing her fingers. 'If you, my treasured Mary, believe a man such as this may succeed where my own extensive enquiries have failed, I will stoop to concur. Thus far I have always found, with Aristotle, that work of that kind ὅσαι πρὸς τὰς χρήσεις κάι τὰς πράξεις τὰς τῆς ἀρετῆς ἄχρηστον ἀπεργάζεται τὸ σῶμα τῶν ἐλεύθερων ἢ τὴν ψυχὴν ἢ τὴν διάνοιαν. Let us hope it will not hold true in this case.'

Maddox eyes him thoughtfully. The young man clearly does not expect Maddox to understand Greek, which is patronizing enough, but cited the phrase in his presence anyway, making him doubly discourteous. And the words themselves merely compound the insult, since regardless of what Aristotle might have opined, the exercise of a profession has never rendered Maddox feeble in either body, or in intellect. If this is how Shelley usually comports himself with strangers, it is hardly surprising he excites such violent antagonism wherever he goes. The fact that he seems completely unaware of the consequences of such behaviour might tempt a philosopher to exonerate him, but it will scarcely soften those he offends, who will expect an apology

270

but never get one. Fraser, meanwhile – to whom this is, indeed, all Greek – none the less has a long nose for contempt in any language, and shows his own in every line of his face.

'Will you come in?' says Miss Godwin, flushing a little. 'I will ask Mrs Butcher for coffee if that is agreeable.'

She shows them into a small sitting room, so squalid it brings a wry smile to Maddox's face; Shelley may boast the blood of a baronetcy, but Maddox is the one doing the stooping here. He had expected to see the third figure in this odd *ménage*, but of her there is now no sign. Having made her offer of refreshment, Miss Godwin seems to be regretting it, but the lodgings clearly afford her no means of making coffee herself, so she whispers a few earnest words to Shelley, and makes her way quickly down the stairs.

Maddox is intrigued to see how the boy will fare on his own, and proceeds to wander about the room, observing the books, the pamphlets, the writing-desk with its untidy sprawl of papers, all the while waiting an invitation to be seated. Shelley, meanwhile, is scuffing the threadbare carpet with his shoe and glowering at Fraser as if he, too, were little more than animated filth.

'Well,' says Maddox, eventually, taking both a chair and the initiative. 'Perhaps you might describe to me what happened at Tremadoc. It is still, I take it, your contention that the man who pursues you now does so at the behest of the Honourable Robert Leeson?'

'Honourable!' cries Shelley, his eyes flashing. 'Such an appellation does barbarity to the word! I despise such illegitimate distinctions, and everything they stand for. Aristocracy is vile, and such mealy-mouthed purse-proud half-measures more than twice as contemptible. There is no

271

justification – moral, philosophical or political – for a system that permits the few to riot in luxury, while the many famish for want of bread.'

'We might debate such a point as lengthily as Aquinas did the corporeality of angels, and to almost as little purpose,' replies Maddox, evenly. 'My time being limited, I should rather devote it to the matter in hand. I have some understanding of the events that may have led to the attack on your household; more such information I can readily come by should I require it. But you alone can tell me the nature and sequence of events.'

Perhaps it is the reference to the *Summa Theologica* that proves to Shelley that he has underestimated this man; perhaps it is the note of authority in Maddox's voice. Whatever it is, when he speaks again his tone is calmer, and his eyes less wild.

'Very well. We retired that night some time after ten. I had received so many odious and despicable threats the preceding days that I had taken to sleeping with two loaded pistols at my side. We had scarce been abed half an hour—'

'We?'

'Harriet.' He flushes. 'My wife. Then.'

'And now?'

Shelley's eyes narrow. 'She lives still. If that is your question.'

A pause. 'I see. Go on.'

'I heard a noise downstairs, so I seized the guns and went down, only to see the insolent wretch attempting to escape through one of the windows giving onto the lawn. He turned, saw me, and had the impudence to fire upon me. Happily, it went wide.'

'You saw his face?'

'I saw only the flash of the pistol. I returned a shot of my own, but unluckily my gun misfired. He then set upon me with blows, and we fell to the ground.'

'In the house?'

'No. We were by then upon the lawn. After some moments of scrapping like savages on the ground, I contrived to free myself sufficiently to fire upon him a second time and – I believe – wounded him in the shoulder. Whereupon he hurled himself upon me again crying, "*By God I will be revenged! I will murder your wife – I will ravish your sister! By God I will be revenged!*" By the time I had struggled to my feet, he had gone.' He puts his hand to his side. 'The kick the scoundrel gave me has never fully healed.'

There is a pause. 'He spoke in English?' asks Maddox.

Shelley frowns. 'Of course. Why should he not?'

'Because if he were indeed in Leeson's employ, and hired thereabouts, I imagine his mother tongue might have been Welsh. Would you not agree?'

Shelley turns away to the window, gnawing his thumb.

'And you can offer no explanation for the words he used?' persists Maddox. 'No reason why he should threaten your wife and sister?'

He shakes his head, still staring down the street. 'None. It is incomprehensible. That woman is not my sister.'

'I do not take your meaning.'

Shelley turns back to face him. 'Miss Eliza Westbrook was present in the house at the time. But she is my sister-*in-law*, not my sister. And besides,' he screws up his mouth in disgust, 'I cannot imagine any man wishing to ravish *her*. I could scarce bear to see her caress my daughter without a sensation of revulsion. As for submitting to such a caress myself—' He turns away again, and leans one hand against the window, tearing his thumbnail with his teeth.

273

'I believe,' continues Maddox, 'that there was a subsequent attack, the selfsame night? Were you again alone?'

Shelley flashes him a look. 'You may judge of the effect of the first attack on a house full of females. Miss Westbrook had a fit of the hysterics, and one of the maids refused to stay another moment in the building. It was past one before I judged it safe to send the rest of them back to bed. I sat up alone thereafter with a servant – a man I knew to be loyal. He had been with us in Lynmouth, and only very lately joined us again in Wales.'

Indeed, thinks Maddox. The same servant, surely, who suffered a six-months prison sentence rather than betray his hot-headed master. How very interesting. 'Pray go on,' he says aloud.

'Somewhere near four o'clock I sent this man to ascertain the time, and the villain chose that very moment to strike again. I saw him standing at the window and rushed upon him. I fired and he returned my shot – my gun did not go off, but his bullet passed so close it burned through my nightshirt. By the time the servant heard the noise and came to my assistance he had gone.'

'So the servant did not see his face?'

Shelley flushes. 'I believe it was the glimpse of a moment only. He had no fixed impression thereafter.'

'And your own impression? Was that fixed?'

He hesitates. 'I did attempt a sketch of his face . . .'

'May I see it?'

Shelley looks at him a moment, then goes to the desk and sifts about in the clutter for a few minutes before dragging a sheet from under a pile of journals. One book falls open as he does so, revealing a page written crossways and lengthways in spiky, illegible scrawl, a rough sketch of a small rowing boat among trees, and a pair of large and slanting eyes. Seeing Maddox's gaze upon the drawings, Shelley shuts the book with a snap and hands him a single sheet of paper.

Had Maddox seen this drawing without knowing its origins he might have thought it a child's imagining of a make-believe monster. The body strangely swollen and elongated, the single arm stick-like, the face a mask of grinning Hallowe'en horror. 'Your assailant wore a disguise?'

Shelley frowns. 'No. Why should you think so? That is how he appeared.'

Maddox places the paper carefully on the table. 'Describe him to me.'

'Is that really necessary?'

'Miss Godwin wishes for my assistance; I can provide that only if I have *yours*.'

Shelley heaves a theatrical sigh. 'Very well. If I must. The night was dark and my thoughts, understandably, confused, but he appeared to be taller than the common, his hair dark, and his stature slender. That is all.'

Much like to you, indeed, thinks Maddox, wondering suddenly what the servant really saw. And what really lay behind that picture, so perplexing and so strange. 'Let me be clear, then,' he says. 'In the course of the night your assailant fired upon you twice, while you shot your own guns three times, but succeeded in discharging a bullet on only one of those occasions. I might say, at this juncture, that should you require advice on the proper handling and keeping of a pistol I would recommend you consult Fraser here. *You* are clearly a novice in such matters; *he* is a crack shot – better even, may I say, than myself.'

He sees Shelley open his mouth to speak, then close it again. Fraser, for his part, is trying – not very hard it must be said – to suppress a smile.

275

'And the weather,' continues Maddox. 'Was the night clear?'

Shelley shakes his head. 'It rained in torrents, and the wind howled like a dæmon.'

Another pause.

'It would appear,' says Maddox, finally, 'that the conclusion I drew from my first conversation with Miss Godwin remains the most likely explanation. This attack was personal in nature, and sprang not from your activities at Tremadoc, nor your neighbours' resentment of them, however well justified, but from some other cause, of much longer date.'

Shelley frowns. 'Upon what do you base such an absurd and ludicrous thesis?'

Maddox smiles. 'It is not so very absurd, Mr Shelley, and a moment's calm reflection on your part will suffice to prove it. For this was not the first such incident to befall you, was it? Had there not been a remarkably similar episode some months before, in a completely different part of the country? Even if Miss Godwin does not appear to be aware of the fact.'

'How dare you—' the young man begins, but there is a noise then behind them and Maddox turns to see that there is another person now in the room, who has entered silently from the farther door. It is a girl. Dark-haired, blue-dressed, softly rounded. Her skin is ashen but Maddox can see at a glance that it is not her customary complexion. And were that not evidence enough, her eyes are rimmed with red, and there are marks of tears still on her cheeks. So this, thinks Maddox, is Mary Godwin's step-sister.

'Claire!' says Shelley, going quickly to her. 'Did I not tell you to go to bed?'

She hangs her head and the tears come again. 'I cannot

sleep – it comes upon me every time when I close my eyes – the horror – Oh, Shelley!'

She bursts now into shuddering sobs and the young man puts his arms about her, pulling her to his breast and kissing her hair.

Maddox gets to his feet; something about the way Shelley is touching the girl strikes an unsettling note. He is holding her as one would hold a child, but she has the full figure of an alluring young woman: even were he a single man Shelley should not have his hands about her body so, and she should not be permitting it.

'May I be of assistance?' Maddox asks, taking a pace towards them and expecting Shelley to release her. Only he does not.

'There is no need,' says Shelley, stiffly, his arms even closer about the girl, and his head resting on hers. 'Miss Clairmont was dismayed last night by a bad dream. We sat up late into the dark talking of magic, and I may – I confess – have indulged myself a little overmuch in my conjuring of the witching time of night. Miss Clairmont is very susceptible to such things.'

So why then, thinks Maddox, did you persist? And where, in all this, was Miss Godwin?

'I ran upstairs to bed,' says the girl, half to herself. 'I placed the candle on the chest and stood looking at the pillow that lay in the middle of the bed – I turned to the window and then back again to the bed. The pillow had gone – it was on the chair. I kept thinking – how could this be? Was it possible I had placed it there myself and not remembered? I came running downstairs again.'

She twists her face up to Shelley, the tears still falling. 'You came out of your room and described my expression in the most horrible way – but I did not feel what you

277

thought I did – and then you looked at me – as if you knew your power over me – and then you said Mary was with child and I – I—'

'Hush, my dear,' says Shelley, hastily. 'Or this gentleman will gain a very odd impression of how Shelley manages his affairs.' His tone is deliberately light but Maddox sees his arms tighten about the girl. 'After all, did we not find that skittish pillow exactly where you left it this morning?' He lifts her chin to his and slips into the sing-song voice one might use with a baby: '*Naughty Mr Pillow, you shall go no more a-roving.*'

She smiles through her tears, and Shelley tips his finger on her nose. Maddox, meanwhile, has noted that he is speaking of himself now in the third person, and wonders if it is an attempt, conscious or otherwise, to absolve himself from the consequences of his own acts. How could any man, far less one of Shelley's intelligence, really be ignorant of what he has done to this young woman who is supposedly under his protection? Sitting up alone with her in the dark, with the quiet tingling in their ears, whispering strange supernatural stories until he has worked her to such a pitch of breathless terror that she rushes for comfort to his embrace? Only to tell her at that very moment that another woman is carrying his child? *In lone and silent hours, when night made a weird sound of its own stillness*, to have so *mixed awful talk and asking looks until strange tears united with breathless kisses.* Not my words, those, but Shelley's own, from a poem he will begin almost exactly twelve months from now. Maddox cannot, of course, know this, but it has not escaped his notice that Shelley did not merely instigate this dangerous game, but took every opportunity thereafter to intensify it. Ever drawing her to the brink, ever pulling away. What perverse purpose – or pleasure – could drive a man to such cruelty?

278

Maddox has been in this man's presence less than half an hour, but he cannot recall anyone who has disquieted him so much in so short a period; he's questioned cut-throats in Newgate who have troubled him less. There is a movement now at the front door, and he looks across to see Mary Godwin undoing the latch and bending to pick up the coffee pot from the floor where she has momentarily placed it. There is ample time for Shelley to release Claire Clairmont before the two of them are seen, but he does not do so. If anything he holds her yet closer, and when Miss Godwin comes bustling into the room, Maddox sees the younger girl's face turn towards her, and a look he cannot fathom pass between them. As for Mary, it appears the sight of the others lover-like gives her no pause, though there is the flicker of a frown as she places the coffee on the table, when she believes herself unobserved.

'Is Claire still in that horrid mood?' she asks briskly. 'I do not wonder the silly miss has frighted herself, sitting up till the early hours gorging on ghost stories.'

Maddox notes her tone – notes how she, too, reduces Claire Clairmont to the status of mere child. This girl who is more voluptuously womanly than many twice her age – or, for that matter, her own step-sister. Is Mary Godwin deceiving herself, or is this her way of defusing what Maddox can see only as an emotional tinderbox, vulnerable to the tiniest spark? However unappealing he may have found the landlady of this place, he feels a modicum of sympathy for her now: if this is how these people comport themselves before strangers, he cannot begin to imagine what goes on behind closed doors. If he were Mrs Butcher, with the reputation of her house to consider, he would have them gone before nightfall.

'Now, will you take coffee?' says Mary Godwin, turning

brightly to Maddox, who gets promptly to his feet and takes up his hat.

'I fear I must away. I have a meeting with another client.'

'But you will take the case?' she says, coming towards him and gripping his arm. 'You will help us?'

He was intending to write to her that very afternoon disdaining all further involvement, but now, looking down into her pale and anxious face, he finds himself saying yes, knowing even as he does so, that it is a mistake, and he will surely regret it. But how much, and how bitterly, he cannot possibly foresee. And as she stands there, so close he can hear her breathing, her hand warm upon his arm, he lifts his head and sees that the two of them are being watched. By Shelley and – now – by the other girl, who has turned within the circle of Shelley's arms to gaze at Maddox. A gaze of such unbearable dark brilliance that, for the first time in all his years of interrogation and investigation, he is the first to look away. And so it is that he does not see the girl turn again to Shelley and her lips part in a wordless gasp – does not see his answering nod, or the change in the young man's eyes as he looks once more towards Maddox, his face burning now with a strange and feverish exultation.

CHAPTER ELEVEN

The Cloud

Two months pass. Months of lashing hail and skies that
dissolve in rain, running the pavements so wet they might
be strips of fallen sky. Ample time, then, for Fraser to travel
to Tremadoc, and return with a report on what he discovered there. Ample time, too, for Maddox to investigate
the murder of an old washerwoman, found in her own
kitchen with her skull broken, and all for the sake of a few
bundles of washing. Thomas Sharpe's father came to Maddox three days after his son's arrest, grey-faced and shaking,
with all the money he possessed wrapped in a cloth, but the
evidence was too strong, and his son's past record too
incriminating, to hope for anything but the worst. Despite
belligerent protestations of innocence almost to the last, they
brought Sharpe to the gallows subdued and terrified, and he
died, as the Newgate Calendar recorded, 'with the name of
God in his mouth'. Brutal, but all too banal in the context of
the contemporary justice system, and worth mentioning
now only because the killing took place less than a mile
from Shelley's lodgings in Church Terrace, but each time
Maddox has called there on his way back to the Strand

there has been no answer, and by the first week in November the rooms are empty, and Mrs Butcher furiously out of pocket.

'The bailiffs must have come a dozen times this last fortnight,' she grumbles, 'and each time *he* contrived not to be here, and *she* comes to the door looking like butter wouldn't melt and claiming not to know where he's skulking. Though he'd come creeping back 'ere quick as a cat on 'eat every Sunday, the minute he knew they couldn't touch him. Wish I'd laid hands on him meself while I still could – *I* don't have a prohibition as to working of a Sunday, even if the gaffmen do.'

Maddox could only express his sympathy, and congratulate himself privately that he had taken Sir Henry's advice and required monies in advance before sending Fraser to Wales. Which makes it unlikely that he has seen the last of the Church Terrace party, even if Mrs Butcher will be lucky to set eyes on any one of them again. And he is right: on the evening of 7th December the maid comes knocking at the drawing-room door to say there is a Miss Godwin wishing to see him.

'I told her as you was eating, sir, and never usually sees anyone at this time of night but she said as she was sorry to disturb you but would you be seeing her if you have a minute.'

Maddox puts down his knife and fork, wondering (not for the first time) if he should invest in a book of grammar for the staff below stairs. But how likely is it that any of them would read it? He smiles to himself, remembering how Samuel Richardson's impossibly perfect Sir Charles Grandison provided a 'Servants Library' at his ancestral seat, with a case of books divided into divinity, housewifery and 'innocent amusement'. In fact he's still smiling when the maid shows in Miss Godwin, who pauses on the threshold, wondering at such a reception.

'Something has amused you?'

Maddox waves his hand. 'I was thinking, hard as it may be to credit it, of *Sir Charles Grandison*.'

'Indeed?' she says, raising an eyebrow. 'Hardly a novel – or novelist – to afford much by way of humour. Though I did find the "Names of the Principal Persons" affixed at the beginning extremely comical. Unintentionally so, of course.'

Maddox laughs. 'I take it you refer to the sub-division into "Men, Women and Italians"? I have never visited the country in question, but I cannot believe it populated by an alien species wholly unconnected with our own.'

It is her turn to smile. 'Nor have I, but I am sure you are right. The French are certainly recognizably human. Indeed, rather too much so.'

He gestures to a seat by the fire and notices she takes it with some relief; her pregnancy now is much more pronounced. The light from the flames throws a warm glow over her face, but he can see that she is thinner than she was, and there are dark shadows under her eyes. 'I believe you have had rather a trying time of late,' he says, pouring her a glass of wine and handing it to her.

She glances at him and then down at her glass. Her lips are trembling. 'It has been – dreadful. We have still not discovered how Shelley's creditors contrived to learn our address. For near a month we could meet only for a few snatched hours each week, and for all the remainder I was walled up in those dingy lodgings, with no creature coming near me from one day to the next. I have been shunned, Mr Maddox, by those who called themselves my friends – by those who commended my mother's principles and yet

283

now condemn *me* for living by them. The only letters I receive are letters of rebuke.'

Her eyes fill with tears and she looks away. Maddox rises from his seat in silence and refills his glass.

'And now,' she continues, her voice breaking, '*she* has had a son, and *he* is all jubilation, sending out to all and sundry, announcing the birth of an heir by his *wife*. A wife who wallows in comfort at her parents' house while *I* am forced to make my own clothes, and go without eating two days in five. That woman absolutely refused to give Shelley money, even when he told her we had sold all we had and were very nearly perished with hunger.'

Her bitterness is as raw as an open wound, and Maddox is impelled to pity her – impelled because from every other point of view he utterly condemns what they have done, and all the more so now he knows the wife Shelley abandoned was with child. And what forsaken wife this side of sainthood would readily offer money to support the woman who had supplanted her?

'You were not wholly alone, though?' he says, after a pause. 'I gather Miss Clairmont is still with you?'

Her fingers tighten on the glass. 'There has been talk of her returning to Skinner Street, but she refuses to go. Even though it is quite clearly the best thing for her – as well as—' She stops, aware perhaps that she is slipping into dangerous territory. 'Claire continues to suffer from nightmares,' she finishes sullenly. 'It is inconsiderate of her to disturb my sleep so. In my condition.'

'Then perhaps,' says Maddox, cautiously, 'you might consider remonstrating with Mr Shelley. He seemed to me to be taking a somewhat perverse delight in provoking such nocturnal disturbances—'

'*She* is the one who delights in provocation,' interrupts

Miss Godwin. 'Those horrors of hers are pure invention, designed to absorb my Shelley's every waking moment. They were out together again when I left. She is now claiming she cannot leave him because he is afraid to walk alone, lest Leeson should attack him in the street.'

Which may explain, thinks Maddox, why Mary Godwin has chosen, after all this time, to brave the cold and the dark, and come here alone. And why she has started to use the word 'my' in reference to a man who does not appear at all constrained by such exclusivities.

'Is this new fear of Mr Shelley's the consequence of a further sighting, or some other incident subsequent to our last meeting?'

'I wished to inform you immediately after it happened, but Shelley would not permit me.'

Maddox frowns. He had asked the question thinking it rhetorical; now it seems he may be mistaken. He takes a seat opposite her. 'Perhaps you might elaborate?'

'It was October. The twelfth, I believe. We returned to Church Terrace that evening to find a letter had been delivered for Shelley. By hand, not by post. It was couched in veiled terms, but its import was only too clear – it was a threat upon his life. Upon *all* our lives.'

'Do you have this letter?'

She shakes her head. 'No. Shelley burned it at once – he said he feared it would distress me. I begged him to allow me to send it to you – I said you might be able to advise us, but he would not hear of it. He began to babble in the wildest and most unconnected way – talking one minute of his daughter Ianthe and the next of a cousin I do not believe he has seen for years. None of it made any sense. But he has always been subject to nervous attacks when confronted with the slightest distress or strain, and fearing a new recurrence, I withdrew.'

'I see,' says Maddox, all his old disquiet returning. 'Pray continue.'

'The morning following he seemed much quieter in his mind, and we determined to go – as we had planned – to see Mr Kean give his Prince of Denmark. It was not, I fear, a happy choice of play. Shelley became increasingly agitated, and insisted finally that we left at the end of the second act.'

She shifts in her chair, her anxiety visible in her fretfulness. 'Imagine our alarm, then, when we returned home to discover that a man had called in our absence. Shelley at once grew white in the face and cried out, "We must leave London! We must go at once – we cannot stay another night in this accursed hovel!" I am afraid Mrs Butcher was much offended by this and said we might go as soon as we liked, as far as she was concerned, and Claire having by then become completely hysterical and threatening to disturb the entire house, we elected to repair to a hotel for what remained of the night, and deliberate there what best to do.'

'You had the money for such an expense?'

She flushes. 'It was Shelley's idea. It was not my decision. We returned to Church Terrace the next morning. It was a – difficult day. We were all unsettled – all disturbed. Shelley began talking rather distractedly of a plan he had conceived to rescue his sisters from their school, and later he and Claire had a fearful quarrel.'

Maddox observes that, as she places her glass carefully on the table beside her, her hands are shaking. 'Was the letter signed?'

'I do not think so.'

'And has this man shown himself since?'

She hesitates. 'No—'

'Or written again?'

'Not that I am aware.'

'I see.'

He gets up and pokes the fire, watching the red-grey embers sift and sigh, then takes a log from the basket and throws it onto the glowing ashes. All the while the girl says nothing.

'And so you are here,' he says eventually, settling again in his seat. 'Hoping I will tell you George Fraser has discovered something in Tremadoc that might solve this mystery.'

Her eyes follow him as he takes a sheet of paper from the table, and scans it again (though that is hardly necessary, since he has a good part of it by heart).

'So long after the event in question,' he begins, 'there was little hope of gaining the class of physical evidence I would normally seek at the scene of a crime. Or supposed crime, in this case. However, by dint of perseverance and a commendable resourcefulness Fraser was able to gain access to the house, and conduct an inspection of the downstairs rooms. He spoke also thereafter to a number of servants who had been in service at the time, as well as the owners of neighbouring properties. He was thus able to verify that there is still the mark of a bullet on the wainscot in the drawing room, which would seem to confirm that at least one shot was fired into the house from the outside. Likewise several of the maids gave corroboration that Mr Shelley appeared wet through and covered with mud when they saw him at midnight, and the grass in the garden had been trampled.'

'You see?' she cries. 'There *was* an attack – it was no illusion—'

'However,' interrupts Maddox, raising his hand, 'the selfsame witnesses also testified that the window in the room where the second incursion took place was broken

287

from the *inside out*, rather than the other way about, which does *not* tally with what Mr Shelley says of the man firing on him from behind the glass. Moreover, certain discreet enquiries among Robert Leeson's household suggest that he had nothing whatsoever to do with it. Plans were afoot, certainly, to drive Shelley from the district, but Leeson and his confederates had not had the time to organize such a concerted raid. Hence his insistence thereafter that the whole episode was a hoax got up by Shelley to excuse his abrupt departure. I should say, also, that Fraser could find no evidence there had been talk at the time of a man in the neighbourhood sustaining a gunshot wound – to the shoulder or otherwise. In so small a place, such an untoward injury to a local man would surely have attracted notice, not to mention gossip.'

She is avoiding his gaze now, biting her lip.

'My conclusion then, Miss Godwin,' continues Maddox, 'remains much as it was when first we spoke. There was undoubtedly one incident of some violence that night. But it was motivated not by antipathy to Mr Shelley's political beliefs, nor resentment at his interference in local matters, but by an intense and long-standing desire for *personal revenge*. What can have occasioned this, only he can tell. And thus far, it seems, he either cannot, or *will not*.'

There is a silence. The new log slides forwards in the grate in a crackle of sparks.

'You spoke of only one attack,' she says softly.

'So I did. Because I do not believe there was another. I believe, in fact, that the second episode that night was some species of hallucination. The isolated location, the darkness, the days of mounting apprehension, the fear and excitement brought on by the first incident – all of these combined, in my opinion, to make Mr Shelley abnormally susceptible to the delusions of an inflamed imagination. My theory – though I cannot substantiate it – is that it was his own self he saw, reflected in the window, and that he broke the glass himself in rushing upon it. I believe, likewise, that the shot he described piercing his nightshirt occurred during the first assault, and not the second as he asserted when he described it to me. One of the servants thought the shirt was already torn when she saw him in the garden.'

'But despite what you say – despite your theory – is it not still possible that it is Leeson who sends this man to torment us?'

Maddox puts the tips of his fingers together. 'There is no incontrovertible proof against it, no—'

'Why, then—'

'—but there is *one* fact which *is* incontrovertible, and which argues too strongly against Leeson's involvement for a woman of your intelligence to continue to believe it.'

Her chin lifts. 'And that is?'

'That an almost identical incident took place in Cumberland more than a year before – before Shelley had ever set foot in Tremadoc and Leeson had even heard his name.'

She starts forward, her eyes wide. 'I do not believe it – he would have told me. It is false.'

'It is *not* false, Miss Godwin. I have heard it from Mr Shelley's own lips. And that fact is itself both instructive and troubling. The former because of what it tells me of that young man's mind; the latter because he has not spoken of it to *you*.'

She gets to her feet and begins to walk about the room, all the while avoiding his eyes.

'I am old enough, Miss Godwin, to have a daughter your age, and I hope you will indulge me if I give you counsel now which might seem to usurp a father's place.'

She throws a furious look in his direction, but he is not deterred.

'I am concerned for your safety, Miss Godwin, yours and your child's. I have been so ever since I saw you at Pancras all those weeks ago. I beg you, leave this man and return to your parental abode as soon as you are able. I do not know what Mr Shelley has done to warrant such a persecution, but everything I have learned in all the years I have practised this profession tells me that it is of a nature – an enormity – such as to place both you and your unborn babe in the most urgent danger. No man practises such a pursuit for so long a period and with so unflinching a tenacity without there being a terrible and compelling reason at the heart of it. From what I have seen of him, I doubt very much that Mr Shelley is in the slightest degree competent to protect you from this nameless persecutor, but even if he is – even if his constant restless movement from place to place does indeed contrive to keep you always one pace ahead of the retribution that stalks him – what can he do to shield you from *himself*? Did you not say he is prey to violent nervous attacks? Have you not seen him walk in his sleep, and not know afterwards where he is, or what he has done? Did his own father not threaten to confine him to a madhouse?'

She is staring at him wildly now. 'I never told you that – how do you know such things?' she cries, her voice hoarse.

'I know,' he says, going to her and gripping her by the shoulders, 'because I have made it my business to *find out*. You know not the risk you run, Miss Godwin, you or Miss Clairmont. Believe me when I tell you there is no happy ending to this tale of love you believe yourself to be living. There is a lunacy in this man that renders him treacherous – to himself and to all about him. *You* may decide to take that risk – do not impose it upon your defenceless infant.

Consult a doctor if you do not believe me – send for William Lawrence: he has made a study of such cases.'

'How dare you?' she exclaims, raising her hand to strike him, but he is too quick, and as he grasps her wrist and feels the pulse of blood beating hard in her veins, his face comes close to hers for a second time. Only now it is not pleading in her eyes, but fear. But is it fear of the man before her, or fear of something his words have awakened – something she has long known, and long suppressed?

A moment later Maddox inclines his head and releases her hand. 'I apologize if I have offended you. That was not my intention.'

She snatches her arm away and marches to the door.

'You may call upon me,' he says softly, 'at any hour of the day. Should you be in need.'

She does not turn but her hand pauses on the handle, before she throws open the door and is gone.

He knows it was a mistake to allow himself to be drawn in by this girl, but now he wonders if it is an even graver one to allow her to leave. He should have handled it better – at least asked her where they are lodging for he has no means to find her – find her or protect her. Because he doubts very much that she will come to him again. Not unless she is in the most terrible extremity.

* * *

Christmas comes and passes. January blurs into February, and Mary Godwin has – almost – gone from his mind in the welter of a murder trial. Maddox has worked many, on both sides of the accusation, but this is more demanding than most, not only because the crime took place in Lisbon, but because the accused cut his own throat thereafter and can now barely speak. After another night in the Newgate cells, slowly extracting what defence he may from a young man seemingly determined to die, Maddox returns early one Monday morning wanting only his breakfast and his bed. What he finds instead is Fraser waiting in the hallway, holding a card.

'What is it?' he says, somewhat tetchily, as he takes off his coat. 'Have Phyllis draw my bath, would you?'

'You may want to see this first, guv. Young fellow left it not half an hour ago. Waited a while getting more and more agitated, then said he'd go on ahead of you. He left about five minutes back.'

Maddox frowns. 'I think I saw him. Turning into the Strand. I thought it odd to see one of his character abroad at such an hour. Thickset, heavy-featured, perhaps twenty-five?'

'And sweating, despite the cold. Seemed to have a lot on his mind.'

Fraser hands Maddox the card. On the face: *Thomas Jefferson Hogg, Middle Temple*. It is a name, of course, that cannot possibly mean anything to Maddox. Though indeed a lawyer by profession, if rather a mediocre one, we remember Hogg now as Shelley's friend and biographer, though in March 1815 the latter is a long way in the future. The former role, however, is both current, and – as Maddox will soon discover – complicated.

'Did he wish to consult me on a legal matter?' asks Maddox. 'Because, if so, I am afraid the hour is far too early for any sort of profitable discussion.'

'No, guv,' says Fraser. 'Look on the back.'

It has been written in haste, and – it appears – at Maddox's own desk, and with his pen:

Mary – Miss Godwin – begs that you will come.
Her need is desperate – I beseech you, do not delay.
    T. J. H.

                              13 Arabella Road, Pimlico

'*Mary*, indeed,' says Maddox, coldly. 'It seems our young lawyer is on distinctly intimate terms with that rather irregular household.'

'An acquaintance of Shelley's at Oxford – or, at least, that's what he said to me,' finishes Fraser, quickly, seeing Maddox raise an eyebrow at the missing 'Mr'. 'Will you go, sir?'

'I am afraid I will be unpopular with the coachman, but yes, I will go. I will change my clothes and be ready to leave in ten minutes. Wait for me outside.'

The journey takes little more than a quarter of an hour so early in the morning. The streets are for the most part deserted, and Maddox looks out of the window, ostensibly watching to see if they overtake their early visitor. But if he is honest with himself he is more concerned to avoid his assistant's shrewdly observing eye, uneasily aware that Fraser already knows rather too much about his entanglement with Mary Godwin, and no doubt guesses even more.

Most of the houses in Arabella Road are still dark, but it is clear even in the half-dawn that the Shelley establishment has raised itself more than a notch since Church Terrace, and Maddox wonders for a moment how the poet came by the money, and how much of his future inheritance he has already borrowed away. Number thirteen, by contrast with the rest, glares with the light of trouble, or distress. But if Mary Godwin is anxious to see him the same appears not to apply to her step-sister, who eyes him with a closed and wary look as she opens the door.

'I hope *you* may get some sense from her,' Claire says at once, 'for she will certainly not speak to *us*. Three hours has she sat there, in silence. She is driving Shelley half distracted – he has had to lie down.'

There is something about her face – something nervous and yet at the same time excited, self-assured.

'What in Heaven's name is going on here?' Maddox says quickly, pushing the girl aside and forcing his way through the hallway to the sitting room, Fraser at his heels.

He will never, afterwards, be able to rid himself of that moment. The girl sitting facing him on a stiff wooden chair in the centre of the floor. Her head bowed, her eyes dry. And in her lap, a swaddle of blankets. The size and shape of a newborn child.

The child does not move, but he knows instinctively that this is not the warm stillness of slumber. It is no baby she cradles, but a corpse.

There is something terribly wrong, Maddox knows that at once. The death of infants – especially those born before their time, as this must have been – is so commonplace as to be mundane. But there is nothing mundane here.

'When was she brought to bed?' he says quickly, turning to Claire.

Claire scowls. She seems impatient, even irritated, which in the circumstances is unaccountable. Or accountable only unsettlingly. 'Two weeks ago. At our last lodgings. We thought the baby would not live – the doctor said we should not hope – but it seemed to rally, only then Shelley became unwell.'

'*Shelley?* What has this to do with *Shelley*?'

'He began to have the most terrible seizures – spasms in

his side that left him shrieking in agony. There was nothing for it but to move here.'

'*Move?* With an infant only a few days old and not expected to live?'

Claire looks up at him, unabashed. 'Shelley did not like the other place. He said it was horrid – that it played upon his nerves.'

Maddox takes a deep breath, endeavouring to keep his anger in check. He has never, in all his years first as Bow Street Runner and now as thief-taker, lost his temper with a client. It has been his hallmark, and a good part of his success, so the fact that he seems on the point of doing so now both infuriates and alarms him. 'Has a doctor been called?'

'No,' the girl snaps. 'I wished to, but *she* would not permit me – she sent Hogg to find *you*.'

Mary Godwin is now rocking backwards and forwards, her child cradled against her breast. More concerned now than ever, Maddox goes quickly to her and crouches before her chair. 'May I see?' he says softly. She seems reluctant at first, gripping the child even tighter, but he coaxes her gently and she eventually folds back the blanket covering the baby's face. The infant is tiny – some weeks premature to Maddox's untrained eye. There are pale blue shadows under her eyes, and flecks of dry foam speckling her lips.

'She seemed so much better yesterday,' whispers Mary. 'I thought – I dared hope – that all might yet be well. She opened her eyes at the sound of my voice – she smiled. I am sure she knew me.'

And as she touches a tiny cheek rigid with death, her words stumble, and the first tears come. 'I awoke in the dark, icy with fear – terrified by my dreams – and I wondered at first where I was, but then I saw there was someone in the room, someone standing over the crib, bending over my sleeping child. I thought I dreamed again – that it was nothing but the continuation of my nightmare – but when I rose this morning and went to the cradle my baby was cold.'

Maddox reaches across and edges the blanket a little looser. The baby's yellow skin is darkening already to a dull purple, but he can see now that there are scatters of minute red marks about her eyelids; marks that Maddox has seen before, even if their full significance will not be formally documented by the medical profession for decades; marks which, if found about the eyes and face, are one of the first signs a modern pathologist will look for in cases of suspected strangulation.

There is a fear now, which clenches Maddox's heart iron-hard, but he must not leap to conclusions – must not allow prejudice to outrun truth. 'Are you sure it was not, indeed, the delusion of a dream?' he says. 'No one could blame you – after days of watching, of broken and intermittent sleep. And did the doctor not say it could have happened at any time – despite all your care?'

And now for the first time she raises her stricken eyes to his face. 'It was no dream, Mr Maddox – I know what I saw. It was as you said – I should have listened. I should not have allowed him near my baby.'

Claire Clairmont rushes forwards, taking hold of her step-sister's arm. 'No, *no*! That is a *lie*! Why do you bring this horrible man here only to tell him such wicked falsehoods? He would never – you know he would never—'

But Maddox has already raised his hand to restrain her. He knows now – has known, indeed, since the first minute he entered this room. But she must say it – he has to hear her say it.

'Miss Godwin,' he says quietly. 'There must be no misunderstanding here – no risk of error. Are you telling me that the figure you saw—'

'It was Shelley,' she sobs. 'Heaven forgive me, but it was Shelley.'

There is noise now behind them and Maddox turns to see the young man standing in the doorway. He looks as if he hasn't slept in months, his shirt half unbuttoned, stained at the armpits and coming adrift from his breeches. Maddox has never seen him look so young, and wonders why that innocent idea should now be so very chilling.

'Ha! *You!*' he cries. 'I might have known! There is nothing for *you* here, Maddox – nothing for you to *investigate*.'

Maddox straightens up and moves towards him. 'I would not be so sure of that,' he says, 'were I in your place. But you may obviate the need for any such *investigation* by answering a single question. One, and one only. What were you doing last night at your daughter's cradle?'

Shelley opens his mouth, then hesitates and looks down at his hands, turning them slowly palm up, palm down, palm up, palm down. And as he starts to speak, his voice high-pitched, hectic, monotonous, Maddox sees Claire Clairmont put her hand to her mouth as if suddenly nauseous.

'Some years since I made a study of dreams, and kept a daily notebook detailing those I had experienced. I became, in consequence, convinced of the existence of two variations of this phenomenon, the Phrenic and the Psychic, the former the dream of the mind, the latter the dream of the soul. I myself have had dreams in the midst of which a pleasant vision has been broken off by a terrifying dream within a dream – a dream of the soul to which the mind was not privy, but from the effect of which I started with horror on sudden waking—'

Maddox has heard enough. He catches the young man by the throat and drags him so close their faces are almost touching. 'So is *this* your excuse – is *this* how you exonerate yourself? You would have us believe you did this in your *sleep* – that you woke in horror in the middle of the night to find your hands about your daughter's neck and squeezing the last breath of life from her?'

'No – no,' cries Claire, rushing forwards and pushing herself between them. 'It was not like that – he remembers nothing – he awoke in his own bed – it is all a lie—'

'I am sorry, Miss Clairmont,' says Maddox, coldly, 'but I do not see how you are in a position to verify the truth – or otherwise – of a single thing he has yet said.'

She flushes, then lifts her head in defiance. 'I know Shelley to be one of the noblest and most exalted beings I have ever encountered – his innocence, his very simplicity make it impossible for me to believe him capable of such a thing, even unknowing. Even in his sleep.'

She places her hand gently to Shelley's cheek. 'Tell him it is not true,' she whispers, 'tell him, Percy, how much you loved that little girl, that you would never harm any baby, far less your own.'

Shelley looks at her, eyes unseeing, then turns back towards the window and starts silently to write across the beads of condensation: *He smiles so sweet and looks so mild but then he kills a little child*.

Claire seizes his hand in panic. 'Do not say such things! Do not let her put such poisonous notions into your head – you *know* why she does it.'

'Miss Clairmont,' begins Maddox, placing a hand on her shoulder, but she shakes him off furiously.

'Do not touch me – how dare you? Leave this house at once – no one wants you here.'

298

Maddox steps back. 'I was summoned to assist Miss Godwin, and it is my intention to do so. And she is in need of that assistance. More, I suspect, than any of you realize.'

Claire looks at Mary and then at Maddox. 'I do not know what you mean.'

'Very well, I will explain. If a doctor comes to see this child he may attribute its death to wholly natural causes. If chance favours you, and he is either elderly or unobservant. But he may – if he is neither of those things – wonder, as I did, whether a human hand might have been at deadly work here. And if he does – if that is his conclusion – do you know what will happen? You will find the Runners at your door, and a warrant for an arrest.'

Shelley gasps, his face white. 'You cannot cast me in prison – I should not survive it. It is a horrible abode for the coarsest thing that ever wore the shape of man – how much more so for such as I?'

Claire turns to him. 'Do not fear – he says it only to alarm you. It is obvious to anyone that the baby died from convulsions. They cannot detain you on so flimsy a pretext.'

But Maddox is shaking his head. 'They will not arrest *you*, Shelley, because the courts, in their wisdom, customarily assume infanticide to be a female crime. All the more so when there is no other credible suspect. And there will be none in this case, I know that full well, because neither of these women will be prepared to accuse you. You have so preyed upon their affections that whatever you may have done – whatever vile crime you may have committed – still they will protect you, still they will keep their silence. And while *you* walk free, it will be the child's mother the law will light on, the child's *mother* who will risk the noose. Are you prepared to take that chance?'

He surveys them, one by one, Shelley chewing his thumb,

his face averted, Mary Godwin, her head bowed, still rocking her lifeless child, and then, finally, Claire Clairmont. She alone will meet his gaze, and she does not, it seems, care that he can read the choice she faces in her eyes. For a moment – a moment only – he sees her waver, but when she speaks her voice is steady. 'So what must we do?'

'Get him dressed. In his poorest clothes. He is the father – he will have to go with you.'

'With *me*?' she says, horrified. 'But where? I had nothing to do with it.'

'The child must be buried before the day is out. You cannot afford gossip, and I imagine you have attracted quite enough of it already. You must give out, if asked, that the child died of convulsions, brought on by a fever. Do you understand?'

She hesitates a moment, then nods.

'There is a graveyard I know,' he continues, 'where the sexton will take your money, and bury the child, and ask no inconvenient questions. It is not a wholesome place, but it is consecrated ground, though knowing what little I do of Mr Shelley's beliefs,' he concludes bitterly, 'I doubt that will concern him overmuch.'

'But why must *I* do it? Surely—'

'Because it will arouse less suspicion if the mother is present, and your sister is in no condition to undertake such a journey.'

And if this is only part of his reason – if in truth he doubts whether Mary Godwin could bear the dreadful sight of her child's last resting-place – he does not say so. As for Shelley, his feelings deserve no consideration; if this is his punishment, it is precious little.

'So I am to be Mrs Shelley,' says Claire, softly. 'I am to say I am his wife.'

He wonders for a wild moment if she is not about to smile. He thought he had the measure of these three – thought he had understood the coils of attraction and repulsion that threaten to drown them all in a wreckage of hearts, but it seems he is wrong: there are darknesses here for which even his experience cannot find a like.

It is scarcely possible to believe this girl is only, what, sixteen?, as she leads Shelley to the bedroom door and whispers a word or two to him. He is as meek in Claire's hands as a small child. She then walks briskly over to her step-sister and takes the baby – without the least tenderness – from her arms. A moment later Shelley appears once again in the doorway, his coat on and his shirt seemly. His eyes are hollow and he is shaking, but he is presentable. And it will do no harm for him to look afflicted, not with the task he has now to perform.

'*I* am going out with Shelley,' Claire announces, taking him by the hand. '*You* are to wait here.'

Mary Godwin looks at her for a long moment, then turns her face away.

'Fraser will show you to the carriage,' says Maddox, and when they are gone he takes a chair and sets it down beside Mary Godwin. He looks around, wondering again at the contrast with Church Terrace. This would indeed have been a delightful place to raise a child. High ceilings, airy rooms, and windows that will soon be bright with the sun of spring. But why the sudden need to move here, with a sick infant barely a few days old?

'Miss Godwin,' he says eventually, 'what has been going on?'

'I told you – the baby—'

'That was not my meaning. I was asking what it was that impelled you to come to this place – who this man Hogg is.'

'He is a friend of Shelley's,' she replies dully. 'They met at Oxford.'

'That much I know, but what is his business here?'

She hesitates, and at that moment there is a noise in the hall and the man they are discussing appears at the door. He manages to look both flushed and pasty at one and the same time, and his face has a squat beadiness that puts Maddox in mind of a toad. His stock is too tight, and there are chafe marks on his neck where he has been poorly shaved.

'Mary!' he says, rushing to her side and taking her hand. 'I came as soon as I could – I was compelled to go on foot the whole way. What has happened? Where is the baby?'

Maddox gets to his feet and puts on his hat. 'I will detain you no longer, Miss Godwin. You know where you may reach me. I shall expect to hear from you.'

Down in the carriage he finds Shelley huddled against the far window. There is a strange smell about him, not cologne but something sweeter and drier than sweat. Whatever it is, it does nothing to quell Maddox's now invincible hatred for everything about the man. He can barely tolerate sharing such a small space in his company, but share it they must. Despite the weather, he almost envies Fraser his place on the box.

'Was that Hogg I saw?' asks Claire, as the carriage starts to rumble slowly away.

Maddox nods. 'It appears he walked here from the Strand. Which would account for him being so late. It would *not*, however, account for him being so early.'

She raises an eyebrow, but does not answer.

'What was he doing at the house, Miss Clairmont, at that time in the morning?'

She slides a glance at him, and seems about to say

something, but contents herself with a shrug. 'Mary sent for him. I imagine she did not trust Shelley to go in search of you.'

'And may *he* be trusted, this Hogg?'

'Oh, he will say nothing,' she replies tartly. 'Nothing that might harm *Mary*.'

There is something implied here – some intimacy – that tallies with what Maddox himself has just observed, but he fails to find the words that will frame the question. Not to this girl, at any rate, with her too-knowing eyes. He glances back at her and sees she is looking composedly out of the window, the baby unregarded on her knee, but as the carriage rounds a sharp corner the dead child slips towards Shelley, who starts at its touch as if scalded. 'Claire?' he says, in panic. 'What is he talking of?'

'It is nothing, my dear,' she answers softly. 'Mr Maddox was just enquiring about Hogg.' And she moves the child away from him, wedging it between her body and the door, as if it were a parcel or a bolt of cloth.

The rest of the journey passes in a brooding silence, broken only by the growl of the wheels on the road, and the sound, faint at first but getting stronger, of rain drumming on the roof.

When the carriage eventually stops the rain is falling hard, and as Maddox hands her down the step Claire pulls her shawl up over her hair and grimaces. 'What dreadful weather – what a truly dreadful day.'

Shelley peers round at the dark and dilapidated buildings, the huddles of grey pedestrians, and the dirt and scrap paper drifting in the gutters, and turns to Maddox with a look of distaste. 'Where is this foul place, damn you? To what corner of Hell have you brought us?'

'I should have thought,' Maddox replies grimly, 'you would welcome such an opportunity to observe the poor and oppressed. You seem all too ready to interfere in their affairs when it suits your own purposes.'

'*Ha!*' he cries. 'I am the friend of the unfriended poor – I claim no kinship with such loathsome uncleanly animals as *these*.'

The latter remark is hurled – far too loudly – in the direction of a group of bricklayer's labourers who are leaning against the nearest wall smoking, their fustian covered from head to foot in dust. Maddox sees one spit on the ground and take a step towards them. 'Who're you calling unclean, you scraggy little by-blow?'

Maddox reaches out and grips Shelley by the arm. 'I should have a care whom you insult, sir,' he hisses. 'If these men are *unclean* it is in the nature of their calling, and proves only that they are worthily and industriously employed.' Which is more than I can say for you, he thinks, more's the pity. The labourers, meanwhile, have put aside their pipes and moved forwards into a closed circle of hostile faces. Maddox glances back to Fraser. He is more than a match for any one of them, but not all ten together. And there is the girl to consider – the girl who is now cowering at Fraser's side crying, 'Shelley, *Shelley*!'

The first man looks across at her, then comes up close to Shelley, feet apart, face insolent. 'She's a nice piece of cunny,' he says, licking his dry lips. 'Is that your kid she's clutchin'? Wouldn't've thought you had the mettle in yer mutton. Look more like a lick-spigot to me, what d'yer think, lads?'

He darts forward and grabs Shelley in the crotch, and the next moment they are rolling on the ground in the mud, Shelley kicking, biting, clawing, and the man beating him off with his fists. The labourers are clapping and whistling as Fraser pushes through the crowd to haul Shelley off the man and push him against the wall.

'How dare you talk to me like that – you leprous scum?' he shrieks, struggling against Fraser's constraining hands. 'I will tear your heart out by the roots – I will wither up your disgusting soul – I will *cut you down!*'

'Don't fink so some'ow,' says the labourer, wiping a scratch on his forehead with the back of his hand, 'not on that showin', anyway!'

The men are laughing as they help him to his feet. The new grime makes little difference to his dirty clothes; Shelley, by contrast, is thick with slime. His lip is cut and he has the beginnings of a black eye.

'If 'e's your dilly boy I'd learn 'im some manners,' the man calls to Maddox with a wink, as the group walk away. 'Though perhaps a bit o' rough is 'ow you like 'em.'

Maddox waits until they are far enough away, then turns to Shelley in frozen fury. 'If you cannot conduct yourself in an appropriate manner, our association will be at an end.'

Claire puts her hand on Shelley's arm. 'Please forgive him – he does not suffer fools easily.'

'And finds it equally difficult to control his own temper, it would seem.'

She blushes. 'It will not happen again. Please, may we go? I am wet through and this is a truly horrid place.'

But there is little pity in Maddox's eyes. If this distresses her, she has more and worse to come. He turns up the collar of his greatcoat and leads them a few yards further down the street before turning suddenly into a side lane that will be unlit and perilous by nightfall. He is following – if he did but know it – the same dismal alley his great-nephew will follow, more than thirty years later, at the beginning of the

305

case that will make his name. The houses of Tom-All-Alone's are not as filthy as they will be then, the tenements not as teeming, but it is a foul and forbidding path they tread here, all the same. The rain is filling the rutted path with puddles, and as they turn the corner and start down the low, covered way, the walls are wet with a sour, year-long damp. Maddox can hear Fraser's heavy steps echo behind him and the quick shallow breathing of the girl, and when they come out into daylight again they are at the iron gate of a small graveyard, overlooked on all sides by tall buildings. The gravestones are sloping and uneven, names and dates mouldering into a blur of lichen and decay. In the farthest corner he can see two rats scrapping over a thigh bone. Too small for an adult's, but possibly – and then he hears the girl gasp, 'No – surely that cannot be—' There are tears in her eyes now, and she is holding her burden for the first time as if it were still a living child.

'It was no doubt a dog, Miss Clairmont. Or, at least, it would be best to think so.' He smiles at her, not unkindly now, and takes her arm. On their left, by the side wall, a grizzled man is sitting sheltering from the rain in a small lean-to. He has a bottle of brandy on a makeshift table, and propped up against the door are the tools of his trade. A mattock, and an old notched spade. The sexton.

The man touches his hand to his filthy cap. 'Mr Maddox, sir. Allus a pleasure.' But his eyes have slipped past the thief-taker to Claire, and beyond her to Shelley. His eyes narrow, and small wonder: the poet's lip is swollen now, and there's a smear of dog-shit on his cheek.

Maddox interposes quickly – the sooner this is done and they are gone the better. He motions the girl forward. 'This poor young woman woke this morning to find her baby dead. She has not the money for a funeral.'

'Is that so?' says the man, pensively. 'It's a wonder she 'as the money to pay for you then. You don't come cheap. Or so I'm told.'

Maddox flushes, then is furious with himself for doing so. 'I do this as a favour, Blackaby. For a young couple distraught by the loss of their child.'

'I see,' says Blackaby. 'Best give it me, then.'

He holds out his gnarled hands for the baby, and the girl's eyes widen as what is about to happen finally comes home to her. She casts an agonized look at Maddox, who can do nothing but nod. 'It is the only way, Mrs – Shelley.'

He stumbles at the name, and wishes at once he'd had the foresight to think of another, but the man seems not to have noticed. Blackaby grips the bundle and takes it into the back of his hut. A few moments later he comes back out and leers up at Maddox from under his grey brows with a gleam in his eye. 'Let's say a sov, then. If you're agreeable.'

'But we don't have—' cries the girl, before Maddox can stop her.

'Your fees seem to have risen of late,' he observes darkly.

'Well, it's a good service I offer, Mr Maddox, as you know. Not many other places round 'ere you could dispose so easily of a little problem like this, and know it won't come back to haunt yer.'

He winks at the girl and she stifles a cry and stumbles away. Maddox takes his pocket-book from his coat and counts out the money, while the man squints at Shelley, who is standing with his back to them, gazing down into an open grave.

'He's a rum one, that,' Blackaby says, nodding towards him. 'Most can't bear to look. And that's a bad one. Water's eaten away the coffin at the bottom, so the whole pit's swimmin' in rottin' flesh. Even 'ad to stand away meself in the end, the smell got so bad.'

Maddox hurriedly concludes his business. 'When will it be done?'

Blackaby shifts his chew of tobacco to the other cheek. 'The one for that pit's arrivin' later today. St Giles work'ouse are sendin' it, so there's not much likelihood of meddlin' relatives. Pox case, they said. Should be room to slip this one in the box with 'im, nice and tidy and none the wiser.'

Maddox looks away, glad only that the girl did not hear this – that Mary Godwin will not hear this. 'Very well,' he says quickly. 'Good day to you.'

He goes back to the gate, where Claire Clairmont is leaning against the iron railings, weeping openly. 'I heard it,' she gulps, 'in the night – I *heard* it.'

Maddox takes a deep breath. 'What did you hear?' he says quietly.

'The baby – she was making strange noises – little choking cries – I did not think – not then – how could I?'

'Did you hear anything else? A footstep perhaps, or a floorboard?'

She shakes her head.

'And you did not go to her – wake her mother?'

Again she shakes her head, the tears running down her face.

'You could have prevented it,' he says eventually, 'and yet you did nothing. Is the enmity between you really so deep that you heard your sister's baby in distress, and yet made no effort to help her?'

She turns away, reaching out blindly to the railings, one hand to her mouth. 'No, no.'

'I hope, Miss Clairmont, that you never suffer the loss of a child. That you are never haunted by the pain of knowing that your baby's death might have been averted, had someone cared enough to intervene.'

She is gasping now, sinking slowly on her knees in the mud and filth of the street.

Maddox watches her for a moment, then beckons to Fraser to take her back to the carriage. And when he turns he sees Shelley, still motionless at the grave that will swallow his dead child. Suppressing his own repugnance, Maddox makes his way among the broken and uneven slabs to where the young man is standing, the rain dropping slow and heavy on his face, and hair, and clothes. 'We must go. It would not do to be discovered here.'

Shelley does not reply, does not even seem to hear. Maddox glances down, despite himself, and has to cover his mouth at once against the stench. The mud in the bottom of the pit is black with putrefaction; shards of sodden wood and half-recognizable bones jut from the slime, and beneath a thin film of sludge, a hand hangs listlessly within its withered skin. Then for the briefest of moments the rain eases and the water stills, and there, where the poet's face should be reflected on the surface, there is a white and grinning skull-face, the eye sockets seething with maggots.

Shelley starts back with an animal cry and Maddox grasps him by the shoulder. 'It is nothing, an illusion of the light. Come – we must be gone.'

And slowly, eventually, the young man turns to Maddox a face aghast and allows himself to be led away, stumbling now and half falling, his hand clutched at his side. And behind them, as they go, the sexton watches them from his lair, muttering something indecipherable under his breath.

* * *

Maddox expects to hear from Mary Godwin within hours –
at the very least the next day – for surely she can no longer
pretend, even to herself, that she can remain safely with
Shelley. But as two and then three slow weeks slip by, his
incomprehension turns to anger, then to indignation at
being so used, and a resolve to forget her – to leave her to
reap the terrible consequences of her choice. A fine resolution, but one that works only in theory and cannot
withstand her actual presence. It is a Friday, and Maddox is
on the point of leaving – on the point of going downstairs
to his waiting carriage and a dinner engagement with the
home secretary – when Fraser opens the office door and
shows her in. She stands on the threshold, hesitating, and he
gives a slight bow. It feels stiff, and no doubt looks so,
because when he raises his eyes again he sees none of her
usual self-assurance.

'Miss Godwin.'

'Mr Maddox.'

She comes a tentative step further into the room. 'I am
aware that my manners have been deficient. That I should
have thanked you – by letter if not in person – for what you
did to help us. Think not, please, that because your
assistance was unacknowledged, it was also unappreciated.
Speaking for myself, I felt your kindness deeply.'

'And Shelley?'

'I am sure he too—'

'I did not mean that, Miss Godwin. You know I did not.'

'You are asking, I take it, as to my intentions regarding
Shelley. They are – unchanged.'

He moves towards her. 'How can you say so, now that
you know the danger you are in? You said, when we last
spoke, that I was right – that you should have listened to
me, that you would never have lost your child—'

'You have not seen him,' she says softly. 'He is tormented by what has happened – he swears he never intended to harm the baby, that he has no recollection of that night—'

'And what happens when you have another child? What happens when you wake in the night and find his hands at another newborn baby's throat?'

She turns away to the window. 'I think about the little thing every day. It is foolish, I suppose, yet whenever I am left alone to my own thoughts I always come back to the same sad place – that I was a mother and am so no longer. I dreamed once that it came to life again – that it had only been cold, and that we rubbed it before the fire, and it lived. And then I awoke and there was no baby.'

Her voice is enough to break a harder heart than Maddox's, but even he notices that the baby is no longer 'she' but 'it'. And that she was never given a name.

'So you intend to remain with him? After everything he has done?'

'What other choice do I have? And even were that not so, I love him so tenderly – my life hangs so in the beam of his eye, my whole soul is so wrapped up in him, I would do anything for him, even – even—'

She is now sobbing bitterly, openly, a woman who does nothing private in plain sight, and holds herself in check from all the world. He goes towards her and stands at her shoulder, speaking so low his words brush her skin like breathing.

'I asked you this once before, and received no answer. So I will ask you again. Who is this man Hogg, and what business takes him to your lodgings at all hours, day and night?'

She is shaking her head now. 'How can I refuse him?' she says miserably. 'It is what he believes – what he wants – that we should – that Hogg and I – that he and Claire—'

Some part of him had expected this; some part of him knew it was the only feasible explanation, but it is wholly different to hear it spoken in such neutral tones by this girl not yet eighteen, who has just lost her child.

'I can scarcely imagine any man capable of such an abomination, that he should sit contentedly by and watch you in the arms – the bed – of another man while he—' He turns and strides to the far corner of the room, unable to contain his fury.

'You do not understand,' Mary whispers, the tears rolling slowly down her face. 'When first we met I would listen to him talking of the freedom and happiness of all mankind and my own passion would rise to meet his. And for man to be free, *love* must be free – Shelley says we should not shackle ourselves to one person for life, that the failure of his marriage is proof of the terrible error of such a dogma, that we, the four of us, might show a new way to live – might defy convention and find a new mode of existence in which all is shared, in which there is no jealousy, no recrimination—'

'And is *that* what has happened?' he cries, twisting back to face her. 'You forget that I have *seen* you, you and Shelley and your sister. Can you place your hand upon your heart and tell me that you are not jealous, not resentful, not bitter to the very dregs of your soul?'

'*Of course I am!*' She sobs. 'I see the way she touches him – toys with him – and I want to tear her apart with my own hands. When she is wretched I rejoice, when she goes out with him, hour after hour, I wait at home, brooding, with poison in my heart. When he goes to Sussex to hear the reading of his grandfather's will, *she* goes with him. When a cradle is to be bought for *my* baby, *she* goes with him. She refuses absolutely to return to Skinner Street, and there is nowhere else. It is almost impossible to bear.'

'And Hogg?'

'He disgusts me. I tried – Shelley begged me and I tried. He said Beaumont and Fletcher had one mistress and why should we not do the same? Surely his genius was a match for theirs. And so I wrote to him.' She flushes. 'You would call it flirtatious – unworthy – and I cannot defend myself from such a charge. I wanted to keep him at bay – to do as Shelley wished and yet postpone as long as possible the moment when I would be expected – when he would ask – I spoke of my pregnancy – that my affections would surely increase with time—'

She sighs heavily and wipes her eyes. 'I think on those words now and I am sickened. For I did not know *then* that Shelley once proposed exactly the same to that little fool Harriet – that *she* should take Hogg for her lover. And now – *now* he dares suggest it to *me*.'

Her breast is heaving with suppressed anger, and Maddox watches her thoughtfully, wondering how much of her distress is to be found rooted there – in insult, rather than injury. And whether it is a coincidence that, having discovered this, she is now here.

'And your sister? Have she and Shelley—?'

'He swears to me that they have not. That he awaits my decision as to Hogg. But I can prevaricate no longer. I am not with child. I *have no* child.'

'But that does not mean you have to agree! He may talk of you as his treasure and his prize but you are flesh and blood, not a possession, however exquisite, to be passed around his friends! A woman like you – with your talents, your intelligence – in God's name do not allow yourself to be so trapped – so used!'

'Oh, Mr Maddox,' she says softly. 'Nothing in that house may be done in God's name. Not even that.'

'Then for Heaven's sake *leave it*!'

'And leave them together?' Mary cries. 'After all I have suffered, all I have lost, surrender to *her*? And even were that possible, where should I go? My father will not speak to me, my friends have disowned me, I have no money. There is not a house in London that would receive me.'

'Then come here.'

The words are out before he knows he has said them. They stare at each other, aware a boundary has been passed, a barrier broken.

'It is,' he stammers eventually, 'a big enough residence. You might be here a fortnight and I should not even know it. And there are the servants – there would be no suggestion of impropriety.'

She smiles weakly. 'As if I, of all women, were in a position to care about my reputation.'

He turns away, desperate to find some small task to perform, all too uncomfortably aware that he is the one who has laid himself open, now, to entrapment and misuse. But when she replies her voice seems very small, and very docile, and very far from devious. 'I am grateful indeed for the offer. Should I have need of it, I will accept it.'

And when he looks up, she is gone.

* * *

It is more than a month before he sees her again. A month taken up with a coining case in Whitechapel, and a murder investigation that has him from the house until late in the night. And it is, indeed, late when he returns home one night to find the maid hovering in the hallway.

'What is it, Phyllis? Have my dinner brought up to the dining room, would you?'

314

'There's a visitor, sir.'

'I cannot see anyone tonight – pray ask them to return in the morning.'

'It's that – that *Miss Godwin*,' she says, with a sniff of disapproval. 'She's been waiting here these two hours and more. Has her bags with her too.'

'Very well, Phyllis. Show her up to the blue room, would you, and I will see her afterwards in my office.'

When he opens the office door there is no lamp burning, and he considers for a moment ringing the bell to have one lit, but then changes his mind. He goes to the window and opens it wide. The moon is full on the Thames, and under the London smell of horse dung and human filth there is the faintest hint of spring.

'Shelley once said that his mind without me was as dead and cold as the midnight river when the moon is down.'

He turns. She is in the doorway, all in white.

'But he is,' says Maddox, softly, 'without you now.'

'And the moon is up.'

She comes to his side and looks down towards the water. 'I remember the night we crossed from Dover to France. It was such a beautiful evening – little wind, and the sails flapping in the flagging breeze. Then the moon rose, and night came on, and with the darkness a slow, heavy swell and such a violent sea that the sailors almost despaired of us making Calais. Hour after hour passed, and we were still far distant when the moon sunk in the red and stormy horizon and the fast-flashing lightning became pale in the breaking day.'

Maddox leans against the glass, his breath misting the pane. 'You should write. You have a gift for it.'

Mary smiles. 'Perhaps. But my talent is but workaday set against Shelley's.'

'You might earn your own living by it, none the less.'

And be free of him. The words unspoken resonate in the air.

'What brings you here?' he asks at last.

'Hatred. Treachery. Violence. Oh, do not fear,' she says quickly, seeing his face, 'I am not harmed – I was not the victim. I was the perpetrator. That is why I had to leave. I did not know myself capable of such rage, such terrible cruelty.'

She turns and walks back into the room, her features dissolving in the shadow. He will wonder, afterwards, whether this were not deliberate; whether she stood so far away that he might not see her face, not read what would have been visible in her eyes.

'After I saw you last – what you said – you gave me the courage to remonstrate with him. To beg him to reconsider. And my loss – *our* loss, his inconsolable contrition – has changed him, truly it has. He told me I was everything, *she* nothing. That I alone can shield him from impurity and vice. That if he is absent from me long he shudders with horror at himself.'

'Good God, what does that mean – what sort of man says such things?'

'Please – let me finish. He promised that he would find a home for Claire, away from us. He has even persuaded her to advertise for a position. And he took me away to Salt Hill, just he and I alone. We had three blissful days among the green fields and the trees and the solitary lanes. I was,' her voice breaks, 'absurdly happy. Happier than I have been for many long bleak months. I even found it in myself to write affectionately to Hogg, now that he was to be no more to me than a friend.'

She pauses, and he sees her raise a hand to her eyes.

'And then, when we returned, it was to new lodgings and

I thought, Surely now things will be different. How naïve I was – how idiotically hopeful. Because now they can hide it from me no longer – I can see it with my own eyes.' She takes a shuddering breath and when she speaks again her voice is raw with rage: 'They have been deceiving me, Mr Maddox, week after week, month after month. No doubt since the very day we first left London together. All the promises he made me were lies – vile, brazen *lies*. All those hours he spent with her – all those journeys they took together – have ended the same way. With him in *her* bed.'

There is a silence. She is breathing hard now, to retain control.

'So,' says Maddox, 'she is with child.'

She nods, and puts her hand again to her eyes.

'And you?'

'I struck her, Mr Maddox. I raised my hand and I struck her. I have always deplored violence, always seen it as the worst manifestation of man's bestial nature, but at that moment, as she stood there, smiling that complacent self-adoring smile, her hand caressing the child *she* will bear Shelley – the child *I* should have had – it was as if a demon had overtaken me. I lost consciousness for a moment, I think, for the next thing I remember was Shelley lifting me to my feet and kneeling in alarm at her side. It was only then that I saw she had fallen. She was in pain – there was blood – but I felt no remorse, felt only that she deserved her pain, for the hurt she had given me.'

Again the silence, again the sound only of the clock on the mantelpiece.

'They sent for the doctor,' she says at last. 'But I had gone before he arrived. I had nowhere else to go, so I came here.'

Maddox goes to the table and pours her a glass of brandy, then returns to the window. As he gave her the glass he felt the cold in her thin fingers. 'I should retire,' he says eventually. 'I have an appointment early tomorrow.'

Yet despite his words he does not move, but remains staring down at the street, and the houses, and the silver river.

'I have often wondered,' she begins hesitantly, 'that first day when I came here – to this house – how it was that you knew my name.'

He does not turn, but senses her approach, senses her nearing warmth in the chilly room. 'You resemble someone I once knew. She had not your colouring, but your height – your face – your features. I thought, just for a moment—'

'And her name was Mary?'

He nods. 'Is Mary.'

'I am sorry. The way you spoke of her, I thought she must be—'

'Dead? No.' He shakes his head. 'She lives and is happy. If she is dead, it is merely to me.'

She places a hand gently on his arm, and when he turns at last to look at her it is as if her words have conjured the ghost he has so long striven to forget. Her hair is as dark as ink in the blue light and this last difference gone she is uncannily, unbearably, like the woman he once loved. Something of this she must have seen – something in his eyes must have changed – for she lifts her face towards him and brings her mouth to touch his skin.

'You do not mean this,' he says in despair, as her cheek brushes his. 'You will regret it – you do it for the wrong reasons. It would make me no better than him—'

'You have not betrayed me – you have not told me lies.'

He seizes her shoulders now. 'And is this not a lie? The worst lie of all?'

But it is too late – she can feel his body deny his words.

318

And as she draws his head towards her and her lips part, he hears her whisper, 'She is gone but I am here. If you wish it, I will be your Mary. I will be the love you lost.'

It is long since he has taken a woman to his bed; longer still since that act was anything but a business transaction, concluded to the satisfaction of both parties, but this coupling is like no other he has ever had.

He tells himself, afterwards, that she has had no lover but one, and that everything that unnerves him can surely be traced to that. For he is unnerved, and profoundly. She is no virgin, but he senses all the same that he is breaching a locked wall, that this is for her an initiation, an opening of places cold and closed. And yet she is no prude neither: his own desire spent, there is a striving for satisfaction – a willingness to ask for what she wants, both in words and in gestures, that he has found in no other woman, and will never find again. And when, at the end, she turns her back to him silently in the dark, and he realizes what it is she expects him to do – to take – the hot blood comes to his face and he buries his face in her hair, murmuring, 'No, not that, not that.'

Hours later he opens his eyes to a shaft of milky sunlight, and a clock that tells him it is past nine and he is late. He sits up abruptly to find that the bed is empty, and she is gone. Downstairs in the dining room breakfast is laid with one place, and when he enquires of the maid he is told, 'Miss Godwin has eaten, sir. And gone out.'

It is a long day in Whitechapel, followed by a bad-tempered meeting with a bad-tempered client, who cannot understand why his case is taking so long. Maddox has to explain

319

several times that he has six good men pursuing different lines of investigation, but that the murder of a banker throws up so many possible suspects it takes time and patience to eliminate them all. He returns to Buckingham Street hungry, tired and out of humour, already wondering what he is to say – what he is to do.

As he takes off his hat and coat in the hall, he sees Fraser coming up the kitchen stairs. There is a scratch on his cheek that wasn't there that morning.

'Good God, how came you by that? Were you not interviewing Mr Orchard today? I should hardly have thought him likely to resort to blows.'

Fraser makes a face. 'That Shelley came here. Two, three hours ago. Accused us of harbouring his – that woman and demanded to see her. Started having one of those fits of his – thrashing about, kicking, screaming. It fair distressed the maids, but not me. I was wise to it, all right. Told him I'd send up for her if he comported himself with the decency as befitted the premises. That sobered him up – enough at least to get him off the floor and onto a chair. But by then she must have heard the noise because she came running down the stairs and climbed on to his lap.'

Maddox stares at him, wondered if he has misheard. 'His *lap*?'

'I know, guv, I thought it odd meself. She always seemed such a chilly one – so clever and aloof, but to listen to her then you'd have thought she were ten years old. Talking all high-pitched and silly like to a baby. Begging him not to be angry with her because "*your Pecksie will never vex you so again. She is a good girl, and is quite well now.*" And a lot more such fatuous stuff besides. It were like eavesdropping on the nursery.'

Maddox turns away, his heart frozen in his chest. Every

320

time he thinks he has understood her, she eludes him; every time he allows himself to believe her, she confounds him.

'Did *you* know she was ill, guv?'

'No,' he says distractedly. 'I had no conception. Where is Miss Godwin now?'

'No idea, guv. Packed her things and left. With him.' *And good riddance*, as his face plainly shows, though how much of that relief is down to personal irritation, and how much to a growing uneasiness on his master's account, you would be hard put to fathom.

'Thank you, Fraser. Ask Phyllis to bring up my dinner, would you?'

His words sound composed enough, but his heart is beating hard as he climbs the stairs to the room she occupied. There is hardly a sign, now, that she was ever there. The window is open, and the muslin curtain catching in the evening breeze. The bed is tidy, the furniture placed exactly as it was before she came. The only trace of her presence, in fact, is the ashes in the grate, which have not yet been raked away by the parlour-maid. Maddox goes to the fireplace and crouches down. The draught from the window has proved too strong for the fire and most of the paper thrown here has not burned through. He takes the poker and lifts the edge of the remains. Pages torn from a journal, it seems. Some from the past three months, some from the past few days. He knows he should not do it – knows no good can come of it – but he reaches out, and lifts the blistered paper in a shower of ash, and takes it to the desk. And then, for a long time, he sits, gazing into the distance, his mind the only thing about him moving.

* * *

Torquay, 22nd June

Sir,

I received your letter, but I chose not, then, to reply. And I write now not to offer excuses, for there are none. Nor do I offer explanations, for you would not understand. My Shelley and I are reconciled – reconciled more irrevocably than any wedding rite could ever bind us. The business is finished. She has gone to Lynmouth for her lying-in, and I hope that we may never more be troubled by her. The issue, if it lives, will be adopted by some people thereabouts, that she might be freed to earn her own living, and forge a life for herself, separately from ours.

They walked out, that last day, she and he, for a last conversation, and the next morning he took her to the coach. He was gone a long time, and I was, for a time, in fear – I even went out to seek him in the rain – but he came back to me at last, and I know now that all my fears were groundless, and he will always return. After what we have suffered – after that insupportable loss for which he still repents – he is bound to me for ever.

And so we begin again with our regeneration. And it will be, indeed, a regeneration, for there is to be a child. A child to be born at the turn of the year. I know how it will be when you hear this – I know you will wonder, and you will question. But I will not answer. There is nothing I could say that would not give you unmingled pain.

I do not ask you to forgive; I tell you only to forget—
    M. W. G.

PART THREE

1850

CHAPTER TWELVE

Death

How much of this does Charles now know? Most of it, I suspect. Fraser, after all, witnessed much of it with his own eyes, and what he didn't see, he was more than capable of guessing. So, as he walks slowly back through the calm sunset from Fraser's door, the light pinking rose the crusting snow, Charles is melding the long past with what he, too, has seen with his own eyes. The last piece has fallen into place: Claire's shame and Mary's deception; Claire's day of horrors and Mary's relief that Maddox, like a winter lion, has in rage forgot all brush of time, her desperate desire that the dead should die and return not. And when Maddox talked, in those words now burned, of the appalling death of an innocent creature, it was not Harriet Shelley he meant, or even Fanny Imlay, but the poet's own baby daughter. *And what happens when you have another child? What happens when you wake in the night and find his hands at another newborn baby's throat?* Did Maddox's words of warning return to haunt Mary, that last summer in Italy? Is that why she was suddenly so desperate to leave, at all costs, a house she called accursed – so frantic to take her last-remaining son away? Only it was not the house that was accursed, but the man within it. When she wrote to Charles of Shelley's love for children – of his own childishness – that was her *real* deceit. Her real blind. And like all the world's most dangerous lies, it was crafted more than half of truth. For Shelley's was not the childishness of innocence and play, but of wanton, unthinking cruelty, and the utter inability to feel another's pain.

And what of Maddox? Maddox who compromised everything he stood for, only to lose a child that could have been his. No wonder those pages were destroyed; no wonder he concealed the secret from everyone, even – or perhaps especially – from the great-nephew who has taken that lost son's place. And no wonder Mary talked so deliberately, in her letter, of Charles as his uncle's only heir – she was luring him, testing the safety of her secret, knowing that if he had discovered who little William's father really was he would never have allowed those words to pass unchallenged.

When he opens the door in Buckingham Street, Charles can hear laughter from the drawing room, and he stands for a moment, wondering how long it is since this house echoed with the happiness of a child. He's about to go upstairs when Nancy appears at the top of the kitchen steps. Her bruises are less angry now, and she is wearing a new dress. Plain and grey, but elegant in its mere simplicity. She sees him looking at it and smiles, then twirls around. 'Like it? Couldn't keep wearin' that old blue one all the time.'

There's another burst of giggles upstairs and Nancy glances up anxiously. ''Ope you don't mind Betsy being up there. I make sure she don't do any 'arm or break nothin'.

326

And your uncle seems to 'ave taken to her. They've been chattin' away nineteen to the dozen this afternoon.'

Charles smiles sadly. 'Don't worry, Nancy. Betsy is no trouble. Quite the opposite.'

He turns to go and she stops him. 'There's a visitor waitin' for you – upstairs.'

Claire, he thinks. And then – But surely she does not know where to find him.

'A gentleman, it is,' says Nancy, watching him. 'Said it were business, but 'e 'asn't been 'ere before, so you won't know the name.'

'It's rather late, surely?' Charles says, with a frown.

Nancy shrugs. ''E said 'e wanted to wait. That 'e ain't often in London so it 'ad to be today.'

A fire has been lit in the office, and there is a man standing over it, warming his hands. A man in clothes that evoke the Church without being, strictly speaking, clerical. He looks up at Charles's approach and comes towards him, hand extended. 'Mr Maddox, I presume? Turnbull, Horace Turnbull. I am an assistant to the Curators of the Bodleian Library.'

Charles endeavours to conceal his surprise and gestures to the chair. 'How can I help you, Mr Turnbull?'

'You are wondering, no doubt,' says Turnbull, as he seats himself carefully so as not to crease his coat-tails, 'what business the University of Oxford could possibly have with a private detective.'

Charles smiles. 'Was it so obvious?'

Turnbull inclines his head. 'I anticipated some degree of surprise. To speak frankly, Mr Maddox – I assume I may speak frankly and in confidence? – it is a somewhat delicate matter. In consequence, and after much private discussion, my employers have decided that the most prudent course of action would be to consult someone unconnected with the university. Someone, in short, in London.'

He pauses, then clears his throat, 'You may be aware,' he resumes, 'that the Bodleian houses an extensive collection of rare books and manuscripts, some of them many centuries old.'

Charles nods. 'When I was a boy, my father took me once to see the Ashmole Bestiary. I was far too young to appreciate it then, of course, but I can still remember that drawing of a basilisk being killed by a weasel. I remember asking my father why we didn't have basilisks in Berkshire.'

'Ah!' says Turnbull, his face brightening. 'Then you know exactly to what I refer. It is, indeed, the manuscripts in the Ashmole Bequest that are in question. The Bestiary has always been rather a favourite of mine, though of course most of our visitors are more interested in the astrological and alchemical treatises.'

'Has there been a theft? Have some of the books gone missing?'

Turnbull is already shaking his head. 'No, no, nothing of that kind. We – that is, the Curators – have received a request from a foreign person, a nobleman of a very ancient lineage, who wishes to consult some of the manuscripts in the collection.'

'And that poses a problem?'

'Not a problem, exactly. There is no difficulty in allowing him to view the collection. The difficulty – if that is the word – stems from the interest he has expressed in making a donation towards its upkeep.' He coughs. 'A rather substantial donation.'

Charles nods slowly. 'And you are concerned to know a

little more about your mysterious benefactor, before you agree to become associated with him in such a public and irrevocable manner.'

'Quite so, Mr Maddox,' replies Turnbull, 'Quite so. And "mysterious" is indeed the word. All that the *Almanach de Gotha* can tell, we have ascertained, but that is lamentably little. We thought of consulting the Foreign Office, but such a course might pose difficulties of its own; and then we thought of you. Well, not of you *specifically*, of course, but a man of your calling.'

'I see,' says Charles. 'And how did you come upon my name?'

'It was your uncle's, in fact. He was recommended by a Fellow of All Souls, who had, I believe, used his services in the past. But I understood from the young woman who let me in that the elder Mr Maddox is no longer well enough to accept commissions.'

There is a brief silence.

'So can I tell my employers that *you* are able to assist us?'

Charles hesitates: he has never undertaken any investigation even remotely like this one. But why should that deter him? And he would give a good deal to see the Ashmole collection again. 'Yes, Mr Turnbull, I am.'

'Excellent,' his visitor replies, with obvious relief, as he gets to his feet. 'I will write to you to arrange a meeting with the Curators in Oxford.'

It is Charles's turn to offer his hand, but Turnbull is now looking past him, towards the doorway.

Betsy is peeking at the two of them round the door, her little face alight with mischief, and her long-suffering doll dandling from one hand. He flushes – it's hardly the most professional impression to give to a new client – but, to his surprise, Turnbull squats down at once on his haunches and beckons to the little girl. 'Your daughter is beautiful, Mr Maddox, quite beautiful. You are a lucky man.'

Charles is about to correct him, but something makes him hold back. 'Betsy,' he says, beckoning in his turn. 'Come and say hello to Mr Turnbull.'

She hesitates, then comes rushing in and clasps her arms about Charles's legs. And so it is that when he sees Turnbull out ten minutes later, he has a small child nestling in the crook of his arm. As he shuts the door he hears a step behind him and turns, expecting Nancy. But it is Molly he sees coming towards him. And now he realizes, with a flash of shame, that he has still not explained what this child and her mother are doing in the house. Molly reaches out her arms to the child, who clambers rather awkwardly about her neck.

'Molly,' says Charles. 'It's only for a few days. They won't be here long.'

She looks at him for a moment, rocking the child from side to side, then nods and turns back towards the kitchen.

Up in the office Charles takes a sheet of paper from the escritoire and pauses a moment before setting his pen to the page.

I know the truth. About Harriet, and about William.
I know how your daughter really died.
I have not decided, yet, what I shall do.

And then he seals the envelope, and pens the address.

* * *

The following morning Charles goes out as soon as the shops are open, crunching through a layer of new snow

330

dusted diamond by the bright winter sun. His letter posted, he's just turning back into Buckingham Street when he smells the aroma of roasting chestnuts. There's a coster on the corner of Villiers Street, crying, 'Chestnuts all 'ot, a penny a score,' as he stamps his feet by his stall's iron stove, the charcoal glowing crimson underneath. Remembering how he had longed for some on Christmas Day, Charles stops and buys a bag, warming his hands on them all the way to the house.

Up in the drawing room Betsy is sitting on the floor by the fire playing with the cat. A slightly one-sided affair, admittedly, as Thunder is far too regal to deign to such kittenish antics, but he seems happy enough to lie on his back and wave the occasional lazy paw in the direction of the knotted string Betsy hangs over his head. Charles crouches down and offers the little girl a chestnut from his bag, and grins as she reaches out, then realizes that the lovely brown shiny things are hot and whips her hand away with a shy smile. The two of them blow big puffs on the bag until the nuts are cool enough to hold, then sit cross-legged together on the floor, munching happily and stroking the cat. And this it is that Maddox sees when he wakes, blinks and focuses slowly.

'And what are you two doing? Making all sorts of mischief, I'll wager.'

Charles wonders for a moment if he is still adrift in the past – if it is Charles and his sister as children that he sees – but there is a clarity in the old man's eyes that was not there before, and when the little girl goes to clamber onto the chair beside him, it is her own name he calls her by.

'I have been talking to Abel,' Maddox says carefully, as the child curls up against him and settles to sleep. 'Though to speak strictly, he has been talking, and I have played a mere listener's part.'

There is still a slur to his speech, still a slight draw to one side of his face, but he is lucid; as lucid as he was – sometimes – before his last attack, before he heard again the name of Shelley and was driven back into the dark abyss of the past.

Charles gets up from the floor and pulls a chair close to his great-uncle. And as the fire burns softer and softer in the grate, and the old man strokes the child's golden curls, Charles recounts the case from first to last – from his commission by the Shelleys, to his stay at St John's Wood, to the visit to the Frasers the day before. And when he is done and he has set out his conclusions, such as they are, they sit in silence for a while and Charles sees the old man's eyes are closed. He has tired him, he thinks, and makes as if to get up.

'He was mine,' says Maddox, his eyes still closed. 'The boy. William. He was my son. I believed that from the first, and when I saw him at her father's house, I knew. He was the very image of my brother as a boy. There was not a shred of Shelley about him.'

Charles is silent, wondering what it must have cost to see that child – that one and only child – consigned to the care of a man who had already killed his own baby daughter.

'But there was nothing I could do to exert my claim. I could not protect him as a father; all I could offer him was my skill as a professional. And that I did. I had them watched. From that day in Skinner Street until their departure for Italy two years later. I never saw my boy again, but I had word of him, month by month, from an agent I employed.'

So there *was* someone watching Shelley, thinks Charles, at

the end if not at the beginning. How ironic that the man once hired to discover his pursuer should have become at the last that pursuer himself.

'My abhorrence of Shelley never abated,' the old man continues, 'not for a moment, but he was by then under the care of a reputable physician, and the boy appeared to thrive. I believed his mother kept him safe.'

He opens his eyes now, and Charles sees that there are tears.

'I wish that were all I had to tell. But it is not. I used my position – my influence – for the first and only time in my career, to further my own ends. I allowed certain facts to come to the ear of the judge in Shelley's Chancery case. With so much already against him – his atheism, his manner of life – I knew the information I passed on would ensure he never gained custody of Harriet's children. I believed she would have wished it so. I believed, and sincerely, that I was acting in those children's best interests.'

'And you were not?'

Maddox shakes his head slowly. 'Not, at least, in the way I imagined. It was only after the Shelleys left England for the last time that I discovered the truth. That whatever he had done in the past that so haunted his steps, he was not the monster I had made him.'

Charles frowns. 'I do not understand.'

'It was some years before I saw Absalom Blackaby again. I rarely dealt with such as he if I could help it, and avoided him all the more after the Shelley case. But there came a day when I could evade him no longer.'

The old man stops a moment; the effort is taking its toll.

'I shall not torment myself with details. Suffice it that I was wrong. Calamitously so. Blackaby saw the child's body unwrapped, as I did not – but that is no excuse. I should

333

have insisted. Because had I done so, I would have seen at once that there were marks not merely about the child's eyes, but all over its body. What I had thought the proof of strangulation was, in truth, evidence only of the infection that was no doubt the true and only cause of death. The man laughed in my face – taunted me for making so elementary an error.'

He sighs. 'And I did indeed merit such derision. I had accused Shelley of the worst possible crime, and I was mistaken. Whatever else he might have done, he did not harm his child. But if he believed that he had, and ever after paid the penance for it in his own heart, it was my own negligence and incompetence that were to blame.'

They sit in silence, the fire cracking softly now and again, the clock ticking in the silence.

'Shelley never knew,' says Charles, eventually, 'what Blackaby told you?'

Maddox shakes his head. 'I wrote to him at the *poste restante* in Pisa but the letter was returned unopened. The hand that had penned my address was hers. Six months later he was dead.'

He is tiring visibly now, his hand fluttering and his voice slowing. Charles clasps the hand that flutters so, and Maddox grasps him tight with the other. 'There is little left to say – let me – there may not be another chance – I beseech you—'

His eyes are pleading. Before his attack – before that moment that seemed to rend the veil of mortal frailty – the most painful part of the malady that afflicted him had been his knowing it. And Charles can see that same terror now – that same fear of the darkness, the forgetting.

'You must not pain yourself,' he whispers.

'It is the *not telling* that has caused me pain.'

He sits back. 'I did not know my son was dead. Not until I heard she had come back to England a widow. She and a child far too young to be mine.'

The words are coming slower and slower now, each breath drawn in distress. 'That journey I made to Italy. I put out that I wished to visit the Palladian villas, and so I did. But I went also to Rome, where they had buried him. It was a beautiful place. The scent of wild flowers, the shade of cypress trees. I asked directions to the grave, but the attendant said that no one knew where his body lay. They had wished to bury Shelley beside him, but when they opened the tomb they found no child's remains. My own boy, and I could not be near him. Not even in death.'

* * *

In the long dark hours that follow, while the rest of the house sleeps, Charles takes his pages of notes and attempts to put them into some sort of order – some sort of connected narrative that makes sense of these tangled and poisoned lives. He knows, now, why his uncle destroyed his records, and why he tried, even in his half-insensible state, to eradicate what Charles had succeeded in deciphering. But one question yet remains – and it is one to which even Mary Shelley seems never to have known the answer. Why was Shelley tracked first to Cumberland and then to Wales, all those years ago, and shot at in the chaos of a midnight assault? What was it that had him seeing the shadow of a persecutor on every street, and an avenging demon at every turn? Was that what he'd meant, that night of storms in Geneva, when he talked to Polidori, half dazed by ether, of a spectre that pursued him wearing his own face?

Charles puts down his pen and looks out at the slowly silvering sky, thinking of Mary, and of Claire. Mary, who will, by now, have received his letter accusing her husband of a crime she has concealed for more than thirty years, but which Charles now knows he did not commit. By rights he ought to write again, and free her from that terrible burden, allow an ill and ageing woman a last peace. But something within him stays his hand, something perverse that whispers she has deceived the world all this time, and it is little enough punishment to leave her fearing, for a few more days yet, that the world might soon discover that deception. And as for Claire, she may have deserved better than she has received, but she has lied as much as any of them. Charles has no more wish to see her again than he has to set foot within that house on Chester Square, with its sham shrine and pristine façade of imitation gentility. He writes Claire a note, explaining that he has not heard from the Shelleys, and that on consideration, he believes negotiations with them would be more fruitful if she conducted them directly. Then he seals the envelope, and has Billy take it to St John's Wood. Though when the boy comes back two hours later it's to say the house is empty and the inhabitants gone.

'I asked around a bit, Mr Charles, but no one seems to know where she went. Left the letter next door in case, but they didn't think it were likely she'd be coming back.'

Charles wonders, in passing, at this sudden change of address. How many homes has Claire had in the course of her life, and not one of them her own? And is she now in flight, or merely – once again – in transit? He, in the meantime, has spent those two hours re-reading Thomas Medwin's *Life*. Knowing what he knows now, this second reading is rather like deciphering the trick of Holbein's

Ambassadors – working out by trial and error exactly where it is you have to stand to turn that strange distorted foreground shape into a perfectly proportioned human skull. Charles thinks he knows now where to stand to scrutinize Shelley, but the image in the centre is not quite clear – not yet. But he is a detective, and this is not the only evidence he has to hand. So he retrieves his volume of Shelley's poetry from the shelf in the attic and sits down in the office to read. He finds the place where he left off and starts to work forwards once more, disdaining anything overtly political, interested only in what appears to him to be personal, or suggestive. And then suddenly he finds it. Stanzas he has seen before, in the paper Maddox found on Harriet Shelley's dead body:

The breath of night like death did flow
Beneath the sinking moon.

The wintry hedge was black,
The green grass was not seen,
The birds did rest
On the bare thorn's breast,
Whose roots, beside the pathway track,
Had bound their folds o'er many a crack
Which the frost had made between.

Thine eyes glowed in the glare
Of the moon's dying light,
As a fen-fire's beam
On a sluggish stream
Gleams dimly – so the moon shone there,
And it yellowed the strings of thy tangled hair,
That shook in the wind of night.

The moon made thy lips pale, beloved;
The wind made thy bosom chill;
The night did shed
On thy dear head
Its frozen dew, and thou didst lie
Where the bitter breath of the naked sky
Might visit thee at will.

It's listed as an early poem, and dated 'November 1815' –
almost exactly a year before Harriet Shelley died. Charles
leafs quickly through the others in the same section but
finds nothing else he recognizes. There must have been
some reason Harriet copied out these words in her last
despair, because if anyone knew the mystery of Shelley's
past, it was her. Did she not say something of the kind to
Maddox, when she spoke to him of Tremadoc? *No one knows
the truth of that night but Shelley and I. Neither what happened,
nor why.* Charles gets out Maddox's papers again and looks
at the page he found on her body, those scrawls and stains
that evoke so painfully her last pitiful hours, that paper
darkened by thoughts of drowning, and the shadow of an
imminent death. But if there is some other meaning here, he
has not the clue he needs to unlock it. He curses softly and
sits back. Perhaps, after all, he's looking at it the wrong way.
Lines about a dying girl might well have impressed themselves on the mind of a young woman distraught enough –
desperate enough – to contemplate the same fate. But what
of the other words on this page – might some of them come
likewise from Shelley's poems? Could that give him the key
to the puzzle? He's left the other volumes downstairs, and
when he opens the drawing-room door a few minutes later
he finds Abel sleeping quietly in the big chair, his hands
folded over his stomach. The fire is low and Maddox is

sitting on the sopha, one of the Shelley volumes open on his lap. Charles walks slowly over to him and puts his hand on his shoulder, and it is not just the old man who has tears in his eyes as Charles realizes what it is he has been reading.

To William Shelley

Thy little footsteps on the sands
Of a remote and lonely shore;
The twinkling of thine infant hands,
Where now the worm will feed no more;
Thy mingled look of love and glee
When we returned to gaze on thee—

There is the sound of laughter then, in the street outside, and when Charles goes to the window he can see Betsy playing down there with Billy, the little girl running round and round him in excited circles, leaving a trail of tiny footprints in the smooth and perfect snow.

* * *

It is Monday morning, and as Nancy and Molly haul the heavy baskets of laundry down to the dolly-tub for washing, Charles is in the office going through Maddox's old cases, in search of anything that might help him in the task he has taken on for the Bodleian Curators. He could ask Maddox himself, of course, and he may yet do that, but the strain of his last disclosures has left the old man restless and occasionally irascible, and Charles knows that the balance of his mind is only too fragile, and judges this latest case not worth the risk.

So absorbed is he, so intent, that even though half his mind hears the knock downstairs – hears Billy's chirpy enquiry and a woman's reply – it is only when the door to the office swings open that he registers who it is he has before him. The little worn shawl he has seen before, a dark silk gown, and a hat the matrons of Buckingham Street would no doubt consider scandalous.

He bows, a little stiffly. 'Miss Clairmont.'

'Mr Maddox.'

Billy looks from one to the other, trying – evidently – to work out what can be generating such a crackle of fractious energy between them.

'Have Molly bring coffee, would you, Billy?'

As Charles takes a chair and sets it for her he finds, to his surprise and vexation, that his hands are trembling. 'You have received my letter.'

'Clearly.'

She is furious, that much is obvious, but as he sees the anger flushed in her face he feels his own exasperation rise to meet it. Has she always known what he has only so recently discovered? And how much effort might she therefore have saved him, had she chosen to tell him the truth? But then he remembers: truth is a commodity Claire Clairmont reserves for her own use, and at a time of *her* choosing.

'When you left my house,' she begins, 'it was on the understanding that you were to undertake my commission to the Shelleys. That you would do so without delay, and return to tell me their response. Not only have you not done so, but it seems you are now attempting to renege on our agreement.'

'I did,' he replies, keeping his irritation in check, but only just, 'visit the Shelleys. And I did, as instructed, convey to them your message.'

'And?'

'Lady Shelley said they would consider the proposal, and inform me of their decision. Thus far, I have not heard what that is.'

Her eyes glitter and she is about to fling her fury in his face when there is a knock outside. He gets up and goes to take the coffee from Molly, and sees Claire eyeing her as he closes the door and sets the tray on the desk.

'I have, therefore,' he continues, calmly now, steadily, 'nothing to report. But I do have something to confess.' He pauses, knowing now he has her attention. And the upper hand; at least for a while.

'And what might that be?' she says, apparently busy about the cups. But she is not fooling him: he can see her impatience in her parted lips, in her shallow breathing.

'When last we met, I told you I had read my uncle's files. That was a lie.'

He sees her gasp, then attempt to conceal it by raising her cup to her mouth. 'This coffee is barely drinkable,' she says, with a grimace, replacing the cup on the tray.

'My apologies. The maid clearly does not know the Italian way of such things.'

'So what has prompted you to this sudden *confessio peccati*?'

He lets a moment lapse, and then another. 'Because I have now discovered what was in those missing papers. They concerned the suicide of Fanny Imlay. And of Shelley's wife.'

Her face goes pale. So suddenly and so completely that if she were not sitting down he would fear she might faint.

'Miss Clairmont?'

'I am sorry,' she murmurs, her hand to her mouth. 'It is so long since I have heard those events spoken of, it is as if

341

they took place in another life. A life I have striven for many years to forget.'

She looks at him with those extraordinary eyes, those eyes that have drowned many an older and a more experienced man, but Charles is not going to be drawn in – not this time.

She takes a deep breath. 'I was very fond of Fanny. She was a sweet, kind creature, and much put-upon. Mary treated her abominably. She knew exactly what to say that would hurt her most.'

'And Shelley? Did he not treat her far more unkindly, by awakening affections he had no intention of returning?'

She shakes her head. 'He told me, years later, that he had no idea Fanny had such feelings for him. That he had never meant such a thing to happen, and reproached himself bitterly that he had not perceived it. You did not know him – he could be very gentle, very encouraging. He would often sit with Fanny – listen to her talk. No one else in that house ever took the slightest notice of her, but he did. It is easy to see why she might have loved him for it.'

'As you did. Only your love, unlike hers, was returned. And your love, unlike hers, led not to death, but to life.'

She reddens now, the contrast deepened by the pale before. 'I do not know what you mean.'

'I think you do, Miss Clairmont. The papers I just referred to are not all I have since discovered. Byron's was not your only child. By then you had already borne another. To Shelley.'

'I bore him no child.' Her voice is small, desolate.

'Please, Miss Clairmont – it is of no use to lie to me! It is not only the papers for 1816 that I have read. I have talked to Fraser – heard his account of how you and my uncle first met. I know why they sent you to Lynmouth. I know it was that the birth might be concealed—'

342

'But do you know what happened *before* I took that long journey alone? When, as little more than a child myself, I was cast out from all I loved into such a lonely and miserable place?'

Charles flushes. 'I know that she – that there was an accident—'

'It was no *accident*! She laid violent hands upon me, lashing out at me in a frenzy of vicious hatred. I have never seen such enmity in another being's eyes as I saw that day in hers. She wished to be rid of me – and rid of my baby. I remember, even now, sitting alone, day after day, on that desolate seashore, without a friend to comfort me in my loss, and being sure of nothing but that my life was already more than I could bear.'

She is silent, so beset by the past that she is struggling for self-control.

'The child did not live,' says Charles, eventually.

'I had scarce been there three months when I was brought to bed. The injury – the fall I had taken – the doctor said—'

She stops and raises her hand for a moment to her eyes, then forces herself to go on: 'My baby was – damaged. They would not even let me see it. When I wrote to Shelley to tell him he contrived to come to see me, but aside from that one visit I was alone. Alone, and utterly miserable. And when at last I did return, wretched and exhausted, I stepped down from the coach to see them both awaiting me, he haggard, but *she* exultant as her eyes met mine and she moved her hand to rest on her swollen belly. He had not found the words to tell me, but *she* needed no language to convey her message: *I* had lost his child; *she* would now give him the son he longed for, the son he doted upon from the day he was born.'

Charles looks away, unable to hold her gaze. How

343

different might her life have been, he wonders, had Shelley known that precious baby might not have been his own? But the truth, told now, will change her nothing, and only render the past more poisonous with lost possibilities.

'The first moment I saw Shelley take William in his arms and his face light up with love of that little boy, I knew she had triumphed. Why else do you think I hurled myself so desperately at Byron that spring, if it were not to secure a life of my own, a *lover* of my own? It was a mistake so disastrous it has ruined all the years that have succeeded it, and I have never once spoken of what drove me to it. But I will do so now. My long silence has availed me nothing, and served only to afford *her* a protection she has done nothing to deserve. And so,' she says defiantly, 'I will break that silence. I will tell the truth.'

Charles frowns. 'The whole truth? You will speak without reserve of all that happened between the three of you?'

'*I* have nothing to fear. It is time an account were given that will speak honestly not only of him but of those of us who shared his life.'

Mary Shelley, too, insisted no such account had ever been given, but she, by contrast, has done all in her power to prevent it. And, given what Charles now knows of her baby daughter's death, he can understand why. Even if she has found a way to live with that, even if she has long since excused that terrible deed as unwitting and unintended, she knows the rude cold world she dreads so much will not be so forgiving. But if her reserve is comprehensible, Claire's new candour makes no sense. Why should this woman, who seems to have loved Shelley no whit the less, be so willing to destroy his reputation now?

He goes to the window and looks down into the street. Nancy is making her way up to the Strand through the snow, the market basket over her arm. He turns back to the room. 'You will speak openly even of those events you say you have striven to forget? Of Fanny's death – and of Harriet's?'

She flushes. 'I cannot speak of what I did not witness.'

'But there were other events, were there not, that you *did* witness? Where your testimony would serve only to harm the man you say you loved.'

'I did love him; I love him still.'

'In that case I am only the more confounded.'

She rises from her chair and walks away. 'I have no idea to what you refer.'

'I think you do, Miss Clairmont. I am speaking of the Shelleys' first daughter. And how that baby died.'

She glances at him quickly, warily. 'She died from convulsions, brought on by a fever. It is all too often so with infants born before their time.'

'That is true, and I know that was the story you all told. But it is not what you believed then, is it, Miss Clairmont? You thought Shelley was to blame. You thought he had risen in the night, in his sleep, and put his hands about his own daughter's neck.'

She turns towards him, 'And if I thought that,' she says slowly, 'it is because *Mary* said so. Because *your uncle* confirmed it.'

'And that is what he, too, believed. But it was not so. Shelley thought himself guilty, but he was wronged. My uncle only discovered the truth years later – when it was too late – but whatever you supposed then, whatever you have written since, it was *not so*.'

It should have been overwhelming – it should have been a revelation to change her whole life, but she merely glances sideways at him and returns, in a rustle of scented silk, to the chair.

345

'You tell me nothing, Mr Maddox, that I have not known these thirty years.'

Charles gapes at her. 'But how, in God's name?'

She raises an eyebrow and folds her hands upon her lap. 'By the same means, I imagine, as your uncle came to know it. That vile man Absalom Blackaby.'

'The sexton at Tom-All-Alone's? How could he possibly—'

'Find us? Know who we were? I am sure that, for a *detective*, a mere moment's thought will be sufficient to resolve that mystery. Your uncle should have been more careful in letting slip Shelley's name. It is, after all, hardly a common one, and when his case came before Chancery it was the talk of London. It was then that that horrible man tracked Shelley down. It was then that he embarked upon his loathsome scheme of extortion.'

Charles can barely absorb so much new information. 'Extortion? But if the baby died a natural death how could Blackaby possibly turn that to his advantage?'

'Because by then Shelley was petitioning for the custody of Harriet's children. How could he hope to win the case if the slightest whisper came to the judge's ear about what had happened to Mary's baby? That he and the woman he proposed as step-mother to those children had allowed their own baby to die, and left it to be buried in a workhouse grave?'

Charles flushes, remembering that word had indeed come to the judge's ear, and it was not only the site of the baby's grave he had discovered by it.

'Shelley was tormented by that man Blackaby for years,' Claire says bitterly. 'Even after we had left England.'

'He told you of this?'

'Not at first. I discovered it later by chance, when I found

346

a copy of a note he had written to his banker, asking that ten pounds should be paid to a person who would present himself with a note signed "A. B.".'

'And Mary – did she know?'

'He made me promise not to tell her.'

Charles can scarcely believe it. 'But if he never told her about Blackaby, surely she must have continued to believe him guilty of his daughter's death. What husband would allow his wife to persist in such an appalling ignorance?'

'I believe he dared not speak of it, because he dreaded to hear the answer she might give.'

Charles frowns. 'I do not take your meaning.'

'If you have indeed spoken to that man Fraser, you will know that she claimed she saw Shelley that night, standing over the cradle.'

He sees the quick flush across her cheeks and that she fears what else he has discovered; but her own long-past shame is not what matters to him now. 'I have not forgotten it, Miss Clairmont, but I do not see that it makes any difference. Shelley suffered from bouts of sleepwalking, did he not, and especially when he was anxious or under strain? Surely it is possible he was indeed at the cradle that night, even if he never actually harmed the child.'

But she is already shaking her head. 'I said this to your uncle then, and I will say it now, to you. Shelley awoke that morning in his *own* bed. In all the years I lived under his roof I never once knew that to be so when he had risen in his sleep in the night. After such episodes we would always find him wandering distractedly in the next room, in the next street, even halfway across the town.'

'But if that is true, you are accusing her—'

'Yes,' she says quietly. 'I am accusing her of lying. I do not think she saw him that night at all.'

347

And as she looks at him steadily, holding his gaze, willing him to believe her, Charles imagines himself for a moment in Mary Shelley's place, that morning long ago when she found her daughter dead. She was not married, she already had a rival for her lover's affections, and now she did not even have his child. She must have been terrified he would consider himself no longer bound to her, that he would abandon her, as he already had his wife. But this woman had for parents not some portly tavern-keeper and his spouse, but two of the most outstanding intellects of the age; this woman had been taught from a child to believe herself the world's darling – the beautiful lure of every eye. Poor little Harriet Westbrook might be casually set aside but not *her* – not Mary Wollstone-craft Godwin. It was inconceivable – she could not permit it – she *would not* permit it. Was it at that moment, as she gazed down at the cradle at her daughter's cold and rigid form, that it came to her that a dead child might be even more useful to her than a living one? Did she realize suddenly that if Shelley believed *he* was responsible for that death he would be bound to her for ever by a bond he would never dare break – an unbearable guilt he could never redeem?

'But to make him believe he had killed his own child,' says Charles, slowly. 'Could she really have committed an act so—'

'Horrific? Monstrous? An act as monstrous, perhaps, as the crime perpetrated by that abhorrent creature in *Franken-stein*? The inhuman wretch that strangles a little child in the darkness, leaving the print of the murderer's finger on its neck?'

'But you claim that *he* wrote that tale, not her.'

'And remember *when* he wrote it, Mr Maddox. It was the summer of 1816. Before we returned to London. *Before* that man Blackaby told Shelley the truth.'

'So that is what you meant when you wrote of Frankenstein as a man tormented by the abominable crime he
believes he has committed—'

'When Shelley wrote that book he still thought himself
guilty of his own daughter's death – it was *his own horror* he
was reliving. I remember, even now, my shiver of dread
when first I read what the monster tells its creator on the icy
northern wastes. *You and I are bound by ties only dissoluble by
the annihilation of one of us*. It was those words – those *exact*
words – that Mary said to him the day she discovered I was
carrying his child – after he had torn her away as she rained
blows down upon me, where I lay on the floor fainting in
my own blood.'

Claire looks down at her hands; her lips are white, but
Charles does not see it. His eyes are on the floor as he begins
to pace up and down the room, re-forming the sequence,
recasting the chain of events. 'Very well, Miss Clairmont. Let
us assume for the moment that you are right – let us
suppose Mary did indeed lie about seeing Shelley that night,
a lie that is not merely believed by Shelley, but corroborated
by one of the finest thief-takers in the land. And as the days
pass and her deception holds, she finds that falsehood has
accomplished everything she hoped for – Hogg is banished,
and Shelley returns to her side to comfort her in the depths
of her inconsolable grief. Grief he believes *he* has caused.
And then she finds herself once again pregnant and Shelley's love for that little boy makes her believe herself, at last,
secure. Yet when his wife dies and he is free to marry her,
she is horrified to find that he hesitates – he seeks to
postpone – and the only way she can compel him to fulfil
his promise is by threatening to destroy both herself and the
new baby she is by then carrying, the new daughter that will
replace the one she lost. And why does Shelley try to evade

349

the marriage? Not because he knows she has lied, because by then Blackaby has not yet tracked him down. No,' he turns to Claire, 'he seeks to postpone because even the black depth of his guilt has not been enough to destroy his love for *you*. And from that moment on she knows her lie is flawed, because even if she can prevent him from leaving her, she cannot eradicate those feelings – feelings so strong that he can never wholly sever his connection with you, never accept being long from your side, feelings so strong, indeed, that they endure even your liaison with Byron, and the child that is its consequence.'

Claire lifts her chin in defiance. 'Allegra was an exquisitely beautiful little girl. Shelley adored her – and William adored her. When I gave him a sweetmeat he would crawl over and place half his share in my own darling's mouth. Then Mary would insist he give some to Clara too, and the poor boy would cry and cry until his sister was taken away and Allegra restored to his side. It was then that Mary started to say my darling should be sent to her father – that it would be for her own good, that he could provide a better future for her than I. *Allegra must go – I do not want her remaining here; if no one can be found to take her, we will have to go ourselves* – on and on, day after day after day. By the time we left England Shelley's health had completely broken down.'

Charles can well believe it, though even his imagination shrinks from the full horror of what it must have been to live in such a household, as the venomous rivalry of one generation began to replicate itself only too unerringly in the next. And as for Mary Shelley, Claire's very presence – Claire with her daughter more beautiful than her own – must have seemed a retribution designed by Fate purposely to torment her. Is this what she revealed in those letters she later wrote to her dashing young friend Gatteschi – letters she claimed would have destroyed her for ever if they saw light? Is this what she meant when she said her whole life had been an endless atonement for some dreadful crime she had committed all unknowing? Only she had not committed it unknowing. She had always known what it was she had done. Both to Harriet and to her own husband. Not merely letter after dreadful letter that helped drive a vulnerable young woman to a terrible suicide, but a lie that she could never take back – a lie she could never after unsay. And her punishment? Claire. Never to have had the life she yearned for without Claire.

Charles goes thoughtfully to the table and pours himself more coffee. 'And when did you and Shelley renew your *affaire*?'

Once more there is that defiant lift of the chin. 'Mary had only herself to blame. She did nothing but carp and criticize, nothing but complain. With me he could be happy; with me he could be himself.'

'I do not doubt it,' says Charles, 'but imagine the unbearable downwards spiral that now entraps her – the more she protests, the more she drives him away, and yet she cannot stop herself, cannot break the deadly circle. And then, after all she believes she has suffered, Shelley summons her on a journey of more than a hundred miles across Italy for what she deems *your* convenience. With her daughter already seriously ill. It must have been the last straw.'

Her eyes narrow. 'I see you have heard the Shelleys' version of that event. But *I* was there, and I tell you, Clara was not so very sick when they first reached Este. Shelley and I had had three blissful weeks alone with my darling – the house was so beautiful, the air almost luminous and the garden full of flowers – and then when Mary arrived it was as if winter had come again. We endured day after day of her furious accusations and all the while that little girl was becoming more and more unwell. It was horrible – *horrible* – as if we were condemned never to escape the past. I knew it was to tempt Providence to call her so.'

Charles frowns. 'I do not understand.'

'They called the baby Clara. It was the name they had given to their first daughter. Only she had never lived to be christened.'

Charles stares at her, unable to credit the evidence of his own senses. 'They called their second daughter by the *same name* as the baby Mary accused her husband of *killing*?'

She sighs. 'Shelley insisted. It was the same superstition he had always had about names – that the past might be redeemed by repeating it. But he was wrong. It was not true, was it? Not for Clara.'

'No,' says Charles, his mind alight with a sudden realization. 'Shelley was not wrong – the past *was* repeated.'

She shakes her head sadly. 'Repeated, yes, but not redeemed.'

'You misunderstand me: the past was repeated because *Mary Shelley made it so*. Think for a moment. When the first baby died she was struggling with events she could not command – a situation she thought slipping from her grasp. But did not the death of her child restore to her a measure of control, even if only for a time? And did she not regain that pre-eminence by ensuring Shelley believed *himself* responsible? And was it not exactly the same with the second little girl? Her own position is under threat, she fears Shelley is turning again to you, but the death of the child restores him once more to her side. And once again it is because she insists *he* is guilty – guilty this time of neglect

352

and reckless delay, because he was concerned only for you, and ignored the needs of his own dying daughter.'

Claire comes towards him now, tears in her eyes. 'Mary always blamed me for what happened but I swear to you I begged her on my knees to stop in Padua and allow the doctor I was consulting there to treat Clara as well. There was no need to go on to Venice that day – we had already been travelling since three o'clock in the morning, and we were all overcome with the heat and the strain. With a child already so haggard – it was taking such a terrible risk. But Mary would not listen. She forced Shelley to take her.'

Charles looks at her. How many times has it happened before? A whole case – weeks of work – turns and opens on a nuance, a glance. Or a single word. Everything he had thought – everything he'd deduced – has just reversed and inverted. Like a photograph changing places with its negative. Dark to light, light to dark. Like Escher's famous woodcut that is at one and the same time black birds flying by day, and white birds flying by night. The image remains the same: it all depends on *how you perceive it*.

'The baby was *haggard*?' he says slowly.

'She was so weak and gaunt I should hardly have known her. Those four days in Este it was as if she was wasting away before our very eyes. Even as an infant she had never fed well – Mary was always saying that her milk would not come or the child would not take suck – that her spirits sank at the very thought of putting her to her breast.'

Charles thinks again about what Maddox told him of Mary Shelley's first dead child – about her skin so yellow, and her body wrapped so tightly that all that could be seen was her face. Did Mary's deceit begin not with the death of her daughter, and the lie she told, but before that – almost from the moment that baby was born? Were the blankets she

353

bound about the child designed to conceal the real truth – that she, too, had been starved? Was *that* what had really driven Shelley so distracted in the days before she died? He, after all, had been a father before – if the child was not being adequately fed, surely he of all people would have seen the signs. Perhaps he told himself afterwards that it had not been Mary's fault – that it was her first child, and the infant already sickly and not expected to live. Perhaps he thought his own guilt so overwhelming that hers vanished into insignificance. And then, years later and all unlooked-for, he opens the door one morning to find Absalom Blackaby standing there before him. A man who saw the baby naked and unswaddled; a man who would have seen – just as Shelley had – the ribcage protruding through the sallow skin, the stomach hollowed with days of hunger. And later when his second daughter dies, and Shelley has to bury another tiny corpse that resembles only too horrifyingly the first, does it come to him, then, that this cannot be mere coincidence – cannot only be ill-luck?

And now Charles remembers, with an icy rush of horror, that there is another baby girl entangled in all of this. Another who fits the same terrible pattern. Little Elena, the baby Mary Shelley begged for, but then refused to feed. Little Elena, who was so quickly abandoned in the Naples orphanage in 1819. Charles had thought that an appalling dereliction on Shelley's part – an indefensible selfishness – but what if he's wrong? What if Shelley did not abandon her at all, but *rescued* her? What if he took Elena to the orphanage because he thought it was somewhere she would be safe? Did he fear, after the deaths of not one but two emaciated little girls, what his wife might do, if left alone? If Charles had not felt it before he feels it now, that electric teeming of the blood as the elements of a case fall suddenly and without warning into place, and the answer – the explanation – emerges with a perfect irresistible clarity from the mire of past confusion.

Charles takes a step towards Claire. 'I think that when the first baby died she was barely more than skin and bone, and Absalom Blackaby saw it when he buried her – saw it and knew only too clearly what it meant. I think *that* was what he really threatened to reveal to the world, if Shelley did not agree to his demands. And I think that was the true reason Shelley sent Elena away. He had failed to protect his own daughters, but there was one little girl he could still save.'

Claire puts her hand to her face, her eyes wide with terrified comprehension. 'No – it was not just one – it was not just Elena. I did not think – not at the time – but years later, when I was begging Byron to let Allegra visit me, he said he did not trust her in the same house as Mary. He said he could not permit her to come to us only to perish of – of neglect and – and *starvation*. Shelley must have confided in him – Shelley must have told him – must have feared what might happen—'

Charles reaches for her hand, knowing what such a realization must mean to her, but she pushes him away. 'Do you not see?' she cries, her voice raw with pain. 'If what you say is true, it was *her* fault my darling was left to die in that freezing, disease-infested convent. Byron might have let Allegra come to me, if it had not been for *her*. She would have lived – she would be here now – I would not be alone—'

'You cannot be sure of that,' says Charles, softly. 'You cannot torture yourself with the past.'

'I have done nothing *but* torture myself with the past since the day I heard that she was dead.'

And as she weeps now in his arms, her body shaking with

a lifetime of loss, Charles wonders if it had been the same for Shelley. Was he, too, haunted by what he might have done differently – by the deaths he might have prevented, had he acted another way, or made another choice? And having watched the past repeat itself so tragically not just once but twice, did he see everything, ever after, through the same dark prism?

'That letter you showed me,' he says slowly, as her sobs subside, 'did Shelley not say you had put off a visit to Allegra because he feared leaving Mary alone – that he dreaded some fatal end?'

Claire shakes her head sadly, her handkerchief at her eyes. 'She was inconsolable after William died – she had always suffered from melancholia, but it was never worse than after his death. She said she wished she, too, had died that day – that she would never recover from his loss. For months she withdrew from us into herself – impossible to comfort, impossible to solace. She would write, and she would sit, for hours, gazing out of the window. I would see her watching me when I was in the garden, like some sort of phantasm, some image of myself in a clouded mirror.'

Charles nods, remembering how he had thought of the two of them as anti-types – dark and light, hot and cool, eager and reticent.

'It was not the first time I have heard her talk of suicide, but I never believed it as I did then.'

'And that is what Shelley feared?' says Charles. 'That is what the letter he sent you referred to?'

She looks at him with a puzzled frown. 'I have always assumed so.'

'And when was this?'

'1820. The late spring of 1820.'

Charles calculates quickly. Percy would have been –

what? Nine months old? Perhaps even less. 'The letter said, too, did it not, that you had been present when Clara died – and when William died?'

She nods. 'I was there, yes – but—'

'Why should Shelley have mentioned that? Why raise it again then?'

She looks at him blankly. 'I do not understand. What are you saying?'

'Miss Clairmont, I do not think Shelley feared his wife would kill herself. Or, rather, I do not think that such a possibility was his only, or even his principal, fear. Why did he talk of William's death in that letter to you – what happened to that little boy?'

Her eyes fill with tears. 'It had not seemed so serious, not in the beginning. A stomach disorder, such as he had suffered many times before. But the doctor said there was no reason he should not make a full recovery. I remember how happy Shelley was that night when he took me with him to hear the music in the Piazza di Spagna.'

'And how long was it before the child's condition worsened?'

'A few days. Perhaps four. Then suddenly there was a dreadful relapse – terrible heart-rending convulsions that seemed to tear his tiny body in pieces. Shelley sat up with him for three days and nights, not sleeping, exhausting himself, willing his sweet Willmouse not to die. But it was no use. He said later he felt as if he had been hunted down by calamity – as if the whole household was somehow doomed. We were all overwhelmed by it – all of us. I loved that little boy as much as I did my own darling.'

'And how did he look,' asks Charles quietly, 'at the end?'

The tears are falling now, lingering heavy tears she does not wipe away. 'He had hardly eaten anything for more

357

than a week. He was barely recognizable as the child he had been.'

'Just as Clara was – just as I believe the first baby also was.'

Claire begins to shake her head. 'No, not William – surely not William . . .'

'You must see it, Miss Clairmont, as Shelley would have done, sitting up all those nights with his son – alone, in the dark, as the child worsened. He must have asked himself if that relapse, that sudden and unexpected decline, was once again *his* fault because he had chosen to spend time happily with you, rather than miserably with his wife.'

She is sobbing desperately now, and he goes to her and helps her back to her seat.

'You think I am blaming you – but I am not. I am not saying William died because of what you and Shelley did, but I believe *Shelley* thought so. I think *he* believed his wife guilty – *he* believed she had allowed his beloved son to die to punish him, a third time, for loving you and neglecting her. Might that not be the real explanation of his refusal to leave his son's side, those last few days? He stayed because he feared what might happen if he left the boy alone *with his own mother*. And when he begged you later to postpone your visit to Allegra it was because he was terrified the same thing might happen again, to his only remaining child. Both his daughters had died, then his precious William. Percy was all he had left.'

She rises from her chair and walks away, as stiffly as an old woman. It is long, very long, before she faces him again. 'Let us be clear,' she says, in a voice as brittle as February frost. 'Let there be no misunderstanding. You are telling me that William's death was not an accident.'

Charles takes a deep breath. Part of his mind is telling him that the boy's last illness was only too horribly like Clara's. Some apparently mundane disorder of the stomach that suddenly worsened, a swift and drastic loss of weight and, at the last, deadly convulsions. Each time the same pattern. And Charles knows – as Shelley, too, must have known – that a stomach disorder is the easiest possible sickness to induce in a child, and convulsions may be the consequence not only of fever but of an adult's choking hand. But there is nothing Charles can do to prove it. 'It is possible the illness was exactly what it appeared to be,' he says carefully. 'That no human intervention either caused it, or could have saved him.'

'But you do think both those little girls were harmed – deprived of food – that Mary must have known it but did nothing.'

'Yes, Miss Clairmont, I do. I know it is hard to believe any woman could so ill-treat her own defenceless infants, but I trained for a while as a doctor, and even in those few months I saw women reduced to a state of abject misery after childbirth, women otherwise gentle and tender-hearted—'

'Mary was *never* that,' she says quickly.

'—who became erratic, even violent after their delivery. I have read since that some turn their fury on their husbands, others on their own babies. If she were already predisposed by an inherited weakness, such an illness might well have driven her to commit these dreadful acts, hardly knowing, perhaps, what it was she did.'

He is trying to make it easier for her, but she is shaking her head now, not in sadness but in grim and fierce refutation. '*You* do not know her. *I* have known her intimately from when she was a child. Mary has a tenacity – a ferocity of resolve – such as I have rarely seen even in

359

the most ruthless of men. Her own father acknowledged as much. He, if anyone, knew of what she was capable. Knew it, and feared it. Do you not recall in that selfsame letter what Shelley said of the injury to her arm when she was still a girl?'

Charles nods slowly. 'And some veiled reference to Godwin and your mother fearing some greater evil.'

'I did not know what that was – not at the time. My mother did not tell me until a few weeks before she died. She said the physician who came to the house thought Mary might have caused the injury *herself*. That she exaggerated its severity – indeed may have prevented the wound from healing by scratching it again and again with her fingernails. There were marks the doctor could not otherwise explain. My mother believed she did it to secure to herself, once more, the whole of Godwin's time and attention. They had been excessively attached to one another after her mother died, and she fiercely resented being supplanted. Especially by a woman like my mother.' There is a settled bitterness in her face now, the scar of an ancient unhealed resentment.

'I could never comprehend, then, why Godwin sent her away so often when she was supposed to be such a favourite – why he would so carefully burn every letter she sent him when they were all those months apart. Once, when she had returned from such an absence, there was a fire in the bookshop downstairs that no one could explain. She had been in the house less than ten days.'

They are silent. Charles is thinking about what Maddox told him. Of a woman who spoke to her lover in the voice of a ten-year-old-child, and promised to be *a good Pecksie and not vex him any more*; of a woman who claimed to be 'quite well again', when of sickness there had been no outward sign. The same woman who had once basked in her father's

360

undivided love, then seen that love stolen from her by another she despised. A woman who may have been willing, even as a mere girl, to inflict an unsightly wound on her own body in a desperate effort to regain the love she craved. A woman who, perhaps, made her own babies sick to secure her lover to her side, and punish him for daring to neglect her. Charles has not heard, of course, of Münchausen's syndrome, and it will be another century before this mental disorder is named, and even longer before it is fully understood that there are women who will harm not only themselves but their own children to compel the attention, the affection, or the sympathy they believe they are owed. But Charles does not need to name it to recognize in Mary Shelley the possibility of the same terrible and overwhelming affliction of the mind.

'That letter you showed me,' he says eventually, 'did it not say she was pregnant again in those last few months? What happened to the child?'

'She miscarried,' Claire says quietly, turning away once more. 'At the house in Lerici. It was not eight weeks since I had lost my own darling. They did not tell me of her death for days, fearing how I would react, and they were surprised, I think, that I seemed to rally so well. But they did not know what I knew. Shelley was going to leave her, Mr Maddox, and be with me. As he had always wished to.'

Charles moves softly towards her, and stands at her shoulder. She seems scarcely to know that he is there.

'Lerici was such a beautiful place – beautiful and haunting. The landscape so wild, and the house right on the edge of the sea, with the waves crashing against the rocks, and the water swelling sometimes right up to the steps. Mary hated it from the start – she claimed to have a presentiment of coming evil – but I loved it, and Shelley loved it. At least at first. He began writing again – furiously, prolifically – a poem he called *The Triumph of Life*. And he had a vision – a vision that troubled him at first, but which he came to see as a pledge of forgiveness, a promise that all would be well for the two of us, he and I. He was out on the terrace one night when he started suddenly as if in pain and pointed out to sea crying, "There it is again! There!" He said afterwards that a little naked child had risen from the water, looking towards him, smiling, its hands clasped together as if in joy.'

'It was a child of his own he saw?'

'I do not think so. A few days later I departed for Florence to collect my possessions. We planned to tell Mary of our intentions as soon as I returned. I left him happy, composed – settled in his own mind. When I entered that house again two weeks later everything had changed. He was ashen with exhaustion, wrung out to his last atom of energy by Mary's unceasing demands. She was one moment in hysterics, the next in a state of near collapse requiring waiting on hand and foot.' She shakes her head. 'It was intolerable to be in that house – to be forced to listen to the endless recriminations, the dreadful repeated violence. Two days after my return the whole household was roused by her shrieks – she was beside herself, screaming that she was losing the baby and blaming Shelley, but in the end it all came to nothing. A friend who was staying with us said to me later that he thought she had made the whole thing up – he remarked rather tartly how strange it was that she had managed to recover so quickly.'

And how revealing, thinks Charles, that this phantom miscarriage should have happened so soon after her rival's return.

'And then we found her lying senseless one morning in her bedroom. There was so much panic and confusion it is hard to remember clearly, but it seemed to me she must have been standing on a chair by the bookshelves, and fallen from there onto the marble floor. Though why she should have done such a thing – any one of us would have fetched her down a book had she asked for it. I thought, even then, that was almost as if she had wished it on herself.'

She gazes down onto the busy street. 'The house was so remote we could not get the doctor for hours. Had Shelley not been there, and acted so decisively, I think she would have died. But the effort – all that time at her side – took a most terrible toll. A few nights later we were all woken by the most terrifying screaming. We found him in Mary's room, staggering about in a half-trance, babbling wildly that he had seen a figure standing over the bed with its hands about her throat. And when the stranger lifted his mantle to show himself, Shelley saw his own face staring back at him in the darkness.'

Charles starts, remembering that he has read a version of this same incident in Medwin's memoir. Only he did not know then what he knows now. It had appeared, then, to be merely one more example of a whole sequence of paranoid delusions stretching back to Shelley's boyhood, but now there may be a meaning in this apparent madness. Did Shelley wish to free himself so desperately from his wife that his sleeping self dreamed of killing her? And surely it is no coincidence that he acted out that phantasy in echo of the murder she had accused him of, all those years before? That by repeating the past it might be exorcized, even if it could never, ever be redeemed?

Claire sighs, her words breaking into his thoughts. 'It was all so strange, that time at Lerici. Everything seemed unnaturally vivid, unnaturally intense – it was as if the rules of the common world no longer held sway. Only a few days previously one of our friends saw Shelley passing twice by

363

her window even though we all knew him to be miles away at the time. And then, that night in Mary's room, Shelley told me that while I was away in Florence he had seen a man coming towards him one morning on the terrace—'

Charles frowns. 'Did he still believe he was being persecuted by some nameless pursuer – even so many years later and so far away?'

'You do not understand. The man he saw on the terrace was his *own mirror image*. And when Shelley challenged him the man just laughed and demanded to know how much longer he meant to be content.'

Charles can scarcely imagine the state of mind that must have generated such a horrifying vision, and for the first time he begins to feel some small sympathy for this man. It was not only the marriage Shelley made that haunted him. What was it he had done, all those years before, that he was still torturing himself so?

'After that he began to withdraw from me. He would no longer talk of the life we had imagined together, and spent long hours alone, on the boat or walking on the shore. I did not know, then, that he had tried to obtain prussic acid. Enough for a lethal dose.'

'Do you think he meant to kill himself?'

'I think he had begun to feel he would never be free of her in any other way – that it was the only means by which he would find rest.'

She leans her cheek against the cold windowpane and Charles can see the tears rolling again down her face. 'I believe now that he went out on that boat looking for death, and that he embraced it when it came. When he left us he was in such brilliant spirits – exhilarated with the sea, and the bright sky, and the prospect of the journey. They told us, later, the day he set out to return, that he must have known the *Don Juan* was over-rigged as the storm came on – that they could have run for safety to harbour, but they did not. The captain of another boat risked his own crew to bring his vessel alongside and take them on board, but he heard Shelley crying, "No, no!" And when the man called to them that they must take in sail or perish, he saw Shelley seize his companion's arm to prevent him. They were none of them seen alive again.'

There is silence in the room, a silence broken only by a sudden noise from the street – the laughter of children playing in the snow.

Claire hangs her head, and Charles puts his hand gently to her shoulder, imagining what it must have been like to wait, day after day, in that isolated house, in that terrible weather, desperate for news, watching for every sail. Only to find more than a week later that the mutilated bodies had been flung ashore, identifiable only by what clothes they wore, and what little they carried.

A moment later she has moved away from him, and is gathering her shawl and her reticule. 'I came here thinking that you still intended to help me; I did not expect you to force me to live again through every dark hour I have ever known.'

'What will you do?' asks Charles, as she moves towards the door. 'Do you still intend to publish your memoir?'

'I do not know. I need time to think. To consider what you have told me, and to decide.'

She holds his gaze a moment longer, then opens the door and sweeps out onto the landing and down the stairs to the hall. Where she barely escapes a collision with Billy, who is racing up the steps, frantic and breathless, but Charles's reprimand dies when he sees the boy's face. He is white to the roots of his hair, all his usual cockiness gone.

'Mr Charles – you have to come. We need to send for the doctor – we don't know how long she's been down there—'

'What in God's name are you talking about, Billy?'

'It's Molly, Mr Charles – she's just lyin' there moanin', not movin'—'

Charles does not stay to hear the rest. Pushing Billy out of the way he careers down the stairs to the basement kitchen where Nancy is kneeling with Molly's head cradled in her lap, and there is a thick dark stain spreading slowly across the dull stone floor.

'I was at the market,' cries Nancy at once, as if afraid he will accuse her. 'She looked pale when I left but she seemed all right, a bit distracted but I had no idea – she didn't seem in pain—'

Charles rushes to Nancy's side, and it's only now, as the two of them start to loosen Molly's skirts, that he realizes where the blood is coming from. And it is a realization by which everything is changed. Not just for today, but always, and for ever.

Nancy looks up at him and sees the horror on his face. 'But you said you knew – that day I started to tell yer, you said you knew—'

'I didn't – I swear I didn't know.'

Nancy's eyes narrow, and there is a hardness in her face now. 'How could yer – how could yer bloody well *not know*?'

'What must I do?' he says desperately, even though he is the one with medical training, she no more than a girl, no more than a common whore.

'Send the boy for the doctor. At once.'

Charles looks up. It is Claire, standing in the doorway, Billy hovering ghost-faced behind her. 'You must tell him,' she says, turning to the boy, 'that the girl has lost a lot of blood, and is insensible.'

'Right you are,' says Billy, clearly relieved to be told what to do – and to be gone.

'Go to Boswell – he's nearest,' cries Charles, as the boy disappears up the stairs, 'and there's another man in Maiden Lane.'

'We must do what we can to stanch the bleeding,' says Claire, coming quickly towards them, taking off her shawl and hat, 'and try to revive her. Do you have salts?'

'No,' stammers Charles, 'but there is brandy in the cupboard.'

'Then that will have to do. And if there is a hip bath, we will need it. And ice – whatever ice you have.'

Nancy runs for the brandy and Charles drags the old tin bath from the scullery to the kitchen, but when he gently lifts Molly into it there is a sudden gush down her legs and she moans softly in his arms. Her skin is clammy to the touch, and the bath now an inch deep in blood and fluid, and something else that Charles does not allow himself to see.

'Pack the ice about her,' says Claire, folding up her sleeves and tying an apron about her waist.

'Are you sure?' begins Nancy, the pewter bowl clutched tight to her breast. 'She seems so cold already. She's tremblin' so.'

'I have seen it done before – we cannot afford to waver – it may even now be too late.'

Nancy hesitates, then up-ends the bowl and drops the chunks of cloudy grey ice into the bath.

'Is this all you have?' says Claire, anxiously, looking first at Charles and then at Nancy.

'Well, we don't go in much for fancy cookin' 'ere – we never buys much.'

'We must hope it is enough,' says Claire, seizing the brandy flask. 'And hope likewise that the doctor is not long delayed.'

She tips the flask against Molly's lips and a few moments later the girl moans again and opens her eyes. But vital as it is to rouse her, it seems now a cruelty to have done so, for she wakes only to terror, and to pain. Claire tries to soothe her, telling her that the doctor is coming, that she has no need to be frightened, but instinct is stronger than words and the girl begins to struggle, pushing Claire's hands away and uttering tiny wailing noises like an animal ensnared. And when she lifts her eyes to Charles and he sees that her greatest fear is not for her own life but the one she is losing, his own eyes sting with tears and he cannot face her.

'Tell me what I can do,' he pleads, grasping Claire by the hand. 'There must be something I can do.'

'Are you sure there is no more ice?' she says, looking down where the bath is already running in thin slush.

'Snow,' says Charles, getting to his feet. 'I can bring snow.'

For the next hour Charles toils tirelessly up and down the stairs to the street, filling bucket after bucket, which they heap about Molly's shaking terrified body, watching – hoping – that this time the white will creep slower red, this time the dark pulse will slow its flow. But though the girl grows weaker, and her struggles subside, nothing seems to stem the bleeding, and each time Charles takes her wrist in his hand the beat is always feebler, the heart fainter. Then, at last, when they have almost lost hope, the doctor comes – toiling ponderously down the stairs with Billy at his heels – and Nancy runs to him with tears of exhausted relief. And even as she watches him make his long, long examination, and even though she must be able to see his features falling slowly into a grim resignation, still she clings to Claire as if all is resolved, as if all can now be made right.

But it is not so.

The doctor eventually straightens up and takes a cloth to wipe his hands. Then he comes to Charles where he is standing shivering by the stove, his shirt soaked, his trousers splashed to the knees with mud and snow.

'You, I take it, are the father?'

Charles has been fighting the word – resisting the reality of it – the unendurable remorse.

'Yes,' he says in the end, his voice rasping. 'I am the father.'

'I will not prevaricate with you, sir. It is clear enough that this is not your wife, but what you do in your own household, and with your own servants, is not my affair. The young woman has suffered what we in the medical profession call a *graviditas extrauterina*. The *foetus* has commenced its development, not in the womb, but elsewhere, perhaps in the *tuba fallopiana*, and in consequence—'

'I know,' interrupts Charles, his mind rigid like a river under ice. 'I know what that means.'

'Indeed? Well, in that case you will know, likewise, that once the patient has suffered a haemorrhage of the kind we are witnessing here, there is nothing a practitioner such as myself can do. Had it been a normal miscarriage, what you have done might have saved her, but in this case it will avail her nothing. The bleeding emanates from an internal rupture, which I can do nothing to treat. All I can recommend is that you have her cleaned up and put to bed. In my experience,' he says, glancing round and dropping his voice still further, 'that will be easier for the women to bear. At the end.'

369

Charles nods, his throat too raw for words, and watches as the man goes back up the stairs. Then he turns back and makes his way slowly to where the two women are standing. And it is only then, as he kneels by the bath and reaches out to touch Molly's dazed despairing face, that he realizes he has blood on his hands.

CHAPTER THIRTEEN

Ianthe

It is February. A drear grey day of misted rain and slumped dispirited trees. Spiders' webs bag like galleon sails on the brown and brittle hedgerows and the air is dead of song. We are on the old road from the capital to Oxford, watching as the London stagecoach labours through the churning mud towards the escarpment on which we stand. It is one of the last stops on the journey and one of the highest points in the Chiltern hills, so it's no surprise to see the coachman stop at the foot of the slope and ask whatever able-bodied passengers he has to walk up and spare the horses. One by one they emerge into the dank air from the crowded and ill-smelling carriage. A man in clerical weeds, small metal spectacles perched upon his nose and a limp white stock about his neck; a sturdy lawyer in a frock coat, hampered by a parcel of slippery briefs escaping from their string; and a young woman, travelling, it appears, alone. But as she comes slowly towards us we can see she is not, in fact, unaccompanied; there, under her shawl, an infant is folded to her heart, and every now and again she stops to cast a tender glance down at the child in its fitful slumbers, its small fist gripped tight against her dress. And now, finally, one last passenger emerges. It is no infirmity that has slowed his appearance; indeed, he seems nimbler than any of them, and weighed down hardly at all. Not by any great physical burden at least, though as he strides towards us, his blue eyes fixed on the ground before his feet, it would appear he has burdens of another kind. It would appear, too, that there is something about the young woman that unsettles him, for when she slips suddenly in the mud he does not quicken his pace to help – easy though that would have been – but leaves the portly lawyer to slither clumsily across to assist her.

It has, indeed, been a trying and a painful journey for Charles. Not just the cold and the damp, cramped seats, but the presence, all these hours, of that mother and child, hearing in the rattling silence her whispered words of gentleness, and watching, as if condemned to witness, her looks of love and pity and the baby's tiny answering mews. He will not allow himself to think – will not permit himself to imagine – that a child might have looked like that in Molly's arms, that he might have reached for such a child and held it in his hands, gazing down at a face all unlike his own, but which would have been, all the same, his warm and living likeness.

He trudges on now after his fellow passengers, trying to bring himself back to the task before him. For the best part of a month he has done nothing – been nowhere – has sat, in fact, with Maddox day after day, in the same room, in the same chair. And while those passing weeks have seen his great-uncle become slowly more mobile, slowly more voluble, Charles has sunk lower and lower into silence and stillness. And after days in which she berated him for his blind and wilful selfishness, it was Nancy, in the end, who arranged the burial, Nancy who had the doctor paid, and Nancy who packed up Molly's meagre possessions and removed them; where, Charles does not know. And it was Nancy who contravened rules of half a century's standing and went through the papers in the office – went through them and found among them Horace Turnbull's letter. And it was Abel, then, who persuaded Charles, for courtesy if nothing more, that he must do as he had agreed and meet the Curators, and Maddox who later – slowly, falteringly – set out for him how he might go about the task they require of him. And so it is that Charles is on this coach now, taking no pleasure in the journey, and anticipating none at the end of it. Hoping only for some long task, and tedious, that will fill his mind and exhaust his body, for that more than anything, is what he craves.

He reaches the top of the incline now and stops a moment, gathering his breath. It is a small, self-respecting village with a church, a trodden spread of green, a line of tidy brick cottages, and a low-ceilinged inn; Charles can already hear the sounds of shouting and the clatter of hoofs as the ostlers and stable boys make ready for the change of horses. The other passengers are making their way towards the golden light streaming from the door and the promise of heat and food, but such things matter not to Charles. He turns a little and looks about him. Up ahead, perhaps a mile, beyond the high banks and the hedges, there is a windmill. A windmill standing among sodden fields and enclosed within a low stone wall, where a scatter of scant and stunted ash trees rise against the darkening winter clouds. Charles stands there, wondering why this landscape should seem so familiar since he has never, to his knowledge, travelled this road before. And then it comes to him. That strange piece in

Medwin's life of Shelley that talked of just such a scene – a scene with a windmill and a low evening sky, a scene encountered on a walk out from Oxford, a scene the poet remembered with such an overwhelming thrilling horror that he fled for refuge to the comfort of friends.

It's weeks since Charles has thought of Shelley – weeks since that name has evoked anything but an unbearable sense of self-disgust. He has not seen Claire, nor heard from her, since that last day, and not placed a hand to the papers that had once so consumed him, since the moment he realized there was something else that should have had first claim on his attention – something else everyone in the house had seen, but none had dared to speak of. Except Nancy, of course: she had tried to tell him, but he had not listened. He can barely remember now that shiver of excitement when he thought he had unravelled the mystery of Mary Shelley, barely recall the exhilaration of discovery, of deciphering. But the detective is not quite dead in him yet, as we shall see, for he hesitates now, then turns and walks, his pace gradually quickening, to the door of the inn, where he dips his head against the low beam and disappears inside.

A quarter of an hour goes by, and the coachman is blowing his horn to alert his passengers to the stage's imminent departure, but when they appear one by one from the door Charles is not among them. The night is fast falling when he emerges a few minutes later, his collar turned against the cold, and heads along the line of cottages to a large house standing alone.

It is an attractive Regency villa, this one, white-faced and symmetrical, with a window either side of a pedimented porch, and another line of identical casements above. If a house can speak of its inhabitants this one conjures both care

374

and carefulness – patches of brickwork have been diligently repaired, and the garden trimmed back for winter, all dead leaves swept neatly away. Charles pulls at the bell-rope and hears an echoing ring somewhere deep inside. He might have expected a maid to answer in such a class of residence, but the woman who eventually comes to the door is clearly the owner, or the owner's wife. Small, grey-haired and closed about herself, she gives the impression of an untimely withering, a curtailment all too early. She starts, on seeing him, but then appears to collect herself. 'May I help you?'

Charles has not had much time to consider what he will say to this, and what he'd settled on had sounded thin even to his own ears, but when he looks into the woman's faded blue eyes he feels suddenly ashamed at the prospect of his cheap lie.

'It's about your daughter, Mrs Smith.'

Again that almost imperceptible start of surprise – or shock. 'All these years,' she says slowly, her voice brittle as if she has not spoken for a long time. 'All these years I have wondered if someone would come, and that it should happen now. Today of all days.' She holds the door open. 'You had best come in.'

The sitting room she shows him into is clearly not the grandest such room in the house, but it is warm and it is comfortable. She has not yet turned up the lamps, and the only light is the red-gold glow cast by the fire in the brick hearth.

'What was it that brought you here?' she asks, moving to what is clearly her accustomed chair.

Charles takes a seat on the sopha opposite her. 'Chance. An accident of coincidence. I was on my way to Oxford and saw the windmill. There is a passage in which it is described.'

She bows her head. 'And when I asked at The Crown, the

375

landlord told me what had happened. But he could not tell me very much. The bare facts, nothing more.'

'He is new to the village. My family have lived here for four generations.'

There is a silence, and Charles senses a hesitation now, a sudden reluctance.

'You said you were travelling to Oxford,' she says after a moment. 'Are you a student at the university, Mr . . . ?'

'Maddox. Charles Maddox. And no,' he says firmly. 'I am not. And I never have been.'

'*He* was,' she says, pulling her woollen shawl closer about her. 'That is the first thing he ever told me. That he was a student at University College. He no doubt thought it might serve to reassure me, but I knew he was a gentleman, despite his strange clothes and his dirty fingernails. It was his voice – the air he had about him that life would always arrange itself for his convenience.'

'How did he come to be here?'

'He was walking. From Oxford down to Marlow. It was a beautiful October day and my daughter was outside in the garden when he passed by on the road and saw her. We lived at the end of the row then, and she would sit for hours on the fence alone, talking to her doll and making up stories to herself. When I went out to call her that afternoon she came running towards me saying she had found a wonderful new friend, who told the most thrilling and delightful tales. I thought it odd, that a man of his age should be interested in a little girl, but he came at once to shake my hand saying he had been reminded, the moment he saw her, of his sister Elizabeth, whom he loved dearly and missed very much. And, of course, her own brother was away at that time, and she was often lonely. She had so few friends. Other children can be very cruel.'

She shakes her head and gazes towards the curling flames. 'I do not think I ever saw her so happy as she was that day. She had never had a friend only to herself – never had anyone listen to her as he had.'

Charles nods slowly. He is remembering what Claire Clairmont had said of Fanny Imlay. *No one in that house ever took the slightest notice of her, but he did. He could be very gentle, very encouraging. It is easy to see why she might have loved him for it.* 'And he came again, after that?'

'Sometimes with a friend, a stocky, rather taciturn youth I did not take to. But mostly he was alone. As the days drew shorter he and my daughter would sit on the floor by the fire and he would frighten her with ghost stories, and wild tales of witches and spectres and raising the devil and I know not what besides. I worried, a little, at her hearing such things, but my sister said it would do her no harm – that children enjoy being frightened, as long as they are in a safe place and with people who love them. And he did love her. Of that I am sure. Despite all that happened afterwards, I am sure he loved her.'

There is a gust of wind then, and a branch outside the window scratches plaintively against the glass like a suppliant wraith. 'It was forty years ago this very day. I have been sitting here these last hours, by the fire, listening to the wind in the trees and remembering, and when the knock came to the door and I saw you standing there, I thought, for a wild moment, that time had been retraced. That you came with news of her. That she was still out there, waiting to be found. Waiting to be rescued.'

Her face buckles now with pain, and Charles feels an answering clasp to his own heart, remembering what it was like to look up and see a golden-haired child hesitating in a doorway, a child so like his own lost sister that it seemed as if his own impossible prayer has been answered, and he had been given another chance – another chance to redeem the past.

There are tears in her eyes now. 'I know I should never have allowed them to go – the weather was poor that day and like to worsen, and I knew she was not strong enough to walk so far, but he said he would carry her pig-a-back, that he had often taken his sisters on such expeditions, bearing them so in his arms when they became too tired to follow him. And she was so excited at the prospect of their little excursion together that at last I agreed. She had so few opportunities of that kind – so few of the pleasures other children take for granted. I remember standing at the window as I watched them go, he with that fine coat of his all torn about the buttons, and she in her favourite dress, with her best blue sash tied in a bow. And I stood there again that evening, waiting and watching as the night and the storm came on, and when I saw him stagger out of the darkness like a dead man, my heart began to beat so violently in my breast that I could scarcely breathe. He was holding her sash clutched against his chest, and he was covered in slime, his hair black with mud, and his eyes starting from his skull like a monster from some terrifying dream.'

Charles can feel his own heart racing as the image conjures itself before his eyes – an image hallucinatingly like that infamous creature formed by unhallowed arts from the offal of the slaughter-house. A monster that murdered the lovely and the helpless, and strangled the innocent as they slept. Now more than ever Charles wonders if the imagining of that monster was the deliberate resurrection of unbearable memories, or an unconscious externalization of everything in himself that its creator most feared.

'I rushed outside,' she continues, 'but my husband was there before me, seizing him by the throat and demanding to know where she was. I truly think Robert would have choked the life from him had I not intervened, and when he loosed his grip he fell to the ground in the dirt, clutching his neck and gasping for breath, the marks of bruises about his throat. He said they had gone all the way down to the river, that there had been a little boat moored at the bank and she had begged him – pleaded with him – to take her out in it, to row her about a little as he had so often rowed his sisters. And it had started so joyfully – she in the prow smiling like a princess and he singing at the top of his voice and scaring the cattle come down to drink. Only then an oar became suddenly entangled in an overhanging tree and he had to wrestle to free it – the boat began to rock – he told her to be still, but she became frightened and tried to crawl towards him – she stood – the oar wrenched all at once free, and as the boat tipped she slipped over the side. He said she uttered not the smallest cry, that her body made not the slightest movement on the face of the water. It was as if she had never been there at all.'

She looks up at Charles, and then away. 'He told us he searched – that he did everything he could. He tried to wade in but it was too deep and he could not swim. He said she must have become caught in the weed and been unable to free herself. He said that with her arm – her infirmity – she would not have been able—'

Her voice falters; she has a little book in her lap, which she touches now as if it is a talisman, as if it might give her the strength she needs to finish what she has set herself to say. 'My husband dragged him down to the river then and there – all those miles in the dark and the pouring rain – but they could not find her. There was no sign. Not then, and not afterwards. We were never able to bring her body home. Never able to lay her to rest. Two days later that friend of his came here. He said he was distraught at what had happened – crazed with grief and remorse, unable to sleep, unable to eat, threatening to destroy himself by poison, or by pistol-shot. He begged us, if we could find it in our hearts, not to blight such a promising young man's life by reporting him to the magistrate. I remember crying out that *our* lives were blighted – that *we* would never see our daughter again, never see her married, never see her a mother – but my husband silenced me with a face of granite, and demanded money. A very great deal of money. The man floundered a moment, then stammered that there was a cousin who might be able to help – a cousin with money to command. That if we could wait a few days he would send to London.'

The room is still, but it is not the stillness of peace. Then Charles gets up and pokes the coals, and as he returns to his chair and the shadows begin to dispel in the sudden leap of firelight, he notices there are two portraits by the window he had not seen before. 'May I?'

She glances up, then nods.

The first is set in an oval frame carved intricately with flowers and butterflies, and the little mice and rabbits so beloved of young girls. She is half turned towards him, her fair hair curled in ringlets, and her dark blue eyes lit with such an expression of pure, enchanted joy that Charles can hardly bear to look at her. But then, as the fire gathers strength, he can see the picture more clearly – see not only the name engraved beneath it, but what the little girl is wearing about her neck.

A string of bright blue beads.

It cannot be a coincidence. It must be the same. The same beads Maddox saw in Hans Place all those years ago, wound about the neck of Shelley's little daughter. He must have found them in the water that terrible night and kept them until he had a daughter of his own. A daughter he gave two gifts, the day she was born. A string of blue beads, and the name of the girl who once had worn them. That the past might be redeemed by repeating it.

Charles turns to Mrs Smith. 'Ianthe Mary. It is a beautiful name. And she is a beautiful child.'

She nods. 'The artist has captured her to the life, but he has flattered her, all the same. You cannot see it in that picture, but she suffered a cruel accident when she was hardly more than a baby. Her arm and shoulder were withered ever after, and she could only walk with her own strange little jerking gait. Other children shunned her and mocked her, as children do who know no better, and do not understand their own heartlessness.'

Charles looks at the picture again, this picture so seemingly insignificant, but which holds the key to so many dark mysteries. So this is the secret that lay buried deep in Shelley's past and cast its shadow over all the rest of his life. This is why Harriet Shelley died with words of death and guilt and a young girl drowned, hidden among her clothes. This is what Hogg meant when he talked so obscurely of a need for repentance – Hogg who must, surely, have been the friend who came here after Ianthe died, just as Medwin must have been the cousin in London who gave them the money. And this is what left Shelley terrified and shaking, that night of ghost-raising in Geneva, when he heard Coleridge's poem of the deformed witch Christabel and talked, half mad, of a tale of his own that would rouse those who heard it to terror, and a dire fear of what lurked unseen in their own souls. A tale of a young girl, in the like way misshapen, whose face still haunted his waking days and would not let him rest. Not then, nor till the hour of his own death. Was it a vision of this dead girl that Shelley saw rising out of the waves from the terrace at Lerici, those last few fevered weeks? Was it Ianthe he saw smiling and clasping her hands in joy, and did he see absolution in that joy – a promise that she was finally at peace, and he at last forgiven?

And as Charles thinks of those last weeks, and of hope dying slowly into a desire for death, his eye is drawn, half unthinking, to the second portrait hanging next to the girl's. A portrait of the same size, but more austerely framed. The portrait of a young man. Charles looks at it for a moment in horrified disbelief then turns, his blood running cold, to the woman.

'But surely this is—?'

'Not the man you suppose it to be. It is my son. Henry.'

Charles looks again at the painting. Despite her words, he can still scarcely believe it. The likeness is more than close – it is uncanny. The same striking violet-blue eyes, the same pale skin, the same wildly curling hair. And now, at last, seeing this, Charles knows everything. Not just what it was that Shelley had done, but how – and how ruthlessly – he was punished.

'You said your son was away when Ianthe died?' he asks, with forced calmness.

'Henry was in London. He came as soon as he got our letter. He was furious with my husband for not going at once to the magistrate – he said we should never have accepted the money, never bought this house with such tainted coin. He swore he would never rest until he had found the man who had killed his sister, and taken his revenge. He did not see why *he* should be content, and *we* so miserable.'

'He was working in London?'

'At that time, yes. He was a writer, for the newspapers.'

Charles wanders, as if casually, to the window. 'Work such as that must be relatively easy to come by. Even in out-of-the-way places. Even in a county as remote, perhaps, as Cumberland.'

She flushes. 'I am sure you are right.'

'Or the north of Wales.'

'Possibly. I could not say.'

'And did your son ever have cause to journey further afield? To Europe, perhaps?'

She hesitates. 'He did travel at least once to Italy. To the neighbourhood of Lerici. Do you know it?'

Charles nods. 'Only by reputation. But I believe the air on the coast there is said to have a magical quality. People see visions – dream dreams – may sometimes even believe they have glimpsed what the Germans call a *doppelgänger*. An image of themselves as like as to the reflection in a glass.'

She looks away and folds her hands. 'I know nothing of such things. But perhaps there is something in what you say. There was a change in Henry, that summer. I could tell from his letters. He seemed happier than he had for many years. It was as if he was finally at peace.'

At peace, thinks Charles, because he had confronted the man he believed had killed his sister; at peace because that man had at long last paid the price, and his task was done.

Charles turns again to the portrait. The portrait that is Shelley, and yet not Shelley. A likeness both of the poet, and of his persecutor. The man who tried to kill him first in Cumberland, and then in Wales. The man whose face

Shelley caught sight of at the window, that dark night, and saw in terror that it was his own. The man he glimpsed thereafter so many times – on the London streets, in the Italian squares – that he began to believe himself deranged. The man whose last appearance, walking calmly towards him on a sunlit terrace, was to precipitate a final reckless plunge towards death and forgetting.

The blurred image Charles has been pursuing fuses finally into focus. What was it the assailant threatened at Tremadoc? That he would murder Shelley's wife and ravish his *sister*. And there is reason now, and not childish caprice in Shelley's later obsession with kidnapping his sisters from their school – he must have seen Henry Smith in London, and feared the girls were in terrible danger. The rape of a sister, the death of a wife; the first threat never came to pass, but what of the second? Charles remembers now, with a terrible foreboding, the name of the man Harriet was said to have taken as a lover before she died. The man seen about her lodgings who was so like her long-absent husband that everyone assumed it was indeed him. The name she was living under when she went to her death. Had Smith deliberately sought out Shelley's wife when she was at her most vulnerable, her most forsaken? Did he get her with child and then callously abandon her, leaving her so desperate at this second desertion that she fulfilled his threat of vengeance by her own hand? Or did he truly love her and return one night to find that she was dead? She and his own unborn baby together. Another death to lay at Shelley's door. Another cause that cried aloud for vengeance.

The woman is on her feet. 'I think you should go now. You have, I take it, found what you sought.'

'When I came here I had only questions. But now I have answers, I do not know what I should do with them.'

'I have lived with what happened these forty years. Nothing you can do now will change the past.'

It's clear this strange encounter is at an end, and Charles follows her back to the front door. She shakes his hand and he is about to leave when something makes him turn back. The empty, quiet house. Those two solitary portraits. All the walls otherwise bare.

'Where is your son now, Mrs Smith? Does he have a family of his own?'

She would never have told him, had he not asked.

'He died, Mr Maddox. That summer in Italy. He was on his way home when his ship went down in a storm. They found his trunk, weeks later, washed up on the sand. There was hardly anything in it – a few clothes, some papers. And this little book.'

She hands it to him. A piece of faded blue ribbon marks the page. Cut, surely, from the sash his sister was wearing the day she died.

A gentle start convulsed Ianthe's frame:
Her veiny eyelids quietly unclosed;
Moveless awhile the dark blue orbs remained:
She looked around in wonder and beheld
Henry, who kneeled in silence by her couch,
Watching her sleep with looks of speechless love,
And the bright beaming stars
That through the casement shone.

Charles turns the little volume over. It is so worn with handling the lettering is disappearing into the dry leather. But it makes no difference. Because Charles has read these lines before, and he knows the name of the man who wrote them.

Epilogue

75 *Gloucester Road*
Hyde Park Gardens
5th February

Mr Maddox,

After so long a silence, after I have deliberated so deeply what I should do, and what I should say, I find that the decision is no longer my own to make. I have heard today that Mary is dead. I will never now discover whether all you told me had its grounding in truth, or whether we have both been prey to the fatal allure of likeness, and seen patterns and treacherous precedents where none were in truth to be found. Had I known she was ill I would have been sure to see her, and I bitterly resent that Percy did not see fit to give me such tidings himself, leaving me to discover the news through an intermediary. What I would not give, now, to know what she said at the last. Did she confess her darkest deeds, or regret her terrible lies? I am told the end was peaceful – that she had lain for days in her bed, unable to speak a word, and the end came at last in a succession of fits and the slow creep of a profound stupor. The physician

*who attended her spoke of a tumour of the brain of long
standing, which he believes has accounted for many of her ills
and symptoms in the last years, and yet it was a letter, I am
told, that precipitated her last attack. A letter brought to her by
her maid more than a month ago that caused her such distress
she fell at once into a series of fits, and was never able thereafter
to speak, or to move. What it was she read that affected her so,
no one could determine, since the letter itself could not
afterwards be found.*

*I have written myself to Percy, berating him for his treatment
of me, and telling him I am myself dying. And because that is
so — because I will not now live long — I have decided that I will
give to you that memoir over which I have expended such pains
and which would, were it known, make so prodigious a change
in the eyes of the world, the vain, cold, dull-witted world. You
will receive it tomorrow, and you must resolve, then, what you
will do. If you choose, you may keep it safe until I am gone, and
publish it thereafter, that the truth may at last be known; or you
may do the great thing and consign it to the flames, page by
long, slow page, watching the fire eat away to ashes the last
witness to our entwined and extraordinary lives.*

I ask nothing, counsel nothing. It is for you, now, to decide.

Claire Clairmont

Author's Notes and Acknowledgements

This section contains details of the plot, so readers are advised to leave it till the end.

I did a great deal of research in preparing for this novel, and owe a particular debt of gratitude to Richard Holmes's masterly biographical study *Shelley: The Pursuit*, as well as to Miranda Seymour's fine biography of Mary Shelley. I also drew on the journals and letters of the Shelleys and Claire Clairmont, the Hogg, Medwin, and Thomas Love Peacock memoirs of the poet, Polidori's account of the summer of 1816, and on various modern studies such as *Claire Clairmont and the Shelleys*, by Robert Gittings and Jo Manton, *The Godwins and the Shelleys*, by William St Clair, Ernest Lovell's biography of Thomas Medwin, Kenneth Neill Cameron's *Romantic Rebels: Essays on Shelley and his Circle*, Daisy Hay's recent work *Young Romantics*, and the book accompanying the Bodleian Library exhibition, *Shelley's Ghost: Reshaping the Image of a Literary Family*.

My book is, of course, a novel, but I have made it a point

of honour not to make free with known events or timings (with one small exception I mention later), even if that might have made the construction of my plot rather easier. Where there are gaps, I have allowed myself to fill them, and I set these out below. But I was surprised, as I wrote, at how little I needed to invent outright, and I think my readers will also be surprised by how much of my story is based on facts and contemporary accounts, even if I have exercised a degree of artistic licence in presenting them, and extrapolated from what we know to what might have happened, or could have been said.

Those who know Shelley's poetry well will also have recognized that each of my chapter titles echoes one of his poems, and that the opening lines of that chapter contain words and phrases taken from that poem. I also weave in some of my characters' own words on occasion, taken from their correspondence, writings and journals, and once or twice one person's words are attributed to another, where I think that is reasonable. All the letters and documents I include in the novel are my own invention (though they draw on real materials in places); the exceptions are the two suicide notes, which are exact reproductions of what Fanny Imlay and Harriet Shelley left behind. You can see a facsimile of the latter on the Shelley's Ghost website.

Mary Shelley
There is nothing to suggest that Mary accused Shelley of her first daughter's death in the way I have imagined, and no details exist about exactly how she died, but it is clear that the atmosphere between Mary, Claire and Shelley was electric with jealousy by that point. On 14 January 1815, Mary's journal entry reads:

Three leaves are torn out immediately thereafter. In the days before and after the baby's birth there are several more references to the fact that Shelley and Claire have been out together alone for hours, even though it's clear that the baby was unwell from the outset. The day after the baby was found dead Mary records 'a fuss' in her journal, which, as Daisy Hay points out, is usually her code-word for an argument with Shelley. Mary's journal also records that Shelley and Claire took the baby's body away for burial, no one knows where, and the two of them continued their private excursions together in the days that followed. There is also an odd episode, much later, in 1821, when Claire amused herself in her diary by composing 'caricatures' for both Byron and Shelley, and wrote under the latter 'He looking very sweet & smiling. A little child [deleted] Jesus Christ playing about the room. He says. Then grasping a small knife & looking mild "I will quietly murder that little child."'

Whatever happened with the first, Mary certainly believed Shelley's absorption with Claire contributed to the death of their second daughter. There are references to problems with feeding this baby, even before the Shelleys left England, and after her arrival at Este Mary wrote to her friend Maria Gisborne that Clara was 'reduced to be so thin in this short time that you would hardly know her again'. It does seem to have been reckless on both parents' part to take such a sick child on that last journey into Venice, when a doctor was available in Padua. I have found no actual evidence that Mary harmed her children, knowingly or otherwise, but I would hardly have expected to. I do, however, think that some of the surviving records are suggestive, as are the silences. In August 1820 Shelley wrote to Godwin that 'On one occasion . . . agitation of mind produced through [Mary] a disorder in [Percy], similar to that which destroyed our little girl two years ago.' And when Byron forbade Allegra to go to the Shelleys that same year he wrote, 'I so totally disapprove of the mode of Children's treatment in their family, that I should look upon the Child as going into a hospital . . . Have they *reared* one? . . . the Child shall not quit me again to perish of Starvation, and green fruit . . .'

I also believe that aspects of Mary's behaviour would seem to conform to what we know now of Münchausen's syndrome. She certainly suffered from periods of deep depression throughout her life, something she believed she had inherited from her mother. At the same time she was both ferociously intelligent and ferociously determined – Godwin did indeed say her 'perseverance in everything she undertakes' was 'almost invincible'. It is easy to see how the poisonous environment in which she and Claire competed for Shelley's affection might have led her to desperate measures to keep Shelley to herself (and my account of that night of 'horrors' in late 1814 is based on fact). But I think there are traces of the same attention-seeking behaviour long before she met him. Her mother died soon after she was born, and she thereafter developed what she herself called an 'excessive & romantic attachment' to Godwin (it is interesting to note in this context that her later novel, *Mathilda*, dealt with the subject of a father's incestuous love for his daughter – a subject that disgusted Godwin).

After his second marriage, Godwin sent Mary away from the rest of the family for months at a time, telling her, as she left for Ramsgate at the age of thirteen, that there was still a chance of her becoming a wise and even happy woman, 'in spite of unfavourable appearances'. We have no idea what he meant by this, or the nature of the 'dreadful evil' that the Godwins feared in relation to the problem with her arm. That is still a mystery, even now, but it was serious enough to require the wearing of a sling, and, as Miranda Seymour observes, Mrs Godwin may have suspected her step-daughter of exaggerating it, perhaps in an effort to regain her central place in her father's life. I have always found this whole episode very odd, especially when one adds the unexplained fire in the bookshop, and Mary's later references to herself in letters to Shelley as 'Pecksie' who is 'a good girl' and 'quite well again now'. I have tried to create a story that might explain it.

The account of Mary threatening to kill herself if Shelley refused to marry her comes from one given by the second Mrs Godwin. Even though she is not always an entirely reliable witness, especially where Mary is concerned, that does not necessarily mean that she was wrong on this occasion. As for the possibility that Mary might have taken a lover, she did believe – at least in theory – in free love, and even if she balked at inviting the unprepossessing Hogg to her bed, I can quite imagine she might have slept with a rather more attractive man, especially in an act of revenge.

Mary was an accomplished liar when it suited her, both by omission and by commission: her journals are full of eloquent silences, and later in life she helped a female friend obtain a false passport so that she could travel as the 'husband' of another woman (there's more on this extraordinary episode in the Seymour biography). As for the blackmail, there are two surviving letters in which Shelley instructs his bankers to make payments to an unidentified person bearing the initials A.B. This I have woven into my own story.

Mary fiercely resisted all attempts to have a biography of her husband written during her lifetime, having been prevented from taking on this task herself by her father-in-law, Sir Timothy. As Charles discovers, the accounts written during Mary's lifetime by Hogg and Medwin are almost as revealing in what they don't – or can't – say, as in what they do.

Though there is no suggestion that Sir Percy and Lady Shelley ever employed anyone to investigate or acquire Claire's papers, Lady Shelley certainly became the 'keeper of the flame' as far as the poet's reputation was concerned. She constructed what can only be called a shrine to him at the family house in Sussex (on which mine is based), and became ruthless in her determination to expunge or destroy anything she considered to be inappropriate, or which detracted from the ethereal image she was determined to bequeath to posterity. She was particularly sensitive to references to Harriet Shelley, or accounts of Shelley's elopement with Mary (whom she called 'Madre') that cast him in a poor light. It's almost certain that many letters and papers were destroyed as a result, and Lady Shelley was also implicated in the printing, if not the production, of at least one forged letter, supposedly from Shelley. This letter repeats the accusation that Harriet lived with a groom named Smith and 'descended the steps of prostitution', and has Shelley accusing 'that beastly viper' Eliza Westbrook of murdering her sister, in order to lay hands on their father's money, though how Eliza was supposed to have done this is unclear.

Late in life Claire offered to sell some of her papers to Sir Percy through an intermediary, only for him to reply that she was 'no relation of mine'. Relations between the Shelleys and Claire deteriorated markedly in the wake of the incident with her niece at Field Place which I describe, and after

393

Mary's death on 1st February 1851, Jane had the coffins of Godwin and his first wife exhumed from the Pancras cemetery and reburied with their daughter in Bournemouth. The second Mrs Godwin was left behind; one can only imagine what Claire would have thought of that.

Mary did indeed have a sudden series of fits at the very end of her life which left her in a coma, but there is no suggestion that this was the result of receiving a letter. These fits took place in late January 1851, though I have this happening a little earlier, to fit the sequence of events in my own story.

Claire Clairmont

As far as we know, Claire never completed a memoir of her life, but Daisy Hay has recently discovered fragments of what may have been an attempt at one, written in old age, in which Claire attacked both Byron and Shelley for their lies, cruelty and treachery; there is more on this find in Hay's book. Claire certainly kept journals at certain periods throughout her life, some of which may have been lost. She did not die in 1851, though she did write to Sir Percy to say she thought she was dying. In fact she lived on until 1879, the last survivor of a doomed and extraordinary generation. By then she was living with her niece Pauline in Florence, and Henry James's *The Aspern Papers* is famously inspired by the relationship she developed there with an American called Edward Silsbee, who was desperate to see her papers, and hear her first-hand account of Shelley, Byron and the rest. The St John's Wood sections of *A Treacherous Likeness* are a deliberate echo of – and homage to – the Henry James story. Before Claire died she asked to be buried with a shawl Shelley had given her sixty years before, which I have her wearing in my own novel.

There has long been speculation as to the true nature of Claire's relationship with Shelley. Many people believe that they were indeed lovers, even if only for a short period. I am not the first to wonder whether Claire became pregnant by Shelley in the spring of 1815 – I develop this from a suggestion by Miranda Seymour, who speculates that Claire's otherwise rather mysterious departure for Lynmouth might be explained in this way. This period is an example of one of those all-too-frequent and extremely puzzling periods when pages have been deliberately torn out of the journal Mary and Shelley were keeping at this time, which may in itself be revealing. If there was such a pregnancy, it surely must have ended in miscarriage or stillbirth, since it's hard to believe Claire would have abandoned her child, given the passionate devotion she later exhibited for Allegra. Needless to say there are no references to any of this in the records that remain, and I have of course invented the episode in which Mary discovers the pregnancy.

The relationship between the two step-sisters was problematic from the start, and for the best part of forty-five years they alternated between periods of comparative calm and outbreaks of wild hatred and recrimination. Claire once went so far as to say that the sight of Mary made her feel as if 'the sickening crawling motion of a Deathworm had replaced the usual flow of Blood in my veins', and to compare her to a woman who would enjoy the spectacle of the killing of a child, and shake the hand of the executioner afterwards. What, I wondered, could possibly have provoked so horrifying an image . . . ?

Shelley
Shelley's personality and childhood were every bit as disturbed and disturbing as I have described them. He was

indeed followed by Home Office agents for a time, and everything I have the fictitious Sir Henry Pearson say is based on fact. Shelley also had what we would now see as an unhealthy fixation with young girls; he contemplated both adopting and, indeed, 'purchasing' them at various points in his life, for the purposes of 'education' (his friend Joseph Merle called the latter project, to involve two girls of four or five years old, 'more than absurd . . . horrible').

The idea of pursuit, and of a dark 'antitype' or likeness of the self pervades Shelley's poetry from a very early stage; as Richard Holmes observes, 'ghostly "following-figures"' were to 'haunt Shelley both in his life and in his writing'. Shelley became obsessed with the idea that he was being pursued by Robert Leeson, as irrational as that notion was. He was said to have seen his pursuer as late as 1821, in Pisa.

Shelley did indeed encounter two men called Maddocks in the course of his life – one in Wales and one in Marlow – and I have woven my own 'Maddox' into what was clearly a genuine and strange obsession the poet had with names. Thomas Love Peacock recalls that Harriet claimed Shelley saw nothing in Mary 'but that her name was Mary, and not only Mary but Mary Wollstonecraft'. Thomas Medwin, likewise, says there was 'some magic in the name of Harriet'. As for the unusual name 'Ianthe', it appears first in *Queen Mab*, then as Shelley's choice for his first daughter's name, and lastly – and intriguingly – as the name of the innocent young girl in Polidori's story *The Vampyre*, a girl who tells the hero 'supernatural tales', and whom he is unable to save from a terrible death.

Polidori wrote that story after the famous night of ghost-raising at the Villa Diodati. At one point during that evening Shelley did indeed react so violently to Byron's reading of *Christabel* that Polidori administered ether to him in an attempt to calm him down. Under that influence Shelley talked, among other things, of how he had looked at Mary and thought of a woman with eyes for nipples. I have added the reference to an unknown pursuer, and a terrifying memory relating to a young girl, as well as the fact that he intended to write a story based upon it, which I have Mary Shelley later destroying. We know Shelley did begin a story that summer, possibly based on his own past, but it has been lost and we do not know how or why that happened, or what it was about.

I am very far from being the first to suggest that Shelley, not his wife, was the author of *Frankenstein*, and he did, of course, initially allow the publisher John Murray to believe it was his own work. Even the most passionate advocates of Mary's authorship will probably concede that nothing she wrote thereafter can match it, and that Shelley played a significant role in its composition – Mary talks of them discussing it together, and the manuscripts that survive show signs of his extensive corrections and amendments. As for Mary's famous preface, and the tale she tells of the book's genesis, Miranda Seymour points out that Polidori makes no mention of her announcing one morning she had 'thought of a story', and by the time her preface was written in 1831, Shelley, Byron and Polidori were all dead, and she must have thought she risked no contradiction. Polidori's account of that summer was not published until 1911.

Richard Holmes refers to the incident at Tremadoc as one of the two great biographical mysteries in Shelley's career. It has never been adequately explained, and even now it is not absolutely clear what happened, or why. One of the original inspirations for *A Treacherous Likeness* was to create a narrative that might account for this incident, and my fictional version of Shelley's past does indeed explain two of the more mysterious aspects of that night: the assailant's threat to rape Shelley's sister when the woman in the house was his sister-*in-law*, and the fact that a good many people believed at the time that the second attack that night – if not the first – was merely an hallucination prompted by seeing his own reflection in the window. The manager of the Tremadoc works, John Williams, was summoned to the scene the following morning and many years later his wife recounted that Shelley claimed to have seen a man's face on the drawing room window, a phenomenon that was by then being referred to as 'Shelley's Ghost'. I recommend Holmes's account for a fascinating description of how the episode was reported by both Shelley and Harriet, and by others who later investigated it.

Needless to say, Ianthe and her brother are my invention, and there is no evidence at all that Shelley was involved in the drowning of a young girl when he was still at Oxford. However, some sort of incident of this kind would certainly explain a good deal, not least that strange and clearly horrifying memory of the windmill against the sky, and his preoccupation with drawing boats in the pages of his notebooks – some of which are sailed by a lone figure silhouetted in black. Images of some of these (including a page with large disembodied eyes) can be seen on the Shelley's Ghost exhibition website, http://shelleysghost. bodleian.ox.ac.uk.

However, there is no doubt that Shelley did suffer some sort of breakdown in early 1811, the severity of which seems out of proportion to the two events we know happened at this time – his expulsion from the university, and his enforced separation from his first love, Harriet Grove. After leaving Oxford he spent a lonely and miserable time in London, and then stayed for a few weeks at Cwm Elan in

Wales. Here he suffered what he called a 'short but violent nervous illness', and wrote a number of poems filled with wild thoughts of remorse, suicide, and despair, and – intriguingly for me – the same notebook he used that summer contains the lines about a girl in a 'yawning watery grave', which I include in the paper I have Maddox discovering in Harriet's pocket after her death. Shelley also made a number of enigmatic references to the fact that meeting Harriet Westbrook saved or distracted him from 'bitter memories', which I have likewise included in the paper found on her body. The lines beginning 'Full many a mind' were apparently written by Harriet herself, but aside from the lines from *Christabel*, all the other poetry in the novel is written by Shelley. The blue beads I have Shelley giving to his own daughter Ianthe are of course my invention, and there is no proof he wished to give her the second name Mary.

One interesting footnote: E. R. Lovell points out that some time before 1812 Thomas Medwin must have run through an inheritance of as much as £3,000 (the equivalent of at least £100,000 today). Lovell can find no explanation other than extravagance and gambling, but I have fed this small fact into the fabric of my own story: if Shelley had needed money to buy the Smiths' silence, he might well have turned to his cousin to obtain it. It was always very hard for people to refuse Shelley, and Medwin was later to say that this period of his life was poisoned by regrets.

The suicides

My account of these two sad deaths is based almost entirely on the facts as we know them, though there are some contradictions both in the contemporary accounts, and the one given by Claire some sixty years later. That said, we do know there was indeed a William Alder who dragged the ponds in Hyde Park, lodged in the same house as Harriet, and gave evidence at her inquest. Likewise the Godwins did pass on to Shelley a scurrilous rumour that his wife had been consorting with a number of different men, including a groom (in their version) by the name of Smith. I have, however, invented the idea that someone resembling Shelley was seen near Harriet's lodgings, and even if Mary did not hound her by letter as I suggest, she certainly believed herself culpable in Harriet's death – in 1839 she wrote in her journal that she believed many of her own sorrows were the atonement Fate demanded for the death of 'poor Harriet'. In my story I imagine a far more detailed and damning confession, which Jane Shelley burns.

One odd fact about Harriet's suicide, which is not easily explained, is that Godwin's journal records her death as 9th November 1816; this was the last day she was seen alive, but it would be another month before her body was found.

The intriguing thing here, for me, was that in the case of both of these suicides a person or persons unknown seems to have intervened to conceal the identity of the two young women, and hush up the scandal as far as possible. Someone removed the name from Fanny Imlay's suicide note, someone oversaw her interment; someone seems to have arranged for Harriet to be buried under her assumed name, and ensured that there was only the briefest reporting of her drowning in the press. When I read these accounts I saw at once that I could create a fictional story in which Maddox becomes that unseen hand. Of course there is no evidence that Godwin ever employed such a person.

As I said, I have given Harriet's suicide note exactly as it was written. There is nothing to suggest that she had another paper with her when she was found – that is my own invention.

Elena Shelley

This is the second of Holmes's biographical mysteries, and has also attracted enormous speculation. Shelley registered the birth of this little girl in Naples on 27th February 1819, stating that he was the father and Mary the mother. The latter was patently untrue, but many people believe Elena was indeed Shelley's daughter, either by Claire, or by the Shelleys' maid, Elise. The evidence is problematic in both cases, and it may be that the baby was in fact, as I suggest, no child of Shelley's at all. It is certainly true that there was (as Mary recorded in her journal) a 'most tremendous fuss' on the day of their departure from Naples, and that she appears to have rejected the child, though why, we do not know. The baby remained in Naples, at the Foundling Hospital, and died there on 9th June 1820. It is a fascinating subject, but too complicated to deal with adequately here, so again I refer interested readers to the Holmes and Seymour accounts.

The last days at Lerici

Shelley's last days were haunted by the visions I describe, including those in which he believed he saw his own *doppelgänger*. I have taken my description of his last moments on board the *Don Juan* from contemporary accounts. There is no actual evidence he was planning to leave Mary at this time, but as early as 1820 he had contemplated an expedition to the East without her (and probably with Claire). The marriage was certainly miserable in those last months, and Mary cursed the day as 'hateful' when she discovered she was once again pregnant. A friend staying at the house was indeed suspicious of Mary's first phantom miscarriage at Lerici, and when she later lost the baby Shelley almost certainly saved her life by forcing her to sit for hours in a bath of ice until the bleeding stopped. There is, however, nothing in the records to suggest that the miscarriage was the result of a fall.

As with *Tom-All-Alone's*, I drew on a number of books and resources for my portrayal of nineteenth-century London, including Henry Mayhew's *London Labour and the London Poor*, Charles Dickens's *On Duty with Inspector Field*, Jerry White's *London in the Nineteenth Century*, and the excellent website, www.victorianlondon.org.

I am grateful to Nigel Wilson, Emeritus Fellow at Lincoln College, Oxford, for his help in the translation from Aristotle in Chapter Ten.

I am grateful to be able to include the full text of Harriet Shelley's suicide note on page 222, which is quoted by permission of The Carl and Lily Pforzheimer Foundation, Inc.

I would also like to thank the first readers of this book who gave me invaluable insight and support, most especially my husband Simon, my friend and former tutor Professor Stephen Gill, and Tom Atherton.

And finally my gratitude, as always, to my excellent agent Ben Mason, and my two wonderful editors, Kate Miciak and Krystyna Green.